THE PARTS

KEITH RIDGWAY

The Parts

Thomas Dunne Books
St. Martin's Press ✖ New York

THOMAS DUNNE BOOKS.
An imprint of St. Martin's Press.

www.stmartins.com

Library of Congress Cataloging-in-Publication Data

Ridgway, Keith.
    The parts / Keith Ridgway.—1st U.S. ed.
        p. cm.
    ISBN 0-312-32769-2
    EAN 978-0312-32769-9
    1. Dublin (Ireland)—Fiction. 2. Millionaires—Fiction. 3. Conspiracies—Fiction. 4. Talk shows—Fiction. 5. Widows—Fiction. I. Title.

PR6068.I287P37 2004
823'.914—dc22   2004041874

First published in Great Britain by Faber and Faber Limited

First U.S. Edition: June 2004

10 9 8 7 6 5 4 3 2 1

for Kenneth

Firstly

Here we are. All mouth. All words and exhalations.

Kitty Flood is unconscious, laid out, undignified, content. She barely moves, lying impressive on the soft pallet of her large bed in her big dark room in the great and ridiculous house up there on the tiny mountains, the hills, south of the city, above us.

She's all mouth, Kitty Flood. Her snoring is riotous. She's held in the gummy grip of a deep, dreamy sleep – her body inhales and her breath dries her tongue, her lips, her throat. She tastes everything. Her dreams exhale. Her dreams and her mind and her memory breathe out, emanate, fill the still air with all her familiar places – the house, the rooms, the corridors, the stairs. But they're turned inside out. Her sleeping logic is tangled, it has everything backwards, reversed, with the walls concentrated in the centre, a sullen mass, and the rooms bared to the hills, and the windows unworkable. Kitty's nose twitches, and her closed eyes dart.

Taste brings in the world, coming and going over her huddled teeth like dark clouds over dry rocks. Her world in her mouth. The dreams themselves are standard, petty, daft. Nonsense items, parades, meaningless. They are sexual or stressed or scary; sometimes involving her parents, rattling incoherently, much as she remembers them, or others now also dead or otherwise lost to her; or more contemporary people, mostly Delly for example, frail and translucent and preceded by bells; or various members of the Cotter family, continually appearing out of nowhere with a duster or a lawnmower or a scribbled invoice; and more recently of course Dr Addison-Blake, George, who tends to manifest himself as a kind of stage American, with a deep southern drawl and a ten gallon hat and a loud good ol' boy laugh, none of which he actually possesses in real life.

Real life.

Is the world no more than a mouthful, do you think?

The wispy plots of her dreams fill the room with pictures. A confusion of homes. Embarrassments and things said incorrectly. Naked moments, occasional falling, secrets betrayed. Random comedy – burying her car in a garden, hosting a chat show, making hats for world leaders.

But it is, all of it, tasted. Her snoring sometimes pauses while she chews. Her dreams traipse across her tongue and fiddle with her teeth. She keeps mouthwash by her bedside, and a basin to spit in, because frankly, it would be unhygienic not to.

She mentioned it to Dr George once, this dreaming mouth, and he told her that it was her sinuses. That she had trouble breathing through her nose and so left her mouth open, which is why she was prone to throat infections and why her dreams were so oral. He went so far as to mention her snoring – telling her that he could hear her in the middle of the night as he passed her room on his way to minister to Delly, or on his way back. And he went so far as to say that this problem with snoring was weight related, or that it was not helped by the fact of her weight, which could, he said, sounding like a man on a television documentary, be classed as obese. He went on to further classify her size, into subdivisions and subcategories and files and declensions, and conjured up some statistics as well, as doctors will, but by this time she had been sufficiently transfixed by the sheer cheek of the man that she did not hear. She would have been indignant enough had he actually been her doctor, and had they been in private consultation, but he was not her doctor, and they were sitting on the terrace having one of their rare shared breakfasts, with Mrs Cotter hovering about, and he was yammering on about her fat ratios. And she had not liked the implication regarding Delly either – that he was up and down all night looking after her while fat Kitty snored and dreamed of suckling. She stormed off. She suspected that he hadn't noticed.

She recognises the truth regarding her sinuses however. They are a mess. It is the price she pays, she thinks, for her angelic singing voice, which she has little chance to demonstrate, these days.

In any case, she is, now, once more, dreaming, awry on her emperor's bed, her head thrown back, her night dress ripped slightly at the shoulder, her mouth wide, her forehead damp, glistening, her chubby hands clutching the corner of a chinoiserie bedspread – and her dream is a flyover dream, a sweep over the foothills, out over the city and the sea, the wind in her armpits, her ankles rudders in the sky, her hands before her, her body stretched newly thin, sleek and aerodynamic and perfect, and she coughs in her sleep and it is changed in her mind into a bird strike, a sideswipe, something knocking her slightly off course, so that the ground rushes up, the horizon spins, and for a scary moment she is on the edge of losing control, on the edge of losing it entirely, the sickening, jagged earth grabbing at her, but her knees lock hard, her elbows compensate, her ass adjusts, and she is back steady, back again in the curve of the thermals, solid in the vortices, checked and corrected and smiling again, flying through the night, seeing all things at once, all the necessary things, all of her domain.

As Kitty Flood dreams her precarious dream, as her flight takes in the sights, her friend, her patron, her benefactor, her urge and muse and constant source of worry, pain and indecision, lies awake in another room. Her hands, thin, cut and scratched, are also clutching, but in her case they clutch an old and yellowed letter, which she reads in the light of a pencil torch held in the grip of her closed mouth. Delly Roche reads with shaking hands, not because of what she reads, not because she does not know what the letter contains (there are no surprises left, she thinks, not where she is now), but because her hands are not her own, not really, in the sense that they shake of their own accord, and can hold little more than slips of paper, morsels of food, that's about all, and are, she thinks, largely useless, and her mouth, though often gasping and with problems of its own, can at least manage the torch. There are lights in the room as well of course – a lamp stand in the far corner, a bedside light – but Delly's eyes are by now, like most of her, a bit of a joke – eyes in name only, unable to pick out anything close to her, and only half comfortable with the width of the room. So she could not really be said to be reading the letter at all. The shake in her hands is such that even if her

5

eyes were ordinary, sensible, working eyes, she might have had difficulties. But her eyes are such that she may well be holding the letter upside down. She tries a by now familiar series of squints, difficult with her mouth full, as it is, but there is no discernible improvement, and though she knows the letter by heart, it is not the same – she cannot enjoy the pretend reading, cannot take any comfort from the recall, she wants to see the hand, to see the line and the curve. But there is only the slightly metallic taste of the torch in her mouth, and the shape of it, which, it occurs to her suddenly, is almost familiar, a thought which causes her to release it, drop it into her astonished lap, and, in quick order, to smile, sigh and faint, the fainting being nothing to worry about, as it has become, these days, her quickest, often her only, route into the brief, confused refuge of a night's sleep. Which she welcomes and resents both. For while it is a break from the thousand pains and aches, and the small stirrings and clickings of the business of dying, it is also the illusion of the thing itself – death, here at last, thank God, good Lord, here at last – the false promise broken then by waking. Which Delly Roche, she would not mind admitting, is sick of.

She sleeps in silence, propped up on her pillows, the dim light of the small torch warm in her lap, the letter resting in her open hand, her hair loosened and long, her frail body waiting for something else to happen. While Kitty, down the hall, noisily follows her flight path – from the exposed innards of the mansion, out over the grounds by way of the great oak, over the heads of the security guards and their sleepy Alsatians, down the hills to the city, her open mouth collecting the night's many tastes and little lights, all of its moisture and its dust, gathering, breathing and sucking, going on and over, probing it all, licking the city with the tip of her tongue.

What does she see in her dream? How can we know? She barely knows herself. But there are sights to see, that's for sure. Familiar and not. There are things which would give her pause, which would cause her to circle and descend, to touch down and wonder. There in the foothills for example, on a stretch of dual carriageway, wide and quiet, is Dr George Addison-Blake himself, young Dr George, dapper thin American, buckled into a bottle green BMW, driving too fast. So fast that his teeth are clenched and his arms are stiff and he feels shudders in the chassis that he has not felt before. He makes the slightest of adjustments, and he screams his car along the pebbles at the edge of the grey road, and loses his nerve on the hard shoulder, beneath the orange lights, and pulls up suddenly, grinds to a halt, the back left corner of the bumper hitting the barrier, and Dr George Addison-Blake seems to continue though the car has stopped, and he seems to disturb the air he occupies, and he punches the steering wheel, slams his hand, his fist, repeatedly, against the steering wheel, hoping for an airbag that does not come.

And further, deeper, on into the wet chambered heart of the city, Kitty would see, if she could, if she were looking, if she were really there, she would see, in a low ceilinged room near the city's messy centre, a boy, like any other boy, who strips bare and folds his clothes and shivers. He lies down on the floor, on his side, with his back to the door, and he curls up a little and closes his eyes and yawns once and settles down to wait. And there is nothing in the room but the small pile of clothes and the boy they have spat out, and there is a window where she can watch, if she wants to watch, or if she prefers she can fly on, down to the river, and along it, over the bridges and under the bridges, skimming the thick, curdled water, flicking her tongue along its wet walls, down the watery passage to the ugly build-ing on the bank – where a radio station revolves through the high air, sending out a pulse, and where a man – the presenter – the presenter in fact of the ten o'clock to 1am show, is preparing himself, sorting through CDs, crying a little – definitely crying a little, there are tears on his face, his shoulders are hunched – while his – what – his assistant, his producer perhaps, his sound engineer maybe, watches through the inner window, swallow-ing hard, unsure it seems, his hands minutely flapping through a sign language of indecision.

These are strange kinds of people. To Kitty at least. To Kitty they would be strange indeed.

She can stay there if she wants, Kitty can, perched in the air condi-tioning vent, watching the radio man console himself with what

7

he thinks are surreptitious sips from a small bottle of Jameson, but which his producer (for that is what he is, that's what he does) can clearly see, and thinks are probably not a bad idea, given the circumstances. Or she can flap off back to the boy and see what progress there is over there in the new high boxes, where people, and this she would have trouble understanding, actually live – in little single bed-roomed or two bed-roomed, apartments, like capsules she'd think, like tiny, impractical cupboards. She can search for that window again, check what the naked boy is up to now. Nothing as it happens. He is motionless, more or less, maybe a small, barely perceptible sigh every now and again – a little pushing outwards of the chest – he's still on his side – a slight parting of the lips to exhale – but that's all. Even if Kitty stays at the window for a decent interval, there will be no real evidence that he lives, that he is alive, that he is properly breathing.

Or she can, if she's up to it, soar back out over the roof tops, the suburbs, to the wide roads, to the orange lights, to where Dr George Addison-Blake steps out of his bottle green BMW and climbs the barrier and walks through wet grass, his shoes and the cuffs of his trousers darkening, his head clearing, his pockets full of money and chemicals, his heart and his mind severely occluded, unhealthy, gone wrong, which would come as some surprise to Kitty. He sits down in the grass and cries.

There are too many men in tears. Kitty wouldn't understand it at all. She would execute a steep climb, her mouth walls, her cheeks, flapping in the cold air, and spin back for a reassuring look at Delly Roche, with the dying torch still in her lap, with the letter now knocked to the floor by her hands which shake while she is awake and jerk violently while she is asleep. Beautiful Delly, her long hair pooled in the half light.

Where next? High past Dr George Addison-Blake, now flat on his back, staring up at the sky, so that Kitty has to move pretty quickly for fear of being spotted, back to the boy, still as before, his skin gone slightly goosebumped now, but there's nothing happening there, back to the radio station, where the presenter has at least stopped blubbing, and has put away his whiskey, and is wearing headphones and seems, well, almost contained, almost in control, and his producer, a nervous, kindly looking young man, stands at the thick glass of the studio window, also headphoned, and he counts backwards, and points then, at the presenter, who begins, with almost a smile, to talk into his microphone, addressing the city, pushing his voice out of himself like it was something he did not want, as if it was annoying him, and the city seems to pause and pay attention, stop and listen, sit up and be still, as if something, at last, maybe, is going to happen. Back at the window where the bare skinned boy lies waiting, there is movement too.

The door to the room opens, and a man comes in, wearing suit trousers, and a shirt, and a tie tightly knotted and loosely hanging, and he carries a towel in his hand, and he looks at the boy, and seems to do a double take, which does not look quite honest, and he cries, *oh my God*, and he drops the towel, and advances towards the boy – he'd run if there was room enough to gather himself up into a run, but there is not. He reaches the boy, and his hands hesitate for a moment before turning the naked body over onto its back, and the man's face is anguished, or makes a stab at anguished, and feels for a pulse, first at the wrist, and then at the neck, and finally in the groin, his big hand burrowing between the boy's thigh and balls, his face simultaneously doing something odd, something between pleasure and embarrassment. And there is a pause.

Delly dreams of dying. Dr George Addison-Blake feels the wet grass through his clothes. The radio presenter plays more music than he usually does, and his producer watches him. Kitty Flood hovers in the dark.

The man employs his hands differently then, and his face drops the anguish, and his voice, all this time moaning and pleading and imploring, settles into a sort of rhythm, *please don't die, please don't die*, and there is in it a hint of hysteria, of giggling under the surface, while his hands move the boy, straightening him out, tilting his head back, opening his mouth. And he takes a short breath and clamps his own mouth over the boy's. And it is clear, seeing this – if Kitty is indeed seeing this, if she is dreaming our dream, and why wouldn't she be, certainly it would be clear to her, with her recent first aid courses, with her home doctor books

9

and her endless questioning of Dr George – that what is happening here is not quite mouth to mouth resuscitation. It is mouth to mouth certainly, but there is only cursory blowing, and the boy's hands, with their drumming fingers, and their slight suggestion of impatience and some distaste, give away the fact that he is hardly on his way out of the world. And then the man's hands press the boy's chest once or twice or three times, lightly, and again it seems fake, but the man's voice, and there is no mistaking it, seems ragged now, breaking up, and when his mouth is not on the boy's mouth, it is making mushy panic sounds, urgent supplications, demands even, and he goes from mouth to chest, from chest to mouth, all the time muttering, dribbling, weeping, *my poor boy, my poor boy*, his hands caressing, gathering, pummelling, probing, working, and his voice, his wet mouth, beseeching and imploring, threatening, praying, *no don't die my poor poor boy please God don't die don't leave me don't leave me don't leave me Jesus Christ no don't go* until he lifts him, into his arms, and slumps back on his heels, with the boy's head hanging convincingly dead from the crook of his elbow, and he bawls, just bawls, just liquefies and flows and empties.

It goes on too long. It's impossible to believe, and if Kitty is seeing this then she's probably laughing, which explains her rolling shoulders and the change in the pitch of her noises, and her shift to her left with her bare leg thrown over the duvet. She thinks it's a howl. A dripping pietà in a tiny apartment, the man's shirt ruined, the boy's skin slick with tears and saliva. Then a gap. A still silence. The man stops the wet despair and the wailing, as if he's sick of it himself. Exhausted, bored. He lays the boy down on his back and crosses his hands on his chest, and he stands up, a little unsteadily, stares, fixes his feet, opens his trousers and takes out his cock and gets to the nub of the matter, cuts to the conclusion, in double quick time, as if in a rush, and the boy's body winces slightly as the last of the man's output hits him, and he turns his head away and makes a face. The man puts his cock away. He staggers a little, pushing his feet across the carpet towards the door, which he opens, and goes through, and slams behind him.

The boy waits for a moment, and stretches then as if waking, and shields his eyes from the light, and opens them. He sits up, holds his knees, spits, stands and reaches for the towel and wipes the tears and the saliva and the cum from his cheeks and his chest, and he gets dressed quickly and enjoys a series of yawns. He stands by the window, stands there and looks out. And it is unclear what he sees, and it is not known if he would be able, had she been able, had she been there, to see the hovering Kitty Flood, her mouth huge in amazement, looking in at him. Or if he would be able to see anything at all other than his own reflection pasted against the night.

They will always just miss each other, these two.

He emerges a little later, on the other side of the building, onto the street, his hands counting money and pocketing it, his nose sniffing the air, his eyes glancing at what he can see of the city, of the sky, of the world. He walks towards the river.

Kitty doesn't know it. She sleeps and her dreams are crazy. She doesn't know it and she never will. But she will see him once. In a way, she will see him. But that is a long time off. She's asleep, after all, and she's dreaming. She will not come to it until the end, until the end of her world, when the walls come down and the floor opens up and she's swallowed by the whole damn mess. And even then she will not know it, but his name is Kez.

It is.

Really.

The boy's name is Kez.

Here we are. Now.

Life

Dr George Addison-Blake pissed himself in the wet grass. And he didn't know it until he tried to sit up. His groin was soaked, and he could smell the dehydrated nature of it and see the pattern of the stain, which meant, could only mean, that he'd pissed himself.

This was interesting. This was a new thing. He drove home naked from the waist down.

Not home. Back. To the house.

He drove back to the house naked from the waist down.

When he got there, as dawn was starting, he threw a jacket over his lap and stared at the guy in the gatehouse. The guy nodded, grim and nervous, and the gates opened. Dr George Addison-Blake drove down the gentle, pleasant driveway towards the unnamed house which Daniel Gilmore had caused to be built, with its long high wings and its domed central bulge – like an oversized buckle on an oversized belt. He glared at the black windows as he drove past, towards the stables, to where the driveway dipped and the great oak in the distance came into view, and stopped, beside the dawn damp grass and a wheelbarrow. He switched off the engine and got out of the car and felt the morning on his bare legs and the first light on his bare ankles and heard the smooth expensive gravel crackle underneath him. He peered into the distance, towards the walls of the estate, mostly hidden behind trees, looking for the guards. There might have been two of them, but more likely just the one. They were lazy and useless. He couldn't see them. He thought he smelled a dog in the west, but it might have been himself he was smelling.

He opened the trunk of his bottle green BMW and lifted out the bundles, the packages, only seven this time, because he was fed up with this wheelbarrow trek and the mess it made of his wrists. He piled them up in the barrow, shut the trunk, and set off across country, down the shortcut path which cut the corner of the road to the stables, then leaving that altogether, through a clump of bushes and a patch of long grass, then through another clump of bushes, to the edge of the high garden, and along the hedges then which bordered it, out of sight of the house windows, across the path from the house to the stables, down the little hill towards the ruined tennis courts and the tennis court hut. It was a ten minute walk. He had tramped down a bit of a trail. Like a pilgrim, a set-tler. A man making his own way through the world. He was approaching the sharp grey stones around the hut before he remembered that he was barefoot.

Fuck it. Didn't matter. He pushed on.

At the door he glanced towards the house and farted. He saw a big shadow with the sky brightening behind it, over it, around it. It seemed unaffected. There was a light in what might have been The Roche's room, and another in the kitchen. Two small lights. He looked the other way, towards the Cotters' home. There was a dull glow shining through the glass in the front door. All mur-murs in the dawn, humming in the last of the dark.

He opened the padlock and propped open the door with the wheelbarrow and unloaded the packages into the grubby little space that smelled of oil and sweat and dust. There was a torch on a shelf and he used it to have a look at the new stuff. It was pretty good.

He walked the wheelbarrow back the way he had come, gig-gling slightly at his bouncing erection and the cuts on his feet.

Damn it. Damn it to hell.

shutdown. Close. Cease. *Stop*. A little shuddering as the switch is flicked – alright – some rattling as the speed decreases, some grinding as the whole thing halts. Then. A moment to settle. A sigh. And a tentative stillness.

Stop.

There is perhaps the final twitch of an eyelid – alright – a minor spasm in the arm. It can't be helped – some muscles will insist on a port-mortem moment. They contract and go boo. Like little fears. The hair keeps on growing. The nails. There'll be leakage and bad smells. Trapped gases. Inner noise.

Never mind. Some things you can fake, some things you can't. *Stop.* Damn it. *Stop.*

The main thing is stillness. Quiet. Don't open your eyes, obviously. Look at the back of the eyelids – you can see little light shows there – minor fireworks and glow worms and sparks. Look at them. *Stop.* Watch the breathing. See the run of blood to the surface of the skin, see the delicate intake, the parted lips – try all the time to slow it down, to minimise, to make all the workings of your body as quiet and small and as close to nothing as can be managed. Tick over. Look dead. Appear lifeless. Don't move.

Stop.

It was sometime in the morning, up in the hills. Above us.

Delly Roche pretended to be dead. It comforted her. It relaxed her. She did it in the same way that people trapped on public transport in winter close their eyes and place themselves on a sun hot beach, the water lapping, a drink in the hand, someone to have sex with smearing lotion on their skin. Delly though, in addition, nursed the dim hope that the pretence would bring on the reality. She thought that maybe if she became sufficiently minimal in her living that her major systems would simply give it up. That death would get the hint, would seize his moment and be grateful that there was so little left to do. But death wasn't playing. Not today. It was as still as she was. It was not interested. It was simply hanging around, waiting, ticking over, unmoving, as patient as Delly. And she thought it ridiculous, and cruel, and childish, and frustrating, *damn it to hell*, and was put in mind of her youth, of a boy for example, a boy too shy to approach her, when she knew that he wanted to, and he knew that she knew, and she had made it known that she knew that he knew, and had moreover made it clear that she would welcome it, that he had been given the nod, the look, whatever it was, the wink, he had been given it, and still he crouched coyly in the corner, pretending indifference, pretending not to notice, for all the world oblivious, unaware, switched off, lifeless. Death pretending to be dead.

Stop.

It occurred to her also, fleetingly, that although she couldn't get death to pay attention, her shallow breath and motionless frame might fool the household into action, might trick Kitty and

George and the Cotters, and although she was vaguely aware that there were too many steps to be taken to get her there, and that it was not possible, she was suddenly flooded with glimpses, visions, of being buried alive, lowered, screaming, nail scratching, into the dank smell of the soil – the morbid equivalent of her friends pushing her physically at the shy boy she fancied, who fancied her, so that they tumbled together, and rose in embarrassment and separated – death mortified, as it were, slinking off somewhere thinking her an eejit now that he wouldn't bother with, who could feck off now after making a fool of him like that, dropped into his lap and neither of them even half way ready, he'd leave her there in the dark, the blood in her cheeks, wishing the ground would open up and swallow her, which of course it already had, that was the problem, and her screaming too weak to be more than whispers, and her arms just hopeless flailing sleeves, and death run off now, leaving her alone in her box in the cold and the dark. He'd saunter back after a few days. When she was properly starved and suffocated probably.

Delly opened her eyes and moaned and shifted on her brittle hips and shuddered. The room was empty, the house quiet, no one watched her, no one noticed. She was alone.

———

Her room was not the room where she had once slept with her husband. That room was now the main guest room, though no guest had ever stayed in it, Delly not much liking the idea of people who were not herself or her husband, or the ghost of one or the other of them, sleeping in their room. Perhaps their children – that might be alright, children being the next best thing to ghosts – but they had not had children of their own. There was a child of course, but he was not hers, not theirs, and she could not, much as she tried to love him, imagine him sleeping in the room where she and Daniel Gilmore had so often failed to conceive either him or anyone else. The room where she currently slept, had been, at the time of her husband's living, the main guest room, and as such had played host, during a five or six year period, to a serving Taoiseach; a future Taoiseach (several times, once with his lover, who had told Delly terrible lies); several ambassadors; an American film director, now murdered; politicians; business people; a Nobel laureate (Chemistry); a bishop;

certain types of writer; certain types of show business people – a procession of influence which had baffled her until her husband's death, when she had briefly become its object, and realised that all it had ever been about, really, was money. She soon put a stop to it then.

The presence of the torch in the bedclothes puzzled her.

It was nearly eight o'clock, which meant that this was the latest she had woken in more than a week. Usually she was wide awake before six, which was, she thought, indicative of a dying mind, unwilling to waste too much time hovering so close to its inevitable destination, which was strange given that she, herself, Delly, quite apart from her mind, was keen to get there as quickly as possible, and it made her aware, again, that there are competing will powers at work in the average entity. She could not decide if the late hour of her waking was therefore a good sign, suggesting that she had maybe nearly snuffed it, or a bad sign, suggesting that the enemy within, that part of her that was so selfishly concerned with self preservation, had been less bothered with sending out a wake up call to the wreck of her body, indicating perhaps that she was not as dying as she hoped to be.

A confusion existed in Delly, triple branched, between wants and needs and hopes. Which was the main line, which were the offshoots? Sometimes she wrestled with it, she sighed and rolled her eyes, thinking that her confusion might be good news, that maybe her mind was going at last. But she was often horrid sharp, and hated it. She did her best to disremember the names of things, but failed. It would be a good day, a fine day, when her triple confusion concerned Kitty, George and Mrs Cotter, and which of them was which. All she had managed so far was a lazy kind of stupidity, aided by her eyes, which made her sometimes gruff and grumpy and caused her to act deaf and to understand slowly.

There was a lot of pretence in Delly's average day, but she was unaware of most of it.

The letter had slipped to the floor and she could see it but did not know what it was, her eyesight not working at that particular range, it being too close to her, and she glanced at the pale colour square of it peeking out from under a fallen blanket without really taking it in. The torch she pawed at, having forgotten already that she had been surprised upon seeing it, it having become by now simply another prop of uncertain purpose which cluttered up the space in which she was dying. Like the jars and bottles of various medications; the books and magazines read to her on an irregular basis; the clocks; the three radios; the television, for which she had a remote control somewhere – maybe that was the thing in the bed – no, that seemed to be some kind of torch; the panic button on the ugly necklace which she had thrown as far from her as she could manage (it lay some two feet away, the button itself lodged in a slipper); the telephone; boxes and packets of tissues; a bottle of mineral water with ice bucket and glasses; glasses – eye glasses that is – four pairs, all of them useless; the book shelves; their volumes; the paintings she could not quite make out any more, and memories of which tormented her, not knowing the veracity, afraid to ask, driven mad by visions of the things which she was sure were warped and distorted and unrelated to the truth.

The whole bloody thing made her mad.

And she was no longer, she now realised, happy to die in the guest room. It was too small. She could not see it. Her eyes had become odd that way – ignoring the close to hand in favour of the distant, which was, she assumed, something to do with dying, but could not decide whether it was poignant or funny, or whether it was both, and whether poignant and funny weren't actually the same thing. What she saw with most clarity in her room was the sky. And not much happened there. All bland blue nonsense with the occasional plane. What she needed was the long room. The once drawing room. The once formal place which had become, sometime before her husband's death, her sitting room, her favourite place, her refuge. That was where she wanted to die. And it had endless windows as well, with views, though she could not quite remember what views, and with a fireplace which they could get going for her, and they could put the television at the opposite end of the room to her bed so that she could see the news or the shopping channels in the early hours.

That, she would like.

It was rare now that they took her around the house. Sometimes they coaxed her into a wheelchair and rolled her along the corridor to the map room, with its view of the driveway and with her late husband's collection of eastern pornography. Which was not pornography exactly – it had historic and, as she understood it, cultural significance, it was called *erotica*, it was worth a fortune apparently, and twice now nervous academics had come to *examine* it – but to her it seemed cold and precise and diagrammatic, too many flash red vaginas and needle penises, all insertion and no warmth. There were no maps in the map room. It had been her husband's little joke.

As well as the button on the necklace, she had beside her, somewhere, another device, a more localised alarm, which served to alert either Kitty or George that she was awake, that it was time to come and prod her with fingers and poke her with horrible little congratulations on having made it through the night. She was forever confusing the two things, the two alarms, and causing widespread panic and putting various emergency services on high alert, though she did not know exactly what the procedure which the more serious alarm initiated was, only that she was scolded by George for putting it in train, and that he would spend long apologetic minutes on the telephone afterwards standing people down. There had been some debate about taking this panic button from her, George arguing that it would not be a bad idea, given that the local alarm was sufficient to raise whoever was in the house and that they could then alert whoever needed to be alerted. Delly had nodded weakly but enthusiastically at this, terrified as she was by the whole horrible notion of being somehow connected to strangers, but Kitty had over ruled the two of them, insisting that the local alarm was not an alarm at all, simply a request for attention, and that there would be no way of knowing whether Delly pressed it because she fancied a cup of tea or was having some kind of seizure, and that valuable minutes would be lost in the time it took whoever it was to climb the stairs from God knows where in the house, and that Delly should have control over her own health care and not have to rely on the quickness or otherwise of others, that it was an issue of self determination, that it was, in the most important sense, a feminist issue and an issue of human dignity and she would not hear of it, would *not* hear of it, that she would not let it happen.

21

Kitty extended this argument into demands for an entire full time nursing staff to be employed. But Delly forbade it. At first, when she had fled the clinic and had hoped for a quick death, she had been almost violent in her opposition. Poor Kitty had suffered. Her endless and exasperated explanations of what was involved, and her insistence that she and Dr Mullen could find nurses who were not incapable of silence did not convince Delly for a moment. Quite apart from the chief danger – that they might keep her alive – there were the lesser annoyances – of having to look at them, of having to listen to them, of having to generally and consistently suffer them. It was too much for Delly to consider. She had had her fill in the hospitals. She had been drip fed their kindness and their pity and their encourage- ment for too long. They were terrible people. They didn't care. They would intervene to keep themselves in a job. And they would talk to her, as nurses had always talked to her, automat- ically, unaware of it, in a slop of English, like gardeners talking to their flowers.

She had felt guilt of course, about Kitty's anguish. But stronger than that guilt was another, older guilt, which she was tired of, which she could no longer carry.

Stop.

The arrival of George from New York had been the perfect remedy. Kitty no longer bore the sole responsibility. Dr Mullen could no longer claim that Delly was without medical supervi- sion. And George had respected her wishes, and had understood her, and had ended the threat of nurses. He could look after her. He kept away some of the pain. She went about her dying, as best she could.

Kitty remained sceptical, and the compromise had been the alarms. Delly assumed that the main one was designed to save her. She might have complained. But it kept Kitty quiet and it kept Dr Mullen away. And Delly was in control of it. So it didn't really matter. She would never press it. Not intentionally. When the time came, when the shutdown started, when the collapse began, she would stick her hands beneath the covers and she would go as gently as a breath released. Oh the joy of it. Clean and blank. New sheets on the bed. Deep sleeping.

Now. She could not find the second device. It was meant to be a bracelet, but it was too loose and was constantly detaching itself from her spindly wrist. She rummaged for it beneath the bed-clothes and craned her neck over the bed, but could not see it. Her eye, which she did not trust, told her that it was beside her slip-per – that the bracelet could be plainly seen. Her eye was not suf-ficiently discerning to distinguish the bracelet from the necklace, and although Delly half knew this, she also fully knew that the bag needed changing, that she could do with a wash, that she would like the remote control and the television on, would quite like to hear the day's newspapers, would quite like to be reas-sured that Kitty and George were still alive, that she hadn't been abandoned, as she sometimes feared she would be, the last living creature on the planet, to an eternity of memories and awful smells. She picked up books from the bedside table, one by one, and flung them, though flung is too strong a word, at the slipper. On the fourth effort a loud bell could be heard ringing some-where beneath her. It was, she thought, like the scream of a terri-ble child, a metal child, made out of cold air and accident debris. She stared at the floor, and cursed. She cursed vicious and vio-lent, and fell back on her pillows in the certain knowledge that she had at least another few hours of living left now. Damn things. Noise and horror and the continuing life. She held her breath and tried to faint. No joy.

And as she did so, in the far distance, across the countryside, in the southern suburbs of the city of Dublin, an operating theatre in a private clinic was powered up, and a three man team of consul-tants – an anaesthetist and two surgeons – were disturbed from their slumbers and their early morning golf, and a specially adapted helicopter started its engines and began the thumping rotation of its blades, its flight crew already on board, while four paramedics moved purposefully, swiftly, tugging up the zips on their green jump suits, towards the machine they had taken to calling, simply, The Delly Copter.

She would not have liked that.

––––––––

What we summon to us comes in any case. What we ask for. What we call.

The letter had fallen to the floor. Near the slipper containing the warning jewellery, beside the book impact zone, in the general clutter of Delly's room, the clutter which splashed out from her bed like the spray of the sea. It was nearly thirty years old. It was a little faded, thumbed thin, but legible to the average eye. It was about the past. Even when it was written it had been about the past.

Kitty Flood was the first to get to Delly. Kitty, with her mouth dry and scratchy so that she could barely talk, with her dressing gown flailing and her mind grappling – with the hour and with the noise, and with the notion, dim but definite, that this was it, finally, already, now, Delly was on her way out and death was coming in.

There had been so many alarms.

Kitty opened the door, which was the worst, of course – her hand upon it, pushing, and the room unfolding before her, and her mind preparing to see Delly, slipped from safety and sprawled on the shore, washed up with all the rest of it, with the tissues and the bottles and the pills and the buttons and the abandoned fruit, leaving Kitty on her own. She prepared for it. Prepared to see it – to see Delly dead and to be on her own. She had it swallowed, so that, of course, the opening of the door and the unfolding of the room was slowed down, to the speed of something appropriate, such as memory perhaps, of something recalled, replayed, so that there was confusion as to what came at the end of it, leaving Kitty somewhat perplexed as to whether the Delly she eventually saw, after the full rotation of the otherwise familiar room, was dead, alive, or dying, so that she had to ask.

'Delly?' she croaked, her mouth grubbying the words like dirty hands on bread. 'Are you dead?'

Delly picked her out, or seemed to. Eyes open. Staring. Perhaps it was, thought Kitty Flood, knowing the same things as the rest of us, a dead reflex, a swivel of old muscles towards a voice, something horrid in the shutdown fixing on her.

'What?' said a voice, like Delly's voice, but her mouth was hidden.

'What?' said Kitty.

They gaped at each other. It took Kitty a moment. It was simply that she was so near to sleep, so recently woken, so soon out of dreaming, that logic remained, for now, a very flexible thing.

'Are you? Oh you are. I mean, you're fine. Aren't you? Nod dear.'

Delly nodded, and it was this, and the fact that she was sitting up now, was clutching the bedspread to her chin and staring at Kitty and had blinked, Kitty thought, yes, had certainly blinked, and there, again, definitely blinking, which meant that she still lived. The fact that she was muttering something did not accrue. Kitty cut her off.

'Oh Delly. Did you sit on it again? It's chaos. Did you confuse the two? What will we do with you? Where's Dr George? He'll have to call them. Oh Delly, Delly, Delly.'

She left her then to her clutching and her mutters, and she set off down the hall, noticing for the first time the early light, the childish light, crawling down the corridor raising dust, towards the American's room. She passed his door and had to backtrack, not counting right, distracted by the racket, and she hammered then, on the door, the doctor's door, for what seemed like minutes, before he stirred, before he shouted something like *'awright'*, while she wittered on, loudly, looking down at the light creeping over her feet, which were bare.

He was a thin man, Dr George Addison-Blake. Dr George. Kitty, who was not thin, did not like this about him. Amongst other things. He emerged from his room in a t-shirt, his hands fumbling with the buttons on a pair of unbelted jeans which clung to his bones, his feet bare like hers, but, she couldn't help noticing, surprisingly dirty, slapping down the dusty sunlight, a mobile phone stuck in the crook of his neck, already dialled. He didn't even look at her.

He was thin in the sense that there seemed to be nothing in him. Hollow thin. She had mentioned it to Delly, in neutral tones, about how slim he was, how he needed fattening up, how he seemed faded, a facsimile, traced. Delly had eyed her, smiling. Thought her jealous. So Kitty had voiced it a little stronger – that it was, well, you could almost say unnatural, how thin he was. Unhealthy. Delly eyed her then without smiling, silent, considering, Kitty had thought, what was behind it. So Kitty let it go. It wouldn't do apparently, to be at all negative about Dr George.

He padded past her, starting to talk into his phone, and made his calm way to the little control box on the wall outside Delly's room, where he killed the alarm and the house went quiet.

She should have done that. She had forgotten. She had even forgotten the noise. The sudden silence was shocking. It woke her. It broke the last thin connection to sleep and flung her into the waking world with a belly flop slap. She wrapped her gown tight and felt a tiny measure of pure malicious hatred seep into her guts as the doctor went to Delly and continued to talk, doing several things at once, quickly, calmly, on his own.

She watched him and tried not to watch him, and smiled at Delly, who looked by now like she had been witness to a haunting, so pale and frozen was she. Kitty wondered how much she could see of anything. Dr George checked her pulse and felt her brow and peeked beneath her covers, but he barely looked at her, all the time he kept on talking into the little box at his neck, his voice clipped, elsewhere, nothing to do with Delly. And he looked awful this morning. Not just thin, but pale, black eyed, ruined. A late night, it seemed. She didn't know what his late nights entailed. He drank, but she didn't know what he drank, or how much, or what else he did, and she didn't want to know, and he didn't tell her. He dropped Delly's hand and began to pace. His feet were black. Did he not wash?

It was then that she saw it. Her eyes on the doctor's feet had led her to the necklace device, the panic button, and she had bent down to pick it up, with the intention of telling Delly once more, again, the difference between the two things, panic and attention, attention and panic, and she was looking at the long string of it, the long red string, sticking out of the slipper, like a string on a whistle, and she couldn't understand how that could be confused with the short white string of the bracelet, and she was down there, with her fingers on it, rummaging, when she saw the letter.

In fact, it was words she saw first. Certain words. Certain phrases. Peering up at her from the carpet. Particular words in particular conjunctions, short black shapes, with tendrils and tails, disturbing her, like living things, like little living creatures, mandibles and eyes, and her in her bare feet.

She didn't think about it. She gathered them up, swept the fallen phrases into her hand, collected them all, the crawling ink and the clicking spaces and all the trails they secreted, and she stuffed them into her dressing gown pocket. She felt that she was protecting Delly. She crouched on the floor and did her best to be discreet, so that she would not alarm her friend, and it is true to say, as false as it sounds, that she did not connect the words on the floor and the woman on the bed. As if the letter had been dropped there by a ghost, by an intruder, had been left as a trap. But by the time she had risen from her crouch she realised that of course it was Delly's letter, that she had dropped it, that she would miss it. But nevertheless. She coughed to cover the sound of the paper, crumpling as she stood.

She didn't know why.

Delly lay still and quiet, with her long hair gathered, and her blurred eyes looking somewhere towards the window, and her clutching, scratched hands still holding the blankets to her chin. She hadn't noticed. Dr George was in the landing, and his voice continued. Kitty sighed. Sighed and shook her head.

'Delly Delly Delly,' she said. 'What will we do with you?'

Drown her. Poison her. Smother her. Take a hammer to her sleeping head. Something. Anything.

She had thought of asking. But it did not seem fair. And she was scared, in any case, of sudden things, or violence. She was a timid little creature, and she knew she was, and it made her mad. Or, more accurately, it made her a timid version of mad. It made her grumpy. She thought that if she had been poor she would probably have died long before. Not as a result of illness, but as a result of her insufferable, maddening gentility. Someone would have murdered her. Someone would have lost patience, finally. Or she would have starved to death in a foreign city, too shy to ask for directions, or food, or shelter. But she had been cosseted, shielded, protected by money. She had been hidden by riches and the magic of the big numbers. Her shy silence and its accompanying bad humour were put down to power.

For Delly Roche was fabulously rich.

Fabulous is not a word she would have used herself. There was an uneasiness in her mind. She shifted uncomfortably under the weight of it. For it was not hers. It was someone else's. Her own past, which she refused to recall, much as she refused to recall anything, had featured a struggling, quiet spoken, industrious and incompetent salesman of a father, an over weight, under educated, overly sentimental and, in the end, insufficiently sane mother, as well as two older brothers and three older sisters, all of them in varying degrees of ill health and neediness, packed unhappily into a two bed-roomed house on Dorset Street.

It was lost to her.

Nobody seemed to know exactly how much she was worth. There were accountants, lawyers, financial managers, brokers, and they all had different numbers, they all disagreed. Probably Millington knew. Mr Anthony Millington, of Ritter & Floyd, Dublin. Though he would have had to cross check. With a man called Douglas Elliman in New York. With Jean Paul Girard in Paris. With the Gilmore Group, in London. And even then, a certain amount of it was incalculable, existing as it did in such intangibles as stocks, stock options, part shares in stocks and stock options, conditional holdings of bonds and futures, copyrights and patents and patents pending, deeds and entitlements to properties owned by subsidiary companies, the companies themselves, often publicly quoted, sometimes constituted as holding companies, often further entangled in the über holding companies of associates and former associates either as part of, or independently of, international corporations, in a system of off shore and global accounting structures, with a network of open and hidden, traceable and non traceable, legal and illegal accounts and trust funds and investment portfolios – as well as the *erotica* of course, which, while modest by Asian standards, was nevertheless often described as one of the best private collections in Europe, and the properties, of which there were, Delly was sure, seven, although for some weeks now, much to her delight, she had only been able to name four.

Her husband, the late Daniel Gilmore, had been the founder, owner, director and chief executive of Gilmore Pharmaceuticals. And even though Delly had sold most of her holding in the company after his death, and even though Gilmore Pharmaceuticals were now based in London and she had not attended a board meeting in nearly twenty years, she was still the main shareholder. Which made her, apart from anything else, just by itself, by any measure, fabulously rich.

She tried not to remember anything. She waited for all of it to come to a halt. But in her mind there was a little gathering of thoughts, huddled in some far corner, to do with that childhood house, the damp in the rooms, the kettle always boiling, the noise of sniffing and the strange, eventually scary rambles of her mother, and her father's plain embarrassment, his terrible incomprehension of how it was he had come to be there, in such a place, with such a wife, with such a family. Such knots of thoughts cluttered up her head. She hated them. They made her feel sick. Some more so than others of course, but all of them, in some way, horrible, abhorrent. She did not like to think why. Asking why was also a memory. She didn't want to know. Some concoction of guilt perhaps, and remorse, and fear, some hard composite of the lot of them, stuck in her throat like a bone, forcing her now as quick as she could, as quick as could be, towards a choking, wordless death. She wanted to die like other people want to sleep. She needed to die like other people need to eat. And in the meantime she would have none of it, no she would not, she would have none of the rotten waft of her own history, she would not admit it, no she would not, and she would not have talk of the years, the galloping years, and all of their cantering events, little pock marks in the trail, sights and smells and interruptions, all of them, interruptions only – the little shadowy death of her father, the weight of her mother gone mad, the loss of her brothers and her sisters, the new home with her bookish, gentle aunt, the schooling, the university, the jobs, the meeting. She would not think of it or talk of it and she would root out any hint of it and spit it to the floor. Meeting Daniel Gilmore. The sudden living, the sudden life. The endless work, and then , the endless money. The childlessness. The house, the travel, the houses, the cities, the ceaseless wonder of it all, and then the helicopter. The whirring blades. The cut.

————

Madness though. Such it must have been. Madness. For a woman who tells herself that the last thing she wants to do is remember or be reminded, to sit in bed at night reading old letters, and to decide in the morning to move from a room which means nothing to her, to one which she knows full well will bring to mind the dead men she sees while she's sleeping. Madness. Timid and afraid.

George stood at the end of her bed talking into a mobile phone. Why he didn't use the one by her side she did not know. He wandered in and out of the room speaking to various people, telling them that it was a false alarm, sounding apologetic, which she thought was for her benefit, trying to embarrass her into not doing it again. She imagined that they were being paid a fortune, whoever these mysterious people at the end of her necklace were, enough certainly for them to suffer a false alarm now and again. Who were they exactly, she wondered. Where were they? What did they do the rest of the time? How many shifts she wondered? Did they have many clients or just her? Did they not get bored? Or were they like part time firemen, who left off working in the supermarket or the office or the garden centre as soon as their beepers beeped?

'Were they off the ground?' George was asking now, wandering out again, obviously, thought Delly, using one of those Americanisms which she had to tolerate from him, like his 'obligated' and his 'time out'.

'Why you don't let us get someone Delly, I just don't understand.'

Kitty was wedged into the armchair near the window, hunched forward, blocking the view. She looked exhausted, Delly thought, an extra blur to her features, an extra shimmer in her outline.

'I don't want anyone.'

'What? Not nurses. Not really. Not fussing. Just someone to keep an eye out. Always here, or not here, I mean, not in the room, but in the next room, but always there when you needed someone. A few nice, uh, carers. They could look after you.'

'I'm fine.'

'What?

'Well tell him that there was no medical nature to it,' George was saying. 'It was pressed in error. It wasn't a medical thing at all.'

'I'm fine.'

'I know you are dear. Now. Now you are. But you might take a turn or need some attention and if there was nursing, if there was staff here you'd know that you were always getting the best attention whereas now I'm not qualified and I wouldn't feel that in an emergency that I'd be, you know, adequate, and Dr George is the only one who is, and he's not here all the time God knows, and even if he was here, he's, well he doesn't have a *huge* amount of experience now does he?'

Kitty did not like George. Delly thought it was probably jealousy, or one of its lesser relations. Some nonsense like that. But she was past caring really. They would have to sort it out.

'I have not made any diagnosis, there is no diagnosis to be made, Mrs Gilmore does not need a consultation, her condition has not changed.'

Delly flinched at the use of her married name.

'And anyway dear,' Kitty went on, 'in many ways it's not entirely fair of you.'

She stopped, and though Delly could not quite make her out, she seemed to be waiting for a reaction before going any further. Delly tried to shrug. It hurt. She thought that her rib cage, over time, was disintegrating, was turning to dust.

'Well tell Dr Mullen I'll talk to him Monday. Yes. Thank you. Goodbye.'

He snapped his phone shut.

'Christ,' he said. Delly squinted at him. He looked worse than Kitty. She thought.

'Don't mind him,' she said.

'I don't mind him. It's fine. Are you alright?'

'Oh yes.'

'Does the bag need changing?'

The bag, it was always, simply, *the bag*. She was the bag lady.

'Yes it does.'

Usually Kitty shied away from the bag, always finding something else to be doing, which Delly understood completely, was a little grateful for in fact, there being in her mind, somewhere, brushed under the corner of her average night's sleep, a memory. Which she could not, in fairness, have named.

31

This morning however, Kitty was all action, and George, who to Delly appeared hazed in a vague sea green colour and who seemed to make a hollow noise like a muffled bell, stood back with his hand to his mouth, shuffling a little, looking almost the same as he had looked when talking on the phone, communing with something, his clothes thrown on, his dreams still active. Kitty, (dressing gowned and pasty, a little bad breathed noticed Delly, a little unctuous in the skin, a little, it was what came to mind, *ripe*), slowly and gently performed what was a relatively simple manoeuvre with whispered assurances that made Delly want to smack her.

'Not to worry. Pop. There. You ok? There you go. Here we are. These wet tissue things are marvellous . . .'

George left the room.

'I think he had a late night,' said Kitty. 'I think he's feeling a little the worse for it. Moisturiser now. But you know Delly you should really let us organise things for you. It would make sense, save us from having to, there's the new one lovely, save you from having us, us useless things, trying to look after you, when you could have a proper nursing staff, with proper facilities, because this room isn't right, it's full of dust I'd say, and God knows, and it can't be good for you.'

'No,' said Delly.

'What?'

'I don't want to stay here.'

'Good.'

'I don't like it.'

'Neither do I.'

'I want to move downstairs.'

'What?'

'I want the long room.'

'The what?'

'I want to move to the long room.'

'But Delly, that's . . .'

'The long room.'

'But that's not a bedroom, it's worse than here.'

'I want it.'

'I don't know Delly . . .'

'I want it.'

'There's no bed there.'

'Well put one there then.'

'But how do we get you down the stairs?'

Delly felt the tickle and the suction and then the terrible permanent presence of the new bag, and she lay there with a hole in her side and a smell in the air and her head full of horrors.

'Throw me,' she said.

It took forever. It took the combined forces of the entire household, and for some time, crouched in the warmth of her bed, her little hands clutching the duvet under her chin, Delly wished she hadn't asked. It caused too much activity.

He put his feet down one after the other. He checked right and left. He checked the sky. He looked behind him, he looked ahead. He could see it all.

First George was consulted, as to whether Delly could be moved, Kitty asking this in her most serious voice. He was against it. Which meant that Kitty immediately took Delly's side, insisting that the long room had more light, more air. That it had a view which might cheer Delly up. That it might encourage visitors. That it would be easier for Mrs Cotter to get to from the kitchens. But George was having none of it. What, he reasonably asked, about a bathroom? Kitty went off to think about it. George came and sat at Delly's bedside.

'It's not really very convenient.'

She said nothing.

'Why do you want to move?'

She almost shrugged again, but stopped herself, and sighed. His face was a beige blur.

'It's a nice room.'

'Does it bring back memories?'

'What?'

'Does it, you know, do you want to be there because it reminds you of something?'

'No. God no.'

She wanted to look out the windows. To see what exactly? *Stop.* Did she hope to see it all again? *Stop.* A wave of nausea passed through her, unbreaking.

'No,' she said. 'I don't want to be reminded of anything.'
He patted her hand. He didn't seem to notice the sickly face she
made.

'Good,' he said. 'That's good.'
And he left her, and she dozed, and tried to empty her mind.

———

Then Kitty returned. Delly had begun to think that maybe she
should stay where she was, and just retreat a little further into the
cosy dent she had made in things, but Kitty was energised. She
had, she said, been downstairs considering logistics. Positions
and placements and angles. She would be, Kitty said, by a window, with her back to a wall, facing the door, with a wonderful
view, through a whole series of windows, of the formal gardens,
and the fields beyond stretching off towards the stables. There
was a heavy pause at this stage, and Delly realised that she was
being reassured that she would not be able to see the pad. She
continued then to say that she was going to get dressed, as the
Cotters were now involved, *en famille*, that some things had to be
shifted, mainly a sofa and a low mosaic topped table, and that
Mrs Cotter was in any case nearly ready with Delly's breakfast,
which would be on its way, and that the rest of the operation
would be carried out after that.

'But Delly dear,' sighed Kitty.
What was this now?
'Bathrooms.'
Delly said nothing. She had her bathroom tied around her
waist, as far as she was concerned.

'You're en-suite up here dear. But downstairs the nearest bathroom is in, well, it's the offices, you know, either the guest one or

———

He ran, sometimes, through the streets, through the streets of
Dublin, even though there was no one chasing him, even though
he had nowhere to particularly go, even though he was in no
particular hurry. He just ran. His feet hit the ground, one after
the other, one after the other, one after the other. He held his
money in his hands, to stop it cutting into his thighs. He put his
keys in his jacket pocket. He almost always wore a jacket. He
used to put his money there too but he stopped doing that after
he lost a roll of about one fifty somewhere around the fruit mar-

ket. What if he lost his keys though? Sometimes he held his keys in his hand as well. But his keys didn't cut into him so much. Not as much as his money.

the inner one.'

Delly rolled her eyes.

'Dr George is being absolutely adamant that they're not suitable. There's no bath down there. There's a stand up shower in the inner office bathroom, but you can't use that. We'll have to move the bath chair from up here down to the basement, to the bigger of the bathrooms down there. I've just had a look at it and it's a bit bleak I have to say. I've asked Mr Cotter to see that it gets a new coat of paint and some brightening up. But it's the only choice. So when it's bath time you'll have to go the width of the house to the lift, and down to the basement. Otherwise we'll be carrying you up and down the stairs all the time. Which we're going to have to do to get you down there anyway. I don't understand why they put a lift in that only went from the basement to the ground floor. But anyway, once downstairs you'll be at the mercy of wheelchairs and lifts and people to work them. It's not ideal, but if it's what you want . . .'

'Oh for Christ's sake Kitty.'

'What?'

'I don't bloody care. I . . .'

She stopped.

'You what dear?'

'Nothing. I want to go down there.'

What she nearly said was that she was dying, that she wouldn't last the week, that taking a bath was not a consideration, that death was the only consideration, and being able to see the gardens, and the television, that she didn't care if she died unwashed, as long as she died. But she knew it would upset Kitty. So she scowled instead, and turned her head to what she thought was the wall. It was a wardrobe.

Her simple request went on and on, and grew, becoming in the end a day long furniture shifting exercise. Eventually Kitty and George helped her out of her bed, and while Kitty wheeled her to the bathroom and helped her into her bath chair, George and Mr Cotter and the Cotter boys moved her bed, their progress punctuated by general shouts of 'mind the wall' and 'mind the vase' and 'Jesus it's a heavy bugger'. Delly soaped herself and let the hot water run on her head and thought about drowning.

When she was dry and wrapped in new things, and fragrant, she was wheeled and then terrifyingly carried, her eyes closed, down the stairs, by George and Mr Cotter, who remarked that she was looking lovely, and moved backwards, his head level with her lap, his face a damp red smudge, glimpsed by Delly as she risked a look to see how far they'd come, which was not far at all, and they rested three times, which Delly appreciated in a theological vein, and wondered whether she should hire a priest soon, for a chat, and decided against it, there being a certainty in such a situation of taking stock, of examining the life, of dredging through the memories and all that muck. *Hang God*, thought half of her brain, *drop me drop me drop me*, while the other half said prayers and commanded her hands to clutch the arm rests with a grip which took its strength from some deep well within her, which she had not known was there.

At last it was done. At last, landed. Safely aground. They rested, all of them, exhaling and in, their arms hanging, heads too, Mr Cotter wiping his hands on his shirt as if applying an unction.

The view from the long room was wealthy and wild, the kind of view only serious money can own. It took in the sea to the east, and at night the glow of the city to the north, and always the beauty to the south – the gardens, then the rolling fields, and the trees in the distance, and the whole of the country going south under the setting sun. And it seemed higher than it was, pushed up – a tip toe room. Delly had always felt a little buzz of vertigo, a dizziness there, and she liked that.

They wheeled her in and immediately she knew that she had made exactly the right choice. She wanted now to be left alone, to take it in, to lie dying in the bay window nearest the fire, to maybe spend the rest of the day dying in her bed, with the countryside rolling away from her, down out through the garden and the trees and past the high walls and little houses and the winding roads, down through the hills towards the sky.

Kitty insisted that she make her own way from the wheelchair to the bed, that it would be exercise, and she did, finding that she still had strength left over from that peculiar descent, and that she could hoist herself up and over and down again, though it left her dizzy and breathless and would be the last she ever moved, she was sure of that, which was only proper, that the last effort she ever made would be to haul herself on to her deathbed – that was alright, she didn't mind that at all. She lay for a while recovering before finally opening her eyes. She could see, vaguely, expensive wood panelling and the lip of the windowsill. Above it, pale blue, featureless. On the other side, the width of the room, all blurred clutter, and a blank blue sky.

'It's wrong,' she said.

'What?'

'It's too low.'

'What's too low Delly?'

'The bed. The bed's too low. I don't know where I am.'

There was a short silence, and she sensed uncomfortable, impatient movements, glances between the lot of them probably, and then there was a little muttering, chiefly she thought, from George, though also, it had to be said, from Kitty, who Delly could plainly hear scratching her head.

'I'm sorry. I don't feel anything. It's wrong.'

'Do you want to go back up then?'

She would never see that room again she decided. She had had it with stairs.

'No no no.'

'What then?'

Who was talking to her? It was Kitty, gentle voiced, a hand on her shoulder. Patient Kitty, putting up with so much, with nothing to gain, not now, not from Delly, with her crumbling body and her need to forget, and her death impending, pending, soon.

'Get me,' said Delly, apparently distracted, eyes unfocussed, her hand weakly reaching for the windowsill, as her mind reached vainly for rage, 'a higher bloody bed.'

———

It was not easy. She struggled in her blind spot for hours while they fiddled and dithered, and she cried with the frustration of it. And she worried chiefly, stuck in her low pallet, that she would die in this trough, with nothing to look at but herself, in a place without air, hidden.

There was much measuring, calculating, comparing, with Kitty

37

and George and the Cotters going from room to room with tape, calling numbers out to one another, until at last, in the attic, they found something that would do it. The attic of course. So she had to wait then, why she was not sure – something about heavy iron and small spaces and difficulty – until the Cotter boys were located again, which took forever, Kitty suggesting that they call in *security* instead, but Delly insisting, again, that she would not have those men in the house (*security* being a term, she knew, she understood, for *men*, big men, possibly armed, with anoraks and thick necks), that she did not want to see them – let them loiter around the grounds if they had to, but she would not suffer them indoors, that the whole notion was in any case ridiculous and that she would, the next time she met with Mr Millington, insist that she would no longer pay for them, for their bad breath (she was sure of it), and their footprints across the lawn.

He could run solid for about half an hour. Jogging, he supposed, but he was in his jeans, and his jacket, and sometimes his boots, and after about ten minutes he could feel the sweat on his back and legs, but after another ten it was gone, it was blown dry, or the cold in the night had taken it away or chilled it so that he couldn't feel it, and it didn't come back until he stopped running. Then he sweated for a while, and he walked, and he looked at his feet and liked them. He liked his feet. He could sprint too. He could sprint for small stretches when there was a clear space in front of him. He could sprint properly – really fast.

He had to be alone before he sprinted. Ideally. Because sprinting makes people nervous. Which was understandable. People aren't used to sprinters in the dark – footsteps coming from behind, big boots hammering like road works. Or even worse, if he was wearing trainers, then there was just the disturbed air, the flapping, the disturbance, the sensation of trouble, then the whoosh of his passing. When there were people around he spent all his time crossing the road, trying to be civil, trying not to worry anyone, trying to avoid the cars.

Even just running people looked at him funny. Even jogging.

So he had his routes. His tracks and circuits. His way around.

He was a good kid. It's what he told himself as he ran. He pretended he was American and he was something in, what, not crime fighting as such, more sort of X files – weird stuff and assassinations. He pretended he was the youngest ever street operative in the National Anti Assassination And Non Human Investigations Unit. The NAANHIU.

He's a good kid.

The Cotter boys appeared, eventually, and the shifting of the bed beast began, with much noise, to Delly's terror. She could hear loud trumpet sounds of big metal on floors, of iron on wood, she could hear the voices of Mr Cotter, and George, Mr Cotter cursing loudly, George directing things, shouting orders, and she could hear the little scraping sounds and low clatters of instructions badly given or badly followed, could hear the rip of the wallpaper on the landing, she could hear the low grunting effort of them all, could hear their sweat start, and she crouched in her little stall with her head half hidden, her eyes staring at the door, Kitty by her side, until they came in, all of them, into the place where she was.

The Cotter boys, were, she imagined, not boys at all, strictly speaking, being probably not much younger than George, but she had seen them around since they were little things, seen them sometimes in the grounds, glimpsed them through shrubbery, spotted them in the trees. Once, and this was probably the root of it, she had seen them swimming naked in the pool. Had watched them, if the truth be told. And since then, or maybe even since before then, they struck her as entirely erotic creatures, with no other dimension, and she was scared of them.

She watched them come towards her across the long room, hauling the brass pieces and the iron base, with one eye on her breakables and another on their shining necks and their arms. With the length of the room such as it was, she could make out muscles and napes, and she could see the tension in the legs as they lifted what she would not easily have recognised as a bed at all. As more pieces arrived it began to suggest an overall look, a shape. She could not remember it. It rang no bells. This puzzled her for a moment and she grasped again at the notion that her mind was going, that maybe it was the bed she had shared with

39

her husband, grand as it was. But she could not linger on thoughts like those. They depressed her. Instead she peered at the Cotter boys while they reassembled it for her, stared at their bodies as they bent and crouched and stretched at the task, their jeans clinging to them and their shirts coming out. George hovered and instructed, and they bantered with him and puzzled over joins and screws and although one of them winked at her, and seemed to point his bottom in her direction, they said nothing to her and plainly thought she was mad, or dead already, or somehow insensible. She sniffed and huddled and wanted them to be gone.

Once the move was made, once she had been lifted and placed and rearranged like a failed bouquet, and when she had recovered her breathing, and was able to focus her eyes and cease perspiring, she looked out over the country and breathed sharp and deep and loved it. She saw clouds of green leaves nuzzle up against the trees, she saw birds veer and flap in the empty air, she saw a blue sky spun with high white strands, and the roll of the green fields and the dark hedges and the cluttered woods down away from her towards the blur in the distance and the sea at her shoulder.

Delly sipped water and dabbed at her lips and coughed for hours, and watched the long day dim. She grew calm and was happy. Nothing prompted, nothing forced.

All she wanted now was for death to come and get her.

Dublin.

Plural proper noun.

There is a Dublin of the rich of course, and a Dublin of the poor. That's standard stuff. But there's more than that. The rich like a little multiplicity after all; the poor are wealthy in variation. And then there's the neither rich nor poor – the getting by, the middle mass, the bulk. Where do they live?

They live in Dublin with the others. A million kittens in a sack, down by the river.

Working Dublin, queer Dublin, junkie Dublin, media Dublin, party Dublin, executive Dublin, homeless Dublin, suburban Dublin, teenage Dublin, gangland Dublin, Dublin with the flags out, mother Dublin, culchie Dublin, Muslim Dublin, the wind ripped rain at eleven o'clock in the morning on Pearse Street in February Dublin, drunken Dublin, hungry Dublin, Dublin of the vice squad and the syphilis outbreak, dancing Dublin, pro-Cathedral Dublin, writer's Dublin, politician's Dublin, Dublin on the telly, Bono's Dublin, Ronnie Drew's Dublin, Bloomsday Dublin, the Dublin of Arbour Hill and Kilmainham Jail, Gandon's Dublin, Durcan's Dublin, Teaching English as a Foreign Language Dublin, Jewish Dublin, the emigrant's Dublin, the immigrant's Dublin, Dublin where they beat you up, railings Dublin, Dublin where they rob you, fanlight Dublin, Dublin where they rape you, golf club Dublin, Dublin where they kill you, the American Dublin, the St Patrick's Day Dublin, the Phoenix Park Dublin, serial killer's Dublin, paradise, scary Dublin, money in brown envelopes Dublin, traffic jam Dublin, property Dublin, inept Dublin, the Dublin you can't afford, the Dublin that needs you, the Dublin that doesn't, Dublin with its view of the hills, Dublin with the sea in the bay and the river stumbling towards it, drunk.

Dublin.

The drunken river. That'll be the seep water from St James's

Gate. That'll be the paint from the prams and the scrapings from the supermarket trolleys. That'll be the odd drowned man, murdered woman, missing child. That's what that'll be.

How many are there then? Seventeen? Seventy eight? Two?

The paramedic on his third night shift in a row waiting for the word to hop into The Delly Copter thinks there's seven. He's been in four of them and he reckons he knows about three others. The woman selling cigarettes and biscuits and milk and newspapers in the all night Spar thinks there's only six. She once saw a couple doing it in a doorway on Northumberland Road, screaming their heads off, bare buck naked except for boots and high heels. The copper in the cop car waiting by the kerb, dying for a cigarette and missing his wife, he thinks there might be as many as forty. He's seen some things. Kitty Flood thinks there's only one, but she's a complicated woman. Delly Roche doesn't think about it at all. Dr George Addison-Blake has found sixteen so far, because he knows where to look.

Kez thinks there's thousands.

It's a big moon night. Bone dry. Warm. The great summer continues, unabated, and all the cities of Dublin lie back and bask in it, taking it in. The exit doors of night clubs are thrown open onto lanes and back alleys and courtyards and side streets, and shirtless boys and heat smudged girls are coming up for air, pressing against the damp bouncers and laughing, glancing sometimes at the skin coloured hole in the pitch black sky. Certain bars are still serving, ceiling fans spinning, swaying like boats, watched fiercely close by certain worried drinkers, certain half hearted paranoid souls, fearing the worst, but ignored by most. Conversations are difficult. People are hazy now, or so sharp that they're through you and out the other side. No one wants to talk. They want other stuff.

At one point though, about 3am, a guy in a city centre club breaks off what he's doing to ask,

'So what do you do?'

'I'm a producer,' said Barry.

The guy looked at him with raised eyebrows, his head skew ways, curious, it seemed to Barry, curious about that.

'You're a what?'

'Producer. Radio.'

The guy looked in Barry's eyes for a second. Then he laughed, quite loud, and disengaged his arm from around Barry's neck and bent forward slightly from the waist, and turned to the front. His hands left Barry and went to light a cigarette.

'Oh right,' he said.

For a second Barry thought that maybe the guy didn't believe him. Just for a second. But he dismissed that, because that would mean that the idea, for him, for the guy, of someone being a radio producer, is so cool, rare, special, that someone like Barry might pretend it.

But this was easily discounted, this idea, the idea that he thought Barry was lying, because, first, Barry hadn't thought that his job was cool since about two days after he'd started, and secondly, he'd never met anyone, ever, really, who thought it was interesting, who showed anything more than polite curiosity, asking maybe two questions about it, that was all. It was a two question job. The questions tended to be *What radio station? What show?* Two questions. And then they dropped it because it wasn't Gerry Ryan or it wasn't a breakfast show and that was it. Not that Barry was complaining about this. Actually he was doing pretty well. Most of the people he knew had one question jobs. *What company?* or *What club?* or *What bar?* or *What magazine?* A lot of them had no question jobs. They had oh really jobs. *Oh really?* Which was not a question. He knew a couple of others who had two question jobs. People in television usually, or radio, obviously. And he knew some people who had multiple question jobs, which was anything from three to endless. These were minor celebrities. They were minor because, although they did something interesting or unique, they didn't do it either interestingly or uniquely enough to be famous for it, so people actually had to ask them a series of questions to see if they could place them at all. If they were major celebrities then people would know. Major celebrities had no question jobs. No questions and no oh reallys. They had *isn't that* jobs. All they heard was *Isn't that so and so?* It was a line that he had seen people cross. From endless questions to none. It was like

43

going through some kind of pain barrier, some kind of speed barrier, it was breaking through something, and he had seen people do it and it looked like it might be fun for a while but ultimately dull. You wanted, after all, people to talk to you.

This guy was not asking him anything. Which meant that he was not at all curious or interested in what he did. So then why ask in the first place? And it was then that Barry thought, with horror, with a really quite large dollop of horror and embarrassment, that what the guy, this guy, had actually meant was not, *What do you do for a living?* but *What do you do in bed? Sexually. What is it you do, sexually?* He looked at him. Oh Christ. They had, after all, been kissing, and they had not, after all, exchanged names, so why would the guy, this guy, break off kissing, move mouth from mouth, to ask him what he did for a living?

What do you do?

Right then. That. It was clearly meant to mean *Which do you do? Are you top or bottom? Active or passive?* Why hadn't he just asked it? Jesus Christ. It was not, after all, as if they were in a euphemistic place – in a club called *Penetration*, at three in the morning, after five minutes of pretty hard, good snogging, to the point of mutual acknowledgement of semi hard–on's, and Barry tweaking the guy's left nipple to pleasantly shuddering effect. And what a stupid bloody question anyway – *are you active or passive, do you take it or give it, are you this or that?* The cheek of him, asking that, reducing everyone to that, as if it was set in stone, as if all that mattered was which one you were, fucker or fucked, and that your answer to that would determine whether you were interesting or not, whether you were what was wanted. What, thought Barry, (with his cheeks burning, all the blood from his cock having rushed to his face in a matter of seconds), what a conservative, restricted, hung up and conventional, practically parental, possibly virginal, conceivably heterosexual, view of sex.

But of course (and this was why his blood had made such a sudden trip), Barry knew that this wasn't what the guy had asked either. Or at least, not so baldly. He knew the question had been broader. That the guy had been asking not for specifics, but for broad suggestions, areas of interest, so that they could both, together, as adults, as intelligent queer grown ups, reach some kind of consensus as to potential compatibility. He looked at him,

44

at the side of his head, at the cigarette poised on the lower lip, at the smoke in the red haze, as the guy scanned the crowd, debating obviously whether to stay or to go, waiting maybe, for Barry to cop on. He could see where the truth lay. But Barry's cheeks burned.

So Barry thought, wait a minute, hold on, hold on just a minute here. Fuck him. Or rather, don't. The cheek of him. To ask that. As if a person could give a precise little two sentence summation of what could be expected from them, sexually, and as if a decision could then be made on that, on that little blurb, as if he, this guy, could decide, would decide, on the basis of Barry's description of what it was he tended to do, whether he was interested in doing it. What if Barry was the best fuck on the planet but didn't have a way with words? What if he was the shag from hell but could charm the devil? What then?

Barry looked at him. At the guy.

Asshole.

And then he thought, Barry did, that actually, maybe, that wasn't quite fair. And this may have had something to do with the fact that the embarrassment (which was impossible for anyone to see, given the lighting and the haze and the drugs and the time), the embarrassment was now seeping away (probably because no one could see it). Which left him, having worked out why the guy was an asshole, in the mood for a little generosity, allowing him to think that it wasn't *necessarily* a stupid question. What if the guy really needed to know whether Barry was *strictly* a top or a bottom for example? There were certainly many who were either one or the other, without any interest in versatility at all, and maybe this guy was one of them, and maybe he needed to ensure, for both their sake's, that it would be a fit. That they weren't going to get to the point of it only to discover that they had two left shoes or two right gloves, all bread and no filling or all filling and no bread, no way on earth of making a sandwich.

Or maybe he had some special interest such as bondage or S&M or water sports which he was nervous about declaring without having first determined whether his potential partner had an open mind or a vanilla temperament. So he asked so as to avoid the potential for embarrassment or fear or discomfort. So the question *was* an adult, honest, straightforward way of going about things, a little blunt maybe, a little lacking in finesse, and those old fashioned, romantic, and it had to be said, heterosexist qualities to which Barry was still attached, in a self conscious and slightly guilty sort of way. He should know what he liked and should know how to say it. They were after all, not interested in anything other than sex.

The embarrassment seeped back a little. The guy took a second drag on his cigarette. Barry laid a hand on his thigh. The guy left it there.

It was, thought Barry, so fucking depressing. The idea that everything would be worked out in advance. It was so fucking precious. As if certain people couldn't function at all unless there were rules, hierarchies, ways of behaving. What did the guy want him to do – fill in a questionnaire? It was like waiting for approval on a loan. What do you do? *What do you do?* What the hell did he mean, What do you do? I do sex. I do it all. I do whatever the hell I like. It depends how lucky you are. I don't do categories. I don't do labels. I do whatever the fuck I like. So fuck off.

He took his hand away.

The guy, however, this guy, was gorgeous.

Barry leaned forward so that their heads were level.

'What do you mean?'

'Sorry?'

The guy turned and looked at Barry, blowing smoke past him, still smiling.

'When you ask, what do you do, what, um, do you mean?'

The guy looked straight ahead again, shrugged a little, took another drag of his cigarette.

'Oh, you know.'

He didn't seem to want to discuss it anymore. As if Barry's time had passed. As if the question, whatever it had been, was no longer relevant. Barry did not quite understand why this should be the case, could not quite figure out why they couldn't just clear the matter up and get on with it, and then he thought that perhaps the wise thing would simply be to get on with it, to stop being so fucking timid, the guy had asked some question, Barry had misanswered it, now could they please get the blood back where it belonged. So he put his hand on the guy's neck, and his other hand back on his thigh, and he moved his face towards the guy's cheek, and kissed him there, moving back towards his mouth, which is where he'd been before the question was asked. The guy stiffened a little, and then relaxed, as if he had asked himself a question and had quickly answered it. He laughed. Pulled away. Stood up. He did smile at Barry, that was true enough. He smiled at him in a friendly kind of way.

'See you later,' he said.

Barry watched him go. Later when exactly? He watched his t-shirt and his jeans bob across the room, watched his close hair and his neck and his hips bob away from him, like, he imagined, a life belt might bob away from you after your ship has sunk.

Later, upstairs, at the edge of the dance floor, he saw the guy again, talking, or shouting, with a young topless dancing boy, whose body was a sheen of sweat, whose eyes were pinned and wild, and the two of them were laughing at something, and it occurred to Barry that maybe what the guy had meant was, what kind of drug would you like. What kind of drugs do you do. Something like that.

And it occurred to Barry also, just there, just then, in Penetration, after 3am, one random weekend night, with nothing to take and no one to shag, with a headache starting, clutching a weak warm beer that had cost him a fiver, in the noise of other people, in other people's noise, equal parts horny and exhausted, not knowing whether to go home or to stay, it occurred to him, quite forcefully he thought, and quite out of the blue, that Joe Kavanagh was taking the piss.

The city was different at night. Entirely different. It was more than the light and the cold and that. It was more than all the obvious stuff. But he didn't really know if it was the people who were different or something in the city, in the actual air and the actual stones and the actual place. He couldn't work that one out. He listened to other people talking about Dublin as if it was a person. Dublin is friendly they'd say. Dublin is stubborn. And he knew that what they were saying was that Dublin had friendly people in it – that Dublin had stubborn people in it. And he'd heard people talk about the city itself – the buildings and the streets and the river. Dublin is dirty. Dublin is squalid. Dublin is too small. And he'd heard people talk about it as if it was the weather. As if it was the weather. Dublin is wet and windy and cold. Dublin is bitter. But there were some things that people said that he could not decipher. Dublin is cruel. Dublin eats your heart out. Dublin kills you. Dublin is great. Great fun. Great craic. Dublin rejected me. I love Dublin. Dublin is tired and winding down. Dublin is dead.

What was that about? The weather or the people or what? The stones or the river or the streets or what? Dublin does my head in someone had said to him. Really? Yeah. And when Kez investigated a little he worked out that really what was doing this guy's head in was his mother.

People were always emigrating when all they really needed was a place of their own.

He still didn't know what it was that was different at night though. Couldn't quite work out why he liked to run. So he thought of non human things. What is this atmosphere at the corner of Fownes Street? The air cut to ribbons and not a soul near. What is that high pitched cold snap that comes in at about 4am in the lane down the side of The Olympia? That is not the weather. It's more than that. That's some kind of creature made of men and the time and the cobbles. He'd seen it.

Sometimes he thought that it was only when he ran that he saw anything at all. In passing. He knew that when people said *in passing*, they meant *not seriously*, *not well*. But he didn't. He meant things that could only be seen when you passed them. As you passed them. Because you needed the speed. Because the speed at which you travel alters your perspective. He knew about things like this because he was a smart kid, he was a good kid. It was like those magic picture puzzles, where you had to stand back and squint before you saw the dolphin or the dragon or the crucified man. When he ran he could see the things that he missed as he walked.

It wasn't much later, or much earlier either, over the rooftops and up and down a few gentle slopes, and out parallel to the Liffey, across the city which was simmering lightly now, gone off the boil, which was getting ready to call it a night and treat it like one, that Joe Kavanagh, in a Dublin all of his own, was approaching the peak of the evening.

He ricocheted around his house with the curtains open and a hat on his head. It was his father's hat, a grey disgrace, almost pork pie, that he had found in his attic as he searched for his daughter's earliest toys. He had the stereo up loud, and sang along with an ancient home made tape which he had just redis-covered. He greeted the start of each song with some confusion, followed either by a whoop of recognition or a horrified laugh, oscillating him between a brief nostalgia or a raucous, mean hilarity at how bad his taste had been, in all things, back then. He wore shorts and a t-shirt and drank warm whiskey from an eggcup, having decided some time ago that it was the kind of measure that best suited his full mouth knock back. He was roar-ing drunk, laughing at his stumbles. He stumbled often, was cul-tivating a bruise on his right shin, picking when he thought of it at a blood dot scrape on the back of his left hand, earned in a futile fight with a corkscrew. The bloody debris of a cheap Merlot lay rubbled and seeping on the kitchen floor. He preferred the whiskey anyway.

He rambled in thought and word, stirring the contents of his mind with a blunt self pity, probing at the places where his life seemed flimsy, on the point of collapse. He was not happy, but he was thrilled with himself. He was thrice divided like a little God – one of him genuinely distressed, distraught, grieving, pulling down the shutters so he could curl up in the back room and die; the second of him filled with thin reeking pleasure, hilarity, pride, enjoying the surplus of humanity that coursed through his innards; and the third watched the others, curious, fascinated, watched them run hand in hand through his little house and his little life and his little minutes, wondering what it made of him, whether it was perverse or self indulgent or tragic.

He had decided to go off the rails.

Joe lived in the minor suburbs, the half eaten suburbs, the ones that were shrinking, were taking on the swell of the city – out towards Inchicore, staring at the Cammock, in his three bedroom failure of a family home. The living room was a peach cream colour that his wife had chosen. The furniture, the look, the whatever, was Habitat in its detail, Cleary's overall. He resolved to redecorate when he was back on the rails. Sometime in the future. If he made it. The floor was cluttered now. With bottles and CDs and tapes and records and toys. There were animals and dolls, little musical devices and puzzles, kaleidoscopes and pinwheels, a confetti of bright plastic and painted wooden horses and floppy sexless creatures face down in the gloom. All the non-essential diversions abandoned. He kicked at things, turned up the volume, ran his hands over his body. He reeled around the fireplace. He flung out his arms, straightened a large mirror that hung there, in front of him, winking at his blurred eyes. He straightened the hat while he was at it – remembered his father in a coal shed in Drumcondra, black hands and bare torso, shovelling and sweating, clearing a space for his gleaming new shiny red Mountfield lawnmower. Cursing. Very little hair on his chest, his father had. Joe lifted his t-shirt. He was not like his father, he told himself, not at all, he was a hairier creature, nocturnal and dangerous. Wasn't he. Just.

His father had died with a creaking chest and a terror less than a year before. Joe was just getting round to thinking about that – finding a place for it in his head - the first item in what he thought was going to be quite a collection.

There was a short silence while the tape player rolled on to the next track, suggesting in the little gap that unrecorded moment years previously when a younger version of the same Joe Kavanagh had rummaged through his vast record collection looking for something which could satisfyingly follow Henry Cimmino's *My Hard Heart*. He hung in the air, ready to dance or to deflate, thinking that, ideally, it should be something raucous but not entirely removed, maybe some Gun Club or Harold Neck. Instead, in a bizarre non-sequitur which made him choke, the opening bars of Wham's *Last Christmas* filled the room, and Joe, for a moment simply disbelieving, thinking that the tape had ended and this was the radio (early for Christmas, but still), just stood and stared, before, slowly, he recognised that actually, this wasn't a bad choice, that in fact it was a good choice, that it was that old post-modern thing, a conjunction born from the time when irony had been on the way up, and that actually, anyway,

Last Christmas was a damn fine song, that it was a better song
than any of that crap the current boy bands put out, and that it
was in fact a perfect song, the perfect song, on a warm summer
night, to dance to, which he did, in his best 80s *can't dance* style (a
kind of slow motion jogging with the torso joined to the hips by
a stuttering hinge), with his hand full of genitals and his hat
pulled slightly forward. As he got into it he detected a problem
with the sound, a dim knocking, a dull thud all out of time. He
stared at the pinpoint green display, could see nothing amiss. He
pulled down his shorts and scratched. Pulled them up and
glanced at the window. A black man stood on the other side –
staring at him, his fist raised knuckles forward, the glass shuddering slightly.

'Jesus fuck,' said Joe.

The man made a motion with his hands, his fingers, at the side
of his head, suggesting madness or something to do with his ear.

'What?'

Joe stepped down off the sofa, smoothed his hair, lost his balance, knocked into the coffee table, a deeper shade of blue running sharply into his shin.

'Hi,' he said quietly.

The man stared at him, his mouth moving, his fingers then his
eyes pointing somewhere over Joe's shoulder. He was a big black
man at Joe's window. He seemed to be wearing a boxer's robe.

'Hang on.'

Joe turned down the music, walked to the window.

'Who are you?'

The man said something that Joe couldn't make out. He
opened the window. The fresh air was a terrible shock.

'Mr Kavanagh. I am next door. It is nearly 4am. My wife is trying to sleep. My sons are trying to sleep. I am trying to sleep.
None of us are able to sleep Mr Kavanagh. This music is too
loud.'

How did he know his name?

'Who are you?'

'I live next door Mr Kavanagh,' and he nodded to his right, to
Joe's left.

'No you don't. Do you?'

'Mr Kavanagh we have lived here for nearly two months. My wife

51

called to you to say hello but you were not at home. Several times.'

Joe nodded seriously.

'What's your name?'

He said something that missed Joe completely. It went through him. He shuddered.

'Herbert . . .?'

'Albert. Will you please Mr Kavanagh keep the noise at a private level?'

He was very black this man. Joe stared at his skin. The dawn was very bright.

'I'm sorry. I'm drunk. I'm having a party but there's no one here. Where are you from? Do you like whiskey?'

Albert gave him a little smile.

'Mr Kavanagh. I have to be up at 7am. I need to sleep now for a little while ok?'

'Ok.'

'I am from Nigeria.'

Joe nodded.

'I am from Drumcondra,' he said. 'Originally.'

Albert clutched the neck of his robe.

'Will it be quiet now for a while?'

'Yes. Sorry.'

'Thank you.'

He stepped back and turned. The robe was a dressing gown. It was navy blue, collared, comfortable looking.

'Call in sometime,' said Joe. Leaning out the window. 'Come and have some whiskey.'

Albert waved a hand vaguely, hopped the low bushes that divided the gardens. He disappeared.

'My name is Joe,' called Joe. 'I'm your neighbour.'

He left the window open. He surveyed the clutter of his living room. Picked up a weird little plastic horse with a long pink mane and a long pink tail. He lay on the sofa and clutched the thing to him thinking that the smell it had, rubbery and run through with something acid, could not be good for kids. He held it and sniffed it and tried to cry. Eventually he fell asleep and dreamed gently of his daughter in fields in the sunshine, with her long pink hair and her bath time scent. And of his wife in a navy robe, shouting at him, one of them behind glass.

———

Later, hours later.

The cities all expand with the day. All those Dublins, the low heat tugging their edges.

Joe snored amongst the non-essentials. He slept as if dead for hours, and woke then to sickness and a scraped brain. He threw up for a while. Drank some water. Threw up again. Went in search of headache pills and had trouble popping them out of their bubbles. Not physical trouble, more a problem of sensation, for it was like popping blisters, pushing against some odd growth on the side of his tongue for example. He got it over with and swallowed with difficulty, and told himself he was not going to throw up again. He immersed his bloated head in a sink full of cold water. He took a shower. He moaned a lot.

After a snooze in his bed he called Barry. Barry was not delighted.

'What's wrong with you?'

'Nothing's wrong with me.'

Joe could hear things.

'Are you with someone?'

Barry said nothing. Seemed to say nothing. Seemed to sigh instead.

'You're so selfish,' said Joe, tiredly, his voice existing entirely in his mouth, not coming from his brain at all. It was a sound his hangover made. 'So tactless. You could, should, you know, curb your sordid little . . . your urges. For a while. Given my situation.'

Barry seemed to grunt in the distance, or clear his throat. Joe could see him hefting the receiver on to his shoulder, clenching it there with his face, raising his eyes, making faces at some guy.

'What do you think I am? Senseless? A stone? Do I not weep? Am I not . . . whatever? You should be worrying about me. It's all you people think about. Isn't it? Sex.'

Barry half laughed.

'What do you want?' he said.

'What time is it?'

'Midday.'

'Christ. Why aren't you at work?'

'It's Sunday. What do you want?'

Joe poked a finger into the side of his neck.

'I'm sick.'

'I know.'

'I got drunk.'

'Probably.'

'I can't do tonight.'

'Tonight is Sunday. You don't have to do tonight.'

'I can't do tomorrow.'

'Yes you can.'

'I'll throw up.'

'Throw up today – get it over with.'

'I will foul the air.'

'People seem to like it.'

'What are we doing?'

'Sylvia from London . . . .'

'Christ,' said Joe, but felt better.

' . . . and some guy with a book, and then a nice My Dublin with a weird little woman who thinks . . . .'

'What guy with what book?'

'I can't remember. A guy, an American, some sort of thing, new book about referral sex.'

'About?'

'Let him tell you. I think it's like a reading group or a car club.'

'Do I have this book?'

'Yes.'

'What is a reading group or car club?'

'I don't know. You're the heterosexual.'

'That's sexist.'

'What is?' Barry was yawning. 'Read the book.'

'*Weird little woman* is sexist. Have you seen her?'

'She wants homeless people given sleeping bags with hoods on them, and she wants them luminous so we don't trip over them, and she thinks we should get rid of our accents.'

'Who should?'

'Us. The city.'

'Our indelible Dublin brogue?'

'Yes. She says it's vulgar.'

'You haven't seen her.'

Joe discovered a discoloration of alarming proportions on his right shin. His leg in the air. It eased his head. The shin was purple. He imagined his liver might have dislodged, relocated.

'*Little* is sexist,' he said. '*Weird* woman you mean. Little is a word. It denotes something of you. Misogyny. Little woman tells me you're a faggot.'

Barry hummed.

'Little women,' he said. 'Alcott.'

'Alcock and Brown. What of them? They flew to Connemara. I have been there. It's nice.'

'You're rambling.'

'You started it. And I'm sick. Is that it?'

Barry hummed.

'I have some great Italian music.'

'You can fuck off. I really am sick. Will you come over?'

'No.'

'Please.'

'No.'

'What's he like?'

'Who?'

'The guy. Currently snoozing at your side, or doing something homosexual to your lower areas. Your low life.'

'Fuck off.'

'Down with the dead men.'

'I'm not talking to you anymore.'

'Don't hang up.'

The pair of them balanced in that space for a while. They said nothing. They had a relationship that did not cope well with silences. They had the kind of relationship that excluded quiet and certain utterances and the direct look.

'Well?'

'I have a big bruise on my leg.'

'Will you read the book?'

'I don't have it.'

'I gave it to you.'

'I left it at the station.'

'Go get it.'

'Bring it.'

'Get it.'

'Come and read to me.'

'I want a raise.'

'I'll cook you dinner.'
'You're a mess.'
'I'm a mess.'
'Give me a couple of hours.'
'You are a wonderful man.'
'You are barely human.'

There it was. Again.

You'd swear, Barry thought, that he was, in some secret horrible oedipal part of himself, somehow, in love with Joe Kavanagh. That in some way, due to a buried erotic confusion about radio studios or microphones or mixing desks or voice levels – some unspeakable fetishistic notion concerning headphones, hidden in his subconscious, that he was out for a shag from his boss. Joe Kavanagh. Radio man.

Which was plainly and obscenely not very likely.

But why else would he be abandoning his Sunday to go and help the old bastard through his hangover? Why the hell else? It was not like Joe could get him a better job, a pay rise, a higher profile. These things were not in his gift. He was just abandoned, collapsing, falling down. All those states. He didn't seem to have any friends. Perhaps it was that. Pity. But whatever it was, it was starting to repeat. It was starting to become something other than his job. Barry stepping in. Barry being there.

He didn't think of himself as a nice guy, uncomplicated. It would surprise him now, to find that out.

There were notches on the front door, the street door, the door of the building where Barry lived. Scratches and grooves and splinters around the lock. He frowned at this. He went back through the building, looking closely at the doors of all the flats. No signs. He went to his own door, opened it, closed it, re-opened it, swung it on its hinges, looked at the hidden edges of it, sniffed the air, closed it again, re-locked it. Shook it solidly. Went back downstairs, slowly, listening. He could hear music from the basement somewhere, thin radio pop, and that was all. He went out into the noise of the street and stood there for a moment considering the difference, and then closed the door after him. He looked again at the scratches. Maybe they'd always been there. Maybe since the lock was last changed, after that strange couple, that man woman cat couple with the 3am trash metal and the cider drinking on the steps, had been thrown out. He shook the door, and then locked the second lock, the low lock, with the second key, the lock that was never locked, the key that he was sure none of the other tenants ever bothered carrying. There would be a gang of them waiting on his return. They would beat him to death.

He had spent the night alone. And he had, as he had listened to them, liked Joe's assumptions. They comforted him. It's nice to know that you seem more than you are – more competent, more interesting. More likely to score. Was that why he was doing this? Because Joe had managed to flatter him?

The traffic sat in a heat haze at the corner, like a melted cake. You pay a fortune for the name of the road, you put up with the sagging floors and the tiny bathroom and the state of the hall and the stairs. You put up with the constant thought that you're living in a hotel room. A cheap hotel room.

Joe had been a wreck for weeks. At first Barry had been annoyed, and had begun to talk to Harry Gordon again about getting a go on the phone in show. Then one night, ten minutes before air time, as Joe sat in the studio staying completely silent and ignoring not only Barry but the guests as well and being a general pain in the ass, Barry had shouted at him. Not much – just a minor, short, to the point, pre-show spasm. In response, very quietly, Joe had told him what had happened.

Some things, Barry supposed, were more important than others.

He walked for a while, in his shirt sleeves, with his bag slung from his shoulder, his feet pressing softly on the pavements, his soft shoe feet – he liked they way they followed one after the other. He listened to a disk he had made for Joe – music he wanted to put on the show. He didn't know why he bothered. Joe would put the disks on but he would not listen to them, and he would tell Barry that everything was fine, 'Everything is acceptable', and then he would shout at him when one of the tracks was played on air, 'What is this crap Barry Jesus?'

You pay for the address. You pay for the short walks to the city centre and the canal and the corporate headquarters and the embassies. You put up with the boiling cabbage woman on the ground floor and the so called double glazing, past which the wind whistles like a kettle. You put up with the breeze over your head as you sleep and the worrisome scratchings behind the skirting. Little clicks and fumbles. You pay a fortune to lie awake listening.

The canal was stationary, an odd attempt at green, lined by sunbathers and kids with ice cream. The sun was keeping things quiet, squinting quiet, and Barry patted his pockets and looked in his bag and cursed because he had forgotten his sunglasses. He walked on the grass for a while, looked at his shoes. Then he moved to the path and looked at the cars. One of these days he would walk all the way. But he got as far as the next bridge and took a taxi.

They paid him monthly and he paid his rent monthly and the rest of it was living. He went to his job five days a week from about 8 or 9 at night till nearly 2 in the morning and the rest of it was living. Except for day work when it was offered, doing one off things, location stuff, writing scripts for the sketches on the drive time show that they rarely used, putting tapes together, editing slots, some advertising, and the rest of it was living. He had spent the night alone, but that was how it worked – sometimes it happened, sometimes not. On weekends he went out and mixed. That's when you live, apparently.

What was this though? Taking a taxi to Joe's house. In the middle of the afternoon. On a Sunday. Through the heat. Which was this?

Further down the canal he saw kids jumping off the lock gate into the water. They windmilled their arms in the air, moved their legs as if cycling a bike, hit their own rippling reflections with everything flailing and splattered. It looked dangerous. Barry sighed, felt uncomfortable, opened the window, thought about submerged and lethal items – tangles of prams and bicycles, gas canisters and shopping trolleys, trapped feet and the oxygen going. The sound of the kids was stop-start and violent, as if they were dying out there, screaming. He felt irritable and dull in the taxi. Ancient and stuck in traffic. He should have been out swimming or shopping, or seeing people. Living or dying or screaming or something.

Joe's house looked like Joe. It was shrunken slightly in the sunlight, somehow odd in its row of similars, standing out by standing back. Its front seemed shy of the fronts of its neighbours, and Barry could never work out whether this was illusion. He had tried to line his eye up with the walls, while waiting for Joe to come and admit him, and had been caught several times, hunched parallel to the side of the porch, plumb line, hooding his eye, like the way you do with shop windows, that trick, lifting your arm and your leg and looking in reflection like you are spread-eagled in mid air. Joe thought he was mad, couldn't see it. The house sulked on its road, glistened with bad paint work, peeling pale with tattered gutters, and a small garden with a plain lawn, cut weekly in summer by a neighbour boy who enjoyed trying to spell his name in the stubble. It was worth a fortune now, the house, maybe twice what Joe had paid for it.

The windows were all open. Barry paid the taxi driver and got a receipt and stood on the path and took a breath. It was cooler here. Or maybe it was hotter. The air was different on his skin. Joe took forever to open the door, and when he did he looked like he had been sleeping. His hair was all over his head. His eyes were bloodshot. He wore a t-shirt and jeans, and his feet were wrapped in bandages, a great bulge on each one, padded, like off-white castors.

'What kept you?'

'What happened to your feet?'

Joe turned and hobbled off, duckish, like a speed walker in slow motion, his elbows viciously thrashing.

'The kitchen has turned against me,' he said, and disappeared into the living room.

Barry closed the front door and followed him. The place was a mess. He saw toys and CDs and bottles and glasses and clothes, crisp bags and video cassettes, magazines and mugs and plates, records and newspapers and furniture set skew ways, disturbed and misaligned. All of it shining in the dusty sun.

'I am so fucking turned against,' said Joe. 'I am lined up and shot.'

'What happened?'

'I talk to you on the telephone, I disturb you in your sordid little love nest. Then I decide that food might be an option. So I trundle downstairs and waltz into the kitchen in my innocence and the floor bites my feet. The floor snaps my feet to ribbons. I have been picking glass out of my feet for hours. I am hated by inanimate objects. I am hated by the floor I walk on.'

'What did you break like I can't guess.'

'I broke wine. Which is a religious thing actually.' He trailed off, and trailed on again. 'A day without sunshine. Don't go in there. It's a trap. It's a scene from Indiana Jones And The Let's Kill Joe. Kill Joe, upwards from the soles of his feet. Thank you for coming.'

'You're welcome. Show me.'

He muttered and obeyed, without hesitation, which made Barry wonder of course, about the whole set up, about the two of them, about asking for a receipt from the taxi driver, about what exactly his job had become, and where it started and where it ended, and which bits of it he should put up with and which bits of it he should enjoy and which bits of it were bits of something else. Joe unwrapped his right foot, gingerly.

'It's terrifying you know, it is the cruelty of landmines, and I so understand the late Princess Thing now, you step in and you feel the cut of the first one but you're already committed to putting your other foot down cos if you don't you're flat on your face, or your hands, and these are both unthinkable, so you know the inevitable horror of what happens next. It's blood all over. Then you have to get away, and the whole problem of reversing your momentum suddenly it's terrifying Barry. It's death by walking, there, look at that, look at that for God's sake, it's ruined.'

There were small cuts along the length of his foot, with one bad gash at the heel and another in the soft flesh of his big toe. He unwrapped the other one – it was barely scratched.

'They're not bad. What did you put on them?'

'Twelve year old Scotch and Vaseline.'

Barry laughed, and Joe, trying desperately not to, joined him.

He had been doing it for ages, forever. He had always done it. He had never done anything else. And he was not very good at it.

He showed his feet to Barry. And what he wanted to say was, *Look, look what I'm standing on – look at them – they're sliced up and useless, and they are what I'm standing on – and everything is built on nothing – and I'm crap at what I do, so fuck off and leave me here.* But he said funny things instead and flirted with the gayboy.

He had started when he was still at school, scrounging bits of airtime from a guy two doors down who ran a pirate from his grandmother's living room. And he had moved on to bigger set ups, people always encouraging him to talk more, telling him that his voice was good and he should use it, while he had continued to mumble introductions to The Minute Men and The Meat Puppets and learned what all the buttons did.

He'd been a DJ then. When DJs had been a different thing, innocent, permed, anonymous, unpaid.

He never thought ahead. As if the whole thing was done in that fuzzy state just after waking. He could not remember making any decisions. Ever.

At some point he started reading bits of obscure

Kez thought that eventually he'd meet every man in Dublin. That they'd all come to see him sooner or later. As if he was the boss. As if he owned the place. Like they were coming to pay their respects. Or they were looking for a job. They came to him to be interviewed. This is what he thought sometimes. That they wanted his approval. That he had some kind of power over them that he hadn't worked out yet how to use. That he was the centre of it all. That the traffic was fucked because it was a queue to get to him; that all the mobile phone conversations were keeping track of him. That the internet was just to keep his details handy. That they were all making money so that they could give it to him. The whole place was his and everyone in it wanted him.

In Dublin he thought that you were always just one step away from knowing everyone. One brain membrane; one simple, basic, entry level telepathy. One guy has the same doctor as another one. The doctor's daughter is going out with another guy's brother, whose ex boyfriend is that photographer who did a set of Kenyan Billy, who works beside Kez whenever his landlord is due to call.

You know everyone. You just don't know you do.

literature
between tracks. He had conversations with other DJs about sound sculpture and aural mosaics. He threw away the literature and lit a joint and rambled. People seemed to like it. Joe thought it was all wank. He thought it was about time he got a job. Then RTE called. He never knew why. They never told him.

Barry had met Christine a few times. She had liked Barry, Joe thought. Women and gay men, that thing.

RTE took him and they paid him money and they gave him an hour and a half every night to play songs from a list and told him to be funny. They wouldn't let him smoke in the studio. He wasn't funny. So they shifted him to the breakfast show. He had no idea why they did that. Why they thought that if he could not be funny in the evenings that he would be funny in the mornings. So he lasted about six months there, hating it, embarrassed, tired, going to the pub in the afternoons, talking to people in newspapers and magazines about what they did, thinking that maybe he could write, thinking that it was not too late to change direction, to start actually doing things. So he started doing bits and pieces in Hot Press, In Dublin, even the RTE Guide, crappy little things, nothing really. Then he did a couple of interviews, for the magazines, and he was better at that, a little. He could tease things out of people. He thought. He thought he was good at it. He told RTE that he was good at it, and by this he meant – I've found something different that I'm good at so I'm going to give this up and do that.

But they had this really annoying faith in him. They persevered.

He did not know if Barry had liked Christine.

'Did you like Christine?'

Barry looked at him suspiciously.

'It's not a trick question.'

'Yes,' Barry said, eyes level, staring at him, as if to say, *of course it's a trick question, how could it ever be anything other than a trick question?*

RTE switched him to a two hour afternoon slot, and he had by then been so indifferent to his radio future that he had relaxed, and had started to be demanding about what it was he wanted to do – so he started asking people on. He started interviewing them. Anyone who took his fancy. A politician. A writer. An actor. His GP. A guy from a garden centre. Mrs Kilbride from his mother's Irish history evening class. He had tried to get Christine on a few times but she wouldn't do it. He'd play some music, and then he'd chat to whoever it was, and then he'd play some more music, and if they were interesting he'd talk to them a little more, and if they were boring he'd get rid of them. And he got to be really good at it. Whatever it was. Better than he'd ever been. Ever.

He and Christine moved in together then. Barry would have been about 10.

'What age are you?'

'What?'

'What age are you?'

Again, that suspicious look.

'Why?'

'I want to know if we can have sex legally.'

'You probably need stitches in the big one.'

'Really? Do you think?'

Barry wandered off towards the kitchen. Joe could hear him muttering over the broken glass.

'Can you put stitches in a foot?'

He got the numbers impressive enough to be poached by a new independent Dublin station for semi-serious money. RTE sulked, their faith badly shaken. The new place had been called *Dublin FM* for a while, then *Life FM* after a re-launch, finally settling down to *FM101*. They had started him in the same slot, in competition with his replacement at RTE, which was a bad move. It meant that he had to work out what it was he'd been doing, which he couldn't. He got married. They bought the house. The show was no good. He thought about it too much, began to resent the whole thing, got bored, let it slide. Eventually they shifted him to the evening slot, after the drive time, before Harry Gordon's phone in show. That was okay for a while. It was the new thing. And they had a child. He and Christine. They had a daughter and they called her Nicola, for no good reason.

But then he was bored with the new thing.

'What are we doing tonight?'

'Tomorrow Joe. Tonight is Sunday.'

'What are we doing tomorrow?'

'I told you what we're doing.'

'I can't do that stuff. Books and trivia and endless fucking guff.'

Barry came back to the front room and just stood there, in the doorway, looking at Joe, silent.

'What?' Joe snapped.

'I'm not doing this anymore.'

'Not doing what?'

'Coming over here.'

'Why not?'

'It's not part of my job.'

Joe said nothing. He just looked at his feet. He did not know what it was that kept him as he was. He did not understand why he could not collapse, fall over, sink. He was terrified that it might be something to do with his voice. With his job. Some show biz ethic. That his voice continued after he stopped. That the show went on. That he was a *pro*.

'Sorry,' said Barry. 'I didn't mean that to sound so shitty. I just mean that . . .'

'No, I know what you mean.'

'You have, you know, personal problems.'

'Private life drama baby leave me out.'

'Which I am not exactly . . .'

'Interested . . .'

'Qualified . . .'

'Oh fuck off.'

'To be meddling in, really.'

'Jesus Christ what am I your mother? Your boss? I thought we were, well, this is embarrassing actually, but I sort of supposed that we were friends.'

'Well that's the thing. I have no idea what we are.'

'I showed you my feet.'

'What?'

'My fucking feet.'

'Yeah. Well. Okay.'

Joe said nothing, let Barry sizzle for a moment. Then,

'There's a black man lives next door.'

'What?'

'He came over this morning to tell me to shut up. I thought he was a boxer. Can you imagine that? I thought he was an American heavyweight boxer at my window. I am deeply embarrassed by myself. He was in a dressing gown, and I thought, being pissed, I thought he was Joe Louis. Leon Spinks. Foreman.'

'What are you talking about?'

'What kind of man am I? What world am I living in?'

Barry shook his head, clearly not playing.

'I don't know my neighbours,' Joe said, quietly.

'Who does?'

'I have no friends.'

Barry said nothing.

Joe said nothing either.

———

Nicola was four. Five.

He was her father. Sometimes, he found, this needed to be stated. Quietly. To himself. *I am Nicola's father.* This was one of the clues, one of those pieces of circumstantial evidence which suggested to him, when he could gather them together, that he was not sufficiently aware of his own life.

It seemed to him, at times (and these were odd times, when he was sober enough, or drunk enough, or in some other way sharpened), to be hypothetical, illusory, as if it were not entirely his life at all but a dull, lazy story that he was either hearing or telling, or a badly remembered joke, or an argument that has not been thought out – that you find yourself in the middle of making without a clear idea of how it finishes, of the point, of the plan.

It occurred to him sometimes that his age had something to do with it. That he was experiencing a very predictable panic, and that he should ride it out and not let on. That to admit to it would cause a certain amusement amongst his peers. At the same time, there was, constantly simmering beneath his often boiling surface, a consistent, low level anxiety, which was now spiking almost daily, and which could stop him mid sentence and reduce him to a pitiful shiver, as if the spirit of some other, better argued self had passed through him, sadly, tut-tutting over his bleary progress, his mildness, his lack of rage.

Why rage? It was the word that came to him. Why rage? Was it just that he couldn't bring himself to admit that what he lacked was actually passion? Of any kind. About anything in his life. There was nothing there. It was missing. And rage was the word that came to him because it was the only passion he could currently imagine. He could imagine himself getting really fucking angry. *Just one more thing . . . and you'd better watch out, better stand back . . . cos I will just not stand for it any fucking longer.* The idea that he could use it on one of his many failures – that he could rage against his circumstances and force a change – occurred to him, but he found it difficult to prioritise. Which failure was most regrettable? Given that he seemed by this time to have a fair collection of them.

He sometimes caught Nicola looking at him. As if she was stating, quietly, to herself, that he was her father.

Why was it that he could not put his disappointments in order? What was it about him that made it seem that the loss of his wife, his daughter, was interchangeable, in his mind, on the scale of disasters, with the downward spiral of his career, with the fact that he was putting on weight, with the matter of his cut feet, with the loose tiles in the shower?

Surely these things ought to have a hierarchy?

———

They had left in the early morning, taking the car and the remote control for the television, having, apparently, packed surreptitiously for days. Christine started the car and then beeped the horn, blew the horn, without interruption, until he came to the window, one of the last on the street to do so. Then she stared at him and waved. Waved. Gave a little polite, meaningless, one of millions, wave – crouched slightly over the steering wheel so that she could see him. Nicola sat on the passenger seat with her hands under her thighs. His wife waved, once, grimaced slightly, then reversed a little recklessly onto the road and charged loudly away. Joe had waved back, sleepy, frowning, confused. He waved back at her, decided he'd forgotten some pre-arranged trip of theirs, and went back to bed.

When he had finally discovered the note, sometime that evening, he went over that wave again and again. What was that about? He thought that maybe she had planned to shout something at him, or give him the finger, but was put off by the neighbours. Or maybe she had wanted to see him again. See his face. Which could be a good thing or a bad thing – he wasn't sure. Or maybe Nicola had demanded it – had wanted another look at Dad, had wanted to see him puffy and squinting again.

Gasping. He remembered gasping, chiefly, that was what he remembered. His mouth wide and desperate, all the air having left his body, all the oxygen having left the room, the house, leaving behind it nothing but Joe gasping, clawing for breath, clutching, his balance going, his mind drifting, taking him to his father, thinking that this must have been what it was like for his father, this must be what it's like for your heart to fail, to drown in the substance of your own life, to slip beneath all the things you've ingested, and sink, the eyes bulging, something inside twisted and stretched and snapped. He had made it to the back garden, and had lain on his side, he thought, and slowly recovered, his mind filled with his father, as if he was one crisis behind himself, as if there were a waiting list of disasters in his head, lined up patiently for him to consider in turn.

That his father was dead. It was the chief realisation of the day his wife left him.

He found himself thinking that his mother had never left, found himself thinking that this was something to be proud of – something he should have congratulated his father on, and his mother too, and found himself, unbidden, discovering a list of things he had never said to his father which he should have said, and as the list grew so did his knowledge that this was an indifferent, clichéd, insubstantial kind of grief, learned probably, from movies and television, from songs, and maudlin confessional novels and memoirs and plays, and that it was the wrong thing, it was the incorrect subject, that it was decidedly irrelevant, that it had nothing to do with his wife, who had just left, walked out, who had taken their daughter. And that lying in the back garden, thinking that he should have told his father how much he liked those walks they had taken on Dollymount when he was a boy, was decidedly, well, peculiar.

And of course, having recognised that his thoughts were disordered, this disorder became the focus of his thoughts, and so it continued. So that, instead of concentrating on the disappearance of Christine and Nicola, he concentrated on his lack of concentration. It was self examination stalled at stage one. His wife had left him, that was as far as the reckoning had made it. His daughter was gone. That was about all he could say. They were, somehow, diverted. He was left with his dead father and his house full of drink.

He needed, he thought, so the logic went, another disaster to befall him so that he could focus on the disaster of his collapsed marriage. He needed to find something else to trip over so that he could have a still point from which to retrace his steps. He needed to go off the rails. He needed to go down. There was about him though, and this embarrassed him a great deal, a kind of buoyancy, a floating nature, a lack of weight. He rose.

Cringing, he rose.

———————

By eight o'clock they had drunk a couple of bottles of wine between them and had shared a joint, and the throbbing in Joe's foot was like a caress.

'What do they call me?'

'What do who call you?'

'The people. Others. At the station.'

'Joe. Joe Kavanagh. Joke sometimes. Nothing bad.'

'Joke.'

'Joke.'

'They don't call me other things?'

'Well they call you fucker and wanker and a pain in the ass and all that, but that's just describing you, it's not names.'

'Right.'

'I mean describing you temporarily. For a moment. They call me the same, everyone gets described like that. Sometimes.'

'Right.'

It would be mad to continue. To go on. He felt that he would die. That someone would take him to the country and cut his

68

throat. That one of the men of Dublin would split him open and bury his corpse. That there would be one bad fuck and he would fade away. And even if he escaped all of that, he would still, one day, be too old. He'd seen that happen. You lose the market. You have to specialise.

Joe monitored his drying insides. It was not names then. Not names.

'Joke,' he said, 'is a name.'

'Hardly.'

'What do you mean hardly? You sound like a little British politician when you say that. Hardly. What do you mean hardly? That's not a word. Hardly.'

Barry seemed to have no idea what Joe was talking about. They smiled at each other stupidly.

'Joke is just your names run together. So it's a name I suppose, a contraction rather of two names.'

'Rather? What do you mean rather? What's wrong with you for God's sake. You're like a documentary.'

'Joe Kavanagh. JoeKavanagh. Joekavanagh. Joke Avanagh. Havin' a Joke. Joke. Do you see?'

'Do I see? Do I see? Barry. You are a seriously fruity homosexual when you're stoned. Jesus. Do you go into darkrooms and exchange aphorisms? You're like Noel Coward with no dress sense.'

Barry stared at him blankly for a moment before snorting out a laugh, a burst of mirth, a little plosion which he caught in his hand and smothered, rocking slightly backwards, gone on a giggle which Joe couldn't bring himself to follow. Barry was laughing at his joke. Which Joe could plainly see was indeed (indeed!) a name. It may have been both of his names pushed together, but what was that only a more efficient way of using them? Of letting them work? It was him – pushed up small and named, as a single thing. Joke. As in something not to be taken seriously. Oh it's just a joke, do you see? It's only Joke. So that, as Joe Kavanagh progressed through his days, this man-made Frankenstein creature, formed of his collided names, buckled and bled and stapled together, unnatural but accurate, crawled after him, with the truth oozing from its gun metal jaws. Joke. Ha ha.

He'd known for some time that people called him Joke. He thought it was years old. A wispy theory circulated in his mind – that it had been Christine who had started it. She had certainly used it. Against him. At times. In anger. Not nice. Because nick names tend to be honest. They tell you about yourself, as you are known, as you are seen. We have met you and we name you so. Stinky. Fatty. Arse Face. Even the obscure ones he remembered from school. Sparrow. Pophead. Eel, or eely. Most of those, when you got down to it, genital related. At least that wasn't the case here. Was it?

'Barry?'

Barry was still rocking, muffling his amusement with both hands now.

'Barry? BARRY!'

He stopped rocking, wiped his mouth, went suddenly stone cold serious.

'Yes?'

'Have you ever seen me naked?'

Short pause. Steady eyed Barry did not blink. Silence.

Then he just exploded in convulsions and looked like he'd burst.

Joke.

———

By ten o'clock they were playing with Nicola's toy piano. Which was not a piano at all of course. It was a piano shaped piece of plastic that played itself. A music box, Joe supposed – a clever little thing. Which led him to wonder why it had been abandoned. He had noticed that most of the toys she had left behind were those ones which he had bought for her himself – the ones which it had occurred to him to buy for her, off his own bat, out of various blues, wandering to or from work, or on odd days when he found himself without her and looking at childish things. Had she left them because her mother had poisoned her against them, or had she left them because they were no good? Was it his wife or his daughter who disliked him the most?

They beeped out Compton Races and Frère Jacques, the little machine straining, the colourful plastic knobs and buttons and keys gone greasy from their big hands. Little plastic music, fitting into the small places, the jangling spaces, like coins or water.

Barry was very badly distorted by the drink and the draw, pulled slightly sideways like he had melted towards the setting sun. Joe thought about murdering him, wondered if he could bring himself to do that, to knife him and cut him up and hide him somewhere in the night. He wished he could. But he could not. Not with his feet in the state they were.

'Do you think I'm a joke?'

'God no, no, not at all Joe, not at all.'

Joe nodded. He pressed the key for London Bridge. It was an optimistic little piano. It cheered him. He pushed it away.

'Do you think the show is a joke?'

'No.'

Barry looked at him quite seriously, as if this was important now, this kind of talk.

'It's your job,' said Joe.

'Uh-huh.'

'So you don't think of it as a joke obviously. How could you? But it's also my job. And it's a joke.'

Barry was clearly having a little difficulty following this. Joe waited for him to catch up.

'No, no, no, it's not a joke, it's a good show.'

'We make people laugh.'

Barry waited for something else, then shook his head a little.

'Yeah . . .?'

'We . . .'

'Oh yeah we make people laugh,' said Barry, clearly, his mind suddenly engaged by something. 'We make people laugh Joe because we're good. We mean to make them laugh. Not laughed *at*, laughed *with*. You know we are. It's no joke at all.'

Joe wondered why he was even listening to Barry. Why he was with Barry. On a Sunday night, without having gone out once over the weekend, sitting in his broken home, a little drunk, a little stoned, background murderous, background falling apart, on the floor with his daughter's piano, his fled daughter, on a carpet chosen by his fled wife, why was he there, fled from and alone, with his feet cut and his leg bruised and his father dead – listening to a gayboy who told him that everything was alright because people laughed with him not at him.

'This,' he said, 'is all wrong.'

'Is good radio' said Barry, appearing now to sulk slightly.

'FUCK IT IT'S NOT,' shouted Joe, the force of the air coming suddenly out of his innards pushing him weirdly up to his feet, stumbling at the edges, clutching bits of air, almost putting his hand on Barry's head to steady himself.

'It's a fucking JOKE.'

He moved for no good reason towards the door of the room, and part of him was lost in memory of fights with his wife, and another part warned him to watch that, be careful of that – that way led to awfulness – and there was another part of him again which shoved him that way all the same, and he felt that it was where he wanted to be, and another part of him piped up that of course it was where he wanted to be, where else would he want to be other than lost in the screams and the silences and all that they had become because it was after all, in the end, what they had become. It was them. And that, poor fucker, was where he wanted to be.

'I tell you what,' he growled, and had to turn around and growl it again at Barry, who was busy trying to stand up. 'I tell you what,' he growled, with his finger out. 'I'm fed up to my fucking back teeth with being a joke, and it stops here.'

Barry did the wrong thing really. He giggled.

'Oh stop being so fucking stoned, you're just pretending, nobody can be that fucking stoned after one fucking joint what's wrong with you for Christ's sake you're a homo fucking sexual you're supposed to be drug capable, so just fucking stop it. It's my show. So I will do what the fuck I like with it. I'm tired of taking the piss out of myself. I'm tired of talking to fucking eejits about their fucking hobbies and their fucking books and their Jesus Christ creative processes and their fucked up notions of what makes interesting fucking radio. I'm tired of anecdotes Barry. I'm fed up to the back teeth with anecdotes, with jokes and rumours and Italian fucking folk music and itinerant poets.'

Barry swayed slightly, and smiled a bit as well, and just looked at him, and Joe wanted to hit him. Nothing personal. He just wanted to get in trouble. He wanted to hit someone or something, hard, to the point of damage, to the point of blood and cracking bone and something shattered. He wanted to hit something in his life – hit an obstacle or a crisis or a brick wall or a disease or a tragedy or something, anything, that would ratchet up his snail's pace, which would wake him and scratch him and splash his face with water and make him hurt and make him central to himself and which would, somehow, in the end, at last, finally, make him live.

'Barry.'

He thought his best feature was probably his shoulders, but no one ever paid them much attention.

'What?'

'I have a plan.'

The house was quiet. Dr Addison-Blake was out. The boys on the gate played cards and watched the screens. Their third man was off haunting the perimeter with his flashlight and his walkie-talkie and his frothing dog, seeing nothing but the high moon and those stars not lost in the dim fire of the city. He glanced at the house, and kept on glancing, wondering what was the best way of robbing it. Not that he had any intention you understand. Know your enemy – that's all. He thought it couldn't be done without killing someone. Probably him. At the top of the mansion, like a lighthouse on a low cliff, there was a single slanted square of light, unblinking, looking back at him. The fat woman in the attic.

In their little house set off to the side, the Cotter family measured out their evening. Mrs Cotter tinkered with her shopping lists, daily, weekly, monthly, adding and deleting, amazed at the amount of bakery items that three people could get through in a single day. There had been some special requests from Dr Addison-Blake, American things she thought, like bagels and Danish pastries and watery beer. Her husband considered a map of the estate and the red marks he had made where the walls needed repairs. On his mind as well was the condition of the stables and the drained pool. They had, in all the years they'd had the place to themselves, let things go, slightly. The return of Mrs Gilmore had been a delight, but a shock as well, to the habit they had drifted into. He enjoyed it though. It was what he liked. It was proper and real and his depression had lifted. His depression had lifted and had settled on his sons. They sat in the kitchen, smoking and complaining to each other about the course of events, about the change that had come, about the kingdom they had grown into being snatched from their grasp. Mrs Gilmore and Miss Flood had been, over the years, nothing more than occasional shy visitors. Now they were returned in full. And for a while the boys had adapted, withdrawn a little, downsized, but had held onto the bulk of their world, deftly avoiding the suspicions of the fat woman. Then the doctor had arrived and their dominion had been torn asunder. All their schemes had ended. The happy days were gone.

They sat in their cloud of smoke and cursed.

Delly Roche took her time, and hoped that time was taking her. Her plan was idleness and a sudden exit. A painless lingering and a quick get out. She scanned the room for last things and wondered once more why she did not simply cut her own throat. Because she was a coward when it came to soreness. When it came to water or knives, when it came to poison or the rope, when it came to jumping or the gun. And suicide in any case, reasoned Delly Roche, was the hard way out. It required a final step forward, a last little push, a last little pull. It was far too active. She was doing nothing now. Nothing anymore.

She had decided to give up food.

Plans are supple things. They bend in the wind, they adapt, they hang back and lean forward, they take certain steps, when the time is right, when the time is altered, as things occur.

Kitty Flood picked up the letter. She swivelled in her high backed tan leather chair, which creaked and scented and clung, and she read it again. She frowned. Coughed. Lit a cigarette. She let the letter fold itself neatly along the creased, darkened lines it already possessed, as old as the writing, and put it in the fridge. She would have to think about it. This was a slow process, it could take days. Thinking. Everything very slow.

It was her office. At the top of the house, in two converted rooms, reached by a narrow slatted staircase hidden behind a panel beside the large bay window at the east end of the main third floor corridor. The third floor she did not like. There was a games room with a snooker table which no one used. There was a music room where Dr George could sometimes be heard troubling the piano, picking out notes like a wind chime. And other rooms which contained cabinets and tables, desks and chests of drawers, bureaux and shelving, all stacked high with dust coated papers and files. These were rooms where the late Daniel Gilmore had apparently done some work. Not business as such. Work. The office was downstairs. Up on the third floor he had gathered and sorted and thought, and had spoiled Delly's weekends with phone calls and paperwork and minor chemistry.

Above it, in the warren of low ceilinged rooms and crouch spaces of the attic, Kitty had made for herself a tiny nest in the eaves. Skylights were punched in, heating installed – insulation, electricity, plumbing, the new stairs. It had taken weeks. She had started it almost as soon as they had returned from New York, and most of the work had been done while Delly was in the hospital. By the time she had come home, and the work had been finished, she was past climbing staircases. She did not make it higher than the first floor. She had never seen Kitty's new office, her new work place. Had never looked in.

Kitty rotated through the night, through the air, above the house, slowly turning on her high circle, in her two room canister. She was not dreaming now. No sir. Her mouth worked a chicken drumstick, dribbled a beer.

Everyone was waiting for her to utter. To say something. To come up with some story. Sometimes this was what she thought of – that she had been sent to her room to come up with an excuse. That she had been told to think about her behaviour. That she was a punished child. Go to your room. And when she thought of it like this she would, inevitably, extend the metaphor, so that she might find herself sitting there for hours on end, frantic, crying to herself, over again, over again, *what am I going to tell them oh God what on earth am I going to tell them?* Or, at other times, she would collapse into the sleepy careless forgetting of the punished child, lying down and dreaming, forgetting to feel bad, learning nothing, forgetting to regret. As if there was nothing to regret. She would sleep then, or doze, or drift somewhere to the left of panic, and nestle close to what must be shock, and she would forget everything, and forget that she was forgetting, and it would make her tired.

There was another way of looking at it, which was the way she was looking at it now. Circular, raised. Slow turning. Stately.

Kitty Flood was a writer.

She thought of something she had seen once, in a book perhaps, or on the television, about an Indian man on top of a pole, a high reedy pole, swaying slightly in the breeze by the river of corpses, and of asking how long he had been there, or of maybe not asking, but certainly of being told, that he had been there for 17 years, or 43 years, or 84 years, or some such number, of years, she was sure, rather than hours or days or months. Years. And she remembered asking, or maybe not asking, but of forming the question in her mind, of how he went to the toilet. Not how he ate, for it would be a relatively simple thing for passers by to hand him food on long sticks, bamboo for example, that seemed clear, she felt no urge to know about that, she did not ask that. She asked only about how he went to the toilet, for while she could see that peeing would not be impossible, him being a man, she could not see how shitting would or could be achieved, without endangering himself, putting himself at risk of falling, his robes around his ankles, undignified, dead, farting. And she had asked this question, or had formed it in her mind at least, and it had been answered for her, by some disgusted person, or she had answered it herself perhaps, in some high tone, unimpressed – that here is a man who has lived at the top of a pole for 136 years, and all you can say, all you can ask, all that you can think of, is how does he manage to shit. What kind of person are you?

But it was what she thought of. She couldn't help that. And of herself she likewise thought, in her new office which no one had ever been in but herself, that she was on top of something precarious – a small circular platform in the shape of her room, or sometimes in the shape of her mind, or of other parts of her – and there she perched, rotating slowly in the high air. And whatever she dropped would be pounced upon. And in those circumstances it was not unreasonable she thought, to feel terror and to worry about shit, and to think that it might well be best to simply sit tight and try to enjoy the view, and not drop anything at all.

She was working, at work, on a historical novel, set in Dublin, in the latter part of the 18th century, based on city planning and murder. Such books, in their fictionalised, non-fiction, half and half, two tone form, seemed popular. The sewers of Paris. Medici Florence. How London built the underground. How New York. This was what she was at. It was a broad book, she hoped. A book with the story of the city in the grip of its teeth. In the sharp vice of its pages. Of which there were currently 38. Pages. There had for a long time been 23, but then Kitty, in a spring flood of fear some two years before, had feverishly belted out 20 new ones, which she had, over the course of a long night last Christmas, edited down to 15. Hence the 38. Ten of the pages related to the arrival in Dublin of Kitty's hero, the sword wielding architect of ambivalent sexuality and hewn marble features, James Gandon, who carried the future as a picture in his mind. Two pages related to a woman with whom it was suggested that Gandon may

---

He had this dream once, that he was President or Taoiseach or something like that. That he was very powerful and respected and he was at meetings and being asked his advice all the time, and he was driven down O'Connell Street in an open top bus, with crowds of people cheering him and waving, and he was travelling all over – to America to see the President and to talk to astronauts, and to China or Japan or some place, where he stopped a war by making speeches, and he was all over the world, and he was the most important person on the planet. And it was a great dream. Except that he couldn't understand why, in his dream, he was stark naked all of the time, and everyone else was dressed, and he was nude, and no one seemed to notice or mind at all.

There he was. Shaking hands with the Pope. Bollock naked and shaking hands with the Pope.

---

previously
have had an affair, though Kitty was unsure as to whether that would keep, and the remaining pages were odd, slightly ana-chronistic pieces of atmosphere building – all slums and disease and sexual violence. She was not sure about the last 15 pages. They seemed a little rushed.

Cold chicken drumstick, a light Italian lager.

She had told very few people what the book was about. Her

agent. Delly. A woman from The Irish Times. Her editor. Enough people to get the word out. That she was working on a huge one, about Gandon and the bridges and the city as it was, and that she had it up to 400,000 words but couldn't let it go, and everyone who'd seen any of it thought it was a masterpiece.

It was easily done – getting that kind of word out. She had not lied. She had simply chosen her words, and known her audience. Which was her job after all.

She threw the bone in the bin and checked the clock on the wall. It was always late. So much of her time seemed spent. Back to work.

She left the lap top on line, ready to start chatting if certain people showed up. On the PC she started a game of Tomb Raider but was fed up after five minutes of trying to jump over a vat of acid and changed to Quake 2. There was a higher kill rate. She liked that. She liked the grunting and the blood. It kept her mind supple. She liked to creep around the ruined interior of the Strogg Prison And Torture Facility, her breathing heavy, her hands like lightning, shooting, slicing and generally killing all who crossed her path – mutant scum. It cleaned out her hatred, like gutting a fish.

It would be her third novel. They whispered about it in three cities. That she was finally coming up with the goods, that all that early promise was now being realised, that it would be out next year, or the year after maybe, and that she was a genius.

She used her hyperblaster on a Strogg hound and side-stepped a lava pool to catch three grenade-throwing dark arms in a lethal broadside from her chain gun. Motherfuckers could come and get it.

The woman was a genius.

————

At some point, over the sound of an aerial attack from a couple of butterfly men, Kitty heard the noise of a car coming onto the gravel at the front of the house. She glanced at her clock. It was nearly 2am. She would soon go to bed. She dealt a quick shotgun death to her two enemies, saved the game, and in the ensuing silence thought she heard a voice from outside. It was what she liked least about her office – that there was no proper window as such, just two skylights in the sloping roof. She could not see the ground in front of the house unless she opened one of the skylights and stood on her tip toes and peered over the edge. She sat quietly for a moment and listened.

Nothing.

A car door slammed and she jumped. There were a couple of quick footsteps on the gravel. She waited to hear the familiar click and thump of the front door, but it didn't come. No more footsteps either. He gave her the creeps. He really did. She thought that probably some people walked through life in such a way that they left a space behind them, a void, some cleared air, into which the devil moved and followed them. This was a new theory, not very developed.

She heard a dog barking.

Three or four loud warning barks, and then maybe a bit of growling. Not close. Out towards the wall, but straight ahead, at the front of the house. It was one of the security dogs. She knew what they sounded like. She thought she heard a dim distant answer from the other one coming from over towards the gates.

She switched off the light, stood up and opened the skylight. She pushed it until it was level, and then stretched and stuck out her head.

Dr George drove a 5 series BMW, bottle green, and there it was, parked at the edge of the wide gravel turning circle. It was in a pool of light from the house, as was the start of the driveway leading off towards the gates. There was no sign of him. There was no sign of the security guard or the dog either. And no sound. Kitty peered, thinking maybe he'd just been very quiet at the front door, when she saw, coming towards the house, just a blur at first, then clearer, moving at speed, through the three quarter dark, over the grey grass, sprinting, with his suit jacket and his tie flying back, with his arms pumping and his legs chopping, with a grin on his face, a huge grin, giggling, laughing actually, snorting a bit as well, Dr George Addison-Blake, American medical doctor, stick thin peculiar, resident alien, three quarters handsome, the adopted son of Daniel Gilmore. He ran past his own car, his laugh not well controlled, a little hysterical Kitty thought, and disappeared from her view. She looked up expecting to see a dog coming after him, but there was nothing. She could still hear his giggling, becoming quieter, as if he was trying to shut himself up, and then she heard the clicking and the heavy swish of the front door opening, and the deep hollow thump of it closing again. There was nothing else. The night resumed.

He really did give her the creeps.

———

Kitty had French toast for breakfast, getting four slices out of one egg, which she thought was pretty good, and they had good coverage too, delicious. It was one of those big, vaguely shit stained free range things from over the hill in Redwood or somewhere – part of Mrs Cotter's underground produce network. Mrs Cotter took deliveries at all hours from men driving old muddy Fords and Toyotas, family cars, coughing thanks for the fiver and asking after the husband and the kids and the rich woman.

Mrs Cotter was quiet. Kitty asked her whether Dr George had surfaced yet.

'He was having his breakfast when I came up from the cottage Miss Flood. He's gone out somewhere. He looked in on Miss Roche.'

Kitty took it savoury. She took French toast savoury. She did not understand why you would take it sweet. She gagged when she saw people get out the syrup or the jam or the marmalade, layering on all that sweet sickly gloop, turning something essentially perfect into a child's sticky weakness, as if as a bribe. She thought it perverse. A pinch of salt. Ideally a couple of rashers and a pot of tea, that was pretty much your perfect French toast meal, but sometimes as well if she felt like it she could have it with a more general fry up, although she wasn't sure really whether you'd have it with egg, with a fried egg, didn't quite know how that worked.

'Did she take much?'

'She wouldn't take anything at all Miss Flood.'

'Nothing?'

'She says she's had enough food.'

She took pancakes savoury too. She didn't, strictly speaking, fill them with anything, besides other pancakes. She liked to roll several together, some salt in the folds, pot of tea again, and let them melt in her mouth. Some butter, maybe. Lemon was a monstrosity. Lemon belonged in drinks.

In New York now, they hadn't a clue about French toast. Not the first idea. She liked their diners and their coffee and their burgers and their other breakfasts – cream cheese bagels, omelettes, even little breakfast steaks, and coffee everywhere, – *m'aw coffee honey?* – hot coffee, not very strong, but hot, and endless, and the chat, she liked the chat, friendly people she thought, in diners, usually, friendly people who'd chat to you. But their French toast, it was, well, it was a different animal altogether.

'May I have some French toast?'

'Shuah honey.'

'Just plain?'

'Just plain honey?'

'No honey. I mean. With nothing on it?'

'French toast plain. Yes ma'am.'

And it arrived then and looked odd for a start, but she wasn't put off by that, they didn't really go for sliced pans over here, it looked like a little collapsed loaf, golden looking, that was alright, nothing on it, no gloop, no mess of sweetness, no sugar. She poked it with her fork, and it wobbled. Which was the first clue, and by sniffing it she knew, she knew what they'd done, she knew it immediately, and she just closed her eyes for the briefest of moments and shuddered, and opened them again and stuck the fork in, and sure enough, the fuckers, they'd put it on the inside, they'd stuffed it somehow, they'd put the fucking syrup inside the fucking toast, they had, in some devious fucking New York way, made maple syrup integral to the actual basic ingredient of the entire French toast concept and had, therefore, got themselves a new and different concept altogether, which was not what it said it was.

'You don't like that honey?'

'It's not French toast.'

'Yes ma'am. It's French toast.'

'It's got . . . . .this stuff in it.'

'Let's see that. That's your maple honey. That's your French. This here's your toast and this here's your French.'

'It's not French toast, it's French toast stuffed with maple syrup.'

'That's your French. You want just toast, no French? Eddie make the lady some toast.'

That had been the day she met Delly Roche. She was pretty sure.

The Island, by Katherine Flood
reviewed by Brian Scallan

Imagine a world in which there was no longer a
need for the illusion of plenty in order to suppli-
cate the many who are in plenty diminished, but a
world rather where prosperity was no longer an
aspiration or a carrot to be dangled in front of the
noses of the proletariat, or a limited resource to be
measured out to all in accordance with their birth
place or their schooling or their race, or indeed
their gender. Certainly many authors have, over
many centuries, imagined such a world – utopias
of varying complexity and conviction – with the
sole apparent idea of creating a paradise so that we
might find trouble there. So Katherine Flood, a
writer whose name is new to me, follows in a long
and largely noble, if occasionally bombastic tradi-
tion, and she adds to it not inconsiderably with her
novel (her first) entitled *The Island*.

The Island is a short (at just over 200 pages) and
eloquent treatment of a small and ostensibly idyl-
lic community on the west coast of Ireland at some
unspecified time (whether past or future is never
entirely clear) where seventeen adults and twelve
children live happily and self sufficiently and in
apparent isolation. Flood uses a terse writing style,
clipped and sparse, with much space on the page.
There is no poetry here though. There is instead a
robust and unqualified physicality, which adds
greatly to the reader's experience of the ocean,
which appears in this book almost as the central
character, oddly restless in comparison to the
humanity which lives at its edge, as if the ocean
knows something they don't. Which, of course, it
does.

It is to Flood's credit that she does not attempt to
shield from the reader the fact that everything will
eventually go very wrong. It is there from the first

page, indeed, it is there from the first sentence ('There was cracking coming down the hill') and it lurks behind every word of the narrator, a small boy named Malachy whose father is the community's most skilled and brilliant fisherman. For a while though all is bright and smooth – very un-Atlantic waters indeed – as the men fish and the women mend and wash and nurture. The women also build, and it is one of the book's best scenes when the women build a kind of extension onto a small house for a new-born. But as Malachy relates, many strange events follow on from this birth, and we begin to see the signs of a community in need of a scapegoat, as first their homes change shape and colour, and then their children fall ill, and ultimately recklessness and the ocean commingle to heartbreaking effect.

It is the arrival of an apparently saintly 'bishop' to take up hermetic residence on a promontory extending from the cliffs near the village which acts as the catalyst for violence and tumult. The portrait of a scheming and corrupted clergy man will jar with some readers, but it is difficult indeed not to feel some thrill of satisfaction when the rocky path to his newly constructed 'cell' collapses into the sea to trap him on the island of the title. The grim horror of it is very well communicated.

Ms Flood has given us a short book which is more full of good things than many an epic. If at times her style is pared back to the point of near pain, it nevertheless does not inhibit either her story telling skills, her eye for the striking image, or her very convincing character portraits. It is a remarkable book, all the more so for being a debut. Hurrah!

At a reading.

Kitty had been in New York for about a month, living with two Italian poets in a very expensive flat in Greenwich Village, trying to convince herself that this was great, this was living. But she was lonely and bored and she couldn't write, and the Italians were driving her mad. One of them was working on Beatrice's revenge on Dante for making her perfect. The other was trying to sleep with famous people and construct a verse diary of her progress. They argued a lot and borrowed money from Kitty, who was living off the American advance for *The Island* and chain smoking and being nervous. New York made her feel small and Irish. All that coming and going. All that banter and consumption and the ride on the trains. The whistle of the high windows, the shoulder hunching corridors of the streets, and then the shocking size of Manhattan indoors. She was preoccupied by scale, by the size of things in relation to her – everything in relation to herself, so that New York seemed, for months, to have been built solely to annoy her. Kitty Flood.

The reading was in a café or bar or something, not far from her apartment, an Irish place, the small middle aged crowd with that fat flush of Irish Americans, expecting something from her, Kitty felt, other than that which she had to give them. She was preceded by an alarmingly sweaty Kerry poet who wore a '*Smash The H-Blocks*' t-shirt. He recited several poems about stolen cattle, wet fields, spoiled milk, and closed his eyes then and hummed a kind of dirge or free verse chant, possibly impromptu, about the hunger strikes. Jesus Christ thought Kitty Flood. Her publicist, who was not there, had organised this one. The audience applauded him, then stared at Kitty.

Half way through her own introduction to herself ('*I am not political, unless politics is that which passes between ordinary people, during ordinary days*') a door opened somewhere and a woman came in, and Kitty saw her, and stopped. She probably did not stop for long. She probably paused only, briefly, a breath. Certainly not enough for the audience, who were shuffling uneasily at the prospect of ordinary days, to notice. But it was long enough for Kitty to see Delly Roche, to see her pale face and her long black coat, her gentle, tied back hair, her blue eyes, her sadness, her fortitude, her homelessness, her wealth. Long

85

enough for her to see a beautiful, honey haired, blue eyed, pale faced, sorrow propped older woman, who returned her short gaze with a nod, a bafflement of her arm, the most timid of smiles. She seemed mortified to have entered a room full of attention, even if the attention was not directed towards herself. She was accompanied by a suited, shaven headed black man. She had sunglasses perched on the top of her head. She hesitated, glanced at her companion, seemed to consider fleeing, settled instead for a rush to a seat at the back, her pale face dropping, disappearing, behind the sloping shoulders of a popped vein Irish cop, or barman, or high school teacher.

Kitty skated over her own prose. Nothing tripped her. It was, she had decided by then, not a very good book, *The Island*. She didn't understand it at all. It seemed thin and preposterous. It was all made up.

He saw a bird crash once – a blackbird, one of them, a raven or a crow or a rook or one of those. It was reeling in the air like it was drunk, tight little circles and jagged little lines, and he thought maybe it had a broken wing, or had been hacked from above by a hawk or something, and was staggering now, wounded, like a soldier shot.

He saw it hit a roof, smack, and roll down it then, the black feathers crumpled on the black tiles, the whole thing rolling and falling from the eaves and hitting the ground.

He thought he was like that bird. Then he thought that was stupid. He wasn't like the bird. He was like the roof. Broken items always hitting him.

Afterwards, a couple of people asked her questions. Like 'Who are Your Influences?', 'Do you See Yourself as a Woman Writer?', 'Are you Political?', 'What does your book Mean?' Kitty rambled. She nodded a lot. She laughed at things that just weren't funny. She was aware that she sounded like she thought she was great, when actually what she thought was that she might, one day, be great, and that everyone should really come back then.

It ended with clapping. With nowhere for her to go, with her head bobbing, trying to see the woman at the back.

Eventually, as she accepted another glass of wine and tried to stop sounding like a fool, Delly Roche appeared before her. She was the same height as Kitty. She was shy. She waited for a gap to open up. Then she said, with a slightly stuttering, apologetic, quiet voice,

'I have fallen in love with your Island.'

The first shock was that she had read it. But this was relieved slightly by the realisation that the voice was Irish. Not American. This was not Jackie Onassis then. This was not an *utterly* exotic creature.

'I mean, with your book, *The Island*. It made me, it made me, well it made me laugh actually.'

She seemed swathed in money, wreathed and garlanded in dollars and diamonds and silver and gold. Though in fact, apart from a simple gold necklace and a couple of small bright rings, she was without adornment. Her clothes were fine, certainly, her coat immaculate, cashmere, the blouse beneath a shining silk, her skirt a velvety, pleated charcoal, her shoes Italian, as expensive as a small car. But it was in her skin, her eyes, her hair. That was were the real money was. Good food. Restful sleep. Daily swims. Massage. A chiropractor on call. Dentist every three months. Air conditioning. Silence. Warmth. Cool spring water and fresh fruit. No subway germs. No buses. No supermarket stress. No getting lost. No tin openers. No crush. No noise.

'Thank you.'

Her companion stood at her shoulder. His eyes on Kitty. It was wonderful to know that if she said the wrong thing, made the wrong move, she would probably be shot.

'I hope that's alright. That I laughed. Perhaps . . . Maybe I wasn't meant to?'

Kitty could not tell, delightfully, whether she was being cheeky, flirty, or just plain stupid.

'You were just meant to buy it. After that I really don't care.'

She smiled. The woman in the money. Smiled and held out her hand.

'I'm Delly Roche, that's my name. Will you come for a burger?'

———

The black man with the shaved head and the secret service raincoat was called Karl, and he sat at the table in McDonalds with them and sipped a milkshake and smiled benignly. At first he talked more than his boss.

'Miss Roche reads a lot. She reads in the car. I don't know how she does that. Give me a headache. She eat a lot too. Lot of this stuff.'

'Shut up Karl,' said Delly through a mouthful of cheeseburger. Kitty had gone for a quarter pounder, large fries, chocolate shake, apple pie. Delly had medium fries, a coke, the apple pie, and a coffee. They ate at the same pace, Delly careful with napkins, taking small but fast bites, watching her clothes. Kitty took fewer bites, but they were bigger. When Delly took a drink, so did she.

Delly questioned her lightly, and matched all the answers with her own. So once the unhappy circumstance of the Greenwich flat and the two Italians had been related, Kitty learned that Delly lived, alone, lonely, in a duplex on Park Avenue, up in the 70s, and that Woody Allen's doctor ('medical not mental' said Karl) had his surgery on the ground floor. Kitty informed Delly that she didn't know whether she wanted to go back to Ireland, that she was free of attachments either familial (her parents dead, her siblings distant and dispersing) or romantic (she offered no history, nor was prompted for one), and that she was hoping to make a career out of writing, which she said (the liar) that she could do anywhere. So Delly told her about Daniel Gilmore. That he was dead (solemn head bow from Karl), that she was alright for money (really? asked Kitty) and would Kitty, when they had finished eating, like to come and stay over?

Kitty was not really hungry. But she was suddenly, achingly, ravenously happy.

––––––––

What will we call it?

What is proper?

It was said by Delly's friends that she had, sensibly, taken on a secretary. They tested the word 'secretary' in front of Delly, and she shrugged, hummed, made New York gestures with her hands. Whatever. So they tried 'assistant' and then, carefully, 'companion'. Eventually, over time, they called Kitty 'friend'. Which made her one of them, an idea that no one much liked.

Behind backs, Delly's friends (all New Yorkers, all wealthy, bored, studiedly unshockable) talked of The Flood. As in before and after. They sniggered, warmly, and talked of the writer in residence, the Park Avenue Poetess, Delly's Little Helper. At first they were glad to see the previously grief wrapped Delly seem to shuffle back into the sunlight and live a little. They were, eventually, jealous, indignant, hurt. Delly was lost to them. She no longer needed their support, their company, their conversation. She seemed to recede. To become a light going out in their lives. In truth she was a light going on. And their loss was of a small dull area which they had failed to illuminate.

Kitty's Italians shocked her with congratulations. As if they saw things clearer than she did. She herself was simply distracted, minutely so. All her days contracted, all her requirements met. And so easily too. As if they had not just met for the first time but had rather been re-united, with the difficulties already ironed out, the problems dealt with, the accommodations made.

It should have been frightening. But it was lovely.

They lived together in New York for nearly eight years. Then London for two, then summers in France and winters in New York, and then home. Home to Ireland and death. Home to the house and the helicopter pad and the Cotters. Home to the alarm buttons and the catheter and the smell of the country and the view of the hills. Home to the past. Back home.

———

'Will you eat nothing?'

'No.'

'An orange?'

'No.'

'A segment even? It's lovely.'

'No.'

She lay with her hands held loosely together on her lap, looking out of the window at the sun on the gardens. Her eyes were milky and unfocused.

'And what does Dr George think of this new policy?'

'I don't know.'

Kitty wanted to raise it. She was so tempted. To go and fetch it and show it her. The letter. Here. I've read it. You never told me. Why? Why did you never tell me? But she didn't. Because she knew what the answers would be. And she knew that Delly's mind was made up. And she knew that really, in the end, it had nothing to do with her. Nothing.

'You're not going to eat again?'

'No.'

They looked together then at the sun shining down on Daniel Gilmore's piece of the world, and they said no more.

Piss poor, paltry stuff. Women's things, insufferable, long winded. Pretty circles in a pond. Simple and quaint and pointless. He lived in the meanwhile, the elsewhere. He lived.

Dr George Addison-Blake.

The women were berserk. They were hideous. The crazy house, its grounds – it felt like a crevice into which he had fallen, the width of his body, with the women on top of him, all hair and nails and endless, scraping voices. He couldn't breathe. He took something to help him breathe.

In the car he could breathe better.

He drove to Bray. He thought it was Bray. He walked along the front, but nothing happened. He drove south then, and did not know where he was. He went into a hotel bar in a town by the sea, and he drank a Scotch and made some calls.

Delly Roche was not his mother. People asked him how his mother was and she was not his mother. His mother was a different thing altogether. And it wasn't important. The fact that Delly Roche was not his mother was not important, and the fact that his mother was someone else was not important either. There was no mother. That was fine. And Daniel Gilmore hadn't been his father either. And he still did not quite understand how he had become what he was. Buried in a crevice under these people.

He drove home but it wasn't home.

He couldn't understand why the security guys didn't have guns. They were piss poor too. A yapping dog and a flashlight. As if. These guys would be wiped out. A half decent kidnapper could make about twenty million out of Fat Flood, about fifty out of the Roche. Dollar money. Team of five, in and out in ten minutes. Fucking on. So George kept his mouth shut, the company he kept. He stayed quiet and he got bored and he drove around. He stayed quiet and he met up with people who introduced him to more, and he bumped into some and he was aware of others. He stayed quiet and he mixed Delly Roche an occasional Brompton cocktail when he wanted a break. He stayed quiet and he ran his little scam and he had his circle and he had his proper work as well. Down there. He stayed quiet and he got what he wanted and he looked around. He kept notes on Delly Roche and drew up charts and kept the others away. He stayed quiet and he wriggled in his crevice and tried to work out how he'd got there. And he smiled at how he'd gotten to be boss without even trying. Cramped but easy.

He loved Ireland. It was a laugh.

————

One night, late, as he was driving home, through some south east town, some inland town, not by the sea, some small dead place, he saw a girl by the side of the road, a narrow road, a hemmed in road on the exit from some ridiculous inland town, more a village, he saw a girl, with her hair wet, and her clothes oddly wrong, standing there, by the side of the road, and he looked at her as he passed, in his car, going fast, with the music turned up hard, the music hammering at his feet, he looked at her face, which looked at his face, her wet hair hanging down the sides of it, of her face, like curtains nearly closed on a window or on a stage, as at the end of a day or the end of a show, or a pantomime, and she stared at him, and did something with her arms, or her hands, some flailing part of her, directed towards him, towards George, through his window, as if she knew him, with the sky above them dark and liquid, and the lukewarm night between them, and he saw her wide eyes and her wet hair and knew immediately what was going on, knew immediately, there was no gap, there was nothing, he knew without thinking about it, knew it without knowing that he knew it, as if he was his car, as if he was the lukewarmth and the sky, and as he passed her he slowed himself, he pressed the brake pedal and stared in his mirror and watched her turn and follow him, start to run towards him, and her wet hair not flying back from, her wet hair not flying back, and her face clutched by something, and her clothes oddly wrong, and he saw her, and he saw the night, and he saw the car, the other car, the car which he had not seen before, the car he had somehow missed, which had been parked in the lay-by, in the alcove off the road, in the dent there, and he had missed the two men as well, evidently, for they were plain enough to see now, they emerged now, after her, and one watched, and the other ran, and her hair which did not fly back and her face, which was window narrow, stage narrow, at the end of something, and her eyes, were running faster than she could, than her feet could, and he saw, George did, in his rear view (larger than it was, or smaller than it was, he could not remember) her body and the dress that clung to it, running, and her arms, her bare arms, flailing, her hair, wet, not flying back, hanging straight at the side of her head, and her legs, bare, and her feet, her ankles and her heels, barefoot, her feet bare, and he sees her running towards him, and this is happening now, and her dress is yellow or green pastel, maybe floral, though perhaps George constructs that from something in his own mind, but certainly she is barefoot and her dress is summery and light and pressed against her running body, and definitely her hair is wet and does not fly back, and definitely she is running towards him, and definitely a man stands and watches, and definitely another man chases her and gains, until, in the end of it, as George has slowed so much as to be nearly stopped, very nearly stopped, going so slowly that he would be a danger to traffic, if there was any traffic, if there was anything at all, on the edge of this ridiculous village in the luke-warm summer night, on this small island in the outskirts of the world, this ridiculous place, and his car is stopped, almost stopped, all that keeps it inching forward is the spinning of the world, the nature of things, the inch by inch nature of things, and her hair flies back.

Her hair flies back, goes taut, and her head flies back with it, and her face is punched from narrow to wide as if a sudden light has come on, show time, and she is stopped in her tracks and flies backwards, all of her, and her hair and her face and her summer dress flies back, back off down the road, and George looks in his rear view, and he sees the man who was running is now dragging, and the man who was watching is now walking forward, and he sees that together they have her, they have her between them, and they half carry half drag her hair and her face and her bare feet and her summer dress into their car, they half carry half drag half throw her, all three halves of her, into their car, he can see them, in his rear view mirror, as if this was not real at all but a tiny film projected on to a tiny screen in the corner of his eye, as if it was a memory, a thing that had already happened, in his past, previously, and which was larger now than it appeared, or was smaller, he didn't know, he could not remember the warnings about car mirrors, he could not remember which way it went, whether up or down, addition or subtraction, and he could not work out likewise his relationship with his own past, whether he had the scale of it right, whether it loomed or diminished, whether he was leaving it or it was catching him, so odd was it, his childhood and his past, so odd, and he smiled at the thought of it, as he looked away from the mirror and back at the road, as he pressed his foot to the accelerator and as his speed increased, he smiled, at the thought of his childhood, at the thought of it following his car, he laughed at that notion.

He drove home in a riot of drums, in a hail of his own making, kicking the island hard, hammering on while his laughter followed, a one car motorcade, past present future, the three halves of him, in a gunshot procession, tearing through the skin of the island, ricocheting home.

But it wasn't home.

Joe Kavanagh hobbled to the doctor and the doctor put some kind of dissolving wrapper on his wounds and showed him how to dress them and told him to change the dressings twice a day and gave him an injection in his arse and charged him twenty five quid. And the doctor didn't think it was absolutely essential but suggested that he might want to walk with a stick for a while, because otherwise he'd find himself doing an exaggerated, involuntary limp which might put his back out, what with his history of backs.

So Joe limped exaggeratedly into Cleary's and bought himself a stout cane with a bulbed head and a steel tip which the man told him was very much the latest thing in sticks. It looked like a good old fashioned hard wood but wasn't apparently. It was made of some polymer or other developed by NASA for the space shuttle. It cost £42.99.

He walked up and down O'Connell Street for a while testing it out. His foot still hurt, but he liked his stick. It made a clicking noise on the pavement like, he imagined, cocking a gun. People got out of his way. He felt he could growl at passers by, swing out at cars, hurl curses at the populous – the track suited, impoverished locals, the old people shivering in their coats in the hot sun, the tourists with their primary colours, the arms full shoppers. He felt he could tell them all to go fuck themselves and get out of his fucking way.

He didn't, but with his clicking stick he felt he could.

Once, on a Thursday, he had called the Tea Rooms and made sure they heard his name and he booked a table for six for the Saturday and then he didn't show, not that he had had any intention of showing when he booked, not that he knew, currently, six separate people, so that the whole thing was, from the beginning, consciously, self consciously, a little self pitying delusion, which shamed him, and which shamed him twice: firstly in that it was, in and of itself, pathetic – booking a pretend night out with six phantom friends – and secondly: the fact that he was aware of how pathetic it was and did it anyway, judging somehow, with some faculty of his that bulged and clawed beneath the skin of his skull, that it was an appropriate level of pathos, of unhinged affliction, for one such as he, fatherless, wifeless, daughterless, one who was, in so many senses, *less*, and that it was the type of thing that he expected of himself, and was conscious of expecting, and therefore detested, there being no question at all that he didn't, for example, know what he was doing.

It was, he thought, that question, once again, that question of audience. Of him and others. Of the sound.

He could not say when he was most himself. He did not know if it was when he was alone, doing these things, making these calls, but it seemed so unlikely – given that his thoughts when solitary revolved around the need for company, around the lack of it or the chance of it or the memory of it. Or whether, and this was a nasty, fetid little notion, he was most himself when in company, and, more precisely, when speaking, when rolling off his

94

tongue word after word, each of them wrong, dishonest, painful-ly and clearly pretended. On air. Off air. Didn't matter. Whenever he opened his mouth, there he was. And when he was quiet, alone, unseen and unheard, there he wasn't.

Welcome. This is Joe Kavanagh, you have to listen to me now. Tonight, what night is it, Thursday, tonight we have, in no particular order, Sylvia Porterhouse from London; Alain Rauber from Paris, he of the hospitalised mother, we'll have him on in a minute; we have a gentleman from Dalkey if you don't mind, to tell us about his Dublin, which will no doubt be a different Dublin to the one you and I live in; we have some nonsense from Angela Anne who's been reading rural papers apparent-ly, I don't know why; we were meant to have an American poet but he's not answering his phone; we have music from Will Grapple, The Great Wall, Miles, Three Versions Of Judas, Ballista, Gardener, Hunk Jewels, and Bob . . . it says Bob Dylan here, I'm not playing Bob Dylan Barry what are you thinking? I won't have that man on my radio show; and most of all, my special guest, Linda Finnegan, she of the famous Lost Dog *and currently sporting a cast on her right arm, we'll have to hear about that; I'm Joe Kavanagh, you have to listen. This is Beck.*

The point was, he thought, that he was never alone. He had swal-lowed his audience. The idea of the audience. Every thought seemed formed for an audience. Every idea, every emotion, every memory. As if his mind was not a mind at all but a pre-recording. We'll be back after the news.

It's 11 minutes after 11, a lovely symmetry. Bon soir Alain!
Bon soir Joe!
Alain, how is your mother?
Ah, she is a little better I think today thank you Joe. She had a bad week-end however, her doctor thought that she might not live after Sunday morning, she . . .
Really?
Yes, she was close then you know, to the end I think, and we were quite worried of course, and prepared in a way, but in the morning, as the sun it came up, so she . . .
She rallied . . .
I . . . she . . . yes . . . improved. What you say? Rally?
She rallied. Improve if you like, rallied is better, it suggests that she was

involved with her own improvement. Clinging grimly to life and all that. So were you with her then?

Yes of course with my brother and my two sisters also, and one brother in law. We waited by her side for her to leave us but she rallied as you say, she is still with us, it is on going.

Are you a bit fed up with that then Alain? We've been talking to you for about three months about your dying mother, and you get all set every week for the end, and then she rallies. Are you, do you wish she'd just hurry up and die now?

Yes of course. It is difficult for us . . .

You do?

Yes. It would be better now if she just dies I think because we are having to make such alterations to our lives to watch her death, and her death is very slow. We would prefer now that she would just go. We have said our adieus and we do not like to waste whole night-times sitting by her bed, with the odours et cetera it can be very dull.

I understand.

Is not so bad for me I am a old man nearly now and . . .

What age are you Alain?

I am 43.

That's quite old.

Yes of course. I am nearly, I am very old now, so it does not matter, but my sister, my young sister, she is still under the age of thirty and she wants, at the weekend, she want to be out, maybe dancing, maybe with friends, but no, she is so busy watching her mother breathing, her chest go up, go down, just watching, it is boring, and she never dies at all.

Are you religious Alain?

No of course not I am not religious. In Ireland I know that you are quite . . .

We're not in Ireland Alain, I keep on telling you.

Ah yes, laughs, *in Dublin, as you are, in Dublin I know that you are maybe more so, more religious than I, than me, but I have never had that in mind, nor my mother I think, she does not believe, and death is not so special for us then. It is simply one person leaves a room, goes out, and my mother now she just stands in the doorway and we are staring at her.*

To his audience he thought – death came up low from the floor-boards, from the slimy pipes, from the earth. It welled up around their feet and then their ankles and it lifted their clothes and did nothing but annoy them until they could no longer breathe because of it.

What, Linda, do you like to read, when you're not writing?
Oh I just love to relax, to wind down and kick off my shoes and maybe run a hot bath and just get lost in something.
And there's a book involved somewhere in there is there?

One of these days. One of these days he would either appear, or disappear.

Welcome back. It's 21 minutes after midnight, which means that it's, um, what time is it there Sylvia?
What?
What time is it? London time?
It's the same. Here. Laughs. *Same time.*
Right. How's your mother?
Laughs.
Sylvia, don't answer that, I'm asking you the wrong questions. I'm asking you questions intended for Alain. I have confused my sheeting. How embarrassing, people think it's all off the top of my head and in fact I can't say a thing unless the staff of writers I employ have written it down for me before hand on this special stationery. I do apologise.
That's okay. Laughs.
Very gracious. Where am I? Rustling paper. *Sylvia Porterhouse. What is it this time? You've solved the Jack The Ripper case?*
No. Laughs.
Why is that here then? Oh I know, it's not Jack The Ripper, but what it is, oh I know, hold on, I can do this right. Ladies and gentlemen, you'll remember that one of the suspects in the Jack The Ripper case was always thought to have been a member of the royal family. The prince of Scotland or something or other, one of those titles they have over there. And there were stories of cover ups and dark deeds and that kind of thing. And now, a hundred and something years later, it's all happening again. Isn't it Sylvia?
Ah, I see where you're coming from now. Okay. Well. I don't know about Jack The Ripper. I think he killed people. What we have now is . . . Jack The Stripper.
Oh God that's awful Joe, you're not yourself.
No I'm not, I'm not, it's true. I'm slightly, um, tilted.

Ri . . . .ight. Well, what this is is this – there's a flasher at large in central London, a little more than a flasher really, but certainly a man who has been exposing himself to people in and around St James's Park and Green Park, which, if your listeners know London at all, will know are two parks which couldn't be more central, right in the middle of London's power centre, between, beside Downing Street and Whitehall and Buckingham Palace. And this guy has been reported about half a dozen times now, exposing himself to a variety of people, from tourists to civil servants to ordinary Londoners.

And they haven't caught him?

No they haven't. And as you can imagine, that area of London is not exactly lacking in police surveillance and general police presence, and yet they haven't, they say, caught him on camera, and they haven't made any arrests.

But he wears a mask.

Yeah he wears a Prince Charles mask, but I mean they haven't even come close to getting near him, he seems . . .

He wears what?

He Laughs *wears one of those rubber masks, like a Spitting Image puppet, of Prince Charles.*

God.

Which is of course, embarrassing enough, but the fact that police seem to have completely screwed up on this is raising a few interesting questions.

People have said that it isn't a mask.

Yeah, well, people have said that, Laughs, *and of course, that's pretty ridiculous, and I don't believe it for a moment, but what is interesting is the idea that the police might know who it is and have been unable to arrest him because they know who he is, if you follow.*

He is someone.

Exactly.

A royal.

Yeah . . . the idea is . . .

He's a member, if you will, of the royal family.

Exactly. The idea is that he's one of the younger royals, and I'm not going to say obviously, because I'd get in big trouble, but the word is, from my sources, that it's one of the younger royals, and he hasn't been seen in public for a while, and there have been separate rumours about him for some time – that he's been receiving treatment for a depressive illness and various things – and the idea is that he's still, well, how can I put this, but he's still getting over the murder, what was to me anyway, always very clearly a murder, of his, of a very close, um, female, um relative.

I think I follow.

Yeah.

Pause.

What you're telling us Sylvia, is that this younger royal member is sneaking out of the palace after dark, wearing a mask representing his fa . . . , a mask of the prince guy, and he's taking out his younger royal member and waving it at the tourists.

Yeah that's about the size of it. Laughs.

Ladies and gentlemen, Sylvia Porterhouse. Pause. *Alright. I hope we're not going to cause a diplomatic incident here. Calm down Barry. Anything else for us Sylvia?*

Yes as a matter of fact. I'm chasing a really big story with a major Irish connection.

What's that to us?

Well a big Dublin connection then if you like.

Really? What?

Well, suffice it to say that I may be in Dublin soon . . .

Really?

Yeah, I need to follow things up over there, talk to some people, but basically what I can tell you now is that we may not have our history straight. Some doubt . . .

Explain.

Some doubt has been cast on certain recent events. And we may be missing parts.

Explain.

Well, there may have been some experiments in the late sixties and early seventies involving a certain drug, and these experiments may well have been hijacked by certain powers that be with the result, effectively, that it removed mankind's memory of a third world war which was fought in the fifties and won by the USA.

Pause.

Ladies and gentlemen, Sylvia Porterhouse. The Dublin connection Syl?

I can't be too explicit, but the development of the drug may have been initiated over there.

Wow.

Yeah.

There's been a war but we've been . . .

We've forgotten.

Wow.

Yeah.

Pause.

You're mad.

I know.

*You think you're a journalist but you're really just an English nutter
we like to have on the show so people can have a laugh.*

Thanks for that.

You're welcome.

Tell them about the website.

They know about the website Sylvia, they're . . .

It's www dot

I'll tell them.

Sylvia Porterhouse dot

Yup.

Co dot

Uh huh.

Uk.

Okay. See ya Syl.

Bye Joe. Maybe I can come on the show when I'm in Dublin.

Maybe I won't let you.

Maybe Sylvia Porterhouse would go out to dinner with him.
Maybe she would come home with him. Maybe she would fuck
him and switch something off inside, kill the microphone, and he
would relax into his life and breathe and feel human and be quiet.

Barry hung his towel on the hook and closed the bathroom door
and tried not to imagine too much. Always there was noise, odd
things, words on the stairs, suggestions coming either up from
the street or from some impossibly perverse part of his mind, his
imagination. He thought that minds were mostly imagination.
That they created the world they watched. That he was nothing
more than a collection of concerns, a bundle of worries and pro-

jections and horrible future possibilities. He knew it was because nothing had happened to him yet. In his life. No one had died. No one had left him. He had not fallen in love (he didn't think). He had not done anything interesting. He was running out of expectation. All the potential was turning sour, and he awaited the inevitable with a kind of terrified resignation. He thought he would probably be murdered.

He showered quickly, turning the water off once because he was sure he had heard something, some crash, and he stood there dripping, naked, in the silence, and could hear only the water and the traffic and the sounds of his own eyes clicking left and right in the mid distance, looking at nothing, seeing intruders and hacksaws through the wall and faces at the window. Then he had to get the water back up to a decent warmth to rinse his hair. The fucking thing was coughing at him, going from full blast to trickle and back again. And the drain was clogged and the water was deep enough to cover his toes. And the towel rail would not take the weight of a towel. And the toilet cistern took half an hour to fill.

He decided, again, to make a list. Two lists. One list for McArdle, on which he would itemise all of the things wrong with the flat, with the stairs to the flat, with the front door, with the washing machine in the basement, with the whole fucking building. And a second list – of the things that he thought would probably happen to him, eventually, suddenly, one night.

He got his hair done and dried himself and thought about shaving and wrapped the towel about himself again and went back into the bedroom and fixed the bed and picked things up and put them away, and looked into the living room/kitchen and forgot about shaving and turned on the television and sat on the sofa and looked at the newspaper and wondered what he could videotape while he was out at work.

When he had people over, anyone, like his sister or a friend, they had to go through his bedroom to get to the bathroom. He could not put that on the list, but felt somehow that the fact of it should make the list longer. They walked past his bed.

Later, dressed, he found hundreds, thousands maybe, of tiny little white polystyrene things, bits, polyps, specks, tiny white balls, like albino couscous, on the floor outside his flat, as if someone had grated some packaging. Coffee cups, water cooler cups, ground down to their parts. Big dandruff incident on the landing. The carpet was a landlord useful dark grey – it may once have been patterned but was now simply smudged, a slop of years, of many weathers, of spillages and God knows. He peered at the plastic snowfall. There were no footprints. It seemed not to form a trail to anywhere in particular but rather to congregate in the few square feet of carpet sludge outside his door. And that of his neighbour, he supposed, equally. His neighbour was called either Tommy or Tony, and his girlfriend was called either Marie or Mary, and they seemed to have an occasional child. Every week-end or every second weekend a small plump boy would turn up and sit on the stairs and look glum. Which alarmed Barry some-what. There would be noises then in the early evenings, of father son activities – shouting and laughing and violent banging.

Barry considered knocking on Tommy or Tony's door, but he was afraid that he would get Marie or Mary, who slept at odd hours and looked frequently like she had been terrified by some horrible thought, and who stared at Barry as if he was wonderful, come to save her. Even if Tony or Tommy answered, he would only say something straightforward like 'new stereo Barry, forgot to tidy up, sorry bout that', and Barry didn't want to know about new stereos in the building. It was something he just didn't want to know about. There would be long worry then, about the noise. Or if it was nothing to do with Tommy or Tony then the mystery would only deepen, widen, broaden, expand in his mind 'til it filled it. Better to assume that Tony or Tommy and Marie or Mary had purchased some new white goods of an entirely silent variety and had depackaged it in the landing for convenience sake and had neglected, through simple, non-malicious oversight, to tidy up after. Okay.

Okay.

As he opened the front door he was sure he heard a drill start-ing somewhere upstairs, a vicious dental uproar in the upper storeys. Work being done. He closed the door and listened instead to the street.

———

Joe, according to Joe, to Joe Kavanagh, Joke, wanted to *drench the airwaves*, the air, the city; he wanted to soak it in his own half-arsed, petty little misery (these were Barry thoughts – half arsed and petty – which came to him guiltily, given his own lack of trauma exposure, but really, Joke was such a drama queen). He wanted to pour his big tears on the roof tops, as if there was some echo he expected to come back to him, of *a deep and widespread,* what? *malaise.* A *societal, communal, depression,* which no one had noticed before, and which he would *expose,* as if it were something purposely hidden, obscured, by such things as *advertising, materialism, the establishment's obsession with traffic* (cars *and* drugs) and the *huge, tidal, tsunami of crime,* which threatened to break over their heads at any moment, *any moment now,* which was already breaking all their windows and fiddling with their *objets,* which Joke recognised, saw it *clear as day,* as *a kind of post Catholic, Celtic Tiger, Celtic Wanker kind of third rate guilt,* or unease, *malaise,* and he knew that as soon as he mentioned it everyone would know what he was talking about and there would be a general calming, a general sigh of *oh yeah, right, that,* and house prices would normalise and he would get a raise and his wife would come back to him and his father send him visions from the grave of pure forgiveness, understanding and love. There. That was the word. That's what's missing: *love.* Say it, hear it: love, love, love *is* the thing.

This, as Barry understood it, was THE PLAN.

And it was Barry's role, his assignment, to scour the city for living examples of a lack of love. Joke did not express it quite like that of course. He spoke instead of real life, of *radio vérité,* of *shaking things up around here,* of rattling some cupboards and dragging out some putrid, local skeletons to get the ratings up and the city talking.

'Get me a prostitute,' he said.

'That's not in my job description Joe.'

'Or a junkie, a homeless soul, something *actual.*'

'Something?'

'Someone.'

Why *malaise?* Why that? It was, thought Barry, disgustingly communal. He was unable, Barry was, at the best of times, he was unable to think of himself as part of anything – community, society, state, family – without it hurting. He could not bear to turn his attention to those ideas, to those constructs, towards those strange theologies of placement, those *things*, could not bear it, literally, in a physical sense, in the lining of his stomach – it made his eyes throb and his head snap sickly backwards, as if he'd stepped in shit and slipped. It was not that he did not believe in them, or did, or had some argument with this or that premise or assumption or *approach*, or had any intellectual or emotional or, God's sake, spiritual axe to grind, it was simply that they hurt him.

So he was, in the best sense, *aware* of THE PLAN, without ever actually looking at the way it fitted in, or the way Joke thought it fitted in. Barry didn't want to see that bit. Those bits. All that muck. He didn't want to be dipped in the slops of Joke's bad life, his circumstances, his crisis. He didn't. The guy was his boss. The guy was a straight, boorish, blunt kind of joke. Let him do that kind of thing with his friends. In private. Not on air. Proceed in private. Joke's procedure would not make good radio, in Barry's opinion. Change the radio show – he understood that. Change the tone. Change the atmosphere. He could handle that. But any talk of social engineering, or of Joke engineering, Jesus, or of doing good, some vague, general, societal good, left him nauseous and tired and misanthropic. Which he believed was the correct word.

'No don't tell me I don't want to know,' he said.

But Joke told him anyway.

'It's about time,' said Joke, 'that we looked,' and here he paused and his voice dropped a register, 'that we looked more closely at the small print of life.'

Barry just gaped at him.

'The small . . .'

'The small print of life. The detail. Where the devil is. You know. All that.'

'All what?'

'The fucking corners. We need to look into the corners. We need to pull up the rug, the rug out from under, we want to examine the small shitty bits of the world that we occupy, you know, us, in our comfort, we want to measure the depth of the grime and the pain and the reality, and that's really the key word here, reality, of Dublin life, now, this year, this month, straddling the future, the past straddling us – us lying on our backs staring up the asshole of history. Get me a junkie. Let him tell us, let her tell us is better, what it's just, you know, like, for her, daily, here, same streets, same neighbourhoods, same buses, as the rest of us. Let's shake up the fucking place Barry.'

'You want to interview a junkie?'

'Yes. And then a homeless, homelessness, a homelessness person, then a hooker, other kinds of addicts, poverty, disability, mental illness. Your thing.'

'My thing.'

'No offence.'

Barry knew that this was a bad idea, a profoundly bad idea, and he knew that it was something to do with Joke's own personal, closely held disasters, something had sprung him into this, and he knew that he should tell Joe, calmly, that he should take some time off, sort out access to his daughter, get over the end of his marriage, go visit his father's grave, that he should not bother the city with it, in whatever form, that the city had problems of its own, that it would not work, and that he wanted nothing to do with it, and that he just wouldn't do it.

'Yeah,' he said. 'Okay.'

_____

Even sober. Even days later, he still thought, yeah, well, okay.

When he got back to the building he lived in (that was putting it a bit strong – it was the building he *occupied*, the building in which he cowered), when he returned, as he approached its black eye windows and its bad teeth gateposts and its splintered railings and its hard paved garden, with the burned stump of a tree stuck into one of the paving stones like the final chess piece, like the queen's sorry pedestal, he noticed, on the air, as if he smelled it, trouble.

Someone was sitting on the steps.

No one sits on the steps in Dublin unless it's trouble. Unless they are trouble. Especially not on a dull evening with a sunny day gone slightly chill and the sky wanting an early night, turned in on itself, grey and retreating. People sometimes, maybe, sit on the steps of city centre buildings in the middle of hot Sunday afternoons. Maybe. Or when something public passes their way, like a parade or a bicycle race or a presidential procession. And you have those who are looking to rent a vacant flat, though the procedure there, properly speaking, is to stand, usually, unless perhaps after a long day, a trek to find it, that kind of thing. But otherwise, it's not done. Why do it?

Barry knew that either one of his fellow tenants believed they lived in Brooklyn, and was in all likelihood hoping for a drive by shooting; or that one of his fellow tenants was pissed, and believed that sitting on the steps was sociable; or that some stranger was awaiting a homecoming debtor, of an either financial, emotional, narcotic or just plain irrational nature.

He tried slowing down, even considered turning around and going to the shops for something, hoping that whoever it was would be gone by the time he returned, but he was tired, he was pissed off, he wanted to get to his own bathroom and shit and read the paper.

He went on. Peering as best he could, trying to appear as if he was not peering – it was awkward.

'Hello Barry,' said the shape on the steps, loudly, as he approached the gate.

Barry said nothing. It was a woman's voice, and he knew who it was, and although he felt a little queasy as a result, he also felt a little relieved that it was not dangerous trouble. Trouble, but not the kind that bruised. He didn't answer her though, thinking that she needed to learn the proper ways of conversing, the polite ways, the quiet ways. She had to learn.

'Hello Barry.'

He turned and closed the gate behind him, slowly, deliberately, quietly.

'Hello Barry.'

'Hello Annie.'

Annie was mad. There was something wrong with her brain which made her both slow and fast, loose and tight, like a lid screwed shut, but off thread, as if she knew what you were talking about but was inclined to believe that you were a bit dim and not to be trusted. She had once accused Barry of bugging the flat she shared with her husband – who may at some point have been sane, but who now, through a stubbornness of caring, through a surplus of love and dedication, was turning up at the edges, starting to rock on his heels, trying to clear his eyes. There was, Barry thought, a lesson there.

'Barry it's a lovely day isn't it? Were you hard at work Barry were you?'

'Yeah. I . . .'

'That McArdle hasn't fixed the washing machine yet, it's terrible isn't it I hope to God, I hope to God that it's fixed soon, I hope to God.'

'I didn't know it was broken.'

'Yes. That McArdle. My husband is at work he'll be home soon, it's a lovely day isn't it Barry.'

He moved up the steps and passed her, not wanting to listen for too long to her too high voice, a piping, metallic noise with an edge of rust in it, from Offaly he thought. And her blurred face, chemically puffed and prodded.

'They've drilled your wall out Barry, all that mess and noise, I'm trying to sleep, I'm not well, I'm only trying to sleep. He'll be home soon.'

'They did what?'

'Oh your wall I don't know what they were doing, McArdle. I'm not well you know.'

'Was McArdle here today?'

She nodded vigorously.

'Drilling hammering noise can't sleep, can't stay in the flat, banging all day long, God it's terrible, I'm not well you know. I'm applying to the government for compensation. I'll tell the health board and the department. I'm not well. It's illegal what they're doing. I'm not well. My husband earns a hundred and forty pounds a week.'

She had left the front door open, and in turn he left it open for her, and thought that was a very kind thing to do. Up the stairs the white mess was gone. Hoovered clean. There was no sign of anything having been done to his door or his wall. He examined it closely, ran his eye over the wallpaper, discovering an ugly smeared insect carcass but nothing else. He looked at his door. He thought that a strong man, or a drunken man, or a man crazed by some combination of chemicals and the world, could put a fist through one of the panels. Easily. He remembered the trick of the hair. From spy movies. A single hair attached somehow to both door and door frame. He had not done that, but he thought that he might do it in future, if he thought of it, so that he would be alerted, when the time came, to the killer waiting in his kitchen.

He was still on the landing. The house was quiet. He stood and listened to it.

Sometimes he suspected that he hated the world. That he was incapable of love. That his heart was a hermit heart, that he was destined to always be clinging, by his fingertips, to the cliff of other people. He looked at the key in his hand. He sniffed, half smiled, fully shrugged, turned and went back downstairs.

'Hello Barry, lovely evening now.'

'Annie,' he nodded. He sat down beside her. 'How would you like to be on the radio?'

Kez met a guy outside the old, what was it called? the old pub on the corner of the quay opposite The Custom House, Kennedy's maybe, he couldn't remember, after this guy had called the mobile, Kez's mobile, from another mobile, telling Kez that he had seen his ad in In Dublin, which was strange Kez told him, because he didn't advertise in In Dublin, he advertised in GCN and sometimes in Hot Press and once, Kez said, 'I took out a full page ad in The Sunday Business Post', but the guy didn't laugh, which Kez thought was something to note, because he was dressed in a suit, an expensive suit, and he was maybe mid forties, and in very good shape, and he was super efficient and a little abrupt, as if he had done this, oh, thousands of times, as if it was nothing at all to worry about, as if he was completely relaxed, and yet, and yet, he didn't laugh at Kez's little joke, and this was something to note, to be careful of, this nervousness, so well disguised. But maybe it just wasn't a laughable joke. Maybe he was so relaxed that he thought he didn't have to do the polite stuff of seeming to laugh at stupid jokes. Which was again, thought Kez, something to take note of. And when he had called he had just said the place and the time and he didn't ask anything at all like what do you look like, what age are you, can I fuck you, do you suck without a condom, can I come in your mouth, he just said – on the corner, Kennedy's, 7.30pm, he said the *pm* bit, and he said Kez would know him by his shirt, which was a deep scarlet, like, the man said on the telephone, on the mobile, like the deep red head of a throbbing dick, at which Kez made some kind of noise which he had not intended particularly as a request for clarification or repetition necessarily, but which had apparently been interpreted as such, for the man had gone on to say cock, knob, like a fireman's helmet, a huge blood and cum filled cock, with which he would want to poke various bits of Kez. Then he said that it would take an hour and that he'd pay £100. And then he hung up.

Kez was not bothered by this so much as by the idea that such talk was in the air, somewhere, in the waves of which the air was made, mixing with other talk – between mothers and their children and those in distress and the emergency services. All that constant bickering between words, the elbowing of one by the other so that his dangerously horny client collided with the woman looking for her daughter. Or some such. He conceived of it in any case as a battle, between the foul mouthed money making and the simple transactions of human love, that cashless society of the family from which he was excluded.

Cash only. He was a shop which did not take credit cards. It made him feel grubby, sidestreet, stall. All that dirty cash, the greasy folding notes, the bundles of them, the smell of them. He had investigated the possibility of credit cards, debit cards, magnetic strip readers, the old fashioned clunky imprint machines, but how did you do that? No one did that. And who would use them? So traceable, so evident. No one wanted him to know their real name. They were not going to hand him a credit card. Dublin was too small for the sexual services to accept plastic. Still air easily stirred. And it was like stirring shadows – it was ghostly, the way all things were connected, the way in which all people seemed to touch all other people – sensual, ghostly, strange.

Kez always knew, always, that whenever he was with one of these men that he was also, and he liked this, with the city, that he peeled off another layer, revealed something more of it, as if what he did was dig in the ground and uncover the world, and that all he had to watch out for was earthquakes, and all he had to regret was the scrappy cash money that curled and tore and sweated in his pockets and his room. He was an archaeologist. Dirty hands. The smell of the earth. Slow knowledge, occasional treasures, rare.

The guy took him in a taxi to a hotel, which was again odd, as it was only to Jury's down past The Custom House, and they could have walked – though these guys never walked if they could help it – but also because he could just have told Kez to come to the hotel instead of this weird standing on the street corner in full view of theoretically anybody. Why do that? The hotel was no problem. But instead, there was all this publicity. And the guy was a Dubliner, so what was he doing staying in a hotel anyway, unless he specifically was staying in the hotel so that he could take Kez there, or not Kez necessarily, but whatever trade he had happened upon. Some guys rented flats just to take boys to. Just so that they would have somewhere to take them. Private. Like a tree house. A den. A hidden cave.

Kez might have asked the guy about all of this, but in the taxi he was boiling, he was red faced and intense and he kept on squeezing Kez's thigh in a way that actually hurt, and Kez decided, about half way to The Custom House Jury's, that he was not going to go with this guy. This guy was not alright.

The taxi driver was glancing in the mirror.

'Show us it then?'

'What?'

'Show us your cock, just the head, through your zipper like.'

'Fuck off.'

He was muttering all of this, and Kez was muttering back, and all the time the guy's hand was pressing into his thigh, and the taxi driver kept on glancing into the mirror and had slowed right down.

'Wait 'til we get there,' Kez said, and he smiled at the guy with his lips parted and his eyes slightly widened, all the openings showing.

'Right.'

He stared at Kez then, sat still and stared at him as if he hadn't looked at him before, on the street or in the taxi, and had never seen anything like him, and Kez thought that he was going to drool. That there was going to be leakage and moisture and too early evidence of what was occurring here. That theirs was a watery transaction as well as a ghostly one and a cash one and a battle, and all of those other things that Kez thought of – that it was a seeping area, a patch of damp and moisture, the river rising. Do not drool, do not dribble, not in the back of a taxi. Not yet.

At the hotel, while the man paid the driver, Kez got out of the car and looked to the left and to the right and wondered which was the best way to go to get away from this situation with the wet man, dangerously horny, about to take him to a hotel room overlooking the river on a warm dry summer's evening.

Oh what the hell. What was he going to do? Run? Sprint to the corner and turn it and be somewhere else? What was the point? Where exactly was the danger here? The man was simply bursting, simply leaking out of his imaginings, his needs, he was blind to everything else, he was not quiet and watchful, he did not smell of violence, he smelled simply of sex – his strangeness was entirely sexual. This was not Chester Haft. This was not that.

The lobby was quiet. The receptionist yawned and didn't even look at them. As the lift doors closed the man put his hand to Kez's crotch. Kez put his hand to the man's. His cock was small but hard as a penknife, hard as a pocket torch. Kez yanked down the zip and pulled the cock out, bent over and put it in his mouth. The man yelped like a dog gone through ice. Kez gave him a couple of swift nods, listened to the rising cadence of the moan and got out of the way. The cum made a noise on the wall of the lift like rain on a roof. Drumming.

He was all wiped clean and re-assembled by the time they reached the top floor.

It is not a tall building.

Joe took Nicola shopping, which involved hobbling up and down Grafton Street with the follower following and Joe trying to pick an argument with his daughter. Who was five. Or six. He wanted to give out to her for wanting branded products – for wanting Barney or Barbie or Pokémon things, for wanting Nike trainers or a Hilfigger bum bag or a McDonalds burger, or something of indeterminate function from Japan with which she would age him. He wanted to educate her about all of that, tell her of the evil in the world and how it operated. But she was happy enough to look at pretty flowers and listen to the buskers, and when asked what she wanted to eat, insisted that a little cake in Bewleys would be lovely.

She had been shy at first, as she always was at first, there now being moments in their relationship which were *at first*. There never having been such moments before – moments which were usually the preserve of strangers and the unrelated, and which were meant to exist between them, father and daughter, only after school trips or business trips, and which were meant to last for a few minutes and be, in themselves, charming and rare and cute and funny. But now they occurred once a week or so, at the front door of Christine's sister's house, and they were awkward and awful and they made Joe sick. To grapple with his daughter over shyness. It made him sickly, as in sentimental. As in the way of old musicals and old films and songs from old musical films, *Carousel*, *Oklahoma*, *Chitty Chitty Bang Bang*, that kind of thing, that soundtrack, which in turn, inevitably, reminded him of his father, so that he found, while overcoming the *at first*, while calming that down and taking her hand and getting on with it, he found himself, again, thinking mostly of his father. Of his records and his films, his singing in the mornings, and his aversion to shopping for anything other than records or books, ideally books about the people who had made the records, and in his later years, the videos. Endless videos. As if his life was documented in these things. As if he was reminiscing. When all he was doing was consuming. When he was being sold his nostalgia in shrink wrap, digitally remastered, with the original cast. Joe found himself thinking these things and was ashamed that he could patronise his father when his father was dead and his daughter was tugging at his stick.

'Look Dad.'

It was balloons in a bookshop window. Balloons and some soft toy dogs surrounded by piles of Linda Finnegan's. But it was the balloons that Nicola liked. There was clearly something wrong with the child. She was not buying. She was not exercising the nag factor. She was not demanding. She had not mentioned a single boy or girl band, not a single cartoon character or television show, she had not even hinted at any preteen fad, gadget, or food group. Somehow, in some scary way, all the messages were going past her, or through her, or over her head. Joe thought he should ask her mother about the school.

'Very nice,' he said. 'I met that lady, on the radio.'

'What lady?'

'The lady who wrote those books. I talked to her on the radio.'

'Why?'

'I have no idea.'

'Did she have those?'

'Balloons?'

'Did she have balloons?'

'No. She had theories about men and relationships and best friends and shopping. You should read her books when you're older. Like maybe when you're eight.'

'Can we go in here Dad?'

'It's just a bookshop Nic. There's nothing there you'd like.'

'Can we?'

'I don't believe I just said that.'

'What?'

'To my daughter.'

'Are children allowed?'

'Yes of course they are. Of course.'

He looked around to make sure that the follower was paying attention. He couldn't just disappear. He saw him yawning over a newspaper outside a jewellers. His mouth dripped and glinted and Joe flinched at the sight. He waited until he looked up, caught his eye and nodded, before pushing open the door of the shop.

113

'In we go.'

The follower was a friend of Christine's sister, a former soldier apparently, who looked like he had been punched into his current shape and bake dried in a hot oven, coming out bright red and cracked. He looked like a man who would hit him in front of his daughter. Would hit him and make him cry out. In front of his daughter. Joe was scared of him. Flinching, queasy, pleading scarred.

Christine had been very up front about it.

'Joe I'm sending this guy to follow you when you're out with Nicola. She doesn't know anything about it and it's very important that she doesn't know anything about it because I don't for a moment want her to think anything other than that she has a father who loves her and cares for her very much, and I don't want anything to come between you and her.'

'But you think I might kidnap her?'

'No I think you might lose her.'

He had lost her only once. In a supermarket in Blanchardstown. She had been gone maybe an hour. It had not been his fault. And the other time, when Christine had come back from a weekend away with some friends in Wicklow or somewhere, she had actually been with his mother, so she hadn't been lost at all, it had just taken Joe a while to remember where she was.

He had not really argued about the whole follower thing. He wasn't sure why. Christine had engineered it so that she told him just after she had made a big concession over access in the first place, going from once a month to once a week, making it seem like she was being generous, every stage of it preceded by wondering out loud whether it wouldn't be better to let a court settle access, given his drinking and his *psychiatry*, about which she was no expert and for which they should probably seek the advice of the professionals. So that by the time the whole thing of the follower was mentioned Joe was sort of astonished and reeling anyway, and he just took it and filed it under *things to be sorted out in future*.

The follower followed them. In a silver Mondeo, from Christine's sister's house, into town, or back to Joe's place, and if they went for a walk he walked behind them, and if they went into a shop he waited outside. Making sure of something. Of what exactly Joe did not know. That he wasn't pissed perhaps. That he didn't go to a pub, take his daughter to a brothel, sell her, leave her by the side of the road, do something unpredictable due to his *psychiatry*. He didn't really want to think of all the possibilities – of the things that might seem possible to Christine, the things she might have thought of. He preferred to think of it as a bargaining position. That she was not serious, not really, she was just positioning herself for the formalities.

In an odd, uneasy way he was grateful. Sometimes he felt he needed a witness. An audience. That.

He wondered if those sometimes moments of affection between them, when Nicola might reach out for a hug, or laugh with him or kiss him, whether they were reported back to Christine. He hoped that they were. And he hoped that the kiss or the hug, and the hope of it being recorded, happened in the right order. But he was not sure.

––––––

Browsing in the children's section, through huge books and pop up books and books that made noises, Joe found himself thinking about sex. There was a small crowd of loose toddlers and some loitering mothers. He was the only man. Every couple of minutes he said something to Nicola so that the women would know he was not there thinking about sex. But he was.

There had not been another. No third party. In his marriage. There was no other. He was alone in the failure – there was only him. Joe Kavanagh. Why had she left him then? He didn't rightly know. But there was not another. He knew this because he had asked her and she had told him, scornfully, in those terms, that no, there was no other – that there was no relocation of blame (and there was certainly blame), that the fault was his and his only, that the failure was his. And she let it be known that she was regretful, deeply so, that there was no other – that another would have been a positive thing, a good thing, something to go to, whereas the truth of it was that she had nothing to go to, only something to go from, and this was, to her mind, a horrible journey. She was all leaving, no arriving.

Joe wondered about that.

He had checked with Nicola. Which took some doing. He had

carefully, over time, constructed the questions and deconstructed the answers, trying to unravel the knots of little girl world, pulling at it, worrying at it, examining the parts. He pored over his daughter's confusions, her half formed memory, her wet sand convictions. He pried at her little Fischer Price life and tried to find a man there. It was like hunting for a rat in a toy box. *Don't alarm the child.* He could find nothing. No one.

If there was no one then it was not the sex. It had not been the sex. This, for some reason which he was afraid of, made him feel a little better. Because he had been worried that it might have been somewhat about the sex. He hadn't worried that it had been completely about the sex, for that would have been too ridiculous, but he had certainly worried, fretted, been queasy about the idea that the sex might have been involved somewhere in there, as part of the mix. Because they had done that. It had happened – all that demise, that standard fluctuation, then the steady decline. First they had fucked – they had run at each other. Then they had walked, still breathless but calmer, making love now. Then they had come to a sort of standstill. And halted. With the odd, increasingly rare lurch, like a convulsion. The muscles of a dead man, twitching. But this was not unusual. This was the way of men and women. This he knew about. It was alluded to in the culture, they were not unique, they were not bad people. It was not, it was not, it was not the sex.

'Daddy?'

That was good. She had called him 'Daddy'. No one would call security now. Nicola had vouched for him. This man is my father. And they would have called security too. He was sure of it. At least two of them had given him hard looks. And it was doubly good that she had called him 'Daddy' because she had taken, recently, to calling him 'Piggy', or more accurately, 'Pigeye'. As if she was mispronouncing 'Piggy' as 'Pig Eye' or 'Pig I'. As if she had read it somewhere. In her mother's diary somewhere, if she kept one now, as she probably did, positioning herself as she was, for the formalities. She probably kept a record. Dates and times. 'Piggy called at 1.23 for Nicola, though he had agreed to be here by 1.' She had never called him that to his face. But she had called him a pig, so he thought that it was not that much of a leap – that she might write him down as 'Piggy'.

'Yes?'

'What's that say?'

'Snowman. Snowman.'

Her reading was not great. Why should it be? At five. Or six. So maybe 'Pigeye' was just some benign naming of her own invention. He looked around for something with a pig on it. There was a small pink pig shaped book on the shelf beside him. He showed it to her.

'Do you like this?'

'Mmmmm. No.'

'Really? Are you sure? It's a pig on it see?'

'No. I like the snowman.'

He bought her the snowman. In the car on the way home she said:

'Pigeye are you going to sell the house?'

It hadn't even occurred to him.

McArdle came with a small girl who was fat and silent and stood with her back to the wall and said, in response to Barry's neutral 'Hello', a very hissed and peculiar 'Sssshh', complete with stubby little finger pressed to wet lips. McArdle himself was the same as usual.

'Were you here during the week?' asked Barry.

There was a barely audible grunt. Impossible to tell if it was a positive or negative grunt.

'No? Well. I have a list. Eh, a list of things that's wrong with the flat.'

This while McArdle was scratching in the rent book, having stuffed Barry's cheque into the obscenely bulging pocket of his soiled grey trousers, which looked as if he had been wearing them since school. Which must have been about thirty years.

'What's wrong with it?'

His voice – McArdle's voice – was amazing. It was a *flat* voice. Which meant, in this case, not only that it was droning and low and dead, but also that it was too small, and it was flaky and falling apart and smelly – that smell which hints at a carcass under the floor. Murder and small rooms, these were the features of McArdle's voice. A nostalgia for the tenements and slum violence. He licked his thumb to count money. Keys took up as much of his trousers as he did. And he was not thin. He was bursting. His belly was just that – belly – potted and overflowing, so that it was impossible to tell when viewed from the front whether or not he was wearing a belt. Or whether or not anything at all between his navel and his knees was any longer accessible. And his head was scruffed half way down its speckled dome with a maniac fringe of grey to white hair. As if it had exploded and lay open now like an egg. His face hatched out of it, albino and squinting. And somewhere in that watery mess was his mouth, as wet and fat as his daughter's or niece's or prisoner's – whichever one of those miserable things she was. And from his mouth, sometimes, there came his voice. His voice was death beds and boiling, rusted locks and cheap paint, chains and plasterboard partitions and second hand cutlery. Barry fumed when he was silent and shuddered when he spoke.

'It's, well, here's the list, and you never gave me the bank details?'

He took the list, barely glanced at it, folded it and put it in his shirt pocket. His striped shirt, which looked like greaseproof paper spread over turkey.

'What bank details?'

He seemed to be on the verge of smiling – something crooked crawled across the runny white, something yellow, maybe the glimpse of a tooth.

'The landlord's? So that I can set up a standing order? I told you this.'

McArdle closed his eyes and rubbed the left one with a finger from his right hand. His shirt was stuck into his grey trousers as if trapped. Under his arm was the usual damp, ringed with what looked like a tea stain. Everything about him pale, not set. The fat girl wore a red jumper and bottle green track suit bottoms and held her hands behind her and rubbed them along the wall. For a moment there was silence but for the sound of rubbing. And though he knew it couldn't really be the case, Barry thought that McArdle's finger and McArdle's eye made the sound of small fat hands on old wallpaper. A muted swish. A suffocated brushing.

'Yep,' said McArdle suddenly, bringing everything to a close. He turned and headed off down the stairs, and the fat girl followed him, and Barry stood and watched them going.

What had happened to him that he had to deal with this? What error had he made in his childhood or in a previous life or in the run-around progress of his soul that he had to deal with this fat fucker and his keys and his odour and his weekly visits, which Barry had begun to dread now like people are scared of heights or flying or death? Which fuck up caused this?

The one his father had warned him of probably. *Buy property now, the prices are going to rise, paying a mortgage will be no more than your rent, I'll help with a deposit, get into the game, now you have a job.* To which his response had been something about freedom. He had always been going on about freedom. As if he knew what it was and how to get it. As if there was some certainty in him. When all there had been was a great fear, and a suspicion that he wasn't up to it. And that the last thing he needed was any kind of responsibility because he would surely fail and he would surely slide into poverty and he would surely be murdered. What he laughed at now was the notion that a mortgage was a *responsibility*. Where had that come from? Most of the people he knew had a mortgage. None of them were responsible.

And so here he was, living in a hole, paying through the nose, hating every minute, scared, preparing for death, unloved, loveless, filled with fear and suspicion and spite, lost in the entrails of a city he thought he knew, slipping on the guts of his own inaction, the muck that had piled around his feet, the stagnation that rose to his knees, the stinking sorry garbage of his freedom.

Time to make a stand.

Flat # 7,
232 Adelaide Road

Landlord : Unknown
Agent : J McArdle

List of necessary maintenance issues to be <u>resolved</u>, and improvements to be made to the above:

1. <u>Cooking</u>. The current cooking facilities in the flat leave a lot to be desired. The grill and rings on cooker are either not functioning at all or are either working at full heat or none at all. The cooker basically needs to be replaced.
2. <u>Security</u>. The simple Chubb lock on the door to the flat is not enough and there should be a Yale lock as well at least. The locks on the front door should be replaced too, and dead bolts should be used. The porch light which used to come on when you walked up to the door no longer works. It should be fixed, and the hall lights need to be maintained, which they currently aren't – the building is often in darkness. It's just dangerous. I don't think that a house like this should be without an inter-com either, and a front door lock that can be activated from within the flats. It is the only house on this stretch of the road without one.
3. <u>Windows</u>. The double glazing in the main room of the flat is useless – it lets in drafts and rainwater. It's even worse in the bedroom. I don't think the windows were properly installed in the first place, and they should be replaced, or at least some kind of insulating job done on them.
4. <u>The bathroom</u>. There are several plumbing problems with the bathroom. Chiefly, the shower water heater is old and probably dangerous and anyway it either works too well or not at all. It's like the cooker. It should be replaced. Drainage from the shower is slow – to the point that a shower of any length causes flooding. The toilet

cistern takes an age to refill.

5. <u>The bedroom door</u>. Since I moved in this door has been in poor condition, with splintered panels and warping. It does not close on its own, necessitating the use at the moment of a bolt on the inside. The door needs repair or replacing.

6. <u>General furnishings</u>. The flat's own furniture is a mix and match of things, some of which are fine, and others are just old and falling apart. The sofa and armchair are heavy, bulky, uncomfortable and could do with replacing. The three lockers are small and practically useless and need to be replaced by a decent bedside table, hall table, and bathroom unit. The bed is actually two single beds pushed together and needs to be replaced by a double.

7. <u>General appearance</u>. The flat has not been painted, to my certain knowledge, in the last three and a half years, and I'm pretty sure, not in the two years before that at least. The carpets and curtains have never been replaced. The light fittings likewise. Re-decoration is long overdue.

8. <u>Facilities</u>. A simple domestic washing machine and tumble dryer aren't adequate, given the level of usage. If there is going to be a communal vacuum cleaner, it should work. Currently it doesn't. As I mentioned earlier, the lights in the common areas of the building should work all the time. At the moment there is no lighting in the porch or hall – none until the first landing in fact. This is inconvenient, as well as being an obvious security risk.

9. <u>Rent Payment</u>. I would prefer from here on to pay my rent by way of a standing order, on a weekly basis if you like but I think monthly is usual. With regard also to this rent payment, I would like to know who my landlord is? I understand that an agent is employed to look after the maintenance of the building and the collection of rents, but things become quite difficult when the only thing that is done is the collection of rent. In other words, there is no higher authority to which to appeal.

And without bank details it becomes impossible to set up a standing order. The whole set up is unprofessional. I am not happy with a weekly visit to collect the rent. If I'm not in I don't like the idea of the agent entering my flat to collect the cheque. This is nothing personal, and I'm not suggesting that there has been anything improper, but I would prefer to have an adult, proper arrangement with a known landlord. I'm not a student, and I'm not paying a student rent.

Please let me know as soon as possible when these points will be addressed.

Yours sincerely
Barry.

And Annie at the door. Always Annie at the door.

Her rapping was rapid but soft, quiet but persistent. As if she didn't want to bother him but she wasn't going away either. He thought he could smell her insanity through the insubstantial wood. He thought that if he ignored her she would seep under the door, through the big gap there, which was snakeless for the summer.

'Hello?' he said, trying to sound bad tempered but succeeding only, he thought, in communicating mild terror.

'Barry it's Annie from downstairs I have my script.'

Oh Jesus Christ.

'What?'

'I have written down what your man needs to ask me so that I can tell him about all that's happened and I have put in words for the parts but I don't know where the ads will be but I've some music he can play as well but I can't remember the name of the song or who sings it *it's after the ball is over after the la de dah, after the lah de dah de, la de dah dah de dah.* Do you know that my husband says you have a library will I slip it in?'

He still hadn't opened the door.

'Yeah ok, slide it under. I'll have a look.'

'Will you have a look? A look. Good man, here it is do you have it?'

At his feet there appeared a single grubby page with an illegible scrawl and what appeared to be a diagram.

'That's great. Thanks Annie. I'll let you know okay? Just leave it with me. Talk to you later.'

'Will you talk to me later? Let me know and I can make changes Barry and I am getting dressed up.'

And then sudden silence, as if she had ceased to be.

The thing about the bedroom door was that it looked to Barry like proof that someone or something would eventually get him. Would do him violence. The whole thing was buckled. And the panels were splintered, and the handle was falling off and looked as if it had one night been locked, and because it was locked it was forced. Hammered at. Pounded upon. It held traces of the noise in its paint work. All screeching and screaming and deep scary voices. And certain words like *fucker* and *cunt* and *kill* and *split,* all uttered with maximum rage. Maximum rage.

Perhaps because it had happened here once it would not happen here again. He thought about that. For a while.

He couldn't read any of Annie's writing. Just the odd word.

Head.
Please.
Sound.
God.
System.
Ill.
Walls.
Doors.
Sick.

The diagram seemed to indicate the divisions of space, maybe of her flat, the shapes of the rooms. But it was all wrong. It looked like she lived in a warren of kitchens and bedrooms and bathrooms – a repeating collection of basics taken to the edge of the page. A mediocre maze.

It was great. It really was. Joe Kavanagh just loved it. It was like religion – like a secret, deeply secret religion, of which he was the chief, of which he was the pope. Concelebrant. It was like preparing mass. It made him feel cavernous of mind, connected to barely understood, ancient truths. He found himself thinking of rain on fields, of the view from hills, of walking in the country. He wanted to play a lot of Van Morrison music. Barry talked him out of it.

'I need,' he told Albert, 'I need to rediscover the fear. The source of the fear. You know?'

Albert nodded. Albert seemed to possess none of the wisdom which Joe had assumed would be inherently his. Joe was a little disappointed. Albert was a modern man, he drove a small Audi. His children were polite. There was a bookcase, full, in the kitchen. Cookery and photography and American crime novels.

His wife, whose name Joe just couldn't hold, something sibilant and leaking, was beautiful, but he thought that she did not like him. She said very little. He was the problem from next door. The volume and the peeling paint.

'So whereabouts in Nigeria exactly . . .?'

The wife clapped her hands and laughed.

'You know the country Joe?' asked Albert, smiling.

'No. Haven't a clue.'

'So we come from Lagos, you have heard of Lagos?'

'Yes of course.'

He had wanted to call over to apologise, and he had apologised, but he had presented them with a bottle of Jameson and it hadn't gone down very well. The wife had raised her eyes and muttered something. Albert had thanked him and asked him in and they sat at the kitchen table drinking tea. One of the boys played with a football in the back garden, his Chelsea shirt flapping, his long arms leaving a pattern against the western sky, the sun going down.

'I just wanted to get to know you, you know, because I, well, I wanted to say sorry for . . .'

'Yes Joe you have apologised, it is quite alright, it is forgotten.'

The wife seemed to disagree with this, giving a barely perceptible squeeze of her shoulders, as if she was letting something pass.

'And just generally introduce myself. Tell you about the show.'

He had probably told them too much about the show. It was just that it was very close to the surface of his mind. It was within easy reach. All his quiet moments now were filled with it. The plan came rushing in.

'Have you heard it? The show I mean?'

The wife shifted in her seat.

'Mrs Cunningham told me about it,' she said. 'I listened to it once.'

'Mrs . . .?'

'Cunningham next door, on this other side.'

'They are the couple with the two twin dogs,' said Albert.

'Twin dogs?'

Both Albert and his wife laughed. Joe was troubled. Twin dogs. Once. He sipped his tea.

'They have Labrador dogs,' Albert said, 'two of them, quite black, not fully grown yet, but beyond puppies. They are very beautiful dogs. Our sons say they are twins. Our sons are fascinated these days by the idea of twins. They have seen a documentary. They want to be twins.'

Joe nodded slowly. He wondered whether it was incumbent upon him now to share some anecdote about his daughter. There was a silence. He didn't want to talk about his daughter. He wanted to talk about the plan.

'I can't stay long. I have to get to the station. With these new changes, well, you should listen to it again over the next few weeks. It's about to get a lot better.'

The wife nodded. Albert smiled.

'You know the way. Sometimes things need to be changed. Revived. What do you do Albert?'

'I am a doctor. I work at St James's hospital.'

'Oh really? Really? What kind of doctor?'

'I am a urologist.'

'Really? Really? That's amazing.'

'It is? Why?'

'I mean that's exactly the type of thing I would love to have on the show. Would you like . . . Actually I have two propositions to put to you now. Which I hope you'll consider. I'd love to have you both on my show actually, to talk about what it is like now, these days, to be black in Ireland. I'd like to hear your stories, your perspectives. You know, what the atmosphere is like, people's attitudes to you. Whether you have encountered any racism, and if so, at what level, you know, kids or stupidities, or whether at a deeper level, or wider, you know, interfering, nasty, even fearful. Has there been that? That kind of thing?'

Albert and his wife looked at each other a little. She half shrugged. Albert swept his hand across the table top. Their son had disappeared.

'Most people,' said Albert, 'are very kind. I have been here for most of the last 10 years. Since I was a student. But there have been moments of horror and abuse.'

'We don't want to be on the radio.'

She looked at the table, and then up at Joe, and smiled politely.

'Horror,' said Joe. 'And abuse.'

126

'There are,' said Albert, 'many other people who would be more qualified to talk about this kind of thing on the radio. We are only two people. We are well off. We have friends and a nice house to live in and we are lucky and we are happy here. So maybe you should talk to some people who are more recently arrived, who have more trouble. People particularly who have to deal directly with the state – with welfare or that kind of thing. I could put you in touch with some of the groups and agencies who assist refugees, or if you prefer more specifically there is a group which supports and helps immigrants from central and north Africa.'

Joe nodded. They didn't want to do it. That was fine.

'What kind of abuse?'

The wife laughed. Albert smiled.

'What kind would you like?'

Joe felt himself redden a little as they looked at him.

'Well, I mean, what have you got? Sorry I mean. Well I'm just curious. Appalled. Sorry. Embarrassed.'

There was a silence for a minute. He could hear a boy's voice, talking into a telephone with a soft but discernible Dublin accent. The house was quiet. The Jameson was the only alcohol that he could see anywhere. He wanted to ask Albert whether he worked with sexually transmitted diseases, whether he could introduce him to some AIDS patients, some syphilis cases, a sex addict or two, men and women with peculiar genitalia or someone who wanted to be an amputee or someone who had sex with horses or dogs or someone who liked to eat shit and be pissed on, or someone who'd arrived to see him with their balls in a vacuum cleaner.

They were still just looking at him. Which made him angry. This was Barry's job after all, finding this kind of stuff. He shouldn't have bothered. He was no good at it. He was, he told himself, too raw, cut too close, he was too bloody and unhinged, he was reeling and he couldn't stand up. But the truth, and he knew it, was that he was an asshole. And he was sober. And he was making a fool of himself. And his wife had left him and he was trying to change the subject.

'Are you going to open that whiskey or not then?'

———

Barry never invited Joe over. Why was that?

Nicola never wanted to bring one of her friends with her when she went out with her father. Why was that?

The friends he had shared with Christine never called anymore.

The friends he had kept to himself sometimes called, but rarely asked him out.

Albert never did open the whiskey.

These thoughts ashamed him.
Why was that?

Delly felt more at the centre of things, though of course, she was not at the centre at all, she was away in one wing like an afterthought. Which was odd. And when she thought about it, she thought that maybe she would, being where she was, tip the house over and roll it down the hill. Those women who walked the flimsy wings of old fashioned airplanes. Something strapped on to something else. But that was when she thought about it. When she didn't think about it, what she felt was that she was more at the centre of things. She was not that far, for example, from the front door. She was close enough to be able to hear people leaving and people coming in, though often she did not know which it was, leaving or arriving, as all she actually heard was the slamming of the door, the noise of it (which it always made, being weighted, and riddled with dead bolts and catches and automatic clacking mechanisms, installed at Kitty's insistence), and she did not know whether she was alone then or had someone else for company. They promised her that she was never alone. That there was, at all times, twenty four hours a day, one of either Kitty or George or Mrs Cotter in the house, and that most of the time there was two of them, and that much of the time all three were there. The door kept on slamming though. All day long. All night long. She heard it in her dreams. She was sure that she was sometimes alone. She simply felt it. And when she felt it, she also felt unable, despite her unease, to press any of her buttons, terrified that her hunch would be confirmed. At these times her breathing would accelerate and her brow would dampen and she would faint, blessedly, and would know no more. Sadly she was forever waking, later, to the sight of one of them peering down at her, whispering something, pushing food or drink or drugs in her direction.

Coming or going.

The house had trapped her.

It had been designed by an Austrian architect in 1965. He had been, largely speaking, insane. Daniel had found him through a Swiss acquaintance for whom he had designed a summer home in Italy. They had gone to visit this summer place, but not in summer, and she remembered only the loggia cut into the cliff, jutting box-like out over the sea, with holes in the floor. The holes were palm sized, irregular, and through them she had glimpsed gulls and white waves and the sharp, distant rocks.

Perforations, he had called them. Mäckler. Something Mäckler. Austria.

They had found the land they wanted, but Mäckler insisted that earth be moved and a line of trees felled before he would agree to take it on. Then he complained constantly that Daniel interfered. But Daniel paid him a huge amount of money and he got on with it. It took four years. They were able to move in after two and a half. But it took four to finish it.

What the papers all talked about was the grounds. They talked about the tennis courts and the helicopter pad and especially the pool, unusual as such things were in those days, in the drizzled countryside. They talked about the stables and the woods; the gardens and the paths and the ponds. They talked about the view. For some reason, over the course of a couple of months in late 1967, their house was news. Which made Daniel furious. He fired various contractors and brought in new ones. He refused to allow Mäckler to import any more marble. He felt embarrassed. Mainly, Delly thought, because the papers hadn't even got around to the house itself.

Four floors, effectively, with the ground floor at the front turning out to be the first floor at the back. In its middle was the huge atrium hallway and its high dome, pierced by a clear eye of glass at its centre, where bats sometimes swooped on summer nights. Beneath, curved like a drum, the back wall was irregularly slashed by windows twenty feet high and four feet wide looking out over the grounds. The staircase spun around those windows like the steel thread of a screw. Mäckler had based it on something nautical apparently, a Russian film about a doomed ship. He had tried to explain, but his English was not good, and Delly, unlike her husband, did not know a word of German, or French, or Italian. He seemed concerned that she think of it as positive, unrelated to drowning or death. There was a dining room and sitting room to the right, both serviced, at the end of the corridor which separated them along their lengths, by what Delly was told had been the first elevator in a private home in Ireland. There was a terrace off the sitting room, she hadn't been out on that in years. On the other side of the hallway there was a smaller, secondary hall, with its own staircase (a simpler affair, this time going down as well as up), and a series of doors leading into a bathroom, Daniel's offices, and the long room.

There were other things too. She couldn't remember.

Upstairs there were two floors of bedrooms, games rooms, store rooms, collections, bathrooms, small lounges and libraries to either side of the central atrium, forming a shape, Delly supposed, like a wristwatch laid flat. Downstairs, there was the kitchen, the laundry room, the store room, the working places. All of that.

What had they been thinking? That they would fill it with children? That they would establish a dynasty and stretch themselves down through history like priests or painters? Had they thought that money could secure that?

They had apparently. Yes. Addition and multiplication. One after another. And yet here she was, in the same huge house, on her way out, with nothing coming in. She would leave it almost empty. She recognised of course that addition and subtraction were, at her age, in her state, tenuous concepts, especially when related to company, which was, itself, an odd notion, given that she was barely keeping her own, most of the time.

She could not find the letter. It had been left upstairs maybe, amongst the books and the magazines. She could not quite remember the last time she saw it. She wondered whether she might have filed it. She wondered then whether it mattered. *That* debate. That endless conversation full of stalling and fakery and fear. About her death and how it could not be reached without living. About what mattered. If she was serious about her death then the letter did not matter. If she cared for her life then the letter mattered. That angry argument that she could not win.

She pressed her bracelet button and looked at the clock. She tried to make herself believe that she did not know which 2 it was. But she did. She was not completely sure however that she had pressed the right button. But there was no noise. And she thought she remembered them telling her that they had done something to the other one so that she would know it. She looked around. She could not see it anywhere. She looked at the one in her hands. She could hardly see it. She could hardly see her hands. There was just the shape of sand in her lap. She poured the sand into the cord of the button, and pulled it tight, and decided that it was definitely a bracelet. No neck was that thin. No living neck. She pressed it again. Nothing.

She looked out of the window. It was 2 in the afternoon. She could see bits of white cloud split by the wind, and a bright blue sky that shifted and pulsed. She pressed her fingers to her living neck. Felt the filaments of her stubborn corpse, felt her own anger at living keeping her alive. She pressed a little harder and stopped because it hurt. It hurt her hand rather than her neck. These things were piling up. She would be smothered soon, she hoped.

The door creaked open and Kitty's head appeared and looked at her, and smiled, she thought. The door was a good sixty feet away, and she could make out faces and expressions though these then disorganised themselves as the person made their way across the room, melted and sank into an indistinct blur, an approaching confusion. Perhaps Kitty appreciated this, for she did not move.

'Yes dear?'

'Were you working?'

'It's alright.'

'Where is Mrs Cotter?'

'She must be outside, I don't know. Did you get your lunch?'

Still Kitty stayed mostly outside the room, and Delly was forced therefore to speak more loudly than was comfortable, which made her anger, which she had not forgotten, a little loud-er too.

'I don't want it. I didn't touch it. Feed me and wipe me, is that all it is?'

This brought Kitty towards her, dissolving, eviscerating, reducing to stodgy colours, a spillage of bad likenesses carried in a wide frame.

'What's wrong Delly?' she asked in a low, gentle voice.

'I need to have my papers.'

The collage tilted slightly, paused.

'What papers dear?'

'All the bloody papers.'

'Delly there's no need to snap at me. There's really no need for it at all. My question is not a stupid one. I have no way of know-ing what papers you mean. You could mean the newspapers for all I know. Or some kind of business papers, and if it's business papers, which I imagine it is, then I don't know which ones, so I need you to tell me and there's no need to talk to me like that.'

Delly closed her eyes, and saw Kitty properly, which was a shock. To see her so clearly, drawn from memory. It hurt. It came from the past, it was wrong. Her eyes held vicious pictures. She opened them.

'I need the file boxes that were in my room, not my room, the guest room, the room I was in. And I need all the files from the locked cabinet in the old office. All of them.'

Kitty sighed.

'Is there something particular dear?'

'What?'

'That you're looking for?'

She seemed to turn in a circle like a column of weather. A tor-nado. But there was silence.

'I mean, between myself and Dr George we know where every-thing is, or if it's something to do with the houses or something it'd be kept with Purcell, or if it's about money it'll be with Millington, or obviously if it's to do with the company, it'll be . . . .'

'Just the files.'

The jumble of colours nodded once, and Delly imagined a frown, and then it retreated slowly, so that after a few seconds, Delly could see her, the back of her, going away. She was getting fat. Delly opened her mouth to say this, to let it be known, but stopped herself.

She felt slightly sorry for the living. For the hangers on. For history and the world.

Slightly.

There were the Fates to be considered. The Fates. These were the way things went, the flow of the day, the good luck and bad, the events, the weather, the tides, the time.

The Fates, as Kez thought of them , were these old guys who hung around the edges of the city in parks and that, and who made things happen to you and got off on it. They were the storm guys. The falling down the stairs guys. The losing all your money or coming into some guys. They were the black eye guys. The earthquake guys. The good looks guys. The bad sex guys.

There were never any earthquakes in Dublin.

There were rarely earthquakes in Dublin.

The way he worked this out, the way it came to him, to Kez, started in the earth of California. Under the soil and the sand and the thin rocks, between the desert and the sea. Beyond that he didn't really know much about it. But it was useful to think of at times, when the plates of his life were slightly dislodged, or all over the place, and the panels all clattered and grinded and squealed, and only the sky stood still – it was good then to think of it in terms of California. To think of the deep rumbles, the shudder and the cracks. As if anything that happened to you could be a place.

Mr Chester Haft arrived in the early part of April, he thought, from San Francisco, he thought, or the general area of San Francisco, Sacramento, all those Spanish names, European anyway, names. He was in his early forties, he dressed in three thousand dollar suits. He growled that out. 'Watch what you're doing kid this is a three thousand dollar suit.' Ok. He rented an armchair car, filled with CD music and leather and little green lights. He was around for about two weeks, taking in the country, always edgy, didn't believe in credit cards or human rights.

'I make money out of fear. Hear that?'

Yes. The car made humming noises that changed with the surfaces and the speed and the pace of his thoughts. Chester Haft's thoughts.

'I find out how scared you are and I work out what your terror is worth in dollar money. I am a big hearted man I have room for all sorts. So I rent you a place to keep your worries. Pass them on to me kid, I charge the going rate, less than the going rate, cos I have a huge capacity for terror. I can take all the terror of the west coast corporate sector. I am Chester Haft and I have half the world on my shoulders and the rest on my chest. I can carry it all. I can store it all. My capacities are enormous. I am the Jesus of the San Andreas Fault. The saviour of the Golden State.'

He worked in insurance.

He turned the wheel with the palm of his hand flat on the rim like he was washing a window. Rolled the big thing onto the wrong side of the road about once every ten minutes.

'What's the point in that? I am the father confessor of the Silicon Valley. Tell me what frightens you. Let it frighten me instead. Live for yourself kid, as if you were the only person left in the world. As if you'll never meet another. Use people up. Never be sorry. Don't get into people, just do your goddamn job. Do you know what I'm talking about?'

Sure.

'Our jobs are similar.'

He wanted valet parking wherever he went. He wanted hotels in the middle of nowhere to have ISDN lines and 24 hour room service and CNN.

'Yes they are. Similar like you don't know. What kind of country is this?'

This is the kind of country where you can be driven around on the wrong side of the road for two weeks on account of the fact that you're a good listener and you have neat hips. Chester Haft dragged him first to Cork, a long scary drive through bits of towns on fast roads at ridiculous speeds. He overtook on corners and did weird things with the brakes that you could feel in your stomach. He gargled out long speeches, everything he said sounding like he had it written down somewhere.

'Fear is blinding and I am your seeing dog. Fear is a flood and I will bail you out. Pass me your fear. The trouble with anything over six stories is basically whiplash. It's the slow down, the come back, the apex that snaps it.'

They stayed a couple of days in Cork. Chester Haft had a speaking engagement. All weekend he wandered in and out of manners, as if everything he said came from a whole long list of possibles, and it depended whether you looked interesting to him, or whether you were just tagging along, as to how he carried himself, how he eyed you, hard or open, narrow or with a west coast, sunshine twinkle. Sometimes he was lovely. Sometimes he raged and his big mouth flecked his suntan with a frosty spittle. That he talked a lot about earthquakes seemed designed to bother people, to make them uneasy, queasy with the notion of structural damage and death by crushing. He reserved his best voice for it, a low, drawling thing, all weight and breath with the words appearing to have a physical presence in his mouth, pieces of information, data matter, shifted around his tongue, collected in the ditches of his cheeks, and delivered then like footfalls, like rain on the roof, cum in a lift, an almost comforting steady threat.

'The Ring Of Fire. P waves. S waves. Compressional. Transverse shear. Subduction-zone. Landslide. The liquefaction of soil. Tsunami. Loss of life. Flattening. Crumpling. Leveling. Swallowing up.

'There is the problem of compression, of real estate repackaged. A man with ten acres is left with three, his ground torn off like paper. The exposure, obviously, the exposure on all levels – the ripping concrete, the wrenching out of foundations, the sudden sight of hidden parts, all the innards of a corporation spilled out in the sun. Which leaves a taste in the mouth of any investor, of any investor in anything. Of any customer. A customer will think twice about you if he's seen your plate glass cluttering up the sidewalk, slicing through his wife. Will see you differently when your neon, block wide, Sunset Boulevard logo has crushed his kids.'

He paused for the nervous laughter, smiled at it.

'The thing an earthquake destroys with most efficiency is confidence. Not personal confidence, necessarily – a lot of heroes emerge from the mess, with an adrenaline that lingers – but the confidence of ordinary people in structures of any kind, from their dream house to their local store to their bank and their hospital and their kid's school. And this loss of confidence costs you money – you men and women whose job it is to inspire confidence in these very structures.

'It is an extreme example of course, and one that you are unlikely, I hope, to encounter here in the Emerald Isle.'

Same smile.

'But the principle is the same, whether we're talking about earthquakes, storms, malicious damage or a tractor run loose in the main street.'

He spoke at a conference on 'investment, risk and growth' attended by suited, accent-less people from all over, drinking café au lait and virgin Sea Breezes, fiddling with cigars and tiny cell phones and sewn up pockets. None of them had cash – except for Chester Haft. He got everything free, made no effort to explain away his 'friend' other than to say that he was his friend, his Dublin friend. Generous cash amounts daily.

After that they spent a couple of days in Kerry and then Clare, looking at the sea, dressing in warm clothes that Chester Haft bought in tourist shops. He was quickly bored, wanted always to move on somewhere else. He kept his briefcase with him everywhere, and when challenged on this he frowned, and then laughed and promised to leave it in the hotel next time, and he told of his Earthquake Bag. Or Earthquake Bags.

'Essentials and some non. A gun. Ammunition. A bottle of Scotch. Plenty of pain killers. Gauze and dressing and bandages and antiseptic and band aids and matches and a torch. Cash. A compass, maps, a short wave radio, a cell phone and charger. Batteries. A knife. Water. Water purifying tablets. All in a Samsonite hold-all, several Samsonite hold-alls. One in the trunk of the Lexus. One in the back of the off-roader. Two in the house. One in the office. And a slimmed down version in the false bottom of my briefcase. Without the gun.'

They headed back to Dublin along main roads getting mainer, and it seemed an anti-gravity thing, climbing, whereas leaving it was easy, all downhill and down river, going back again was upwards, hard on the lungs, rising hand over hand to the nail from which the postcard places hung.

And in Dublin (where there are rarely earthquakes), when Chester Haft was free for several days, with nothing to do with himself but be shown around, and relax and unwind, he wound up so tight that nothing could disperse his tension, nothing could cap him or divert him or stop him from splitting. So one morning, when you're supposed to be lazy in your bed, reading the papers and sipping orange juice and hoping that they won't come too early to clean the room, he lashed out at his Dublin friend, knocking him to the floor with an out-swung arm, roaring in the first light, a twenty second burst of violence that brought down the light stand and cracked the bathroom door, leaving a smear of baby blood and a broken tooth in the deep carpet. He subsided onto the bed, settling in the soft give of the mattress, breathing sharply, panting out with a grim smile the same sentence a dozen times, the words clipped short so that it was hard to make them out.

'This is what I'm paid for.'

Or

'This is what you're paid for.'

Or

'This is how I pay whores.'

Or maybe

'This is all the Fates' fault.'

Either way, it was time to leave Chester Haft. Time to evacuate the area.

———

Kez moved back in with his mother after that. He said to who-ever asked that he had thought it would be nice for a while, to be largely looked after, pampered and maintained. The truth was that he was terrified. It had never happened before. Nothing like it had ever happened before. It cost a fortune to get the tooth fixed, almost exactly as much as he had made from Chester Haft, which meant that he had just about broken even on the entire deal, which was not good, no matter what way you looked at it, it was not good. And he was convinced that Chester Haft, knowing where he lived, would be back. Which was not a reasonable fear, and was therefore compelling. So he moved out, went back to his mother's for a month.

Which was not all bad.

It was there in his old bed, where he used to fall ill, used to cry himself asleep, where he used to experiment with his body, where he had lain from the ages of six to sixteen, that he con-jured up the Fates. Or that they conjured him. For a while he called them Faiths, but corrected himself when he read in a magazine interview with an actor whose name he had now for-gotten, that the Fates had willed his marriage and his movie to fail. And people talked of Fate. But there were Fates. They were plural. There was, Kez was sure, nothing singular in the world. In the worlds.

In his bed he thought about Chester Haft. About that sudden blur in the hotel, about the way the room had vibrated and his jaw had seemed to splinter into pieces that he had tried not to swallow. He thought about that rupture. He thought about the end of the world. He thought about earthquakes.

He could remember the only earthquake there had ever been, in Dublin, the only one in living memory, in recorded history. He remembered it. Or thought he did. He had been told loads of times now that he was too young to remember it, that he had made up a memory from things he had heard from his mother and from Vincent. That meant nothing to him. He remembered, clearly, sitting on the edge of his bed, a small creature, perched in the half light, yawning, his head in dreams, thinking about getting dressed, and there was a barely sensible rumble, a tiny little shudder that he thought at first was inside his own body, but seemed then to affect the air – as if a giant hand had swiped at the world and missed but only just – and he went out into the landing and met his brother coming out of the bathroom with his mouth full of toothpaste, and they had stared at each other. And their mother had joined them then, her dressing gown clutched around her, her face annoyed, suspicious that one of them had broken something, and he remembered questions then and Vincent being sent up into the attic to see what had fallen over, and while he was up there he and his mother heard the DJ on the radio saying that the studio had just shook. There was grinning. All day there was grinning and great pride. Later in the week his brother came home wearing a t-shirt that said 'I survived the Dublin Earthquake.'

He had told that story to Chester Haft.

'That wasn't an earthquake kid that was a fucking Godfart.'

Sometimes still he thought that his jaw hurt. It ached, like it was remembering. Then he would console himself with what it was he had learned from the whole Chester Haft disaster. He had learned that the Fates were dull and fickle. They fucked things up. They were stupid and mean. They could flick a switch, anytime, anywhere, just when you least expected it, and you'd be in the dark, hopeless, hunted down.

He spent a while imagining what it was that could happen to him. How the Fates would act. But that was useless. He would never think of it. That was the point. So he created his bag. Not an Earthquake Bag. It was more general than that. It was a Disaster Bag. Sometimes he thought of it as his Getaway Bag. And he found it a hard thing to do – crouched by his new bed, in his new flat, where no punter would ever set foot, with the noise of kids in the street and the long rumble of traffic and the voices below. Putting things in a bag.

It was simple – sensible. No drugs. Just new clothes, shirts and underwear still in their packaging, some photographs, bathroom stuff, money of course, his passport, his birth certificate, some of his favourite CDs, bought a second time, unopened. Also pieces of paper, cards, beer mats, matchbooks – all with addresses scrawled on them in various hands. Addresses in London, Glasgow, Amsterdam, Paris, Rome, New York, Chicago, Toronto and Sydney. The Nine Cities Of The Kez Disaster. He kept a map there too, a map of the world, so that he would know where his friends were when it happened, when his life was over and shut down and closed and he would have to find a new place to open up a new one.

He didn't tell people about it. He told nobody. It would be a hard thing to tell – it would bring questions and long looks, and maybe it would make people laugh and they would talk about him as if he wasn't there. People would look at him differently, as someone they probably shouldn't trust too far, as someone who might not be there too long. It would make him transparent and temporary to others.

There were things he liked to keep to himself.

Joe and Barry set about it as if they were involved in something spectacularly controversial, risky, a huge change in the nature of not just the program, but of the station as well, of broadcasting even. For the first time in their working lives they wrote memos to each other.

The Real Sound Of Dublin

Of JK. V1.976,,, // 14th // reconstruction item # 7

Phase One :

• Sotto voce. An adjustment of the equipment equivalent to Vaseline on a camera lens. Take that decibel out of the first ad. This shall proceed over the course of the first week.

• Speaking of ads – bookend them, as in the old days, start this with the last slot, working chronologically backwards over the course of the first week so that the first slot will be bookended by the Monday of the second week.

• Bookend should consist of opening two bars of Angel Throat by Closing, track three of Politics Please.

• I don't know what a bar is – you know what I mean. The opening two notes, beats. It sounds like a knock on a door from a weird opera.

• Change the lights in the studio before each show to two thirds the current wattage. Just dim them generally. They're on a dimmer aren't they I think they are.

• Begin introduction of agreed set list. Nothing gets played anymore unless I approve it before hand. Yes I will listen to tapes.

• Guests remain as before, during phase one, and phase two too.

Phase Two:

• Maintain phase one changes and see if anyone notices.

• I'll maybe ask unusual kinds of questions of the usual kinds of guests. (See V1.921)

Phase Three:

• First new guest. We can't slide into this. It just happens. From here we are on to what I described in reconstruction item # 3.

They put them in sealed envelopes and handed them over in corridors. Nothing was to be opened in the studio. They met a few times in town. They did not drink. They sat and sipped coffee, and Joe, mostly, clarified his items. Went through Barry's ideas with a green pen and a squint.

B to J 15th [re reconstruction item # 7]
Bookends for ads can't be Angel Throat it is very distinctive and we'd
have to do a per needle drop and I'm not willing to get into that. I can try
and find something either unrecognisable or free, or we can use the old
theme which is still cleared, the Proof song that you used to like. I can get
something out of that. Or we can commission something from my friend
Tom Kilburn, he'd love that and he'd do it for a fiver.

There's a mad woman lives in my building. Do you want her on?

of V1.921 JK TJC000900101 item # 3
What do you think of the economy?
What are you ashamed of?
What is your house valued at?
Have you ever thought of suicide?
Do you believe in God?
What's the worst thing that has ever happened to you?
What does your sexuality mean to you?
And, obviously, a selection of difficult questions pertinent to each individual guest.

They made a slow start, testing each step with little pauses, moments of listening, straining to hear something set off after them, the following footstep, the increased interest in their progress. But there was nothing. Barry sat through two meetings with the Production Manager without hearing a word. Which led him to suspect that the Production Manager did not listen to their program. Or that he was stupid. Or both. On the Tuesday of the second week someone called in to say that the music was a bit depressing and could they play some De La Soul. Joe thought this was a good sign. A very good sign.

The Real Sound Of Dublin

Re B2J15 (Please number and catalogue your memos better)
How mad is she? I don't want to be accused of anything.

He didn't put it in a memo but Joe, through all this, while impatient to be underway was, increasingly, infected by his own health. By the suspicion that this was not really what was needed. How come, for example, how come he was paying more attention to his job than he had for years? How come he was suddenly drinking less? He was becoming infected by his own health, by the corruption of it, the stench of it, the perversity of his middling happiness, his dislocated pain. He was, he quickly admitted to himself, in denial.

And Barry was possessed. The flat, Barry's flat, had entered his head. It squatted there, in occupation, in opposition to his spirit. It was dug in deep, with paranoia and worry and horror and fear of the dark and terror of morning. He left the windows open in the night and he could not sleep. The short warm nights. He found himself wondering what he might have dreamed of, clapping at flies in the half light, towards dawn, hunched in front of the television with the windows open.

McArdle returned the following Saturday, without the fat girl, in the same clothes, and he took Barry's cheque and stood in his doorway writing in his book and Barry had to ask.

'Well?'

'Well what?'

'The list. The list I gave you. About the flat.'

'Oh yes,' he said, and he was suddenly animated. 'I gave it to the boss, and he said he'd get back to you. Directly. He'd see to it. Yup. That's it. A done deal. Fair play.'

He smiled, revealing a row of tiny yellow teeth. He winked, Barry thought.

'He'll see to it. It's all in hand. He'll be in touch. Bye bye now.'

McArdle had never said so many words at once as long as Barry had known him.

'So I'll hear from the landlord?'

'You will.'

'When?'

'Directly.'

And he was gone, descended, his head sinking beneath the grey carpet like a seal in winter.

B2J 0002 Re SP (ex London)

Joe –

Sylvia Porterhouse called me today to say that she is going to be in Dublin
from the 24th, she doesn't know for how long, and she wants to come on
live for a change. I said I wasn't sure because the whole point of it is correspondent, distance, etc. But it's up to you. And anyway she's being very
hush hush about it all, about why she's here, she's a bit mad.

But she mentioned the writer Kitty Flood? I said that I thought you'd met
her on the RTE show – you interviewed her didn't you? So SP wants an
introduction. Anyway, you can have her on the show, SP that is, but we
are <u>not</u> having her talk about her conspiracy theory. We don't need
lawyers.

B.

Joe was bored. He didn't want Sylvia on ever again. No more trivia. No more rubbish. It was time. Show time. He was going to begin. And he was going to continue.

B2J 0003 RE: MADNESS

Her name is Annie and I don't know exactly what her problem is sometimes she's quite coherent, other times she's not. Maybe it's not such a good idea. I'm not sure now. Do you want to meet her?

Barry had recognised as soon as he'd said it that it was a terrible idea, but by then it was too late, it was unleashed, it was off and running and Annie was like a dog, her sharpened teeth getting hold of it and running and a ferocious noise came out of her and the smell of excitement and the whole horrible possibility seemed to have altered her world.

She waited on the steps for him. She knocked on his door.

'When Barry when? Will there be something done of it? It's the only way. Because they never listen. I'm not well. I'm not at all well. It'd be great. It'd be like Gay Byrne but it would be full of life. I know then that they'll listen to me that's great Barry, will I need to bring my husband, I can't go on like this, when Barry when, when will you do this of me, me Barry, me, when?'

Why had he said it? A momentary thing he thought. An old anger about Joe. About Joe and how pliant Barry felt in relation to him. Bandaging his feet. Indulging him. Looking after him. He had thought that he'd give him a fright. You want a little despair? You want to see how the rest of us live? Here – meet my neighbour.

It had not been fair on her. Showing her straws. Her clutching leaned him sideways and he could not shake her off.

Re: Madness
No.

'We'll have to wait a bit Annie. Joe wants to put it off for a bit. Sorry about that. I was a bit previous. I shouldn't have mentioned it. Just put it out of your mind for a while. Ok?'

She sat on the stairs.

'Ok yes. When I'm a bit better maybe. When I have my story right. When I have it right. Sometimes I know I have too many things going on in my mind. All kinds of different things like a mess of stories and I don't know where one start and ends and I'll get it right though I will, thanks Barry, thanks so much, it'll be great won't it, it'll be great.'

She seemed to stay all day on the stairs, in her dressing gown, getting it right, waiting for the moment to tell it. Barry thought eventually that she had forgotten him, that she was lost instead in trying to separate out her own story from the story of the world.

Which was a mad thing to be doing.

Kez leaned sideways. He tensed his left thigh to keep his balance and his hand slid a little on the shiny bar as the bus turned the corner. He thought it was a bit like skateboarding.

'All this,' said the woman again. She was at his side, sweating in the evening, with the dark coming up out of the ground. He didn't understand why she sweated.

'All this,' she tried, for the third time, and got it out, 'bollocks.'

He nodded, watched his reflection in the black window, flashing over the buildings, his face dragged over the doorways and the windows and the holes in the walls and the posters on the hoardings. Little lights snapped at him.

'About the rent never raised since year before last and my Eddie tells him to feck off 'cos he never fixes a thing, like the fan in the toilet hasn't worked in months, you know, the fan in the bathroom, for the steam and all that, you know those things, they're a legal requirement you know Kevin, and he always says he'll do it next week, and my Eddie tells him we'll pay the extra the same week that he fixes the fan, and of course he says oh right so I'll get that done and Eddie thinks he's got the better of him but sure all he's done is caved in to an extra fiver a week for a fixed feckin fan. It's not on Kevin is it? Is your mother better?'

'Better?'

'She had a cold.'

He lost his face in the window, and saw a kid on a bike that was too big for him try to turn a corner too quickly and come off the saddle and land on the crossbar.

'Ouch,' he said. 'Yeah she is.'

The kid doubled over and the bus moved on, and Kez picked up his reflection once more, and watched it clatter over the railings like a stick. He touched his hair.

'Your mother is,' said the woman, and stopped to let someone squeeze past for the next stop. She wiped at her forehead and looked at her palm and rubbed it on her coat. Why was she wearing a coat if she was sweating?

'Your mother is a lovely woman.'

'Isn't she.'

Kez couldn't remember this old one's name. He was barely sure that he knew her. She knew his mother obviously, lived around there somewhere, in his childhood places, where Kez was now headed. Off to see his mother, with his day's work done. His week's work done. He had money for her. He had money for his brother as well. There was five hundred quid in fives and tens, rolled tight and stuck in his jeans pocket, creating a long thick bulge that made him half proud and half embarrassed.

'She is,' said the woman. 'And you're a handsome young fella now Kevin.'

Kevin was long for Kev. Which was different to Kez. He had dozens of names. He thought he should write them all down. Twice in the last month he had got it wrong with regulars. He couldn't keep track of himself anymore. He was multiple. He was summoned up by varied words. He was like God. He watched his face on the sides of the city and thought about being Jesus, and about being a thousand different things all at the same time.

'I am,' he said.

————

He got back to his mother's house as the sun was finally leaving, and he liked the shadows and the ink blue sky, and he found himself humming tunes amongst the small houses on Blackhorse Avenue, walking back past the English soldiers' cemetery – having gone an extra couple of stops so that he could stretch his legs and get rid of the talkative woman who thought he was handsome.

His mother never made a fuss about the money. She took it and thanked him, and she never counted it in front of him and she never asked him what exactly it was that he did. If she had to talk about it she pretended confusion and muttered vaguely about tourists and guides and hotel rooms at cut rates.

She knew what he did. She tried to believe that he did the same kind of things as his brother, but she knew.

She gave him a great hug and fussed about the kitchen with tea pots and cups and the biscuits he had brought, and she asked him earnestly how he was, and told him he looked great, and took her money and put it in a drawer. Two hundred pounds. Together they wondered who the woman on the bus had been, and Kez was asked to describe her and guess her age and state the colour of her hair and so forth, and they had great fun with all that, giggling at the table, spilling the milk, until she decided that Kez was making it up, that he had met no one, that he was gone mad, and he decided that she was being spied upon, her movements recorded, the state of her health monitored, everything known to the government and the park rangers.

They slumped together in front of the television and watched the videos she had rented – two American things with guns and girls. She seemed to want her youth back, thought Kez, so that she could fling it around. He watched her watching, her lips parted, her eyes pinching and opening and squinting again, muscles somewhere in her upper body tensing and relaxing with the shots and the leaps and the love making. She loved action.

They went to bed before midnight, Kez settling down into the room where he had been a boy, his mother calling to him from her nest of pillows and throws to 'dream nice dreams son'. He dreamed of the river, of being upon it in the sunshine, in some kind of boat that turned out to be his body.

———

He was woken by his brother, Vincent. Not by his voice, but by his being there. Kez didn't move though, or open his eyes. He listened and he waited. And there was nothing for a while, no sound or motion, as if Vincent also listened and waited. In the gap the brothers breathed. Kez almost fell asleep again, then :

'KEV, KEV, JESUS CHRIST, KEV.'

'What?'

'It's nearly fucking midday. You lazy fucker.'

He opened the curtains, and he perched then on the corner of the bed, and picked a magazine from the floor, OK!, and flicked through it.

'Stinks in here.'

'Shut up.'

'Jesus look at this. What's her name. Fuck.'

Kez groaned and turned, his foot finding his brother's body.

'Is Kathy here?'

'Yeah. Do you owe me?'

'My jeans. Pocket.'

Vincent rummaged.

'How much is mine?'

'All of it. That's the last two weeks right?'

'Fair play. Thanks. You must be raking it in. You alright?'

'Yeah.'

'Busy?'

'Fairly.'

Kez sat up and smiled.

'Your man by Christchurch is fucking mad.'

'Who?'

'The guy in that flat by the cathedral. He's one of yours. The one I meet in the pub, what's it called?'

'Oh him, Quigley, he's harmless.'

'He's fucking mad. He gets me . . .'

'I don't want to know.'

'No, he gets me to play dead.'

'What?'

'You know, pretend like I'm fucking dead. Stone dead. A dead body.'

'Well . . .'

Vincent said nothing for a moment, just looked at him.

'I don't want to know I said.'

Kez rolled his eyes and clicked his tongue, and swept a hand across his chest and scratched his ear.

'Anyway,' Vincent said. 'You'll be getting a call this week, so check your fucking messages right? Cos you never do. And don't forget to call Handiman or Hardiman or whatever the fuck his name is. Don't look at me like that.'

'I'm not interested.'

'Oh just talk to him for Christ's sake see what he has to say, it's great money.'

'Yeah and I get to have my face all over the fucking internet for the rest of my life.'

'It's not your face they're interested in kiddo. And on Friday there's a gig for you if you're into it, Deano's cousin again. Usual.'

'Alright.'

'I'll get Ray and that black bloke again. Bring your mates, those two guys I met last week. But not that fucking spacer from the last time – what was his name?'

'Pete Woo. I haven't seen him since.'

'Alright. So don't forget it. I'll pick you up early. I'll call later in the week anyhow, dozy git, you yawn like that I can see your fucking lungs.'

'Bring me up a coffee will ya?'

He stood and messed Kez's hair.

'Your mother's happy you came over. Couldn't give a shit about me. Seventeen sugars right?'

'Thanks.'

Vincent left the room and cantered down the stairs. Kez lay back and looked at the shelves by his bed. There were books there, mostly comic things and annuals. He pulled one down. Started to read it, and started to remember it. When his coffee eventually arrived, Vincent laughing at him, he was already half way through it, half way gone.

———

Later, Kez sat with his feet in a basin of water, his shirt open, in his boxer shorts at the kitchen table reading the end of his comic book while his mother peeled potatoes and his brother lay in the garden smeared in vegetable oil. Kathy, his brother's wife, was feeding their baby, sitting on a rug on the grass with the child at her breast. Kez was embarrassed.

'Eh eh eh,' muttered Kathy, happily, nodding at the kid. 'Eh eh eh eh eh eh.'

The baby seemed to want to clutch something and found a button. Kez peered out from the side of a south American mountain range, where the boy reporter was chasing kidnappers through the snow.

'You'll be hospitalised,' said his mother.

'What?'

'Not you. Vincent. He'll be cooked. He'll have his skin hanging off him like a sausage.'

'I'm only doing it for a minute.'

'You've been there five minutes already. I can smell you. It's like walking past Macari's.'

Kez laughed.

'Eh eh eh eh eh eh eh ow ow ouch. God she's stuck to me. I could stand up and let go of her and she'd hang on.'

She looked at Vincent and smiled. Kez watched her through the door, around the corner of his book, like a kid. He got annoyed with himself. He coughed, put it down, scratched his chest, stood up in his basin and looked at his feet, splashed a bit.

'Will you come in Vincent,' his mother whined. 'I can hear you sizzle.'

'I will in a minute.'

Music came over the wall from the couple next door. It was a jazzy thing, laid back, quiet and low. Kez stepped out of his basin and did a little dance because no one was looking at him and because he could. He just stood where he was and swayed his hips and pushed his shoulders up and down and let his arms go swimming like in a dream. His head tripped one way then the other. It was good.

His name.

He was christened Kevin. They all called him Kev. Vincent was two when he was born and he couldn't say his name right. It came out as Kez. So he'd been told. While everyone else in the world called him Kev, his brother called him Kez. Then Vincent had become embarrassed about it, or thought it was stupid, or just forgot. But he stopped calling him Kez. Gradually. For a while he'd say 'Kez, I mean Kev' so that it sounded like Kez's name was Kezimeankev. From what he could remember, he'd been about ten the last time he'd heard Vincent say his name. Kez. Since then no one had ever said it. No one. No one knew. No one remembered.

It had been like a game when he was a kid. He had his secret name, and he decided that anyone who used it would be rewarded, would become his best friend. He thought that Vincent would remember it one day, and blurt it out. Or that his mother would say it. Or that someone who had once heard it used would think of it suddenly and would ask what had happened to that silly name that Vincent used to call Kev. But no one said it. So that he stopped thinking about it as a game, and it became just something he remembered that everyone else had forgotten.

Except Vincent. He knew somehow that Vincent hadn't forgotten. That one day he'd stop calling him Kev and start calling him Kez again. And that all that they were doing now was just the gap in between.

They had always thought that they had the same father until their mother told them once when they were about 12 and 10, about the same time that Vincent stopped calling him Kez, that they had different ones. Different fathers. So they were half brothers. She said that.

'You're half brothers,' she said.

'And half what?' asked Vincent.

'What?'

Kez knew what he meant.

'What's the other half' he said, not as a question, but he just said it to help his brother. His half brother.

'Jesus Kev,' said his mother, but she was smiling. He was tip toeing outside, with his basin in his hands, and a shush face on him. Kathy was smiling at him too. Vincent had his eyes closed and the music made everything slow. Kez tipped the water out onto his brother's body and ran. The women laughed and the baby cried and Vincent jumped and fell at the same time, slipping sideways onto the ground. He didn't run after Kez. He just stood and went into the house, saying nothing, but later on, in the afternoon, he thumped Kez across the back of the head while he watched television.

160

'There,' he said.

Kez flinched and smiled. He could leave then, so he said goodbye and kissed the women and went to take a bus across the river.

The guy was fiddling with the door. Fiddling as in trying to open. The guy was trying to open the door.

Dr George Addison-Blake knew so many things that nobody else knew. He knew about the tennis shed. He knew about the stash of chocolate bars that Fat Flood kept in the glove compartment of her car. He knew about her bread rolls. He knew that The Roche needed a colostomy bag about as badly as he did. That she was no closer to death than any woman her age. He knew that the Cotter boys had been busy boys. All that time and the place to themselves. All that place and the time to themselves. He knew that Mr Cotter knew nothing.

He knew about the place. Down there. That place.

The guy tried the door a couple more times, rattling it, jerking the handle, and then stopped. Dr George waited for footsteps but there were none. The guy was looking around, considering his options. This could be interesting.

The way the money worked was simple. The Roche was paying him the salary which he would have been earning had he stayed in New York. She had also set up an expense account for him. This he alone had access to, and it was meant, as had been explained to him, to cover the purchase of a car as well as general living expenses and also all expenses incurred in his treatment of The Roche. The first time he had gone to the bank to see what kind of car he might be able to afford they had been all over him. Managers, coffee, private office, chocolate biscuits. There was a hell of a lot of money in that account. Even in dollars. A hell of a lot of dollar money. So he bought the BMW, got himself a couple of nice suits. He also, to be fair, spent quite a bit on making Delly comfortable. He bought a wheelchair. He bought a variety of crutches. He fitted out her bathroom with handles and grips and low things. Wasted now of course. He stocked up on various non-prescription pharmaceuticals. Colostomy gear. Creams and ointments and dressings and gauze. Remedial mattresses. Remedial pillows. Thermometers and blood pressure gauges and monitoring equipment. He was as well equipped as a small town surgery. He spent a lot of money on it. To be fair. When the first statement arrived it was all debits, and a single credit at the end, bringing the balance up to where it had been to begin with.

The money was simple.

He could hear the guy up to something else now. Rustling. Something. He thought he might be trying to look through the window. Which was dumb, given that the window was painted black. There was a slat missing from the northern side of the shed though, and Dr George could see that outside the sun was setting, and the house was lit in yellow, and the windows glinted. From the back, the house looked as if its right side was sitting on a low hill, as if it was cut into a slope. The main sitting room and the terrace, on the left, sat over the windows and doors of what was usually thought of as the basement, while the long room, on the right, sat on the rising ground, with nothing below it at all. It was beautifully done. He smiled as he studied it.

There was a sharp cracking noise. A crowbar, maybe.

There was a pause and the door creaked open. The light flooded in, and the shape silhouetted in the door was a single one. They were not together. One of them, on his instructions, was off in the BMW buying a TV and VCR and getting the car washed. The other one, the uglier one, was skulking around the grounds, plotting, trying locked doors, thinking that it was Dr Addison-Blake he had seen driving away.

Stupid kid.

'Ah!' said Dr George, in his bad Irish accent. 'Hello there, young Cotter. And what can I do for you?'

Kitty Flood could hear the forgettable melodies of Dr George's piano, tuneless, repetitive, but flowing, quietly flowing. The notes hovered below her, somewhere in that empty air beneath her feet and her floor.

She was busy with Caroline in Montreal who wanted some advice about boys. There was this guy called Reeves, imagine that, and he was giving her a hard time, and he was 16 and Caroline was only just 15, like Kylie (Kitty), and she wanted to know what Kylie (Kitty) would do about it, and anyway, how was Kylie's (Kitty's) mother now? Did she have her sight back? And was her father still missing?

Kitty was a little bored with Caroline.

There was always a pattern to these kids, to the real ones anyway. They were predictable and stupid. The genuinely young were appallingly bad at it. They all used the same words, they all had the same problems, they all over-estimated the importance of their lives, and none of them noticed the plot. They never seemed to realise that their sincerity and their seriousness and their sense of the world was entirely false, fake, constructed, cleverly designed, provided and compiled, packaged and purchased and consumed. By their parents. By their guardians. It was software, the best selling of software. It was Childhood Version 2.8; KidWorld, The Millennium Edition; Youth2K; Teen Age Simulator 2002; MaxTeen, the 21st Century Girlboy. They were virtual kids. They were a game that the adults were playing. Can you enter level 4? The Adolescent Fun Palace? You bet you can.

Kitty guffawed, and snaffled on a Mars bar. Maybe she would give Caroline a fright.

yeah my mum is ok but she cant see so good
>is she still at the hos?
yeah
>i think ur so brave to go thru this on ur own
yeah
>did the police catch the guy?

Kitty had to consult her notes. Hit and run or weird acid attack?

no they havent but they found a witness this guy from a shop who saw it happen so now they have description and they might be able to find him
>cool

yeah
>what was the decription like?
its not my dad
>oh im relived
yeah me 2

Kitty opened a carton of milk. She rooted around in the fridge for something savoury. Behind the letter there was a cooked sausage gone a strange human colour. She extracted it and put it in the bin. She took a bag of crisps from the box at her feet.

so has r made a move on you??
>u mean?????
yeah!!!!!!
>well hes a good kisser!!
wowsie wow!!
>so thats all so far but hes cute so i dont know
did he grope?
>no he was good. we were pressed up against each other tho it was pretty neat
could you feel his wanger?
>kylie!!!
hehe – well?
>not really im not sure maybe
jesus kid eithre he had a hardon for u or he didn't – did u feel it?
>kylie!!! stop!!!!
was ur pussy wet?

well?/

u there?

o for fucks sake.

She logged off. She made a note. 'Apologise to C. Mother/ acid attack stress manifesting as highly sexualised and inappropriate outbursts. She should go for that. Good lead into "think I might be gay" conversation.'

She moved chat rooms, ducking her head and crouching, stepping over a couple of alleged teenagers with alleged incurable disorders, sidling along past a fully declared kiddie porn sniffer, and settling down to lurk discontentedly in the dank rectangle of

TeenFun#2, while deciding who to be. Besides Kylie (an edgy and eager 16-year-old Dublin lesbian with a life unfolding in a remarkably similar way to the plot of Kitty's first abandoned and unpublished effort at a novel), she could be:

- **John** – a thirty seven year old writer of crime fiction living in Chicago, who had a wheelchair bound wife, a fondness for guns and a sweet and vulnerable nature, with a dark twist in the small hours.
- **Polly** – a fourteen year old rich kid from New Hampshire, unformed and terribly sincere.
- **Alice** – a housewife on the Irish west coast, early thirties, tired, depressed, sometimes suicidal.
- **Nathan** – a teenage London homosexual with a liking for older men and extreme bondage.
- **Ciaran** – a Dubliner, in his sixties, retired from the army, right wing, abstract, demented.
- **Lisa Wheel** – an American healer living in West Cork, full of bright ideas for cancer cures and aura repair.
- **Gossamer** – a sexually rapacious New Yorker (female) seeking fulfilment and hard core porn.

They were all pretty well filled out. Kitty had constructed biographies, family trees, psychological profiles, had even found photographs for five of them (Ciaran and Alice remained elusive, still, despite everything, a little improbable), and each had a fat file and a set of guidelines. She loved them all. She was good at them all. She was consistent and solid and impressively adept at switching from one to another. Click. Flick. Her fast fingers taking on forms.

And each of them had friends, correspondents, lovers and foes. All binary variation was theirs. All manner of memories and motives and means. They occupied the world. They could do anything. Nathan for example had recently done extremely well in his exams. He was heading for Cambridge he was. And Alice, after her last long stay in Ennis general hospital, had taken up painting, and seemed, to her on-line support circle, for the first time, to be approaching happiness. Lisa Wheel might even have a book deal ('The Wheel Of Life – How To Spin Your Own World'). That day alone there had been six e-mails for Nathan, four for

Kylie, three for Gossamer, one each for Alice, Ciaran and John. There were twelve for Polly.

For Kitty Flood, there had been nothing.

She heard a bell. Mid way through the crisps. Milk on her lips. Just as she was about to assume the shape of an appalled and vengeful Polly, and have the entire population of the room reported to the chat police of lovepotion.com, there was suddenly a bell ringing, somewhere in the house, one she had not heard before, not associated with either of Delly's alarms, as far as she knew anyway. She cursed the sting of limited dimensions, the little lock up of the natural world. She shut herself down, and stared for a moment at the blonde wood slats beneath her feet. Then she stood and brushed the crisps from her dress. As she opened the door and headed down the narrow stair to the floor below, the sound of the piano ceased, finally, and she heard Dr George opening the door of the music room. She saw him from above, his shoulders tightened, paused on the threshold.

'What the hell is that?' she called.

He jumped, startled, and looked back at her. He was sweating, his eyes were wide, he was pale. Something in the music, she thought, was bad for him.

'Christ,' he said.

He looked awful.

They proceeded together along the corridor to the stairs at the end, and as they did so Kitty began to smell the burning, distinct and acrid.

'Something's on fire,' she said, and quickened. Dr George did not quicken. He lingered. 'Jesus,' said Kitty. 'Jesus Christ. Delly.'

The first thin scent of burning, the first whispered smell, Delly took for cooking. Mrs Cotter somewhere below, making something light for Kitty. Had she had her tea? She couldn't remember. Ah! That was good. She couldn't remember if she had had her tea. Now if only she could extend that uncertainty backwards, gradually, over the previous ten, twenty, fifty years. Back say to Brittas Bay maybe. She could stay in the water. She could bob there, smiling . . .

The smell of burning seemed to her at first to come from within her own mouth. As if she had trapped and bitten down upon the past, as if it crashed in flames on her tongue. But this had not happened. The past would not be tasteless. Delly moved her hands, sniffed. Cocked her strange head to one side and sniffed again. Something was, very definitely, on fire.

She wondered if she was on fire. She looked. It would not have been the way she would have chosen, ideally. But beggars cannot. She could not see herself very well. She did feel, suddenly, quite uncomfortably warm. An interesting bumpy rash seemed to have appeared on her lower arms. She peered into the room, looking first, not unreasonably, at the fireplace, and the television beside it, without seeing anything, and then trying the more difficult items closer to hand. She was, she suddenly realised, or remembered, surrounded by papers and documents. Oh God. She had knocked a candle. Or one of those bizarre insects had clicked its hind legs on one of her husband's ancient files. Or some chemical he had hidden in a shoe box had ignited. She looked for her buttons. She felt around her neck and around her wrist and there was nothing in either place. She cursed to herself horribly, trying to remember the worst kind of things. It was not the idea that she would burn, that she would die a terrible death, consumed like a dry leaf, run through with fire in an instant, all her blood sizzling on the hot grill of her bones; it was the fact that she had not found the letter. It would survive her.

She heard a door slam. Not the front door. A different door. She tried to shout but her mouth was dry.

She slapped at the covers around her. She smacked down on the bits of paper she could reach, hoping to hit an alarm somewhere while she was about it. She thrashed her legs, or she gave her approximation of leg thrashing, which was really just a restless stirring below the knee. The blur which surrounded her seemed to glow orange at the edges, blue in the centre. The smell in her nostrils was all consumption, the gulp and swallow of raging heat, of death become passionate, over eager, pawing at her and panting a scorched and blistered breath. Delly Roche whimpered lightly.

She looked, perhaps something caught her eye, out of the window and saw, quite clearly, a naked man, an entirely naked man, though headless, and missing a foot, drift towards her through the blue evening sky, floating easily and calmly, rocking a little, side to side, with his strong legs apart and his muscles glinting in the late sun, with his chest rigid and hairless and slick, and his right hand, fisted, clutching a large and hard and rope veined penis. He hit the window with hardly a sound, and seemed to stick there, pointing at her, as if glued on by lust.

Delly, her astonishment ringing in her ears like a bell, gave one sharp shriek, and swooned.

🍴

Kitty Flood ran down the stairs. She held her skirt and ran, two steps at a time when she dared, which was only twice, near the bottoms of the lower flights. Behind her, by some distance now, came Dr George, and she hated him for his laziness. In her mind she saw Delly on a pyre, burning through the wall of the house and out to sea, a Viking boat going black in the water. She could smell the skin on Delly's stomach curl like paper and lift. She was, by the time she got to the small hall and the door to the long room, convinced that she could taste the grease of Delly's melted eyes, that it was all over, that nothing mattered anymore, that it was serious now, her life, back – as she was – on her own again.

Mrs Cotter was ahead of her, administering. Delly lay crumpled and unconscious and pale as a flame, but she was not burning, she was breathing, she was not singed in the slightest, she was simply slipped under. Alive.

'Oh Jesus Christ Almighty God,' said Kitty in a prayer of one breath.

Mrs Cotter turned.

'She's only fainted Miss Flood. She's fine. She probably smelled the smoke. The fire brigade's coming, it's all alright, and it's away from the house anyway, no worry, it's destroyed though, and God only knows what was in there I've never seen the like of it and I just hope to God that Mrs Roche didn't see any of that, poor dear.'

What was away from the house? What was burning? What was destroyed? Seen any of what? But all that Kitty could utter, submerged as she was in a sudden release and a simultaneous realisation that she'd really have to get her act together, was a strangulated 'Oooooomphf'.

So that when she turned, or was turned, caught by something in the corner of her eye, towards the south facing windows, she was at a loss to explain to herself, to understand, what she saw there. A small hut, some kind of shed, off to the left, with flames coming out of it like water out of a fountain, with smoke fleeing it in a panic, upwards, then blown back curling towards the house, carrying on it hundreds, thousands, millions, of pieces of paper, singed, grilled, roasted, a speckle of them stuck to the glass, a great swathe of them, some blank, some blackened, others skin coloured, and still others carrying the naked shapes of copulating humans, all cocks and cunts and cum covered asses, cooked in the barbecue of flash bulb and gloss.

Someone had lit a bonfire of hardcore pornography in the back garden.

———————

Dr George had not followed her into the long room. She could see him now through the window, making his way across the grass towards the blaze, and she went closer and saw Mr Cotter and one of the boys and two of the security men carrying buckets. The bell still rang, furious.

She thought for a moment, with a surge of sickly horror, that the porn belonged to her. That it had somehow been made real. That it had been deciphered, spooled and printed from the hidden folders of her hard drive. From amongst Gossamer's things, or Nathan's. Hard drive, hardcore, hard luck. And that the resulting reams, the pages and pages of wide open skin, of binding and mouths and chains and emissions, of leg arrangements and face assaults, of fissures and fucking, had been thrown from her window and set alight on the lawn by some puritan among them. She even thought she recognised some of them. Some of the faces.

But there was too much. She had not gathered so much. She did not think she could. Settling on a small hedge near the steps was an unfolded double page spread, with the crease clear and the

169

staple holes gaping. It was clearly from a magazine. From some difficult to obtain publication. She stood at the window and heard herself muttering 'fisting for fuck's sake' and was startled at what she knew and how she knew it. Closer to her were more fragmentary pieces, little face shots and tit shots and money shots. There were a lot of burned naked men in the garden. A lot of burned naked women.

Dr George made her jump by shouting something. He wanted her to turn off the alarm. She shrugged, mouthed that she didn't know how, didn't know where. He had to come back in and do it himself. She had been in the house so much longer than he had and yet she did not know these things. But they hadn't felt much need for alarms until his arrival. When the din was eventually silenced, Kitty could hear the approaching sirens, low and reassuring. Delly woke and looked out of the window and fainted again. Mrs Cotter drew the curtains. Stayed with her.

Outside, Kitty followed Dr George towards the heat. They tip toed their way through the orgy, across the lawn, down the first steps, around the little pond (where a bearded man floated, his leather harness turning grey), down the other steps, and as they moved, Kitty noticed that Dr George tried not to look. At anything. Mr Cotter and two of the security guys however couldn't help themselves. They were staring at the ground, having given up on the blaze, their faces bright red.

'Oh Miss Flood,' said Mr Cotter. 'You shouldn't be out here really.'

What could she tell him – that she'd seen it all before? That she'd seen worse?

'What the hell is all this?'

She motioned vaguely, but what she had meant really was, what the hell was going on, why the fire, how had it started, what had the shed been for? Mr Cotter misunderstood.

'Some men Miss Flood,' he said, 'some men will do this kind of thing, as a sickness, a sickness. You should really go back inside.'

Kitty felt the men's embarrassment as a comfort. It was nice. It reflected well on her.

'Yes. Well. I mean, what is *this* thing? Where did it come from?' She pointed at the shed.

'Um, it's always been there Miss,' said Mr Cotter.

Dr George was making beeping noises on his mobile. 'No it hasn't.'

'Oh it has Miss. Used to be we kept all the tennis gear there Miss.'

'Tennis?'

'Hello?' said Dr George. 'Can I, um, can I cancel a call to the emergency services?'

'These was courts,' said the younger Cotter, a slightly bewildered look on his face.

She had never noticed. She couldn't believe that she had never noticed. They were standing about five hundred yards from the house, two levels down, on a kind of plateau, some fifty feet from the burning shed. Tennis courts. Beneath her feet she could feel the hard flat surface, overgrown with scanty grass.

'Of course,' she said, making no sense.

'No, ok, no, yes,' Dr George was rattling, 'yes, I know, no, it's still burning but it's going, yes, ok, right, uh-huh, yeah, got it, never mind, yeah, yeah, they're here anyway. Never mind.'

And it was going out. They was nothing for it to spread to. The firemen arrived, eight of them, swaggering their heavy way from the flashing engine parked on the Cotters' driveway, stepping on flowerbeds and rolling something heavy which looked like a radiator over the flat grass. They were already laughing by the time they reached the others.

They used the mains outside the Cotter house and trained water on the fire for a few minutes and it spluttered and retreated and the air turned damp. Then they sort of forgot about it and wandered around the grounds giggling. Kitty heard Dr George giving out to Mr Cotter for having set off the alarm which had summoned them, saying that it could never have spread, but Mr Cotter was firm.

'Fire is fire sir. You can never tell.'

There was a small moment of panic when the younger Cotter mentioned rather casually that he had no idea where his brother was. Mr Cotter and the chief fireman looked at each other.

'Right,' said the fireman. 'Get in there Mike and check it out.'

Mike put on some extra gear, including an oxygen mask, and took an axe to the smouldering door. One blow and three of the walls collapsed. Inside there was a merrily burning stack of cardboard boxes and a little hill of ashes and charred timber and shapeless black debris. Mike poked around for a few minutes before shaking his head and emerging, pulling off his mask.

'There was no one in there,' he said, and burst out laughing. The cover of what looked like it might have been a video tape called 'Oriental Orgy' fluttered from his axe head.

They knocked down the rest of it and raked the ground and soaked it until there was only ugly staining smoke and a mess of charcoal. At one point the chief dragged something rectangular over to Dr George and kicked it with his boot.

'Petrol can,' he said. 'Who was last in there?'

Dr George shrugged.

'I don't know,' he said, but Kitty saw him look at the Cotter boy, whose red face turned away. 'I'll be finding out.'

The fireman considered him a moment and shook his head.

'Well that's the way these things usually happen. Someone leaves something daft in there like a can of petrol or white spirits, surrounds it with,' he grinned, 'flammables, someone else goes in there for a,' he smiled fully, 'smoke, and there you have it. Hot stuff.' And he laughed. Dr George didn't.

When they had gone, attention turned to the question which all of them had formed and passed back and forth by way of suspicious glances and noting of behaviour.

Who owned the porn?

It was not clear. They stood on the grass with the smell of it surrounding them – Kitty, Dr George, Mr Cotter, the one son, the senior security man, and then Mrs Cotter, who was happy that Delly had now been restored to consciousness and would be alright. She was watching the television apparently, and had made no mention of fires or nudity at all, assuming, Mrs Cotter thought, that it had all been a dream. And it was probably best that way, said Mrs Cotter.

Explicit sex acts leered at them out of the evening gloom. Everyone denied it. Dr George didn't say much, and kept his eye on the boy. Mr Cotter, after a few declarations of his opposition to all kinds of pornography and most kinds of sex, informed them that he hadn't been in the shed for months. Maybe even a year. And he insisted that he didn't store petrol or white spirits or anything even vaguely dangerous anywhere other than the locked windowless room off the garages. Mrs Cotter spoke disparagingly of the sick minds of men, and stood shoulder to shoulder with Kitty. By that time they were all ranged against the younger Cotter, whose worried eyes and increasingly plaintive reminders that his brother was missing, spoke innocence to Kitty. Anyway, he informed them, he'd been out in Dr George's BMW, as instructed, on various errands. Dr George confirmed it, scowling.

They reached a kind of consensus – that the missing Cotter boy was a dirty little pervert who had run off in shame and that as soon as he was found he would be punished most severely.

The Cotters were slightly odd about this Kitty thought. They were embarrassed certainly, but they weren't *mortified*, they weren't appalled. They appeared to have conceded that it had been a fairly predictable risk – that a child of theirs might accidentally set fire to his vast stash of hard core pornography, exposing in the process the rather shocking fact that he had managed to construct for himself, under their very noses, a remarkable masturbation facility on the disused tennis courts of their employer.

Maybe they were in shock.

Kitty, with her own stash (minor though it was, and devalued slightly by virtue of it having been collected *in character*), felt some admiration for the missing boy, for his energy, his application. She half decided to herself that once he'd slinked back, she'd take him to one side and tell him not to worry about it, that she thought he was an alright kid. Meanwhile his brother was sullen, and stared at Dr George, and would say nothing. Mr and Mrs apologised profusely. Dr George played the grown up, tut-tutting and muttering darkly about the embarrassment of it all. Kitty peered at the grass.

What a collection, she thought. What a collection. It must have taken years.

———

Delly was alright. She sat up, leaning a little to her right, away from the window, as Kitty explained what had happened. She had been through some of the papers, Kitty saw. She had moved things around. Most of it was on the floor. The page in her lap was upside down.

'And what was in it?' she asked.

173

'In what?'

'In the shed.'

Kitty hadn't said.

'Um, bits and pieces, old magazines, rubbish really, I don't know. Why?'

'Headless.'

'What?'

'There were men. All their clothes ripped off.'

Kitty giggled.

'Oh okay then. You're right. It was a stash of porn. Can you believe it? One of the Cotter boys has run off. We think it was his. Busy boy.'

Delly was silent for a moment. Kitty thought she might be thinking of that time . . .

'Do you remember Delly . . .'

'No.'

Little things. Simple things. Old jokes. Old stories.

'Do you not remember . . .'

'No.'

'Yes you do.'

She looked away. She turned and faced the far wall. Her eyes closed and she shuddered.

'I remember,' she said, and seemed to swallow something big and awkward, 'nothing.'

Delly felt spliced to the blankets which covered her. She felt that her skin had grown into them and their fibres were meshed with her withered muscles and her eyes. She could see nothing. Her ears were blocked with bells first and silence later. She could smell only the crash and the splinter and the burn, as if everything was on-going. She thought Kitty was lying. That Kitty sought to deceive her, fool her, blind her, save her from the truth of it. She thought that it had not been the over grown and unused tennis court that had exploded at all, but the unused and overgrown helicopter pad. The helicopter pad.

And that slamming door. Who had that been? And that dying

man who had clung to her window? His head gone. And later, when she had revived, briefly, she had seen the smoke and the body parts and she had been thrown back, of course, how could she not, to that night, and she had wondered since whether she was being told the whole truth of her days, all of her days, since then, since that night. She wondered whether it was still that night now, and whether everything since was a simple dream, clutched at in those few dazed minutes between the sudden silence and the sirens. And she was nervous.

And she was right. For everything, really, had been a dream since then.

The smell drew her back. Chiefly it was the smell. Burning. And not just burning, but a rapacious, wild consumption, flames which smelled like danger, like death, with a chemical, in-organic fuel. Not the rustling, warming, gentle smell of wood or coal or leaves, but the stench of something gone badly wrong with the man made world. It drew her back.

And why is it that memory is always *back* – always backwards, retrograde, negative? Because it is. It is exactly that. She knew where the events of her life were situated. In the past. Behind her. And she did not want to face them. It was not that she did not want to think them through, evaluate them, consider and understand. No. She simply didn't want to know they were there. She wanted to forget them. Discard all knowledge, disregard and ignore them. She wanted not to know. And she was willing, no problem, to let go of it all. To dump the lot. She didn't want to be difficult – selective – to remember the love or the joy or the happiness, and forget the death and the pain and the lies and the hate and the horror. She would forgo it all, forget it all, slide content into a blank place, with nothing on her mind but the moment, and the next one after it, and the last one, the last of all, approaching. That would be fine.

And there was a way. She was sure there was a way.

But then. Sudden in the lazy evening. Just as she was edging towards a light amnesia, it had come to her. The noise in the air. The slightest billowing in the glass of the windows, as if the world pressed up against them, breathed against them. As if the world was against them.

Everything came back. Always the memories were like that.

One sneaked through and then let in the others. And they flooded, they hammered in.

The smell of burning.

———————

She had met Daniel Gilmore in the water of Brittas Bay, about
fifty feet from the shore, their bobbing heads exchanging mildly
salacious pleasantries, treading water, looking at each other. He
swam around her then, so that later, when sharks circled her boat
off Cape York, she thought of him. They had emerged together,
walking up onto the sand side by side, showing their bodies to
each other, dripping and fine. She had thought him beautiful. It
was the first time the word had occurred to her in respect of a
man. Beautiful.

The smell of burning.

He asked her out. She went. She suspected she was falling in
love with him. She didn't mind.

It was ages before she realised that he was brilliant, that they
were going to be wealthy. She had believed that he would eventually open his own pharmacy in the city, where he would sell
corn plasters and headache tablets and that they would have a
quiet, middle class life. They had nothing of the sort.

The cracks.

He went off to London for about six months. At the end of it he
came back wearing a suit, and he had more money than she had
ever even heard of. That was the start. He had patented a gel fil-
tration technique. Apparently. Which he had then sold. For a lot
of money. With the money he created Gilmore Pharmaceuticals.
He owned three primary patents within two years. Chemical
patents. Within five years GP was manufacturing the world's best
selling non addictive sleeping tablets.

The smell of burning.

They had a helicopter pad. Yes they did. They. They had tennis
courts and a swimming pool. They had stables, two mares, a
gelding, a staff of twelve. They did. They. Yes. Delly went over in
her mind all the things they used to have. She had none of it. She
had abandoned it all, she had let it go. She didn't want it, she did
not trust it all, it was too much. It had bruised her. Items, all of
their items, all of their things, all of them gone, or rusting, or
dead, or sent away, or grown over. Done with.

The smell of burning caused her to faint. It was not the shock, it was the memory. Of another shock, of the real shock, the actual shock, the shock after which, in time, all other shocks would simply be reminders. Aftershocks. Such is the spite of life. The rack of living. So thought Delly as she fainted and hoped for death. Consciousness was a Cromwellian bastard who wandered her towns, hacking and cutting and sipping her pain. It was. That's what it was.

The helicopter pad had been seldom used. Mostly it had been used by visitors. By the board members, by politicians. People who had not the time to drive from Dublin. Who could not afford that hour. She could remember going out to it, going out to meet him, only twice. Once in 1972, after he had been away, and they had been particularly desperate for each other, when he had brought with him, from Italy she thought, a case of wine. They had dropped the wine, Daniel and the pilot, as they tried to hoist it up on their shoulders coming across the tarmac towards Delly, a great soft smash, and a seeping out of red against the yellow markings and the spindle shadow of the blades. Not a single bottle saved. And the second time, in the middle of that stupid night in June 1979 when the machine somehow tripped over a treetop and gouged into the ground like a corkscrew, sideways, with a grind that Delly could hear still, did hear, still, nightly, in her dreams. The crash killed her husband. It killed Daniel. It killed the pilot. It killed Frank Cullen too, their accountant.

She had been in the house, sleeping, not sleeping, restless, listening to the wind. She had not expected them until the next day. But the letter had arrived, the letter had come, and she was not surprised when she heard the whipping of the blades as her husband passed over her head. She was out of bed and downstairs before the crash. She was making her way through the sitting room towards the terrace and the gardens, she was there in the solid luxury of their house, when it happened. Her feet on the dark carpet suddenly lit. The flash of all their silver. Then a dim noise growing bigger, a roaring that she rushed towards, which seemed to open up in welcome.

By the time she got to them, across the lawns and down the steps and through the formal borders, past the tennis courts, past the covered pool, along the path towards the debris and the gash in the ground, there was a silence settling down. Even the wind seemed to pause while she found them. While she discovered them.

Daniel was decapitated, not as she might have imagined, cleanly, through the neck, but bizarrely, so that she stared for a long time trying to work it out. All she saw was a body with a chin, a tiny anvil shape on top of her husbands suit, bony white and threaded red, cut through the mouth and out the back, leaving a messy little platform, like the miniature floor of a slaughterhouse. Frank hadn't a scratch on him, but when she touched him he was soft and cold like wet leaves in a winter sack. The pilot was still alive, she thought, but he died with his eyes open, burning and silent, before the ambulance arrived.

There. There you have it.

The smell of fire and petrol and the dancing lights. Their clothes all ripped. She imagined horrors behind her drawn curtains. She imagined all the dead of the world scattered on her grass.

She had left after that. Gone away for years. Found Kitty in New York. She had come home to die. It was taking forever.

She spat. She spat and lurched and looked for something she understood. Some proof. She squinted at the papers close to her and her ruined eyes fished for dates. What year is it? Frank? Frank? Is that you, are you alright? Jesus. And where was the rest of his head? Daniel's head? Where was that?

She found a button and pressed it.

A shadow passed the window. She heard a hollow sound below her.

Who slammed the door?

Who is here?

Frank?

Daniel?

Who?

Delly chewed at her lip. Her belly was full and it needed to be emptied.

Her life too.

Kitty's dreams had been of men. Men tied in a knot like a daisy chain, their limbs interlaced. She woke and washed her mouth out.

Dr George announced, mid morning, over coffee, the day after the fire, that he thought the Cotters should be fired. They were sitting on the terrace, the two of them. He had asked her down. Had called her on her phone. Sitting in the attic, taking a phone call from downstairs – Dr George pacing some room with his mobile stuck to him, in his bedroom probably. She suspected he was just up and that this, this coffee, this was breakfast. Mrs Cotter had just brought them a pot, as well as some pastries, and the early sun was coming round the corner, warming a rectangle of Kitty's neck, just below her ear, and he announced it, in a whisper, a dry American hiss. There was still the smell of burnt wood, of charcoal. Before sitting down she had plucked a partial blow job from a flower pot.

'What? Why?'

'Because,' he said, glancing back through the French windows to make sure Mrs Cotter was gone, 'because they're strange.'

She just stared at him. He was probably the strangest person she had ever met.

'What are you talking about?'

'Yesterday,' he drawled, low like a sick cow. 'The fire. The boy. You know.'

She gaped at him. He was still looking rough. He had not been out she thought. At least, not in his car, which had remained parked on the gravel where the Cotter boy had left it. But there had been no sign of him. Of Dr George. Nothing. She had been up until nearly 2am, patching things up with Caroline. There had been no sound. No noise. No piano. Just the dogs barking in the distance.

'What are you talking about?'

She noticed some grey in his hair, she thought, but he ran his hand over his head and it disappeared.

'You know, yesterday.'

'We don't even know it was him.'

She didn't know his name – the Cotter boy. She didn't know either of their names. They were always 'the boys', always together.

'Well,' he chirped, and stood to pour himself some more coffee, his baggy cotton drawstring trousers pressing against his hips. She thought he was naked beneath. She looked off sideways towards the trees. 'Who else was it? And anyway, they're ass-holes.'

He laughed when he said it, as if what he had said was self evident, given, already agreed between them, as if there was no possibility that Kitty might argue the point.

'They are not.'

He shrugged.

'They've been here forever' she continued. 'They've been here as long as the house. Which is longer than Delly has been here, longer than me, and a damn sight longer than you, so you can forget about it.'

He considered her quietly, shrugged again, drank his coffee.

'Well,' he said eventually, slowly. 'I suppose he hasn't showed up this morning?'

'No. And Mrs Cotter is upset. So don't bother her. Don't say a thing.'

'They look for him?'

She supposed they had. She had not seen the other boy, or Mr Cotter, all morning.

'Yes of course they have.'

'What age is he?'

'I don't know. Twenty four? Twenty five?'

'Really? I thought he was younger. Well okay.'

'Why?'

'Police won't want to know will they?'

'Jesus he's just gone off for one night. Wouldn't you if your porn stash burned down in your parents' boss's back garden?'

He laughed. She hated that.

'Yeah. Probably.'

She knocked back her coffee.

'Was there anything else?'

'Yeah. How's the writing?'

She knew some things that Dr George did not. She knew that he would get his own way with the Cotters. Eventually. That their days were numbered. That the number matched her own. That the number was Delly's. Like everything else.

She and Delly had never fought over money. Not really. But there had been a row nevertheless. Which was ongoing. Kitty was having an argument with herself. Loudly. And it peaked into a rage roughly once a month. The menopause in sight and then this.

It was her own fault. Kitty's. Where had she learned her embarrassment about money? Where had that come from? She was like a twelve year old being told about sex. She blushed and fidgeted and tried desperately not to pay attention. It had always been thus. From the moment they had first met, Kitty had been immensely careful never to give the impression that she wanted money. She had never asked for any. Ever. Yes she had lived in Delly's homes and travelled with her and had benefited from all of that, but she had never accepted any cash. Until they returned to Ireland.

On Delly's insistence, Kitty was now paid a nominal sum per month. Nominal. Monthly. Delly of course had wanted to pay her more than a nominal sum to begin with, for coming back to Ireland when she really would have preferred to stay in New York, for being *around*, for being there, for being a companion, for listening to the rambles and the coughing, for carrying and fetching and wiping the arse of, and all the rest of it. Kitty of course, completely, utterly rejected the idea of payment, for being, after all, simply, truthfully, a *friend*. At least to begin with she rejected it, pointing out that she still had substantial savings, given that, since living with Delly, she had incurred virtually no expenses, and that she still had, though diminishing, an income from her two novels, both of which were still in print, and the second of which was still selling rather well, and the first of which was used by schools and universities, which meant that the income, though not exactly what you would call a living wage, not now, not these days, was, nevertheless, quite respectable, given that it was, as she said, not going on actual day to day expenses, spending, living, given that she lived, courtesy of Delly, rent free, with everything she needed, everything and more, as she said to Delly, more than she could ever dream of, that she was not spending virtually anything, that all of her (now tax free) income was converted almost completely into savings, and that there was no case whatsoever to be made for paying her anything at all. But still, Delly had insisted, simply to make her feel better, to make things easier for her, she knew it was selfish, but there, what could she say, she wanted to give Kitty a small something, on a monthly basis, and she would, and that was the end of it, and if Kitty didn't like it she could give it to charity, but Delly wanted to do this little thing, it would mean so much to her, she would be better for it, please. So Kitty allowed for this, and this had been nearly two years ago now, not too long after they had come back to Ireland, and now every month, at the end of every month, sometimes the beginning, if the end was over a weekend, Kitty received into her bank account, in the form of a standing order, a little midnight machine transfer, the sum of one thousand pounds.

Which made her feel like a fool.

Kitty genuinely had little interest in money. And when she said that she did not care about money, about having any or getting any, she was telling a broad truth. But the fact was that she had no interest in money in the same way that other people have no interest in oxygen. She expected that there would always be, somehow, plenty of the stuff. Enough anyway that she could indulge her natural tendency not to care about it.

So there was something annoying about that one thousand pounds. It was like a reminder – a monthly injection of what she did not actually have, a monthly breath suggesting a sweet room elsewhere, a monthly little nudge in the ribs to look at someone's else's honey. It made her mad, that thousand pounds. It made her miss what she had never missed, it made her feel employed, and adversarial, and made her consider trust where she had not considered it before, rolling it around in her hand now like a piece of clay, wondering, where did that come from, look at that now, that's an interesting thing. Something connected to the world. She took it on board. She took it through a forest of different associations, blaming it sometimes for her inability to write, praising it sometimes as the comfort which allowed her to write, when she thought she was writing, when of course, she was not, she was simply caring a little less about it, one way or the other, she didn't mind, writing, not writing, blah, I'm alive dammit and it's good.

Which of course it wasn't.

It was tenuous and it ached. She had to think about things now. She had to think about money and she had to think about writing and she had to think about the future.

As a result, taking the path of least resistance, not wanting to waste too much time on it, she had slipped into something of an assumption. Which ran more or less along lines which she did not think unreasonable. She thought she'd inherit the lot. And she estimated the lot to be quite a lot.

And sure enough, as Delly had settled comfortably into her long decline, her homecoming, her dying, she had taken a couple of days off from death to consult, behind closed doors, with her accountant, Mr Anthony Millington of Ritter & Floyd, Dublin; with her lawyer, Mr Greg Purcell of Purcell Daly, Dublin; and with Mr Douglas Elliman himself, of D.E.L. New York, flown in specially with two secretaries. And Kitty had paid hardly any attention, other than remarking to herself, mildly, without much excitement, that there had to be a hell of a lot of money around to summon such a coven and to keep them cocooned for two whole days.

The men dispersed. Delly was silent. Dr George was due the following day. Kitty cooked lasagne. She brought a tiny cooled portion up to Delly, who seemed embarrassed and who told her to sit down, to sit down and listen.

It came as something of a shock. The depth and breadth of the fortune, of the cash and the property and the stocks and the shares and the holdings and the options and the patent royalties and the deeds and the accounts and the preposterous, ridiculous, scandalous wealth – would be going, almost entirely, to Dr George. Kitty would get the proceeds of Delly's investment of the insurance money she had received after Daniel Gilmore's death, as well as a one third share of the sale proceeds of the French property, and a free lifetime tenancy of the New York apartment. Both of which had been bought after her husband's death, but with his money. It seemed that Delly did not wish Kitty to have anything of Daniel Gilmore's. She wanted all that to go to Dr George. Kitty would get the leftovers.

'Is that alright dear?' asked Delly, nervously. 'You always said you wanted to live off your own work, and I respect that I really do. So the main thing is that you get to go back to New York and you have the apartment. It's your home. And the money will just be to get you on your feet after I'm gone. To make sure you're

183

comfortable. Because I need to know that you'll be okay. Please don't say no Kitty dear. Please don't say no.'

So she had, red faced, her breath terribly difficult, as if the air was suddenly thin, said yes, I will, yes, of course, don't worry, I will, I do, there there, let's say no more about it. And she had rushed to her office and burst into tears and wondered at the world she found herself in, where a Park Avenue apartment and $40 million could be *such* a disappointment.

She had never really understood Delly's reasoning. Until she found the letter.

'How's the writing?'

She sneered at him and left the terrace and stomped her way through the sitting room and the hall and walked briskly up the curving steel staircase, only slowing herself after a near slip on one of the perforated steps. The huge windows to her left took in the gardens and a corner of the terrace. She did not look, but was aware that the bastard might be able to see her. Dignity. Calm.

She looked down between the gaps. The empty air. This was were she placed him.

There were several sections to her average day. Breakfast. Ablutions. Work. Lunch. Out. Home. Work. Dinner. Work. Supper. Bed. Into these sections at any random point Delly could insert herself. And over the course of the week there were dealings with the Cotters or with the bastard on the terrace, and phone calls, though not frequent now, to New York and London. And Out could mean a walk in the grounds or a drive into the city or lunch with a friend. And Work meant the attic. Work meant being on-line or being immersed in a game. Work meant these things now. It was not that she no longer worked, it was just that the nature of the work had changed. For what was she meant to be doing except creating characters? What was she meant to be doing other than telling stories and lies, fabricating a world based upon what she knew and what she imagined? She was, she had decided, a pure writer. Far purer than she could ever be with the nonsense of books and publishers and agents and shops and sales and readers. All that was paper. She was story. She was a writer who was writing herself into the days of the world, into the minds of people so completely that they didn't know that it was happening to them. The story she told was immediate, direct, instant, intravenous. It rattled off her keyboard and straight into the soul of her audience, each of them – Caroline in Canada; little Sissy and her drunken mother in upstate New York; Ryan the gayboy, for whom she had uncovered the joyous despair of love; Tom Nelson, with his rooms filled with photographs; Maureen, very close, up the coast a little, with her terrible marriage and her search for a binary God. All of these people. And dozens more. Myles from Kenmare; Fabian from Paris; Josef in Rio; Dominic in San Francisco; Virgil in Nebraska; William in Cape Town, Maxwell in Sydney. She knew every one of them. She could, if she dared, count them. She did not dare. And then the countless others for whom it had been a brief, fleeting tale. Something flicked through, glimpsed. Unrecorded, not repeated. They were happy with a couple of minutes, an hour or two, parts of days – then gone. Her audience. Each of them catered to. Each of them responding to a different character. Identifying. Changing the story subtly, simply by hearing it.

What was it if it was not work? Great work. Literature.

The world should be told.

Sometimes, usually in the Out section, driving badly through the narrow lanes trying to find the motorway, or in the Ablutions section, dripping, her eyes squeezed shut, or in Bed, or in Supper, Dinner, Lunch or Breakfast, she told herself a story about that. About why she couldn't reveal it. Her new work. The new literature. It was because of the money. Because no one could make any money out of it. No one would pay. It would not fit. It was not marketable. It was not product. Gandon and the great change. That was more like it. Plots, murders, mysteries, storms.

She found the motorway. She came home. She bathed. She dried her hair, fell asleep, ate. And she did not believe a word of the story she told herself. And in the pit of her stomach, panic grew.

———

Kitty lay in the bath and chewed a third of a Gateaux Chocolate Swiss Roll, and sipped cold milk from a pint glass. Crumbs floated in the water.

She had seen the Cotter boy, not the missing one, the other one, the one who was not missing, in the bushes. He had been, she thought, crying, as he peered, arms folded, under shrubs and hedges, looking for all the world like an old woman who has lost her lapdog. She had watched him from her bedroom window, and it had been close to dusk, close to dark, and the curtains had been open and the mirror light was on, and he had seen her. He glanced up at the house, and his eye caught hers. As far as she could tell anyway, in the creeping gloom, and he shuffled and turned away slightly, as if embarrassed, and as he turned his eye seemed to catch something else in the house, somewhere she couldn't see. He seemed to gape. His face grew longer, as if his mouth had dropped open, as if his eyes had widened. For a second he didn't move at all, not a muscle. Then he gave a strange face altering shudder, and twitched, as if disgusted, and turned furiously and stomped off.

He had been looking somewhere off to her right, on the same level, as if at another window somewhere else, down near Dr George's room maybe.

Like a whale she slipped down into the water and opened her mouth and let the crumbs wander in, plankton in the clear sea.

He cut the chain with chain cutters. He melted wax. He used a scissors on the dusty strings. He took an axe to a buckled trunk. He found everything. None of it was his.

Dr George Addison-Blake.

He was underneath her. He thought of a car mechanic, down in his pit with his pliers, fiddling with the underside. He gave a short cough of laughter. He was covered in grey dust and he was choking and he was sweating and he wanted a beer. Bad times in the burrow.

He had found it by accident. He had thought, from his first glance at the large outer office, where Daniel Gilmore had held meetings, where the board had sometimes gathered on fine weekends in summer, and at the more spare inner office where Daniel had worked, telephoned, negotiated, dealt, that there were secrets here. It was in the dimensions. It was in the leather volumes and the deep carpets and the panelled wood walls and the thick double glazing. There was power. And power always has a hollow space, an inner chamber, there is always a safer place for it to be.

In the inner office, he rummaged in the drawers of the desk. There was very little. In a cabinet he found an unlocked cash box. Inside there was a receipt from a hardware store with some garbage scrawled on the back –

~~fidelma~~

~~delly77~~

~~dg01~~

2208

~~greatoak~~

~~0210~~

~~280609~~

It was Daniel Gilmore's writing. He could tell because he had spent many years reading Daniel Gilmore's writing. And the numbers which his writing contained. The dates which headed each letter. The figures on the cheques. He knew his fat threes and his jagged twos. His skinny eights and his teardrop zeros.

Days later, when he had almost forgotten about the numbers, still exploring, he found a safe dial under a fake light switch, in the inner office this time, near the end wall. It was an old fashioned mechanical dial lock, the kind that was found in the movies, but usually behind paintings. He spun the numbers from the back of the receipt. Something beside him clunked. The wall shifted, slid sideways, opened up. There was a door, it led to another, which was locked. It made him laugh.

He said nothing.

He looked for keys everywhere. In the inner office, in the upstairs study, in the endless drawers of clutter in The Roche's old room, and in the room that had been hers and her husband's. He found plenty, but none were right. Eventually he bought a sledgehammer, waited until Kitty was out and the Cotters down in their place, slipped a couple of Mogadon into Delly's lemon squash, and, with his shirt off, cracked the door across the middle, leaving the lock fairly intact but the hinges swinging.

Behind the second door was a cold damp air and a narrow stairs going down to darkness. It made him giddy. It was ridiculous. The stairs were long, shallow, winding awkwardly at one point. They led to a long corridor. Off the corridor were three rooms of equal size, more or less. There were no windows. There were vents which he later traced to grill outlets in the gable wall, above the windows of the long room. All of it was under the long room. He found an office and a bathroom and an old laboratory. Nothing was working but the electricity was still live. He replaced the ball cock in the toilet cistern and it worked. The taps stayed dry in the bathroom. In the lab they coughed and spat a brown mucus and rattled and ran, eventually, clean and cold.

That had been in the first month. A long time ago now. He might not have stayed if he had not found it.

He remembered when he was a boy, perhaps about eight, or eleven, that he had been afraid of death. Suddenly, as if he had just realised that he would die. Maybe someone had said it to him, convinced him of it finally, but he couldn't remember that. He could only remember the fear. Terror. It had lasted a few days.

Then it had stopped.

———

He was born in Alabama in 1971. They were not sure of the date. They reckoned on the summer. His birthday however was celebrated, traditionally, on February 23rd, the day on which, in 1972, he had been taken into the care of Gilmore Pharmaceuticals.

He knew nothing of his parents. He feared trailer trash red necks. They had decided, apparently, that a child with a certainly fatal blood disorder was not worth it. They took him to Addison-Blake Memorial Hospital in Montgomery and left him in reception. The porter who found him wrapped in a red towel was called George. His name father. His name mother was the hospital. On his birth certificate, a much annotated document, he was named George Addison-Blake.

His blood ran watery in his veins. It was thin and weak and could not carry what he needed. He did not thrive. He was prone to infection. They hooked him up and ran their tests and were able to tell that he suffered from thalassaemia major, Cooley's Anaemia, and a particularly unusual and complex form at that – the Cagliari B variation – which did not respond well to the usual treatment of long term blood transfusions and subsequent desferrioxamine therapy. His red blood cells were malformed. They were hypochromic and they didn't live long enough. They died in his arteries. Years later, in medical school, he had found out what would have happened to him. His growth would stop. The high proportion of nucleated red cells in his bone marrow would mean that it would never reach maturity – it would proliferate, making his bones thinner, brittle, distorting his skull, his face. He would take on a mongoloid appearance. His liver would enlarge. He would die young, warped, squeezed like an empty can – one of the intercurrent infections eventually doing for his heart or his lungs or his brain. In the hospital he was named after, they made him comfortable and waited for him to fade. To leave nothing but a couple of certificates and an anecdote for George the porter to tell when maudlin.

What was killing him though, was to save him instead. For his condition was rare, and his prognosis bleak, and his welfare was in the hands, not of protective, grief stricken and troublesome parents, but of a sharp eyed young paediatric surgeon who happened to know that Gilmore Pharmaceuticals were starting trials of a new set of treatments for haemolytic anaemia and ineffective erythropoiesis, and were on the look out for hopeless cases. He made the call. Within a couple of months George Addison-Blake went from being a dying Alabama baby with no one to care for him, to being an upstate New York guinea pig in a drug trial which was so successful that on the day he was finally detached from the machines and the monitors and stretched his little legs and turned on his side and fell into a blissful sleep, Gilmore Pharmaceuticals estimated value shot up by nearly 18%.

Everyone did well out of it. George got to live a life. The surgeon who had tipped off Gilmore was given a nice little cash donation for his children's ward. George the porter got a $1,000 thank you and a nice story to tell. Only George's parents failed to benefit. They obviously didn't read the papers.

Of the seven babies included in the trial, six survived. All Cagliari variation thalassaemia cases. They had re-unions every few years until they were into their teens and were fed up with being referred to as miracle kids. Of the six, George was the only orphan. More good luck. Daniel Gilmore had taken a personal interest in the trials. He knew, George guessed, that there were public relations pit falls to be avoided. Dead babies. When he knew that they had a happy ending on their hands he wanted to be close to it. Maybe as he stood surrounded by babies in a bright room of his company's research and development complex near Albany, he felt that his own and his wife's failure to conceive had been somehow reversed. When he learned that one of the children, the quiet one with the big brown eyes, would be going to a Home rather than a home, he made his decision. He started adoption proceedings.

As it was George went to a Home anyway. But it was a good one. There were legal problems. The courts decided that the original parents should be sought out. Why this was the case George was not sure. He had heard the story of why he was left to spend the first seven years of his life living in a dorm, but he had never quite understood it. The adoption was finalised in the same week that Daniel Gilmore was killed. By that time he had met his adoptive father about a dozen times, and his adoptive mother once. He supposed it was better than nothing.

When Delly came to New York he went to live with her for a while. But they had not got on. She pretended that it was her grief that kept her distant, but George guessed that it was simply that she didn't much like him. And it tied in with her previous absence. As if the adoption had been Daniel's idea, not hers. George went to boarding school. During holidays Delly encouraged him to take a friend and go somewhere else. If he wanted to be in New York she would stay a couple of days with him and then find a reason to be in France, or on the west coast, or somewhere. He used to ramble around that place, pissing off people like Karl and fat Mary. Later Kitty moved in. Then his chances of becoming close to Delly seemed to fade. Which meant, strangely, that they got on a little better. He went to school down in Washington. He had his own place. It was fine.

He had two theories, George did.

One: Daniel Gilmore was really his father. His actual father. That the red neck story was made up. That he had had an affair with some New Yorker and Delly knew or didn't know (but her knowing might explain why she didn't like him much), but that would explain why the adoption was difficult – because it wasn't an adoption at all, it was a hoax, a fake, and there was no such person as George Addison-Blake, there was only George Gilmore and he should stop feeling so damn grateful and lucky.

He had gone to Montgomery. The hospital existed, but no one remembered a porter called George, and the paediatric surgeon had only been there two years. They couldn't find records relating to a George Addison-Blake. But they said that those records could well have been transferred to Gilmore Pharmaceuticals in Albany. There was a record of a $50,000 donation to the paediatric department in 1973. It was anonymous though.

Two: Ok, the Alabama story was true. He was the son of southern fried souls. Then why this strange line that the story, as related by Delly, always included – that there had been a delay in the adoption because they had to go looking for his parents? And she never followed that up. And when he asked she said she didn't know. She assumed that they had not been found. He wasn't buying that. Who would look for them? Some kind of adoption agency? Some court appointed private eye? The cops? Who? And whoever it was, could they match the resources of a man like Daniel Gilmore? He knew that the first thing Daniel Gilmore would have done was to find those parents himself. And pay them off. Buy them. Absolutely. It just made sense.

Whichever of his theories were true (and they battled with each other for the upper hand constantly, all day, every day, a dirty little war in his head) he knew that he could probably find out. If he could find the documents. Because there were bound to be documents. There always were.

He had been through everything. Everywhere. In the upstairs study, which had been his first target, using the music room as his base. In the store rooms. In the bedrooms. In the office. In the inner office. And then. The passageway. That funny basement. And he had known, as soon as he had gone down there, giggling and shining his torch, that he had found it. Whatever the answer was, it was there.

Except it wasn't.

And what was there, in a sheaf of paper and tub of tablets in a locked drawer, had made him realise, in some perplexity, and with some admiration for the late great Daniel Gilmore, that the secrets of his own parentage were not, in the grand scale of things, really, when you thought about it, all that important.

The Cotter boy had caught him at the window, looking up suddenly from the grounds with his stupid ugly face and staring for a full minute. The Cotter situation was the worst thing that had happened since the night with the black girl and the knife. At the party. That night he had nearly died. He was sure of that now. As time opened up between him and her, he became more and more convinced that she would have killed him.

He had rumbled the Cotter boys. He had closed them down. It had been funny. Now it was a pain in the ass.

The first he knew about it was a small stash of cocaine he found down at the stables. Just half a dozen bags, like $50 bags from back home. It made him curious. He started snooping. He found some more cocaine, and a load of porn, and two rusty looking handguns. Hidden. In various places out in the grounds. He thought about it for a while, watched the Cotter boys and their father, tried to work out the angle. He chose his moment, called the boys into Daniel Gilmore's old office and told them he'd stumbled on their porn stash. Didn't mention anything else. He threatened police and firing and making their parents homeless. It did the trick. The same day he got a phone call. From a man in Dublin called David Martin.

George and Mr Martin hit it off right away.

It turned out that the Cotter boys had had an arrangement with Mr Martin, a kind of warehousing deal, by which they stored whatever he wanted them to store. Mr and Mrs Cotter had known about it, vaguely, but had not been involved themselves. Mr Martin was not big on detail, but George could see that in the years when The Roche had been away, the scope for storing things would have been pretty wide. Drugs, money, guns, maybe people. And porn. They had scaled everything down since her return, no longer using the house itself for example, and in compensation for the lost revenue, Mr Martin had let the boys take surplus porn off his hands. Because nobody wants paper porn anymore – it's all CDs and DVDs and internet now. They sold it to various small-scale non technology customers down the country.

Mr Martin assured George that all this would come to an immediate end. And would Dr Addison-Blake like to go out for a drink some time? He went and met him in the weirdest pub in the world, down a side street, a place called The Pony Bar, full of smoke and stories and wet mouthed whispers. They got on like old friends. They half smiled and bantered. They came to an arrangement.

Mr Martin needed a doctor who could look after his 'little family' whenever they needed it. Dr George needed a reliable supplier of prescription narcotics. It was a deal. With little bonuses involving ecstasy and cocaine and the occasional party, the occasional woman. And one night, when they were gloriously pissed in The Pony Bar, Dr George had caused widespread hilarity by suggesting that he wanted to get into the porn distribution business, taking over the Cotters' tennis shed empire. Mr Martin had loved that. He'd started supplying him. Not that George had done anything other than stockpile. He wasn't going to ask the Cotter boys for a list of their old customers. They were pissed with him as it was. Back to being handymen, hammering, fixing, holding a ladder for Dad.

He had been summoned only twice in three months. The first time was for three broken fingers caught in a security van door, and the second was a minor gunshot wound in the left buttock of an otherwise skinny suburban track suited youth, elaborately ugly, who seemed to think that Dr George was going to kill him.

The party though. It had been bad.

The party was loud, obnoxious, searingly hot, and, by midnight, as if something had been slipped into the punch, or the crates of beer or the wine, as if the pot or the coke was a GM crop, as if the E's stood for something else, it was already beginning to sweat out violence. The air rippled. The music was all wrong. The sky stayed red eyed. People seeped through the doors and the windows. There was so much noise that a silence built. The air ruptured, buckled, gave. The house bled profusely. In the hall the host was in his boxer shorts, swinging wildly with a golf club. He hit nothing but a porcelain dog and a carriage clock. In an upstairs bathroom a Romanian girl was set upon by three men, her clothes stuck to the bath as if left over from an old fashioned wash day, her dignified terror lost on most, but a treat for those who noticed. In the kitchen, where the weapons always are, a woman was stabbed, her thigh split, and her chest punctured, and a black girl was blamed. She, George knew, was not the guilty one. But these Irish guys, he had to laugh, they were real ground floor racists, cartoon racists, unevolved, old fashioned racists. They saw the black face and they found they knew the script. They beat her partner first, her husband or boyfriend, who tried to run, faltered, ran again, faltered, ran a third time, made it. By the time they turned back to the girl she had armed herself, deciding to cling to the error, make it true, and was holding everyone at bay while she backed towards the garden. Dr George was on the floor busy with the original casualty, a woman in her late forties, who was screeching so loud that he knew she was lucky. The knife had missed everything but the breast. He was down there thinking, these people, these people, they get wounded in the buttock and breast, buttock and breast, because they have no structure, no bones, no organs, no essential parts. They were, he was thinking, down there, all flesh. The black girl stepped on his foot. She was surprised, but he, Dr George, he was furious. Fury.

She would have killed him had it not been for the fury. He was sure of that now. She would have interpreted his presence, which she had forgotten, as something surreptitious, aggressive, an attempt to trip and disarm her, and she would have lashed out with the knife, the bloodless knife, which she held raised, pointing downwards, in a microphone grip. But he stood and screamed and kicked at her knee and she fell and dropped the knife and it clattered on the floor and the crowd clattered and fell on top of her and he, Dr George, was left to one side, raging, lucky, damn lucky, blood on the soles of his shoes.

The Cotter boy had seen him at the window, like a fool, like an American tourist fool, sitting on his high stool with his shirt off, staring at the moon and shooting up.

One time he was rented by a guy who was the same age as him. Exactly the same age. They shared a birthday. He thought this was a bit special. He hadn't been doing it for long and hadn't really grasped just how special it was. Though *special* was the wrong word. He hadn't been doing it very long and could still use words like *special*. He hadn't understood that it was almost completely unheard of to be rented, at his age, by someone the same age. It was peculiar. But this guy had called his number and had met him in town and had bought him a drink and then taken him to a sauna. They had the same birthday. And it wasn't mercy. The guy was a little overweight maybe, and he wore thick glasses, but apart from that he was fine, he was even good looking, in a cartoon kind of way – like a Bash Street Kid.

He'd been very happy about it, Kez had. It had seemed like it might be a good arrangement. A good find. But he'd never seen him again. He'd never called. And he'd never seen him in the pubs or in the clubs or anywhere. He wondered whether he'd just been trying it out and that's why he'd paid for it. He thought that was probably it. But maybe he hadn't liked Kez. He had seemed to like Kez, but maybe he hadn't. Maybe the whole thing had been a trauma for him and he had killed himself. Or taken to his room with some computer games and those extra large bags of crisps. Maybe he had needed Kez to be something gentler, older maybe – not a guy his age who talked too much and took his money and was completely cheerful. He probably needed something else.

It bothered him sometimes, with some guys, when he never saw them again.

He knew the guy was the same age as him because he asked him what age he was and the guy said what age he was, and Kez smiled and asked him what month his birthday was, and the guy told him, and Kez laughed and asked what day and the guy told him and Kez probably made too big a deal of it, thinking it special.

'Hey,' called George. His shoes were collecting dew and charcoal.

'Doctor,' said the Cotter boy, with a stiff nod.

He was shovelling ash into a wheelbarrow, the last of the shed, the last of the collection.

'What did he do it for? Huh? Why, do you think?'

'I don't know. I don't . . .'

'Because it's a fucking embarrassment, you know.'

'I don't know he did it.'

'Well who the fuck else?'

The kid just glared at him, leaning on his shovel. George tried to measure distance and reach. He stood at the edge of the ruins.

'You're lucky I don't fire you. You're lucky I didn't spill the beans last night. Wonder what Miss Flood might have made of it. Wonder what Mrs Gilmore would think.'

He stayed quiet.

'I gave Mr Martin a call. Told him to keep an eye out for your brother.'

The boy flinched a little.

'So we'll see what turns up.'

'We heard you were selling the porn on.'

George allowed himself to smile a little. He couldn't lose really. It was like he'd stepped out of the television.

'So you decided to burn me out of business?'

'No.'

'You thought you'd teach the American a lesson?'

'We never did.'

'Well your brother did. And anyway. You heard wrong. I didn't sell a scrap of it. I mean. What the fuck do you think I am?'

The kid said nothing. Stared.

George smiled at him. It was early in the morning. It was about eight o'clock. The sun was up. He turned and turned back again, doing a little circle on the cinders that crunched like snow.

'I'm diabetic,' he said.

'What?'

'I'm a diabetic. I have to inject myself every day with insulin or I'll die. I haven't told Mrs Gilmore because she has enough to worry about without worrying about me. Alright? Just in case you were wondering. Ok?'

He nodded. Didn't smile or frown or look like he believed or disbelieved. He just nodded. Went back to shovelling.

George went back to the house.

This place was easy.

He took Nicola with him. She was bored. She sat in the back, seat belted, staring out the window, asking him a series of questions which he couldn't help thinking had come from her mother, and for which Nicola had been briefed during bath time, while eating soldiers, putting knots in her shoelaces.

'How's your job?'

'It's fine thank you for asking. How's school?'

'Do you get lots of money?'

'Yes. I'm very rich. How's school?'

'Who is Slavia?'

'Sylvia. She's from London. She comes on the show sometimes.'

'Why?'

'To tell us what's happening in London.'

'Is she nice?'

'Yes.'

'Is she. Is it. What's the stuff in your mouth?'

'What stuff?'

He glanced in the mirror, bared his teeth.

'Sly . . . Sylvia.'

'What?'

'Is it the stuff in your mouth?'

'You're thinking of saliva.'

'Oh.'

'Sylvia is a name. Saliva is the water in your mouth.'

'What's it for?'

He didn't know.

'It's to clean your teeth,' he said. 'It's to clean your teeth and to stop your mouth drying out.'

'When does your mouth die out?'

'Dry Nicola dry. To stop it drying out.'

'What is dying anyway?' his daughter asked him.

What is dying?

He thought maybe he should pull the car in to the side of the road and switch on the hazard lights and get in the back with her and tell her the terrible thing. The terrible truth. About death and the size of her life. He could see the silver Mondeo behind them, its snub bumpers in the small of his back like a muzzle.

'Going to sleep,' he said. 'Ask your mother.'

She sighed, went silent, looked out of the window.

'Is your mother well?'

'No she's dying.'

'Nicola, don't say that, it's not funny.'

197

She giggled and kicked his seat.

————

Sylvia Porterhouse turned out, wandered out, emerged, to look like nothing he'd imagined.

His imaginings had been rather complicated. He had hoped initially that she would be black, or not white anyway, so that when she came to stay with him (and he imagined very loud sex, and then the two of them lying out in the back garden, in the sun, and him kicking a football back and forth with Albert's boys) she might serve as a demonstration to Albert and his wife, and his children, that Joe was alright after all, that he was not the fool he had appeared.

He was in no doubt but that she would come and stay with him. That they would sleep together. At some point that had ceased to be something he wondered about. They might even, he imagined, have discussed it on the telephone.

They hadn't.

He imagined as well that she would be a smoker, and a tall woman, thin, and that if she was white, she would be pale white, and that she would be able to drink him under the table. He thought she would probably be hugely adventurous, sexually, and would exhaust and revive him, several times. He imagined that she would always be on the phone, always be talking, that she would continuously send him to the off licence, that she would run out of cigarettes at four in the morning and he would have to drive to some garage half way to Naas to restock her supply, that she would not sleep, that she would sit at her laptop for hours, belting out reams of damning copy on the corruption of Irish politics and society while knocking back tumblers of Scotch and telling filthy jokes. He imagined that she would scare Nicola and that Barry would hate her.

He also imagined that she would be tender and light. That they would walk on the beach (some beach, somewhere) in the early morning, that they would cry together in front of the television, and laugh about the fact that they were crying, that they would be charming and funny and gorgeous and make toast for each other in the afternoons. He imagined that their relationship would make the newspapers – RADIO STAR FINDS LOVE WITH LONDON BEAUTY or THE JOKE'S ON ME ADMITS SYLVIA. He imagined that their relationship would make friends.

She came through the arrivals gate and stood still, blocking the people behind her, and scanned the crowd impatiently, and he knew her immediately. He would have known her even without the Arsenal baseball cap which she had told him she'd be wearing. He would have known her even if it had not been her he was there to meet. Oh look, he would have said, there's Sylvia Porterhouse, obvious as anything. Obvious.

'C'mon,' he said to Nicola. 'Let's go.'

'Where?'

'Home.'

'Where's Saliva then?'

'I don't know . . .'

He took his daughter's hand and turned towards the exit. She dragged at him slightly, looking behind.

'Is that not her?'

'No.'

'She has a red hat, like the arse hat you said was red.'

'Nicola . . .'

'Da-ad! It *is* her. She's waving.'

It was his own fault. He had insisted on collecting her. She had not asked. She had even been a little reluctant, as if there was something about the way he had asked it that she could smell down the telephone line, as if there was something vaguely obscene in the notion, rancid. He had, he realised, made a mistake. The mistake was now at his elbow.

'Joe?'

'Oh Sylvia? Hi hi. God we thought we'd missed you. How are you? Good flight? This is Nicola. God. Well. How are you?'

She was about 5´2″. Maybe less. Her face, which was very white, very pinky white, was an almost perfect circle. Her mouth and nose looked like they had been stolen from a small boy. Her eyes, magnified quite a lot by her round, wire rimmed glasses, were brown. Her hair, he thought, was fair. It was cropped and almost completely covered by her cap which read 'Arsenal – Gooner Army'. She was overweight, and shaped a little like a tea bag dropped in a sink. She wore some kind of light, silky, blood red trousers, baggy but tapered over the top of old black boots. She wore a pale purple jumper and carried a bulging sports bag.

'It's so lovely to meet you Joe. And Nicola,' she said. She beamed at them. Nicola held on to her father's leg, which prevented him, he supposed, from holding on to hers. He could feel his face continue to redden. His mind had been so filled with expectation that it had raced ahead of the actual, of the reality, to the point where it was busy imagining Sylvia naked, manoeuvring the actual body into all those fantasised moments. It was not a good fit.

'Well then. Alright. Alright. The car. Let's go.'

—————

In only one way did she match up. She talked a lot.

'So the latest on the whole Green Park Flasher case is that it's stopped and no one knows now whether it ever actually happened, so that changes the angle of the story do you see from a story about the story to a story about who would put out that kind of story? Do you see? That's the new journalism really, it's like physics, it's about seeing the spin and trying to work out the velocity and the rotational variance and the distance travelled and the angles and see if you can't find the source. The spinner. Who benefits from the lie? Do you see? That's what it's like here now. I mean there. Where do you live?'

In the rear view Joe could see Nicola with a strange blank look on her face. After the first greeting Sylvia had completely ignored her.

'Live? Oh I live in, um, Inchicore. It's near the centre, but slightly, um, east, I mean west of it. It's not close to you. Your hotel I mean.'

'Oh ok.'

She was staying in one of the new hotels just to the left of Temple Bar, which was actually, he supposed, quite close to where he lived, in London terms anyway. That's what he had thought before he had seen her. He thought he'd be able to tell her that in London terms, by London measurements, they were practically neighbours.

'I don't know Dublin at all, I've never been here, isn't that mad?'

She seemed to have traces of an Australian accent. All her phrases finished upwards? Like a question?

'I live in Cunt Arf,' said Nicola loudly.

Sylvia Porterhouse gave a shriek of laughter and slapped the dashboard. Both Joe and Nicola jumped, the car doing a little sideways shimmy on the narrowing motorway, and someone beeped them from behind, possibly the follower in his Ford, and Joe glanced and imagined him taking notes, if he could do that while driving. *The subject demonstrated carelessness on the motorway, endangering his daughter's life.*

'Jesus Christ,' said Joe, as Sylvia jiggled violently in the passenger seat, still squeaking. 'It's *Clon*tarf Nic. Clontarf.'

The child was silent. In the rear view mirror she seemed terribly watchful, as if she was sitting up in bed, having been awoken by a strange noise.

'Cunt Arf,' said Sylvia, shaking her head. 'Well I just know I'm going to like it here.'

They hit traffic and hardly moved for half an hour. The follower sat directly behind them. Joe wondered what he'd make of Sylvia, what he'd log her as.

'I cycle everywhere now, myself. Wouldn't bother with a car, it's hopeless in London. The tube gives me panic attacks due to an incident in my teens, I'll fill you in later, spare the child, but I can't go near it now, it's like descending into hell, it's horrible. Have to take a bus when it's pissing down or too cold, but it's never as cold now as it used to be. The environment's fucked basically. Oh sorry. Car is part of the problem. You can be sweating in January and shivering in August and you'll be soaked by the rain at any time. London will be under water in twenty years, they know it too, plans are afoot, evacuation, re-location, devolution by natural disaster. I've spoken to a guy in the Home Office, they have a timetable. Are you divorced then Joe?'

He looked in the mirror. The follower hadn't shaved. He was yawning too.

'Separated.'

'Oh yeah it's illegal here isn't it?'

He wondered if he braked suddenly in the five mile an hour traffic whether the follower might go into the back of him, give Nicola a little mild whiplash, get himself fired.

'What is?'

'Divorce. All that. Isn't it? Being gay. Having an abortion. Black people. All that's illegal here in'it?'

'Um no actually, not any more. We're very sophisticated now. We're even good at dancing. Except abortion. That's illegal.'

He wondered whether Nicola knew what that was.

'But,' he added, to confuse her, 'it is maintained purely as an indirect subsidy to the ferry companies and the airlines in the form of hundreds, thousands maybe, of additional trips to the UK every week. Gets around various European injunctions, strictures, rulings and um, derivations.'

'Really?' said Sylvia Porterhouse smiling, impressed with something. 'Clever you.'

They dropped her off in her hotel after a hour and a half journey from the airport. Longer than her flight, she pointed out, by 35 minutes. In his imaginings, in his plans, Joe had envisioned waiting while she checked in, then taking her, and Nicola, for ice cream. Showing Sylvia his city. Taking her on a little tour, a little wander, down to the river, back up to the Green, feeding ducks, laughing, their hands sometimes touching as they watched his daughter on the swings. As it was he didn't even go into the lobby with her. He would have, despite the fact that he would have gone no further, if Nicola had not been silently and urgently mouthing *I want to go home* in his rear view mirror.

She asked him for his phone numbers, home and mobile. She said she wanted to meet him the next day so that they could talk about her doing the show, and also because she wanted to discuss why she was in Dublin. He tried to tell her that he didn't think he could help, but she wasn't listening.

'I'll call you tonight actually, or maybe, maybe sooner.' She was looking over the seat at Nicola. 'There's something odd . . . well . . . I'll tell you later. Nice to meet you Nicola.'

She got out of the car. Slammed the door. They watched her climb the hotel steps and disappear.

'Da-ad!'

'I know. I know. Let's get you home.'

'She's mad. She's very rude. Very bad language.'

'Well she's English.'

'You gave her the wrong number.' It was true. He had given her Barry's numbers.

'Well,' he said. 'She's rude.'

There you go, Joe thought. That's what happens. You lose it to this degree, the degree to which he had lost it, you lose it that bad, and there is really only one thing that can happen, at any given time. Not the worst thing. That would be good. That would be fine. If the worst thing happened, then at least he would be jolted forward, or back – one way or the other, he would be moved. But no. What happened was the useless thing. Always the useless thing. The thing that gets you nowhere, that simply turns you once more on the spot you stand on, simply grinds you in a little deeper.

It was, he thought, astonishing that he was allowed to live. To think that he had planned a lame seduction, with ice cream and his daughter as props, in front of a proxy audience – a bored man in a silver Mondeo – all in order to somehow get back at, or make jealous, or somehow, one way or another, to prod, poke, provoke, make sad or sorry or sick, his abandoning, absent, all together missing, wife. And then to flinch and waver – not because he did not find the prospect of Sylvia Porterhouse attractive (there was something after all in that slightly manic good nature that he liked – perhaps its level of definition, when compared to his own fuzzy edged, foggy outlines), but to reject her because he knew that the follower would find her ugly, ridiculous, laughable, would assume her to be a dyke (something Joe would have to check on, granted, but which he felt from all their previous conversations, not to be the case, though with his luck, and his stupidity, she may well have been), and would pass those judgements on to Christine, who would not be jealous or sad, but would either laugh at him or rage at him, both of which he had already experienced, had had enough of, thank you, that's alright, he'd leave it.

Sylvia Porterhouse had not been a tall beautiful black woman with a lap top. Joe would have to think of something else to do with his life.

Barry rose that Saturday at a little after eleven thirty. He had for breakfast a bowl of gritty cereal, two slices of toast with marmalade, two mugs of instant coffee and a glass of orange juice. While he ate he watched television. He went to the bathroom, sat on the toilet for a good fifteen minutes reading *The Popular Murders*, and then showered, for almost twenty minutes, paying particular attention to his balls and his arse, both of which he had shaved before going to bed, and which seemed to have come through the night ok. Once out of the shower he shaved his face, used the nostril trimmer on both his nostrils and his ears, cut his toe nails, plucked three stray hairs from his left eyebrow, moisturised his elbows, brushed his teeth, gargled with mouthwash, and applied liberal amounts of deodorant to his underarms and a lesser measure to the small of his back. Then he walked naked to the bedroom, pausing briefly to consider his reflection in the full length mirror in the hallway.

Barry had a date.

His name was Bernard, and Barry wanted to call him Ben but wasn't sure that it was the correct contraction – that Ben could be short for Bernard. He knew that it could be short for Benjamin. But couldn't it be short for Bernard as well? He did not even consider Bernie or Bern. But he wanted to call him something. He would, he decided, if it came to it, create a nickname.

Bernard was from somewhere else. He wasn't from Dublin. He was broken nosed, about six foot, slim, dark, his eyebrows were a bit bushy, but apart from that he was fine. He spoke slowly, seemed content. He worked in publishing, and they had talked on the telephone several times, Bernard trying to get various authors on to the show, Barry being difficult, before Bernard had finally showed up in the studio earlier that week, accompanying a nervous first novelist from Belfast whom Joe had been interested in because he thought she might have had someone close to her shot. While he interrogated her, demanding to know where she, the author of *The Weekend Lover*, stood on the re-naming of the RUC and the decommissioning of arms, Bernard stared at Barry and Barry felt oddly that he was being tickled, and laughed.

'What?' he asked.

'Sorry.'

'For what?'

'Can I go out with you?'

'Ok.'

'Saturday?'

'Yeah.'

'The Front Lounge? Daytime obviously. Say two o'clock?'

'Alright. Two o'clock.'

'Good.'

If he had not been busy monitoring Joe, worrying about getting another ad break in before the news, slightly concerned that the Belfast novelist was going to either start shouting or crying, and looking for a missing Stiff Little Fingers CD (Joe's idea), Barry would probably have made a mess of it. As it was all he did was smile, nod and be completely impressive.

A date, imagine that, in this day and age.

He dressed in a light blue hand made Italian shirt, black mole-skin trousers from Postillion, tan canvas runners, and a brand new Rubicon denim jacket, black, that had cost him nearly two hundred quid.

He wrote out a cheque for the amount of his weekly rent and left it inside the rent book on the little locker in his little hallway. He left his flat and locked all of its locks. There was nothing out-side his door or on the stairs, or anywhere in the building, or in the porch, or on the steps, or in the front garden or on the street, that could affect his mood. He was optimistic. A little excited. Quite horny. He positively beamed at the blue sky and the sun, at the traffic and the trees, at the warm air that nuzzled him, at the bright day ahead. It was time to forget the week just gone, and the week before it. To forget completely Joe Kavanagh and FM101 and all the crap they created. The city was good. The city was happy. The city was his.

The chief problem of the previous weeks, for which he really had no one to blame but Joe Kavanagh, and, he knew it, himself, was that of his task. His task. His assignment. His new orders. Go out and find the hopeless and the damned. Go and have a rummage in the scary places and see what you can find. Joe of course claimed to be doing his own share of this, but it seemed to amount, so far, to nothing more alarming than a moment of embarrassment in front of his next door neighbours. Barry mean-while, was knee deep in trauma.

So what do you do? Given this particular chore? Where do you go to find them, these little demon Joes, the flakes of his predictable despair, the slivers of his nightmares? Barry thought first that he would have to go to the *authorities* – that he would have to ask those who look after the jails and the hospitals and the treatment centres and the rehabilitation programs, and all of that, all of that sweeping up that went on behind his back that he had never really thought about before – he thought he would have to approach them and ask them for *examples*. Which he just could not contemplate. He had visions, for some reason, of men in pyjamas and women in flowered, pastel frocks, of the delicate trace aroma of human excrement and the squeak of bright corridors.

So he found himself, good God, one night, late, wandering up and down the quays looking for rent boys. This, he thought, would be a relatively straight forward thing. He had seen them often enough, their ever changing anoraks, their pale faces, the ill look of most of them, hungry and, he imagined, somehow ancient, like vampires. He thought that they would be glad to see him, someone like him, come just to talk. Joe had been so keen that he had offered Barry one hundred quid cash and the use of his car.

'For what?'

'To pay them.'

'I'm not actually going to have sex with them Joe.'

'No. Ok. Alright. They'll want something though.'

'Joe I can't offer them money, that would be unethical.'

'Right. You're right. Take my car.'

'I can't drive.'

'Ok. I want to help. Take my jacket.'

So there Barry was, all wrapped up in the 2am chill, after the Thursday show, Friday morning, worrying that he'd be spotted by someone, a scarf around his neck, a baseball cap pulled down low, wearing Joe's leather jacket, good, he supposed, as a kind of disguise, finding three loose cigarettes and a linty mint in the pockets.

It was all very obvious. He could see two boys. They loitered. One by the river wall, one at the corner opposite. Cars crawled by them. Not very many, and after a while he noticed that they were the same ones each time. Two boys and three cars. As he watched from a doorway, the boy by the river was picked up. A car stopped, the window came down, the boy crouched and said something, the door opened, he got in, the car drove off.

Barry decided that if he stayed where he was he'd be next, so he left his little alcove and walked towards the boy at the corner. He walked and watched him, kept his eye on him, his eye with the cold air hurting it. The boy seemed to watch him back. Maybe. His skin was blotchy in the street light and he looked scarred, splattered, a large port wine and a bloody Mary. His back was to the wall, his head down a little, and Barry thought he looked freezing and awful. Ugly and wretched, never possibly attractive. Not ever. Not in a million years. He wore a cheap jacket the colour of the river, and loose jeans, and white trainers. He spat, and then lit a cigarette, and as Barry passed him he nodded. A very civil nod. Very grown up. The kind of nod you got down the country from a stranger. Formal. Curious. Barry couldn't return it, clutched as he suddenly was by a not unfamiliar sensation. He tremored up the middle, from the crown of his head down the centre of everything, eyes, nose, lips, throat, chest, stomach, genitals. All gone sudden raw, a parting of his self, as if he was stapled to a page and opened up for reading. He clucked bad tempered with a high pitched yelp in the back of his throat and stared at his feet and pressed on.

Round again.

He considered crossing to the water where a new figure had now appeared and crouched eating chips off a car bonnet, but he was not ready for that. Or rather, he decided against that. The wall of the river, the salt and vinegar, the shadow of the guy, his folded swagger – it all added up to something. And in contrast, the seemingly ugly boy with the nod and the neat shape, the intelligent stance – that was proper. That was as it should be. Eating chips on the job was just not on. Chip boy would be snarly, slurred. He would snap and do odd things. He might threaten and curse. He might explode. Whereas the other one would be nice. He thought. Or he would be nice to begin with. He might stay nice and then do it on air, go weird on them under Joe's pokey questions. He might be insulted, or traumatised. He might implode.

Barry crossed the river and thought it through again.

It had turned out, it had become clear to him, he had realised, that he didn't have to look any further than his immediate surroundings for the ghosts of Joe's bleakest fantasies. And this, it struck him, was a little sad. That he had been able to put his hand so easily to this kind of thing. There were rent boys by the river, girls by the canal. Alcoholics and gamblers were in the telephone book. The insane lived in his basement. And the poor, the really poor, they were just *everywhere*.

The first of the new guests had been a junky. Joe decided this. *Get me a junky.*

Barry had remembered, he didn't know why, a guy he had met a couple of times in Out On The Liffey, whose name was Derek, who had been largely *frightening*, in the retrospect sense, who Barry had spent a first night with, and been a little surprised that he had gotten out of it alive, and had promised himself, Jesus Christ, never again, and sure enough had, maybe a month later, spent another night with him, in Barry's flat, watching German bondage porn and taking some speed and doing a lot of poppers, and doing things which were, to Barry at least, extreme, though not, apparently, to Derek, and generally coming out of it bruised and incoherent and largely *scared of Derek*, and swearing the never again swear, again. He found Derek's phone number in the little locker beside the bed, the one with the *equipment*. Which was not completely surprising. Nor was the fact that yes, Derek knew loads of junkies, nor was it completely surprising that Derek was not at all surprised that Barry had thought of him in connection with junkies, and it wasn't much of a surprise either that Derek suggested his sister as being the easiest to ask because of her actually being in Derek's place when Barry called. One phone call, one junky.

Joe of course had leapt upon this. Had jumped at the barest glint of ruin which it contained, that smallest, child sized impression it gave that things were falling apart, decaying, city wide, at least city wide, broken and abandoned. Thus were Joe's words, his eyes wide, his head shaking, his hands opening and closing and his mouth coming and going. 'Doesn't that just tell you something though Barry, doesn't it? Doesn't it just scream at you, that? It's like that film.' And Joe had used this single click phone call as a kind of confirmation, encouragement, blessing, and had put his head down and gone looking for old Joy Division albums and played a lot of Persuade and Guru Seven, especially after the news.

So Barry walked up to the boy, straight up to his face, and with his eyes unfocused, so as to be less, he thought, interested looking, less furtive, more professional, acting in a professional capacity, direct, he said,

'Excuse me?'

The boy said 'Hi', and smiled, half smiled, this much Barry could make out, this gentle reforming of the mouth so as to look more, or less, he didn't know, like he was available, he didn't know which, but there it was, causing Barry's eyes, momentarily, to focus, just so as to check, and yes, it was a half smile, flirty, and the eyes were with it too, so that it didn't look particularly forced he thought, and he allowed himself to consider that, given the type of men that these guys usually had to go off and have sex with, given the type that would be the norm, Barry thought, that as compared to that, he, Barry, would be quite a welcome relief, maybe even half fancied. And it occurred to him, as he momentarily focused on the smile set into what he could see now, in close up, was quite an attractive face, with no hint of scarring or staining of any description, it must have been the street lights, that he, Barry, would be quite sought after among rent boys, if, of course, rent boys sought after anything other than money, for he had none of that, Barry didn't, but he had his youth and his little bit of looks, which would in themselves, he thought, if rent boys paid any heed to that kind of thing, be quite valuable on the whole rent boy and their customers scene, if there was such a scene, and if he was on it, and if they, the boys, were into looks or youth or anything other than money at all, at any time, whatsoever.

'You looking for business?'

'No no, no I'm not actually, I . . .'

It sliced through Barry's mind that he might actually in truth be looking for business. Sliced in cross section so that he could examine it, see where it entered and the parts it touched and where it left him. It was a long time leaving him, or a long time at least in the relative frame of those sudden odd thoughts which occur to us, fully formed, between one breath and the next, one word and another. Those little gaps where we live our little lives.

'No I'm not as such, I'm . . .'

The boy frowned as he looked at him, impatient, his lips disappearing, chewed, his eyes flitting off elsewhere. He had no curiosity for this. Barry had assumed that he would, be curious that is, as to what he wanted, but he was not, he even took a step away.

'I'd like to talk to you really . . .'

The boy looked at him again.

'Oh yeah, okay, you have a place?'

So. This was obviously a euphemism then, wanting to talk. This was obviously something that he had heard before, meaning nothing at all to do with talking, used maybe by nervous types like judges, maybe it meant a particular act, rimming maybe, or some generally oral thing, and the phrase, the word, being unique to rent boys, to rent, to that.

'No I, well, would you like to go for a coffee or something?'

The boy looked at Barry.

'You're not a fucking writer are you?'

'No, I . . .'

'Cos I have had it up to here with writers and researchers and fucking film makers and fuck knows. Are you making a documentary?'

'No, I'm not, I'm from . . .'

'Cos I have been in about a dozen fucking documentaries and about six fucking books and Christ knows how many fucking newspapers, and I am tired of being a fucking story.'

Barry coughed. The guy's voice was too loud. It would be easier just to have sex with him.

'I work for radio . . .'

'I knew it.'

'And I'm looking for a rent boy to go on air and talk about it.'

The boy squinted at him.

'You want me to go on the radio to talk about you working on the radio?'

'No, I mean . . .'

'Cos I'll do that, that's no problem. I can do that. I can tell them about how your job is to go looking for trade to put on the radio so that the general population can get off on me without having to fucking pay.'

'No, I . . .'

'Piss off.'

'Right.'

He nodded. Felt ashamed.

'Sorry.'

'Piss off.'

The junky interview had gone very well. Joe, Barry had to admit it, did good. He was at his best on air – this had always been the case. All of his stupidities and his insecurity and his fraud were not left behind, they were carried with him. But on air, in the air, off the ground like that – they found their own gravity. They settled well and were impressive. They became his tone of voice, the music that he played, the words he strung together. They made Good Radio.

He treated the junky, he called her Mary, as if she was anyone else, or, more accurately, as if she was a B list celebrity. He asked her about her favourite song (*Walking On Sunshine* – he didn't play it), her favourite food (lasagne and chips), her favourite book (*Hello*) and he joked with her and let the listeners get confused. Ten minutes in he asked her when she had had her last fix. From then on, in the extended silences, in the pin drop studio, Barry could sense people sit up and listen. It was good. It worked. It ended in an awkward monologue from Joe, in which he seemed to try to make himself cry, and failed. But by then it didn't matter.

Mary, a little startled, nicked five CDs and a set of headphones.

Since then though, there had been a large amount of crap. A stilted conversation with a gay poet about his attempted suicide (in 1976). A drunken actress who howled with laughter at the notion that she might be troubled by playing an abusive nun in a new play. The playwright himself, with a bitter and scary rant against the church. The station manager remarked to Barry one evening that they'd had 'a bad run of guests'. He said it without much sympathy. They let it cool off for a while. Joe insisted they were heading in the right direction, they just needed to be more careful with the stops along the way.

Barry was sure suddenly, as he turned his back on the rent boy, that the place was under surveillance, that the van parked off to his left was full of listening equipment and bored cops. That there were cameras trained on him. That the words he had used were now being analysed by late night lawyers for their legality or otherwise, and that at any minute he'd be picked out by a helicopter searchlight and his photograph would be in the papers and his mother would die.

So when a voice behind him said 'Hey', he hesitated between sprinting and stopping, and stumbled instead, his feet getting caught in his conscience.

'Hey.'

Turning, he was surprised to find that there was only one figure there, not a line of them, and that there were no flashing torches or reflective jackets or holstered guns. And that the voice, which had boomed in his head like a bullet, was quiet and gentle, and belonged to a boy. He stood with his head to one side, a bag of chips held in his hands, his breath salty and warm.

'Don't mind him,' he said. 'He's a bit of a gobshite.'

Barry squinted. This guy was almost his height, not skinny like the other one – he looked healthier, his eyes glinted, his jacket was padded, expensive, he half smiled.

'You want a chip?'

He held out the steaming parcel. Barry shook his head.

'No thanks.'

'Ok.'

'Are you, um . . . are you here . . .'

'Yes,' he said, smiling fully this time.

'Right, well actually I'm not looking for business at all, I'm from a radio station, a radio programme, and I was just looking for a guy to come on and talk to us about what he . . . about this.'

He nodded. He looked a little disappointed maybe, but not much. He ate his chips.

'You a DJ?'

'No, I'm a producer. But my boss is Joe Kavanagh – do you know him? FM101?'

'No.'

A car crawled by them. Barry caught a glimpse of a pale face leaning over towards the passenger window, staring.

'Can we walk?'

The guy shrugged, looked around and started walking slowly, Barry by his side.

'Have you been doing this for long?'

With his mouth full of chips, he nodded.

'You make good money?'

He nodded again, swallowed.

'What's a producer do?'

'Everything. Prepares the show, research, and then all the technical stuff as well, on-air.'

'You make good money?'

'It's ok. Not really. Joe though, he's a good guy. He'd just want to chat for a while, real relaxed, no pressure, it'd be fine.'

'Chat about what?'

'What you do.'

He seemed to frown at that, but perhaps there was a chip lodged somewhere awkward.

'You'd be anonymous of course.'

'Does it pay?'

'Well just the standard appearance fee, it's not much, like £30 I think.'

'Wow.'

'Is that good or bad?'

'That's terrible. For thirty quid you get a hug.'

He crumpled up his chip wrapper and tossed it in a bin. He looked back down the quay.

'I have to work,' he said.

'Well. Are you interested?'

'I'm not a very good talker.'

'That's ok. You just be yourself.'

He said nothing. He stared down the river, following cars with tiny movements of his eyes.

'How about,' said Barry, 'How about I give you my number? And then sometime when you're not working, during the day sometime, you give me a call and we'll meet for a drink or whatever and we can talk about it. You can come down the radio station if you like, have a look around. No obligation.'

'I don't drink.'

'Coffee then.'

He pulled a mobile from his pocket.

'Ok,' he said.

He punched in Barry's number, and then pressed a few more buttons.

'My name is Barry,' said Barry.

'I've called you Radio Boy. On my phone you're Radio Boy.'

'Fair enough. What's your name?'

'Rent Boy.'

'No really.'

'Kevin.'

'Kevin. Nice to meet you Kevin.'

'Ok.'

He wandered off fiddling with his phone, and Barry watched him go, thinking dark thoughts about the world but surprised, a little shocked, by cheerfulness.

———

Bernard was sitting at the bar, perched on a high stool, a half pint of lager in front of him, reading the paper. He wore a black t-shirt, black jeans, black boots. At his feet was a Brown Thomas bag, and neatly folded on the stool beside him was a slate grey Armani jacket. His hair was lightly gelled. His aftershave had lime in it and was perhaps a degree too strong. He shook Barry's hand, and insisted on buying him a drink, so Barry ordered, it was just after two o'clock in the afternoon, a Bloody Mary, and asked Bernard what was in the bag, joking that he shouldn't have really, but Bernard didn't seem to hear that or get it, he just took out a small powder blue Versace top with an elaborate curl of black filigree up one side, held it up to his chest and fluttered his eyelashes. Barry thought it was horrible but told Bernard that it was lovely. He also thought that Bernard was trying way too hard, and that relaxed him a great deal. He knocked back his Bloody Mary and joined Bernard on halves of lager.

They talked about publishing and about radio. Bernard asked him about Joe, but Barry said very little, loyalty having become something of a habit. They complained about the gay scene. They complained about where they lived (Bernard shared a house off the South Circular Road), and complained about the amount of money it would take to buy anything, anywhere. They complained, in a perfunctory kind of way, about the traffic. Apropos of nothing in particular (they had been discussing, he thought, where they had been on their holidays) Bernard announced that he found Barry very attractive. He was, he said, intrigued by Barry, on a very sensual level.

It was, by then, coming up to three thirty. Barry knew, from Bernard's conversation, that going back to Bernard's was impossible. One of his housemates was looking after her sister's children. This meant that they would have to go back to Barry's. The problem with this was that it was Saturday afternoon, the time of McArdle's weekly rent collecting visit. He found that he was unable to tell Bernard this, because he was somehow ashamed that he lived in such circumstances. That a man like McArdle had a key to his home. That he let himself in weekly. He thought however, that it wouldn't be a problem. McArdle was usually gone by five. Six o'clock at the latest. He had never been there after six. All he had to do was slow down the drinking, extend the conversation, and keep them there for another couple of hours.

So by way of a tactical ploy, and, he thought, very neatly conceived of and executed, he did not respond to Bernard's admission of sensual intrigue by admitting that the feeling was mutual. Instead he smiled brightly, and thanked him for the compliment, and asked Bernard, calmly, with the silent promise of some eventual (about six o'clock) reward, to tell Barry all about himself.

It did the trick but was deeply tedious. So much self regard. All decisions huge, all lovers bastards, all events conspired to trip him. And he was well practised, as if he had thought long and hard about his own story. All the phrases lined up neatly. Barry had to stifle yawns, drank more than he properly should have, went to the bathroom more than he had to, simply for the diversion of it. He consoled himself with long hard looks at Bernard's crotch, with a close examination of the nape of his neck and the sweep of his chin, a consideration of his lips, his mouth, his lips, and the occasional and frustrating suggestion of nipples beneath the ribbed black film of his t-shirt. Eventually, at about five o'clock, Barry ventured so far as to ask Bernard what he was doing for the evening. Nothing. Would he like to come back to Barry's, for his tea? He would. And what was it, did he mind saying, that he did?

Barry had been so looking forward to the moment of confusion which that would provoke. He was all set. He was ready with a belly laugh for the 'I'm in publishing' reply. He was prepared for the stutters and the blushes. He was primed for the blank stare and the confusion. But he got none of that. Just a tiny pause, the merest beat, and then 'I fuck. I am the greatest fucking fuck on the planet.'

Right then.

They took a taxi.

The state of the front garden. The rubbish in the corner, the broken tree, the railings bent and buckled. All of it looked just awful. Barry hurried Bernard through it. The street smelled of dog shit and fear. He got him up the steps and in the door, which was scratched, clawed, interfered with.

There was no sign of anyone inside, which was excellent. Either McArdle had been and gone, or, horror, had not yet arrived. It was ten to six. He led Bernard up the stairs, which thankfully someone seemed to have hoovered, past the closed doors and the filthy windows, up to his own floor, his own little plateau, his place. He could sense with every step Bernard registering all the little things, all the big ones. The crap carpet. The wallpaper and its stains. The boiled vegetables. He knew that Bernard would now be wondering whether the flat itself would match the rest or would prove to be an oasis of style and taste and sensuality.

It matched the rest.

But once inside it Barry sighed loudly, and relaxed at last, and allowed himself, for the first time, to enjoy the idea that he was about to have long, noisy, wonderful sex. The cheque was gone. The rent collected. The scene was set.

Bernard was trying to say something, wanting a tour or some such, but Barry stopped him. Put a hand on his shoulder and leaned in and kissed him on the mouth, which Bernard responded to, Barry thinking, let's just have sex, you can see how bad it is afterwards. He pushed off Bernard's Armani jacket and let it fall to the floor. Skilfully, he manoeuvred him towards the bedroom door with its hacked panels and its bad handle. It swung open. In its frame they stood for a couple of minutes, mostly snogging,

216

Bernard getting Barry's jacket off, opening his shirt, getting fingers to a nipple. Barry let one of his hands, he didn't know which, drop to Bernard's jeans, finding there the solid outline of a really very big cock. This, he promised himself, was going to be good.

He broke away to pull the curtains and switch on the bedside light. He took off his shirt. He turned and watched Bernard roll his t-shirt up over a moderately hairy chest and kick off his boots. Barry did the same with his runners, and undid his belt buckle. Bernard came at him, launching his mouth on a slow meander from Barry's neck to his navel, his hands meanwhile undoing the moleskin nonsense of Barry's jeans.

As he fell back on the bed, finally naked, and felt his cock taken into a warm and accommodating, loving and lovely, murmuring mouth, Barry closed his happy eyes and moaned, smiling. This was very good.

They progressed over time through several different variations, exploring, checking all the views, kissing roughly, unconcerned, sucking, licking. Bernard's body had the muscular heft of an occasional sportsman who would, in a couple of years, start to fatten. For now he was almost perfect. There was a wonderful upturn to his penis, exaggerating the size of his low slung balls, which Barry found, through application, that he could completely accommodate in his mouth. After a while Bernard began to pay increasing attention to Barry's ass, so Barry obligingly opened the bedside locker and let Bernard have a rummage around for whatever took his fancy. He made little appreciative noises, as well as a couple of tut-tuts, and emerged back on the bed, now kicked clear of duvet and pillows, with a condom, a squirt bottle of lube, two leather, button down cock rings, and a bottle of poppers.

They had a lot of fun.

At some point, wearing his cock ring tight, his nipples bruised, his head set sideways by the nitrate, Bernard's perfectly curved cock swinging in and out of him like a battering ram, trying desperately not to come, not yet, not just yet, Barry became aware of a distant drumming, which he assumed was his heart, sending out the reinforcements, marshalling the strength to deal with this. It took a couple of minutes for him to realise that it wasn't an internal noise, it was an external one, it was knocking, like knuckles on a door. He opened one eye. All he could see was the headboard, the wall, the window to his right. He collapsed his elbows, dropped his face to the bed, reached back and grabbed Bernard's balls, squeezed them, made steam engine noises through his teeth. So there was someone at the door. They could fuck off.

Bernard was holding Barry's cock, while his thighs made loud slapping noises against Barry's ass. He was hooting, with occasional words escaping – unsubtle invocations, bad prayers, good curses.

'Hello Barry.'

This was not, Barry understood, Bernard's voice. It was someone else's. He had not, he realised, a little drunkenly, screwed insensible, locked the door.

'Hello Barry did you read the script?'

Bernard seemed to have disappeared, his battering ceased, the siege suddenly lifted. Cold air replaced him. Barry opened his eyes. About two feet away, crouched slightly, her hair in a haystack of incalculable horror, her eyes shielded by her modest hand, her purple tracksuit bunched up at the knees as if her entire life were flooded, was Annie.

'I'm not looking,' she said.

He made some noise. He flung himself upwards and hit his head on a shelf, painfully. He attempted to cover his genitals and then could not get off the bed. He glimpsed Bernard, backed into a corner, a look on him not unlike that of a man who has been shot in the face and survived.

'ANNIE JESUS CHRIST GET THE FUCK OUT OF MY FLAT.'

'Sorry to bother you Barry. Did you read the script?'

He wanted to hit her, and probably would have, but he could not stand, his head was reeling, and she was already cowering, quivering, her hand, then both hands, clenched tight over her eyes.

'I haven't looked. I haven't at all. I never saw a thing.'

Barry retrieved the duvet from the floor and covered himself.

'Out,' he said. 'Now.'

She turned, silently, and walked a couple of paces, straight into an armchair.

'Ouch,' she said.

'GET OUT,' screamed Barry – his blood already cooling, a sharp post poppers headache cutting in, a vague nausea rising, various parts of his body and his mind in shock.

She let her arms drop and scurried, not looking at Bernard who was still naked, his hands cupping his considerable cock. She left the bedroom. They stood and listened until they heard the flat door close.

'Jesus Christ,' said Bernard. 'Jesus Jesus Christ.'

'Fucking hell. I am so sorry.'

Barry went and locked the outer door. The house was almost quiet. Softly, from somewhere below him, from somewhere down there, he could hear Annie sobbing as she made her short way home.

———

He shouted apologies through the bathroom door, but in return he could hear only the sound of Bernard cursing the shower and splashing about in the rising pool at his feet. Barry's mobile rang. He retrieved it from the bedroom, walking there with his lubricated arse uncomfortably swishing. The calling number was withheld.

'Yes?'

'I think we were followed?'

'What?'

'From the airport?'

'Who is this?'

'Who is this?'

'What?'

'Believe me Joe, this Gilmore crowd are big serious fucking shit. And they're on to me.'

He'd read some books about management. About executive strategies and marketing tactics. About the profit to risk ratio. About adding value and energising the exchange. They were boring and stupid and they all said the same thing.

The transaction is at least as important as the product. You're selling the sale.

This is what he told them.

Eighteen, smooth body, nine stone, 5'10', brown hair, blue eyes, seven inches cut cock, great ass, versatile, out calls only. He had it stored as a text message but most of them wanted to hear him say it.

Yes I suck. Yes I kiss. Yes I do like poppers. Yes I do like videos. No I don't rim. Yes you can. No I don't do watersports, bondage, scat, dressing up, blood, bareback, parties, groups, your wife, your dog, your drugs. I don't do overnights. No I don't. Yes toys are fine.

I'm the best there is.

None of this of course was strictly speaking true. Not all of the time anyway. Nothing was ever completely true, all of the time. Nothing.

Joe was awoken from a detailed pornographic dream. He found himself on his sofa, confronted by a game show. For the briefest of moments he thought he might have been a contestant, but then the phone rang again. The noise it made had entered his dream as something which, even now, already, he had lost. A woman. His thighs. Her breast. Some delicate chains. A hand held bell. Something.

It startled him.

He hated falling asleep in front of the television. It reminded him of his father. And it was also, by the way, and in connection with his father, but also in respect of his wife, and his daughter, and all that wreckage, and everything else – a clear demonstration of his undeveloped grief, his trivial mind.

He had had a trivial day. He had spent most of it in traffic, driving first to Clontarf, then to the airport to collect Sylvia, then into town, then home, then back to Clontarf, then home again, alone. There had been nothing in it that mattered. He had been polite and constant. He had driven cautiously. All his sudden turnings, his speed, had been imagined. He had been mild. Nicola had declared that it had been the most boring day *of her life*, which had delighted her mother. Even then, on the doorstep, relinquishing his daughter, sneered at for being unable to entertain her, there on the threshold of all his humiliation, he had been silent meek. And had inherited nothing but a television snooze and a filthy dream and a useless hard on.

It was Sylvia. She had tracked him down. She had done her investigative thing.

'Why did you give me Barry's number?'

'Oh I thought that's what you wanted.'

She said nothing. On the television he could see a woman he recognised from his dream.

'I thought you wanted to talk,' he said, 'you know, about the show.'

'Well. Anyway. I don't know if you noticed but we were followed from the airport today.'

'Oh yeah.'

'Which means that I'm definitely on the right track, and to be honest I'm a little nervous, I'm getting paranoid, yeah? I keep hearing things at my door, footsteps, scratchings. I've just been staying in my room.'

He was going to interrupt her, reassure her, but he was sick of the details of his paltry life. What would he say? That his wife did not trust him with his daughter? That it was he who was under surveillance? But that she should not misunderstand – she should not misconstrue and believe that there was something about his life, about his comings and goings, which was inherently of interest to someone else. She should be clear in her mind that he was not under surveillance for the *whole* of himself, but only for that part of him, that small and ever shrinking part of himself, that affected the child. The rest of him, it seemed, was unimportant. It didn't matter what he did then. That was a game show that nobody watched.

He said nothing.

'I made some phone calls, but then I got paranoid about that, about the phone? So I went out and bought a mobile. So I'm talking to you on this mobile, but I don't know if that's better or worse, so I'm not going to say anything to you right? So I have to meet with you and Barry cos I need to ask you a couple of favours yeah? And I know you're going to want to be in on this Joe, as soon as you hear it you're gonna wanna know more. So that's the first thing.'

'Sylvia what the hell are you talking about?'

'Gilmore Pharmaceuticals. Katherine Flood. Fidelma Gilmore. I mean I would have told you about it today but frankly I didn't want to scare your daughter. So can you meet me tomorrow? I would have said tonight but Barry isn't really up for tonight – seems to be having some kind of row with the boyfriend from what I can gather, he was pretty stressed anyway, so I thought we could, the three of us, meet up somewhere tomorrow and I can tell you what I know so far, yeah? And I can ask my favours and you can only say no, right? So where's good and what time?'

'Barry has a boyfriend?'

'Well whoever. I don't know who he was. A lot of shouting.'

He had a headache starting now. All the dull items.

'Ok, tomorrow, 2pm, we'll meet, you can tell me what you're on about. There's a place, a restaurant, does a nice brunch. Let me tell you.'

It had been such a terrible day. A day with so little in it. An empty day. He had driven back and forth across it and had not reached anywhere good. Could he not be interesting? For once, could he not surprise someone? Could he not disinherit himself from the endless, useless, pointless day?No he could not.

When he had given Sylvia Porterhouse her set of instructions and had sent her happily back to watching her door, he knelt in front of the game show girls on his television, and in a spasm of deep and shameful boredom, with a dead pan hand, he put an end to his dream.

He called Radio Boy. It was engaged.

He wondered whether he was allowed to be famous. Whether he had ruled that out of his life now, after a couple of years on the game. You couldn't just turn up famous after that could you? Couldn't make it into a boy band or be a TV guy or even a radio guy. Maybe a radio guy. You couldn't be face famous though. Not after being in trade. They wouldn't let you. The Fates wouldn't let you.

———

A guy asked him once over the phone whether he picked pockets.

'What does that mean?'

'I just wondered.'

'No I don't know what it means – what does it mean, pick pockets?'

'Steal stuff from guys.'

'Oh. No.'

The guy had hung up. Maybe he didn't believe him. Or maybe that was his thing – he wanted to be robbed. A lot of men loved it when he was surly, mean, bad tempered, half dangerous.

'Don't tell my wife sure you won't?'

'No I won't.'

'Please don't tell her.'

'I won't.'

'She'd only kill me if she knew. You won't tell her will you?'

'I don't even know her.'

'But if you did I'm saying. If you did, would you tell her?'

'No.'

''Cos what if you told her, Jesus can you imagine? Can you just imagine it?'

'I won't tell her.'

'If you told her she'd have to know everything. She'd have to see you and see your thing can you imagine, she'd have to see your cock just to see what had been in me, I'm sure she'd demand it, can you imagine that?'

'Yeah.'

'Oh please God don't tell her. If you told her we'd have to have a meeting the three of us, and you'd have to get your thing out just to show her, and, oh Jesus can you imagine, and she'd make it hard just to see it, I'm sure she would, she'd make it hard and she'd make us do what we did in front of her so she could see your thing going into me and she'd probably slap your bum and all, oh Jesus can you imagine, can you just imagine it. You won't will you? Will you tell her?'

'I might.'

'Oh Jesus Christ oh lord God oh Jesus save us, you won't will you, Jesus, God, will you?'

The second time, it rang, and a voice said 'WHAT?' real loud and annoyed, and Kez nearly hung up but didn't.

'Radio Boy.'

'What?'

He was having an argument with someone. Kez could hear a man's voice shouting at him – something about a door.

'It's um, I'm the guy you met in town. You know, the other week. Last week?'

'Who? Hold on.'

Then, through Radio Boy's fingers Kez could hear, he thought :

'You're ove . . . acting.'

' . . . was a loon . . . the room watch . . . us fuck. ..ow shou . . . I react?'

'o . . . uck off.'

The fingers lifted.

'And your top is fucking ugly. Now. Sorry. Who is this?'

'Rent boy. I've got you at a bad time.'

'Sorry about that. Is this, um, this is, I don't know your name.'

'Kevin,' said Kez.

'Kevin. Shit I did know that didn't I? Thanks for calling. I'm Barry.'

'Ok.'

There was a bit of faffing around then. He asked him how he was, yada, how was his weekend, all that. Kez asked him about the domestic. He wasn't telling. The Fates were over at his place.

'Well you wanna meet me?'

'Sure.'

They fixed a time on Monday afternoon, in Bewleys on Grafton Street. Kez almost told him his rates, it was so like the usual. But he didn't. It would be nice he thought. It would be like a meeting. That people with proper jobs had. Coffee and a cake and a progress report. Quarterly targets. Market projections.

On his mobile he changed 'Radio Boy' to 'Barry'.

Then he made himself a nice cup of tea.

———

One time he was sucking a guy in a car parked in a lane way down the quays somewhere near Ringsend and he was really working on this guy, giving him the full tongue and teeth, squeezing his balls and a nipple with his hands, moaning the full come on moan, trying to get it over with because he didn't know the area and he didn't know the guy, and it was late, nearly first light, and he was tired and the guy was trying to finger his ass and the next thing there's this massive fucking jolt and Kez has his head slammed off the steering wheel and feels something click in his neck and he nearly bites the guy's cock off.

Kez is out cold for a minute. Maybe a couple of minutes. When he comes around he's slumped back in the passenger seat, a big bump coming up over his left eye, his neck killing him so that when he turns to look over at the guy he gets a full cold injection of agony, but he turns anyway because he can't really believe what he's seeing, which is his guy, his customer, lying back in his seat whimpering, while a youngish woman, who's leaning her pale face through the window – a perfect red dot in each cheek, maybe the hint of a grin – is clutching the base of his cock and administering a gauze dressing to the tip, which is covered in blood like it's the stump of something bigger that's just been amputated.

They'd been hit from behind by a pissed nurse in a Mazda hatchback.

The nurse was terrified that the police would be called and she'd be breathalysed. The guy was terrified that the police would be called and he'd be arrested. Kez was terrified that he'd swallowed some of this fucker's actual cock and that his neck was broken.

She was nice, the nurse, as it turned out. She told the guy to go to casualty and get it seen to. She told him to tell them he'd got it caught in a zipper. She said it happened all the time. Then she had a look at Kez, who by this time was out of the car, spitting furiously and trying to hold his head up. She gave him a bottle of mineral water and had a look at the bump over his eye and felt his neck and told him to go see his doctor if it was still sore in a couple of days.

Then the three of them examined the damage to the cars, which was minimal, and the nurse was apologetic, but so was the guy, and they agreed to say no more about it, that it was an accident, that nothing could be gained by exchanging details, and that neither of them wanted to lose their no claims bonus.

The nurse drove Kez home.

'You should look after yourself,' she said.

'You should look where you're going.'

'It got rid of my hiccups.'

They laughed but they stopped then because she swerved and nearly hit a telephone box. It was only when he was home and had used up an entire bottle of mouth wash and had held a bag of frozen chips to his head for twenty minutes and had climbed into bed and spent half an hour trying to get comfortable, eventually putting his pillow under his shoulders so that his head hung over the back of it like he was waiting for it to be cut off, that he realised the guy hadn't paid him.

A bad day at the office, all told.

Sylvia Porterhouse told them everything while Joe and herself ate eggs – Florentine and Benedict – and sipped stout. Barry had a standard full fry, with tea. They were gathered around a corner table, their backs to the wall, in the smaller, darker room of The Major Sirr. Barry sat in the middle. He felt, after a time, like something in parentheses, an afterthought, an aside.

He had been the first to arrive, astonishingly tired, cold (despite the start of the heat, the midday humming), and bruised. His elbow was black, scarlet, clotted, blue on the bone. He had sprained his ankle. The world was a hammer. He had sat by the window, hoping to turn warm. But Sylvia had manifested herself before him, somehow knowing who he was, immediately – somehow picking him out. She shrugged at that and tried to joke with him – that he looked so obviously like a homosexual on a Sunday before 5pm that she couldn't miss him – which he thought was terribly *sudden* of her, and neither very charming nor funny, not with him so fucking *cold*. He smiled politely, and sighed a lot when she insisted that they move to a more 'discreet' table, and he resisted the urge to apologise for not being a more discreet queer. She ranted on, dribbled out personal details that he didn't want to hear, told him that she liked Joe a lot, significant pause, and asked how long he'd been separated and how he was taking it.

'Oh he doesn't take it at all. He gives it.'

She shook her head airily. She was easily perplexed.

'I don't follow.'

'No. Well. He's not dealing with it. He's in denial. So he might be pretty good for a shag but I wouldn't count on a relationship.'

She burst out laughing, giving great guffaws that seemed to Barry to be entirely false. He really didn't like her.

'I'll keep that in mind Barry,' she said, rocking. 'Thanks.'

Joe apologised for his lateness, citing parking difficulties. Sylvia kissed his cheek, and Joe frowned at that as if it puzzled him. He sat beside Barry, insisted that they drink stout, flapped about the menus, made the waitress wait while he translated terms like *potato cake* and *rasher* for the English woman, who giggled at him across Barry's chest. They would have none of that they decided, going instead for their various eggs, as if agreeing to forget their islands and become, for the moment, Europeans.

Joe asked Barry where he had managed to find a boyfriend.

'Is it anyone I know? That skinhead who does the traffic? Does he cook?'

227

'What are you talking about?'

'Oh yes,' said Sylvia. 'That's my fault. When I called you. I heard . . . um, someone else. I just assumed . . . didn't think.'

Barry felt himself redden. As he had left the house the night before, too abjectly mortified to stay at home, he had heard Annie in the basement in one of her rocking, wailing rants, repeating the words 'I never saw I never saw' to her loudly unsympathetic husband. That morning there had been a solid silence, as if the basement had been sealed off.

'It was um, just a friend.'

He had spent the night being extremely slutty in The Boilerhouse. He had made it home at 5am, complete with his injuries, which he had acquired by slipping in an embarrassing manner in the steam room. His ankle was now killing him, and he reached awkwardly under the table to take off his shoe.

'What are you doing?'

'I hurt my ankle. Where's your stick?'

'What? Oh, I, uh, I'm healed. What friend?'

'No one,' said Barry, 'actually, just, you know, someone.'

Joe smiled at him horribly. Sylvia looked somewhere else. He marvelled that what had been such a private moment had exploded so violently into a public event, known fully by a lunatic and guessed at by his boss and their London correspondent. It was his own damn fault.

'Right,' he said. 'What's this all about then?'

Sylvia took a moment to examine the room, which was empty except for a couple who silently read the Sunday newspapers, and an obviously hung-over middle aged man sitting in the shadows with a fry up and a large coke. She crouched forward, her hand in front of her mouth.

'Ok. You both know who I'm talking about, right? Daniel Gilmore?'

'Pharmaceuticals millionaire,' said Joe, matching her whisper. 'Killed in a plane crash.'

'Helicopter. 1979.'

'Jesus is it that long ago? Barry was barely thought of.'

'What about him?'

Sylvia coughed.

'Wait,' she said. 'Til we get our food.'

They waited. Barry hugged himself and tried to fall asleep. Sometimes he wanted nothing other than warm wool and winter. Joe, he could see, was deciding whether to be charming or grotesque.

'Do you know?' he wondered. 'Do you know what I'd do with refugees?'

'Oh Christ,' muttered Barry, and let his head fall back on the seat.

'I'd allocate, isn't that it? I'd allocate for everyone entering the country, for every single soul, I'd allocate an old person, a person over sixty say, or even under sixty in special circumstances, who would anyway have been adjudicated by a panel of independent experts to be a complete pain in the arse, and that person would be exported. Expelled. What's the word? Demoted?'

'Deported.'

'Deported. Deport the elderly and the pains in the arses. Deport the crocks and the bigots and the priest lovers and the scum of the townlands and the middle classes. It'd be a great re-mixing of the population.'

Sylvia laughed, and her hand reached past Barry and flapped at Joe.

'You could basically do it,' Joe continued, trying out a bored voice now, 'by having a referendum you see, asking people if they thought we should send all the refugees back, and the people who answered yes would thereby be allocating themselves. And the overall population would stay the same. It'd be great. Great stuff altogether.'

Barry closed his eyes and drifted, his ankle throbbing in half time with his heart, hi-hat to bass, and his elbow feeling like someone was at it with a potato peeler. Joe and Sylvia started cooing and humming at each other, Joe apparently having decided to be, if not charming, then not entirely unpleasant. She seemed to like it. Barry did not listen, but he heard the watery, bath time sounds of the radio man and the audience of one, he heard the narrow-cast, the patter, the play back and the plug. There was a sale in the air. He wanted to go home.

The food revived him a little. He ate without manners, snorting at least once when his mouth was filled with toast and his nose was blocked. He listened to Sylvia's account of Daniel Gilmore, about whom Barry knew nothing other than that he was dead and that there was a building in Trinity named after him. Apparently he was a genius.

'He started Gilmore Pharmaceuticals on the back of a couple of technical patents that he developed himself. Process patents. They made him very rich, very early. He set up GP here in Dublin. And pretty quick he divided it in two. It became almost two different companies. The first, based here, now in London, was strictly business. He bought, acquired, merged and took over. There was a real tough little band of business minds at work – Gilmore, Frank Cullen, Robert Poole, John O'Connell, a couple of others. They were very good. Very aggressive. Very hot.'

Sylvia sipped her stout. Barry was surprised, a little wary. He waited for the punchline. The first he had heard of Sylvia was when he read a piece she did in a Sunday supplement about an S&M restaurant. They had called her up to tell them about it. A relationship had developed. It was usually nothing more serious than celebrity gossip and simple politics. He didn't see where this was going.

She forked some soggy toast into her mouth. Dabbed her lips with the napkin. She lowered her voice. Joe's head appeared at Barry's shoulder.

'The other side of Gilmore Pharmaceuticals was the, um, pharmaceuticals. It was pure research and development, and on pretty odd stuff. They bought, hired, whatever, the best people they could find, from all over the world, and put them in these incredible, state of the art labs in the UK and Italy and the States. And they had the best funded research programmes, and they funded all the top people, and they really did it full on. And the clever thing was that they didn't bother researching what everyone else was researching. They weren't interested in standard stuff. To keep themselves covered they just bought up companies who were doing well in your common or garden drugs – your sleeping tablets, pain killers, ulcer zappers, all that. And that meant that they could indulge the way out guys, on the basis I suppose that if one out of ten of them is on to something then they could hit the big time. So they had guys, like this one Sicilian guy they had who was researching the effects of zero gravity on cancer cells. In 1967. Another guy in California who was trying to revive ostensibly dead brain cells by bombarding them with microwaves. They concentrated on weird things. Blood. Brains. Death. Gilmore himself apparently tried to persuade a couple of Italian hospitals to let him monitor dying patients with all kinds of apparatus, trying to find out exactly how it is the brain manages to die. He said that it was one of the most impressive things the brain ever did – shutting down. The hospitals agreed, cos he was offering a fortune, but the papers got a hold of it and it didn't happen.'

She paused. Barry looked at Joe. He seemed content.

'Then he got killed trying to land at his house, south of here, up in the mountains apparently, during a storm. He was killed, the pilot was killed, Frank Cullen was killed. And after a while Gilmore Pharmaceuticals fell back in terms of research. A series of new chairmen didn't see where that was going at all. They're still huge. Still worth a fortune. But they're not cutting edge now. They're a real safe investment.'

She drained her pint. Folded her arms. Sighed.

'And . . .?' prompted Barry.

'About six months ago I did a piece in the London *Evening Standard* about some of the wackier conspiracy theories that I had found on the internet. I think I even talked to you guys about it. Didn't I? There were all the usual Kennedy, Monroe, Princess Diana ones; all the alien ones; the faked NASA missions; all the religious ones; AIDS is from the CIA, Robert Maxwell, Rudolph Hess, the Florida election. It's a complicated world. There is a search ongoing for the unifying theory of everything. The complete conspiracy. The one that gives rise to all the others. Or that covers them. Explains them. And this guy e-mailed and said he knew what it was.'

She looked at the leftovers on her plate.

'Daniel Gilmore,' said Joe, whispering, 'was an alien intelligence in human form and his helicopter was a UFO and it crashed because . . .'

'No,' said Sylvia, smiling at her crusts. 'No it's much better than that.'

Barry wanted to go back to bed. He'd had his food. He wanted a snooze and a black and white film.

'This guy told me that Gilmore Pharmaceuticals, and Daniel Gilmore in person, developed a powerful memory inhibitor which could target and destroy memories in individuals or groups of people and that this drug had been tested in the USA in the early 1970s and that it has been used by the American government ever since to wipe out memories in entire populations by placing it in the water supply.'

'Oh for fuck's sake,' said Barry.

'Oh bollocks,' said Joe.

'Look I'm going to go home, I'm completely knackered.'

'Do you want a lift?'

'Yeah great.'

'Ok.'

Sylvia smiled at them.

'Go on then,' she said.

They didn't move. Barry yawned. Joe played with a butter portion.

'I didn't pay it any attention. Loads of people sent me details of all kinds of daft things after I did that article. So I included them in a follow up. I mentioned the memory inhibitor, without mentioning Gilmore Pharmaceuticals obviously, in one sentence in the middle of all that – amongst Freemasonry and the flat earth, and the hollow earth, and the occult theory of European history, and the Knights Templar and The Holy Grail and all the Eco crap. Just one sentence. Oblique at best right? And what happens? I get a letter.'

She nodded seriously. Remained silent.

'Yes? From who please?'

'Frank Cullen's widow.'

'Who,' asked Barry, 'is Frank Cullen?'

'Started as Daniel Gilmore's accountant. Was financial director of Gilmore Pharmaceuticals at the time of his death, which was, you'll remember, by his boss's side, in the helicopter, in 1979.'

'So what did she say?'

'It was a very nice letter. She said she enjoyed reading my stuff. Said I was very entertaining. Told me who she was, and said, as a by the way, as if in passing, sort of – you wouldn't believe it would you but, Daniel Gilmore did actually develop an incredibly powerful and targeted memory inhibitor. Yours sincerely Siobhan Cullen.'

She sat back and folded her arms and smiled.

'Is that it?' asked Barry.

'Did you go see her?' asked Joe. 'Talk to her?'

'I tried. I asked to see her. She was surprised to hear from me, and when I told her what it was about she hummed and hawed and then said she wasn't well, and that anyway she couldn't really remember much about it, that it was a long time ago, and she didn't think anything had come of it. That was it. She hung up on me actually.'

'Wow,' said Joe.

Barry looked at him, expecting incredulity, boredom, the same level of scepticism and disinterest as his own. It wasn't there. Joe looked intrigued.

'So then what did you do?'

'Research. Loads of research. Do you have any idea how complicated this stuff is? It's a fucking nightmare I tell you. I didn't know where to start. Company records, annual reports, medical and pharmaceutical journals, patent indexes, the Chemical Patent Index for example, with non-plastics BCE Chemical codes, Markush TOPFRAG, the DWPI, which is the fucking World Patent Index, which has, get this, 14 million patent documents, 8 million patent families, but is not the same as DWPIM, which is the Markush version, which don't ask me what that is I forget, which involves specialised software and fuck knows and I have two A-levels and a bad law degree.'

'You have a law degree Sylvia,' said Joe. 'God I never knew that. That's great.'

She paused.

'Yeah. Right. Anyway. What I did find out was this. He was, Daniel Gilmore that is, and I think it's pretty certain that it was him, personally – he was doing research into sleep first, that moment of falling asleep, the one that you don't remember, which acts the same as at any time when the body loses consciousness, especially during a trauma – but the thing he was interested in was the fact that whole minutes or hours or in some case even days which precede a trauma, like a car crash or something, are forgotten by the person who suffers the trauma. Yeah? He was interested in this from the point of view of psychiatric therapy apparently, and also from an anaesthetic point of view. And I know now as well that he was carrying out research, directing an entire programme of research, in Chicago, from 1968 to 1971, on childbirth, and on trying to pin down the exact sequence of chemical and hormonal events in the mother from the moment of the start of labour to days after the actual birth. Why?'

Neither of them said anything. Barry glanced at Joe. He looked primed, full of anticipation.

'Because women forget the pain of childbirth. We do. We completely cannot remember just how fucking painful it is. He never stated it, but that's what he was after, I'm sure of it. And maybe he was after the same kind of thing with those dying Italians. Anyway, according to my source, he got it. He found it. He tracked it down, and he did whatever it is that they do, and he bottled it. So to speak. Think about it. A drug that allows you to forget, completely, as if it never happened, to the extent that you don't even realise that you ever felt it, the pain of something. Maybe even the thing itself. It's astonishing. The bad things in your life? They haven't happened. Getting hit by a car or breaking up with your . . . oh sorry Joe. You know. The end of something.'

Joe's smile faded. He paled slightly.

'Oh,' he said. 'That's ok.'

Sylvia was silent. She stared at her empty glass. Barry stared at her. That was it?

'That's it?'

'Oh Jesus Christ Barry,' Joe turned to him. 'Every two minutes you ask is that it, you're like a kid in a car for fuck's sake – *are we there yet are we there yet*? Shut up and let the woman speak.'

Barry rolled his eyes and tried to pour more tea, knowing that the pot was empty, spotting the signs already, knowing that here was a new thing for Joe now. A woman with a secret. He'd love that.

'The problems start here though. How far along was he in the development of this? He had certainly got to the point where he could kill sensational memory – he could do the childbirth trick. He talks about this in an interview with some obscure Californian journal in 1972. He talks about administering the drug at the right moment and the sense of pain, horror, torture will be forgotten. He says that you'll know you went through it, but only vaguely, in the same way that you might know – this is him talking now –

that you once drove your car through Carmel. But he says in this interview that the next step would be to reach the point where he could erase the knowledge that you had ever been to Carmel at all. Just that very specific memory. And that then he'd have to overcome the timing problem. That he'd have to be able to back date it. He said he needed to get it to the point where you could take the pill three years after being in Carmel and from that point on be convinced that you'd never been there at all. Ever.'

'What the hell is Carmel?'

'Shut up Barry. California. Clint Eastwood. You don't know about it.'

'But he says, in this interview, that he's real close to this. Then there's nothing more about it. Not from Gilmore anyway. I got back in touch with my e-mail correspondent. Turns out he's a former environment ministry guy. He's, well, let's say that he's furnished me with pretty impressive evidence that the British Government have, on two occasions, once in the early eighties and once in the late eighties, fiddled with the water.'

Barry laughed.

Joe shook his solemn head.

'Jesus God,' he said.

'My guy is convinced that before he died Daniel Gilmore had developed a targeted treatment. All you needed to do was be in a state of recall when you took the drug. You needed to be remembering your trip to Carmel. And it was taken in combination with, or included, an anaesthetic, so that it knocked you out and you didn't end up wiping out the memory of where you lived or what your name was or something that you wanted to keep. My guy thinks there's a chance that he was killed because he wouldn't hand it over. In any case, since his death it's been further developed, by the US government. And it's been used.'

There was a long pause while the waitress cleared their table. Joe quietly ordered two more pints. He didn't ask Barry if he wanted anything. Barry tested tiny movements of his foot.

'Well Sylvia,' said Joe eventually. 'That's some story.'

While they waited for their drinks she went over details, repeating things she had already said, laying emphasis here and there like licks of paint. It still looked to Barry like a cartoon. He suspected that it didn't look much better to Joe but that he was being careful now because he was considering shagging Sylvia Porterhouse and didn't want to piss her off.

Sylvia sipped her new pint.

'There's certain things that I can track down while I'm here. Company records, that kind of thing. Maybe some former employees if I can tfind them. So what I want from you guys. You guys. Is. Well Gilmore's widow right is Fidelma Gilmore, though she calls herself Delly, and mostly uses her maiden name, which I can't remember, and she lives outside the city somewhere in a great big mansion that he had built in the sixties by some famous German architect. And . . . she lives with this writer woman. Kathy Flood.'

'Kitty,' said Joe. 'Kitty Flood. I interviewed her once on RTE, in the afternoon. She was fat. I didn't know she lived with Delly Gilmore. Are they, you know? Are they?'

Sylvia sighed.

'I don't know. It's very difficult to get anything on either of them.'

'Well from what I can remember she was completely up her own arse and one of the most boring people I've ever done, ever, and I've done some.'

'Did she like you?'

'I'm not sure she even saw me.'

'Would she talk to you?'

'To me?'

'Well. The thing is, I can't get close to Delly Gilmore. Any enquiries are just completely ignored by Gilmore Pharmaceuticals, so my only chance is to see Flood and to maybe get to her that way, but Flood's agent says she's working at the moment and is not available for interview.'

'Well then she's not going to talk to me is she?'

'I thought that she just even might take a call from you, you know. That you might have a personal number for her or something.'

She looked hopefully at Barry.

'Before my time,' he said. 'Anyway, why do you want to talk to her? Why would she know anything about it? Even the Gilmore woman might not know the first thing about it.'

Joe told him not to be so negative. He insisted that they would do everything they could to help her. That there was every chance that Kitty Flood might remember him. It had been, as far as he was aware, the last interview she had given. And now that he thought about it, he said, he believed that she had liked him quite a lot. That she might well take a call from him. Might return a call from him. All this was delivered, spoken, in his best 2am voice. His head was in front of Barry's left nipple. Sylvia's was in front of his right. He looked down at Joe's expanding crown and Sylvia's mild dandruff and felt both above them and in their way. He had had enough sexual tension for one weekend.

The announcement of his departure was barely acknowledged, which he did not mind. He hobbled home wrapped up in the sunshine, shivering and weary, his mind filled with worries and embarrassments and the horrors of his life all lined up to laugh at him. He heard in his footsteps Annie's sobs. He imagined that the faces which passed him were witness to his naked moments, his humiliations, his history.

He had forgotten nothing.

———

That evening Barry was woken from a doze by sirens which seemed for once to come to a loud halt outside his window. He sat up, and his Sunday newspaper slipped to the floor. It was still light. It was early. His windows flashed blue, and the grime and the dust and the oil spill of a million hours of traffic pulsed like low cloud. He stood and yawned and lifted the corner of the blind.

It was an ambulance. It went silent, but the lights continued. A uniformed man emerged from the passenger door and opened the gate to Barry's building and crossed the barren ground and disappeared from view. Sleep left Barry slowly. He rested his forehead against the glass and considered going to the door of his flat to listen for voices from inside. He heard no buzzers. But then the second man emerged, the driver, and he stopped at the back of the ambulance and opened the doors. And climbed inside. Barry expected a stretcher. Instead there was a moment of quiet, and he saw faces in a couple of passing cars press themselves against their own windows and he considered for an instant that he himself had been murdered, and that the first ambulance man was on the way up the stairs to his flat, and that he, Barry, was dead, and had left his body, and that if he turned now and looked at the bed he would see that thing there, his body, pale in the blue light, the blood collecting in his back, gathering in his arse and his elbows and the heels of his feet, all his blood finding rest at last, free from his lusts and his embarrassments and his humours, subject now to nothing more than the law of gravity. And drying at the edges of his cut throat, or the multiple wounds in his chest, or the blunt blow to his head.

He turned one eye and saw the bedspread bare of anything but shadows, and he knew from that that he was alive. It caused his breathing to differ.

Down in the street the ambulance driver climbed back out of the vehicle with a bulky shoulder bag, pulling gloves onto his hands. He too crossed the threshold and disappeared.

This time Barry left the bedroom window and made his way through the dusk of his flat to the door, where he crouched and cupped his hand to the wood and pressed an ear against it. There was silence. He knew of course. He knew that he couldn't hear anything because they were down in the basement, that all the action was down there, that the noise of it, if any, would not reach him. He knew that it was Annie.

He thought of course that she was dead. That she had taken too many of her tablets, or that she had gassed herself or had done some fatal damage with the kitchen cutlery or the bathroom taps. Or that the husband had had enough and had crushed her skull with a loving hammer; had strangled her gently, while she slept.

He stepped back to the window. There was a certain lack of urgency he noted. And an absence of the police. So maybe she wasn't dead. Maybe she was dying. Maybe the ambulance men were involved in an emergency stomach pumping, a kiss of life, a shock to the heart. Perhaps she had simply lost it completely. Perhaps she was writing verses from the Bible on the bathroom wall with a crayon of her own shit. Perhaps she was rocking wildly, naked, on her damp bed in the corner, her wails internalised, hell made real in her innards, an entire world taking shape in her terrified mind, complete with armies and governments and impossible creatures and the hideous language of devils and a thousand years of war.

He went back to the door. Nothing. Unless there was, perhaps, a slight sighing in the distance, though that could have been the traffic on the road, or the breeze coming after the ambulance men. He could hear no voices nor movement.

He went back to the window. The ambulance looked a little obscene, with its doors wide open and its lights flashing. Barry thought about pulling on his jeans and opening his door and going downstairs to see what was wrong. What had happened. Whose trouble this was.

He suspected, or knew, that it was his. That he had caused it. For who else would summon sirens in the early dusk, in the warm summer, on a sleepy useless Sunday, if it were not Annie and her shoe horned life? What other panic did his building hold, really? None. And what had provoked her? What had brought her to this – her face pressed up against the world, her mind racing to find the words to tell her story, her script demanded, her words demanded, her silence ended? Who had said it to her? Tell us Annie, tell us all about it, explain yourself now, take your time, tell us your life, tell us what you are, where it all begins, tell us everything Annie, tell us now.

Him. He. Barry. It was him. He had asked her. Told her. He had done that.

She came out wrapped in a pale blue dressing gown, with boots on her feet, with her track suit bottoms rolled up again, to her knees, and her head bowed, and her face averted, and her hair ruined, back combed by wire, exploded. Her steps were tiny. As if she was an ancient creature, or a brand new one. She shuffled, and in her hands she held her hands. She cupped them. To her breast. A secret thing in her grasp.

The ambulance men held an elbow each. Her husband followed with a packed bag, his coat on. She made the street and the path and never once looked up. Barry stood back, in the shadows, and stared at them. She climbed up into the ambulance, the men all helping her, and he imagined her voice going with her into the ambulance, on to the stretcher, lying there or sitting, her hands still held to her breast, her voice going with her, her muttering, her life. She never once looked back. He knew because he stared at her, watched for it. Never once did she look.

Her husband, though, he did. He looked up at Barry's window. Stared at it. For quite a moment.

Barry though, with his hands at his breast, and his mouth wide with guilt, and his eyes on Annie, did not notice.

Joe Kavanagh, who rarely noticed anything, noticed that life was a series of decisions. He noticed this on the Sunday afternoon, after Sylvia had explained herself and her conspiracy, after Barry had disappeared, and he was left, on his third pint and the car parked outside, with this English woman whom he did not find attractive telling him that his voice was like the sound of a zipper going down.

That is what she said.

'Your voice Joe,' she said, purring, nestled slightly into his chest, 'is so seductive. It's just so seductive. It's an undressing voice. It's like pulling down a zip. It's that deep low thrilling noise, it's the sound of skin. Being revealed.'

His instinct here was simply to laugh. To laugh and shrug her off him and tell her not to be so stupid, that zippers made horrible farty noises and were more properly associated, in his world anyway, with having a piss than with anything even vaguely seductive, and anyway, he had never been seductive, he had never been smooth, and if his voice was those things then that was the only part of him that was. And he didn't fancy her. And he didn't fancy it. And he would really rather just go home and watch TV.

But he was conscious of his life as something unfolding, and he was conscious of his place within it, and he knew that it should, properly speaking, be disastrous, and that he should, if he were any kind of man at all, be lost to despair, flung down by failure, doomed and demented and out of control. It was only right that he should be getting pissed on a Sunday with his car parked outside, in the company of a woman he didn't care about but would fuck anyway. This was, he told himself, he decided, how it should be. Even then it was mild. If he was doing it properly he would be spending serious money, taking serious drugs, considering serious violence. If he was any kind of man at all he wouldn't even be thinking about all of this, his decisions would be made, and they

240

would not even have been decisions – they would have been inevitable, because he would be mindless, and he would, without thinking about it, without even noticing, he would take this routine that Sylvia Porterhouse was giving him, and he would fast forward it into one of his own, and he would yank her back to his place and make her share in his life for a night. See how that sounded.

He decided not to laugh.

He decided to have another drink.

He decided to drive.

He decided to take Sylvia home.

He decided to make her hate him.

Yeah and verily.

He managed the first of his decisions. He didn't laugh. He stared at her instead with what he imagined would be a terrifying intensity. Sylvia considered this for a moment, then smiled, then yawned, then looked at her watch, and announced that it was time she was off, she had someone else to see, someone who had known Daniel Gilmore, someone she was hopeful might be able to get her an introduction as well. She said that she thought Joe should not drive and should call a cab – in fact she'd get the waitress to call one, which she then did, and then she said she might see him the next day, she wasn't sure, she'd call, if she could, and she kissed him on the cheek and was gone. Gone.

Joe decided to argue the bill, which he did, loudly, until a manager came and whispered calmly in his ear, taking on a voice which seemed interior, 'Fuck off out of here before I call the police. And the papers. You're making a fool of yourself.'

That at least, thought Joe, as he climbed into the back of his taxi and barked his address, was something salvaged from the day.

———

He remained drunk as long as he could, but he did not have the heart for it, and he knew it. Eventually he showered and had some coffee and some food and felt more sober afterwards, but bored. He went to see Albert and his wife. This time he took them a tin of biscuits, and it seemed to go better. He was slightly blurred, and his edges were softened he supposed. For the first time he met the two boys, two shy and very beautiful creatures who spoke in Dublin accents.

'You're putting that on,' he said.

'Wha?'

'You're putting that on. You're imitating me or something. It's very good.'

Thankfully they didn't seem to understand what he was talking about, and Albert and his wife were just at that moment fussing over the cooker and hadn't heard him. He asked the boys if they'd like to visit the radio station sometime, and they didn't seem very enthusiastic, but agreed nevertheless. So he made plans with them for the following Saturday, and promised to introduce them to his daughter.

'I mean you could come in when I'm actually doing my show but that's probably after your bedtime, and you'd have to ask your parents, it's an adult show you know. Which one of you is the youngest?'

One of them pointed at the other.

'Well you can't be that much older than my Nicola. Do you have a girlfriend?'

They both giggled, and Joe giggled too.

'Nicola is very nice. She's very quiet you know? And she's not materialistical. So she'd make a very good girlfriend all told. I'm sure. What do you think?'

The younger one shrugged and smiled.

'What do you think Albert? My daughter and your son? Will we splice the families, form an alliance?'

'That would be good Joe. But maybe they will think differently.'

'That's kids for you isn't it. They think differently.'

The boys looked like they were going to leave.

'Would you like a biscuit?'

'No biscuits,' said Albert's wife. 'Your dinner is nearly ready.'

Joe stayed for as long as he could, which was to the point where hot soup was being ladled into green bowls while Albert sliced a loaf of soft white bread. Joe was offered nothing. He thought that this was strange. He felt hurt. They did not, it seemed, like him. But they did not dislike him enough to bar him from their house. Maybe he was on probation. Perhaps he was being tested, and if he behaved well enough he would be welcomed more fully into their home. He had, after all, made a bad start. He decided, and it was a decision he liked, the first one he had made all day which he felt he might admit to, if pressed, he decided to become best friends with Albert and his wife, whatever her name was, and their two boys. Their houses would be open to one another. Their meals would be shared, their stories mingled, their troubles halved.

He left them quietly, thanking them for their hospitality, patting the younger boy awkwardly on the head, saying that he'd let himself out (but Albert took him to the door) and inviting them over to his place the next weekend, 'for supper'. The wife said nothing. Albert mentioned his work schedule, and promised to find out in the next couple of days whether he would be free, and let Joe know.

Good. Great. That was great.

He went home and could find nothing to do. He opened a bottle of wine, carefully, and watched television. He stayed up late and kept on drinking. And he crept closer and closer to the television as he turned the volume down further and further, worried that he would annoy his new friends, that he would keep the boys from their sleep, that he would make Albert's wife angry so that Albert had to defend him to her. He pictured the two of them lying there in bed together, staring at the ceiling, wanting to sleep.

Eventually his cheek was pressed to the static and he could hear nothing but the dimmest hiss, as if his inner audience was booing him at last.

He met Radio Boy, Barry, outside Bewleys. Monday. He was standing there, Barry was, like he was selling something, with a bag slung on his shoulder and a magazine in his hand. He didn't look up, so that he didn't see Kez coming, and that annoyed Kez a little because it meant that it was up to him to do the recognising - it meant that he was supposed to remember what Radio Boy looked like because Radio Boy wasn't going to try and remember what he looked like, and it had been dark that night, and it was, thought Kez, a bit unfair to expect him to remember what this guy looked like, especially when he hadn't even looked at him very closely, that night. As it was there was only one gayboy hanging around the door of Bewleys just then. Only one white t-shirt with cropped hair and a short denim jacket and his jeans ironed.

Kez thought he probably would have recognised him anyway. He stood in front of him and said his name.

Barry smiled, shook his hand – which Kez thought was crap. It put him on edge – the only people who ever shook his hand always wanted to save him or treat him or have some of his money. Rescue or rob. Bewleys was crowded and noisy so Barry suggested that they find somewhere else, and Kez thought that yeah, it was crowded and it was noisy, but it was always crowded and noisy and he thought that maybe Radio Boy was a bit worried about being spotted by his gayboy friends chatting to a bit of trade. So they went up to the Green, Radio Boy limping. He said he'd slipped and sprained his ankle. Kez was suspicious of all such things. Physical things. Something in him just automatically assumed that it was faked and fetishistic. He changed his mind about Barry not wanting to be seen with him though when they went for their cake and coffee to the café in Habitat, which was full of young queens measuring sofas and staring at lamps. He thought then that maybe limping towards a public snack with a male prostitute was the kick, was the thing, was the reason.

So he was a bit grumpy to start with, Kez was. He couldn't shake the idea that somehow this was business. And if it wasn't, then it was *about* business, which was of course worse. He just wanted to relax and eat his cream meringue and find out about radio. But instead he felt vaguely sick, as if on a clinic visit. Sometimes he thought he'd rather have the clap than the understanding, the compassion, the caring, the endless fucking *listening* – all those temporary, watery things – those ideas. And it was always scared looking gayboys and papery old queens, so busy not judging him that they were never quite sure who he was. They never remembered him from one month to the next. He preferred the nurses with their vicious country smiles who jabbed his arm and his arse. *You again*, they snarled.

Radio Boy though, Barry, was alright. He didn't ask him anything until way after the cakes and into their second coffees. He just nattered on about his boss and his flat and all kinds of crap. He seemed obsessed by his flat. He had landlord problems, neighbour problems. He had window and appliance problems. His problems were endless. Kez was getting bored. So eventually, after he had spent a couple of minutes just staring out the window while Barry told him how he thought someone in the building was somehow stealing his cable television signals, bleeding his feed, making his reception of Channel Four and Sky News practically impossible, Kez just interrupted him. Just asked him straight out what it was he wanted exactly. And Barry apologised and hesitated and went quiet, and then apologised again. Kez saw that he was blushing a little. He realised then that Barry was *embarrassed*. He was shy. He didn't know how to ask Kez about what it was he did. He didn't know how to say it. He hadn't mentioned it once. Kez felt sorry for him.

So he took up the slack a little. Led him through it. Told him what he thought he would want to hear. He didn't tell him anything true.

'Me and a guy I knew from around the corner got into it years ago when we used to go hang around in the park during the evenings in the summer and we'd see all sorts going on in there and then guys would offer us money, so my friend couldn't get into that but I thought it was easy and a bit of a laugh so I ended up spending most of that summer just doing that, then I learned most of how everything works from the punters, you know, where to go in town for business, how to keep out of the way of certain people, who to look out for, what not to do, all that crap, and then I just kept on doing it and got regulars and I don't mind it I make more money than you do probably and I can take weeks off anytime I want and I don't pay taxes, I advertise now, don't go to the park ever, and I'm not much on the quays either, you were lucky you found me, haven't been down there in months before last week, and I just do all my business on the mobile and that's about it.'

Barry let loose with the questions then, permission given. These were mostly standard punter questions. The ones that tended to come on the drive back from the punter's place, or getting dressed, or while Kez was waiting for a taxi. The afterwards questions. Which were different to the before questions such as *how big is your cock* and *do you take it up the ass*. The afterwards questions were all basically the same question. Which wasn't a question at all, it was more a kind of faulty apology. He had learned to not really give them much thought, the afterwards questions. They never led anywhere. It was their repetition, and Kez's boredom with them, that had drained all his answers of the truth. So he told the usual half lies, full lies, the right answers to the wrong questions. It was aftercare. After sales service. Pay for the sex, get to care for free.

'Do you work every day?'

'Jesus no. Do you? I work when I like.'

'How much do you make per week?'

'Depends how much I work. If I want to, I can come away with over a thousand.'

'Do you practise safe sex?'

'Always.'

'Is there an upper age limit?'

'No.'

'Are there guys you won't have sex with?'

'Violent guys, drunken guys, stoned guys, guys with a bad atmosphere.'

'How many regulars do you have?'

'About a dozen.'

'How regular is regular?'

'Anything from once a week to once every three months.'

'How long have you been doing this?'

'About two years.'

'Do you live at home?'

'No I was thrown out by my Dad. I have my own place.'

'Do you have any brothers and sisters?'

'I had a brother but he died in a car crash.'

'What do you, you know, what do you, uh, what do you do?'

This was not an afterwards question. Interesting. Kez didn't want to get into it though.

'I'm a rent boy.'

Barry laughed at that.

'No, I meant . . .'

'I know what you meant. Will he ask me that then?'

'Who?'

'Your DJ boss. Will he ask me to describe the sex when I'm on the radio?'

'Uh, no he won't. I wouldn't think so. Sorry. I was just . . .'

Kez smiled at him and he blushed deeper. He was kind of fun, this radio boy.

'Do you get much hassle from the law?'

'No. I've been stopped twice in my life. First time they gave me a lift home. That was from the park. Lectured me, threatened to tell my mother. Second time I was given a summons. I keep out of their way though. And as I'm not ever on the streets much anymore . . .'

'Has a uh, what do you call them, punter? Has a punter ever been violent?'

Kez glanced out the window, at the sky, checked it was there.

'No never. I've been lucky. But I think you can see those guys coming, you know? I just avoid them. I've heard some stories though. I've had guys who wouldn't pay, told me to fuck off, gave the impression that they'd have liked to knock me about a bit. But I just get out of there.'

'Do you have a pimp?'

'No.'

'Do you have a boyfriend?'

'Yes.'

'Does he mind?'

'Does he mind what? Being my boyfriend?'

'No, does he mind your work?'

'Apparently not.'

'He knows then?'

'Of course he knows.'

'What does he do?'

'He's an architect.'

There was a pause. Where had that come from? He was usually a barber.

'At least, he's studying to be an architect.'

He thought Barry was going to ask where. Where did he study? That looked like the question that was taking shape, that looked like it, and that Barry knew some architects or something, or his boyfriend was an architect or something, or that his boyfriend was a fucking architecture teacher or something. But Barry just smiled, and his blush faded, and Kez could feel one of his own beginning.

'Do you,' asked Kez, 'have an arch . . . do you have a boyfriend?'

'No. How did you know I was gay by the way?'

'It's a gift I have.'

'Yeah.'

They decided that Kez would come in to the studio on the Thursday night. That he would meet Joe, and, if everything was ok, he'd go on air that night and chat. Kez was pretty sure that he wouldn't do it. That he wouldn't, when the time came, want to do it. But he thought that it'd be interesting to see inside a radio studio, and that it would be fun to see how close he could get to going on the air, to opening his mouth to millions and telling them all that bullshit.

It wouldn't be millions. It'd be thousands probably.

Including his mother. Or Vincent. Or Kathy, who'd tell Vincent. Or some regular would recognise his voice. They could disguise voices though, make them sound metal, retarded, scary. Which would be crap.

There was basically no way he was going to do it.

Barry went to shake his hand again when they were splitting up on the top of Grafton Street.

'No, can we not shake hands? No offence.'

'Oh, right, ok. Why not?'

'I just don't do that. Or, like, if you want you have to pay extra. Two coffees and a cake doesn't get you that.'

Barry smiled. Kez had been trying to get him to laugh, and felt his blush come up again.

'I have your number,' said Barry.

'Yeah.'

'I'll call you on Wednesday sometime, make sure you haven't changed your mind.'

'Yeah. Ok.'

'Thanks for meeting me. It's been really good.'

'Ok. Right. See ya.'

Barry headed off towards the south, which was actually where Kez could have gone as well – he was going to go home, he could have walked to the other side of the Green with him at least, but he didn't want to really. He didn't know why. He wished he hadn't made that last joke. It had sounded wrong, as if it was true, when it wasn't, it wasn't true. Nothing he said was true.

He turned towards the river.

Joe Kavanagh's week was spilled salt. It crunched and burned. It got into his wounds. He was thirsty and his heart was strained. He didn't like it.

He was going to be hard – to match it. He was sticking to his decision to sleep with Sylvia Porterhouse. He still felt that rigorous and casual sex might cure him of something, or, equally as good, might bring the fever fully on. Bring it on, he thought. Bring it fucking on.

She was clearly up for it, but she obviously expected a little effort on his part. Which was, he thought, fair enough. He thought that if he got her in touch with Kitty Flood that it would pretty much secure the deal. This was a sober thought, formulated while retrieving his car on the Monday morning, at some ridiculous hour which he had not seen clearly in about a year. He couldn't believe the traffic. So he set about tracking down a phone number for the fat novelist. This was not easy.

He hated calling his previous colleagues at RTE, but he did so. He could never work out if they thought he had been a fool to leave or were jealous. Whichever it was, they seemed to hate him, in a very quiet, grown up kind of way. They were unswervingly polite. His old producer insisted that they had never interviewed Kitty Flood. His old sound engineer remembered her breathing. Her breathing had been technically difficult for him. She wheezed a lot and had tended to lick the microphone, inadvertently perhaps, but he had his suspicions. He remembered her though because he was a fan, and she had signed a copy of *The Mythology of Noise* for him, her second novel, and, he said, her best. He recalled also that they had not had their usual producer that day, but a stand in, a woman who was now quite big time, having become the series producer for Pat Kenny. Gosh thought Joe.

He called her and she was surprised to hear from him, and commiserated on the break up of his marriage, and asked him seriously how things were going on FM101 and would he ever think of coming back 'home'. Joe dithered, and then accepted an invitation to dinner 'sometime soon'. He had to talk to her for a half hour before she told him that she didn't have Kitty Flood's number. But she knew someone in the *Irish Times* who almost certainly did, and she'd call Joe back.

So it went on.

He had to talk to these people all day long. It gave him indigestion and a headache and involved him in seven different invitations to drinks or dinner 'sometime soon'. He was appalled at his ability to get certain people on the telephone. Editors. Columnists. Television personalities. His name opened doors to all the useless places.

But he got the number.

———

He didn't call Sylvia. He decided to wait until she called him. This involved him in a game, and he was glad of it. Better, he thought, to be playing with someone else than with himself. By Wednesday though he thought that she'd forgotten about him. Then he thought that maybe the whole story had been true and that she had been murdered, kidnapped, her tongue cut out, her memory erased – something exciting like that. But she called him in the evening at the studio, about ten minutes before he went on. She told him that she had met some very interesting people who had told her some very interesting things. That, Joe told her, was great. But she had been unable to get in touch directly with either Delly Roche or Kitty Flood.

'Ah.'

'So I was wondering.'

'Yeah?'

'Whether you might have had any luck?'

'Luck no. I don't do luck. Or luck doesn't do me. Me and luck do not have a relationship. Currently. What is the opposite of luck?'

'Bad luck.'

'No I didn't have any of that either.'

'Did you get a number or not?'

'I did.'

She screeched and screamed, and Joe's eyes closed and he thought of other things. She said she'd come to his house the next day.

'Sylvia, that would be great,' said Joe, trying to make his voice a slow as possible. This was game on. 'I can't wait. We'll have a wonderful time.'

'Um, yeah. Do we need Barry?'

'What?'

'Should we record it I wonder? Cos if she refused to meet, you may just have to drop a hint and see what happens.'

This was not game on.

'What are you talking about?'

'Well what if she just refuses to meet us?'

'Us?'

'I think you should then just say something about what we've got – what we know – and see how she reacts. You know, or else I've got nothing.'

'You want me to talk to her?'

'Of course I want you to talk to her. She knows you. She hasn't a clue who I am. She's definitely not going to want to meet me.'

'Ah Jesus Sylvia I thought all you wanted was a phone number.'

He could hear Barry laughing softly at the desk behind him, the little queer.

'No Joe! What good is a phone number? I want you to call her. I need you to call her. You're my big hope Joe. Joe? Please Joe.'

Barry was now tapping his watch.

'I have to go Sylvia. I'm on air in about a minute.'

'So will I see you tomorrow?'

'I'm not. I don't. I haven't. Fuck, call me back will ya?'

'Ok, thanks Joe, you're a star, I really owe you one I do. Put me on to Barry will you?'

What did she owe him he wondered? What exactly did she think she owed him? He would like to know.

Barry grunted something into the phone and then put it down on the desk. He didn't pick it up again until Joe had done his intro and they were half way through *Flowers For The Dead Flowers* by Ecce Homo. He liked Barry's occasional loyalty. He liked the way it rhymed with his own occasional needs.

———

She had tried to persuade Barry to come to Joe's as well, with his *gear*, assuming that he would somehow be an expert at recording telephone conversations. Barry, thankfully, had told her to get

252

lost. Or something similar. He had then spent most of the evening giving out about Sylvia Porterhouse ('She's not even entertaining crazy, she's just low key sensible crazy. She's so fucking boring') and singing the praises of some rent boy he'd discovered. ('He has a dry humour as well, which you'll love, and he's very matter of fact, straight forward, and his voice is perfect.') So that by the time he got home, and the phone was ringing as he came in the door, and it was Sylvia again, asking what time would suit, he was no longer in any mood for anything.

'Anytime. I don't care.'

'Are you alright?'

'No.'

There was a big pause. A really really long one.

'Would about one o'clock be ok?'

'Whatever.'

'Ok. Have a good night's sleep. It'll be worth it. Wait and see.'

What would be worth it, he wondered? And what was the *it* that it would be worth? He twisted into a horrible dream in which he chased his wife with a machete.

The whole week came at him with mild shocks, one after the other. Variable shocks. As if the world was preparing him. His bruised arm looked like the start of something.

Barry.

He slept badly, and rose later each day. His energy seemed rationed out, and he felt that he was either recovering or getting ready. He was nervous. He was lonely. He thought someone was following him. On Monday afternoon, after he had met with Kevin, he heard someone call his name on Earlsfort Terrace, he was sure he had, but when he turned there was no one there.

He soaked his swollen ankle in a basin of water for hours each evening, going to work then with one cold foot and a loneliness which he experienced mainly as a taste. As if this new sense of solitude was a flavour in his mouth. His foot pain and his bruising and the taste made him slow, and his mind matched his body, and he found himself thinking about things that he wasn't accustomed to thinking about, like suffering and death, like isolation, creepy-crawlies, religion and illness and getting old. He decided that he would go to his parents' house at the weekend and try to find his copy of *Lord of The Rings*. He felt the need of a long journey and great wars. He thought he might be depressed. He hadn't been properly depressed since he was about 14. It alarmed him that he began to understand, almost admire, Joe's attempts at despair.

Annie was the chief problem. Annie.

He felt enormously guilty. As if he had killed her. He felt that he had probably killed her. Even if she wasn't actually properly dead, there was probably, he thought, a very thin line in a mind such as hers, between useful living and a sealed up, catatonic, rocking back and forth, dribbling hell. He felt that he might have sent her there. He relived again and again that moment when he had gone to her on the steps and had asked her if she wanted to go on the radio. What had prompted that? Because there was no doubt in his mind that it had led, directly, to the interrupted fuck and the sirens on the Sunday, and the only thing he could think of now was that he had been trying to shock Joe out of his plan. Or that somewhere in his messy head he had imagined the interview and had thought that it would be a scream.

A scream.

Or that he had wanted to punish her for the discomfort she caused him. With her night dress and her track suit. With her cropped hair and cut voice. With her words.

In his own itty-bitty defence, which he prepared but did not believe, he thought that he could remember having joked with Annie, previously, about her going on the radio. He was sure that she had talked about it. And that she had thought it ridiculous and funny and had laughed at the notion. He was sure he remembered that. And he certainly remembered times when she had been much better, far more lucid, when she had chatted to him easily and lightly, about the weather or the news or the state of the building. He guessed that had he said it to her at a different time, at a different point in her medication chronology perhaps, that she would have laughed and exposed those weird sharpened teeth and coughed and writhed and wrinkled and shuffled off and not minded it a bit. But he had timed it wrong. Or maybe it was that he had asked it in a certain way. Maybe it was because as he was saying it he was serious, and somehow, in the mis-wiring of her brain, in the switches and the routers, she could, uncanny, read intent. And so she had taken him seriously, and had bundled much of her life into the acceptance of the offer. Her life.

He thought about going down to speak to the husband, but he couldn't face it.

On Tuesday morning, early, he thought he heard knocking at his door. But he was still half asleep, and perhaps he dreamed it.

Another reason why the world moved slowly, why his mind was stalled and his steps were short – he thought Kevin was beautiful. As the week progressed and his bruises changed colour, the thought became stronger. Kevin was beautiful.

He had not looked forward to meeting him on the Monday. He thought he had done something stupid. He thought that he might ruin another fucked up mind with his trivial devotion to his triv-ial boss. He couldn't even remember what Kevin looked like. He had gone to Bewleys and hoped that he wouldn't turn up. He had stood there reading a magazine, not looking, hoping that if he did show up he'd change his mind and piss off again. Then he'd heard his own name spoken, softly, but without hesitation, and he had looked up, and his first thought had been, *Jesus, this guy is beautiful.*

He had wondered about this a lot since then, and he had con-sidered whether it was really the case, whether he might not sim-ply think that Kevin was pitiful, or forlorn, or tragic. That he saw a wounded youth, a despoiled innocence, a broken promise – something heart breaking in a Diesel t-shirt and cargo pants. But no. Kevin was genuinely beautiful. Barry had limped alongside him feeling old and hideous. And in Habitat his words had sounded grubby and deformed next to Kevin's simple story, his lack of guile.

He guessed that he was about nineteen or twenty. Maybe a lit-tle older. Maybe a little younger. A lot younger than Barry any-way. He had big wide eyes, brown, and dark eyebrows which seemed to arch slightly, and his lips were always a little pursed so that he looked like he was about to smile or like he was holding back a laugh. And his eyes sparkled and his skin shone. And his

255

hair was dark, and it curled over his ears and on his forehead. And his body was muscled but not worked on – it seemed naturally occurring. And his arms looked strong. And he was slim and neat – his waist, his hips, his ass, his legs – all of it was conspicuously perfect, so much so that Barry resented the whole damn set up. He was pissed off that the only faults he could find were a nose that was a little big around the nostrils, and an obvious need for a decent hair cut.

He assumed from the looks that he would be a nasty little queen. Because he could get away with it. But Kevin was quiet, polite, shy, a little nervous. He tried to pay for their coffees. He was embarrassed that he couldn't decide what cake he wanted. He stood there at the counter, reddening, as he dithered between a coffee slice and a cream meringue, apparently unaware that his presence had completely halted conversation at three tables, and that half the staff of Habitat were staring at him lustfully.

All of this combined to make Barry feel a fool. A voice in his head sought to warn him. This is a teenage hustler, for Christ's sake, a rent boy, a disaster area – keep your eyes peeled and your libido locked up. But another voice, perhaps from his heart, he wasn't sure, told him that it would be good to offer friendship to Kevin. Because of that smile, because of those wide eyes, because he looked like he was a little lost. A third voice, from somewhere lower still, wondered what he charged, and whether there might not be some kind of discount scheme.

It was depressing. He wanted good and evil, trees and mountains, hobbits and orcs.

On the Wednesday morning he was woken once more by the sound of knocking. This time he made it out of his bed and stood naked in his little hallway, but it had stopped. By the time he pulled on a dressing gown and opened the door he was not sure anymore that it had not been another dream.

By Thursday the bruise on his elbow had turned yellow, and the pain he felt when he put pressure on it was pleasurable, but his ankle was ruined. He worried that he could not run away from whoever it was who was following him. He nearly said it to Sylvia when she called the studio on Wednesday night, nearly told her that he was being followed through the streets by a man or a spirit or a private detective, but he knew that she would believe him.

And he knew as well that what was following him was in fact his conscience, given shape and shadow by his poor understanding of Freud, and by his having watched *Fight Club* on video. He had turned down her request that he join her on her Gilmore investigations, on the basis that he thought it would be the end of him if he actually began to take her seriously.

He tried to snap out of it in time for Kevin's arrival at the studio. He tried to snap out of everything – his depression, his paranoia, his guilt, and his erotic fascination for a teenage boy who had probably been sexualised quite enough already thank you. But nothing snapped. He knew it wouldn't. He knew that it couldn't in fact, from the moment he had heard Kevin laugh on the telephone, at some minor joke of Barry's, while they talked on the Wednesday afternoon. It was a laugh that hit his mind at such an angle, at such a speed, that it felt like it was emerging rather than incoming, as if it were a thing remembered, from the best of days, from somewhere bright and perfect, in some imagined past. Happiness.

He felt followed from the phone to the fridge, and when he closed his eyes he felt examined. Look at you now. What do you think you're at? What kind of trouble are you after now, as if you don't have enough?

She arrived with a bottle of Dom Perignon and a box of hand made chocolates. She looked ok. He thought that maybe she would look better naked because her clothes were so awful.

She had a script written out for him to follow in his conversation with Kitty Flood. There were several A4 pages covered in her large loopy writing. She went through this about three times while he drank the champagne and wondered what she was into exactly. What exactly. Precisely.

'Just turn on the charm though is the main thing Joe. That charm you have. That voice. Use it on her. That's the key. Flatter her. Flirt with her. And it's important that you don't mention Gilmore at all. Just talk about her books and her writing, and we only mention Fidelma if she's not going for it. Ok?'

'She probably won't even be in.'

She was in. She answered on the second ring. He recognised her voice immediately. It was a horrid nasal vaguely Cork wheeze, with New York squawking on the short vowels. He thought from the sound of her that she had probably put on some weight.

'Kitty Flood?'

'Yes?'

'Ms Flood, I hope you remember me. My name is Joe Kavanagh. A couple of years ago you were good enough to do an interview on my radio show on RTE.'

She said nothing.

'It was an evening show, we had a lovely chat, you spoke about your work.'

'Yes I remember.'

'Oh good. How are you?'

'Fine.'

'Good. I'm sorry to bother you out of the blue like this. Is it a bad time?'

'Well I'm working . . .'

'Ok, well I'll tell you what this is about. I'm a huge fan of your work Ms Flood. I really am. And I . . .'

'I'm not available.'

'Pardon?'

'For interviews. I'm not available.'

'No, I realise that, I know that Ms Flood, I'm not asking you to do an interview. What I had in mind was this. I don't know if you've heard my show recently. I'm on FM101 now, and the show is a little more, uh, highbrow as a result, and I get to do more of the kind of thing I find interesting, which tends to be a juxtaposition of great literature, ordinary people and timeless music.'

He glanced at Sylvia. She was mouthing the words as he said them. He realised with a pinch of surprise that she was not a very successful journalist because she was not a very good writer.

'And I would dearly love to have some of the major scenes of your novels read on the show.'

'Oh right, well let me give you my agent's number.'

Quickly Sylvia plucked away the sheet he was reading from and pointed to a place half way down the next page.

'No, I, um, the seriousness of your work. Oh. Here. And I would really like you to be the person to read them.'

'Pardon?'

'Would you like to read them?'

'Read scenes from my novels?'

'Yes.'

'On the radio?'

'Yes.'

She wheezed horribly, and Joe guessed it was a little bit of laughter stuck in her throat.

'You must be joking.'

'No, I, well. No?'

'No way José,' she said. 'I hate reading. I have a terrible voice you know. But it's nice of you to ask. Do you want my agent's number anyway?'

Sylvia was frantically riffling through the sheets now, and handed Joe one with 'HINT' scrawled across the top of it in deep red marker.

'Um, no, that's ok, I think I have that already. But, um, are you sure?'

'Yeah. Very sure.'

'Ok, well, maybe we could meet up and I could tell you a bit more about my vision of it?'

'No thanks.'

'That's a pity. Actually another idea I had was actually to do an interview with you, and with Mrs Gilmore as well.'

There was a silence.

'Because I think that would be a very interesting story too.'

'She's not well,' said Kitty Flood, and her voice was harder.

'Sorry to hear that. I met recently with someone who was telling me something of the story of Mrs Gilmore, and it was fascinating. And I thought that in combination with your own wonderful gifts for storytelling and the power of words that the two of you would make for wonderful guests.'

'Who were you talking to?'

'Siobhan Cullen.'

Joe was embarrassed. To be reading such crap down a phone line to a woman who plainly thought he was mad, at the behest of a woman who seemed genuinely to be mad, with the schoolboy intent of getting a cheap inconsequential shag. It was all a bit sordid. He thought of that evening's rent boy. He thought he would mention in passing that all men are whores. See how that went down.

'Cullen?'

'Yes, Frank Cullen's widow.'

The silence extended.

'Ms Flood?'

'What is this about?'

Her voice was strange. The wheeze had stopped. Something else had entered into it. A kind of hushed fear, he fancied. Or maybe it was threat.

'Well. It's mostly about what Mrs Cullen had to say.'

'Really?'

'Yes.'

'What did she have to say?'

Joe didn't like this now. This was starting to sound serious. He looked at Sylvia. She seemed delighted. Her clenched fist was jabbing the air in front of Joe.

'Well . . .'

Sylvia poked the sheet on his knee.

'We can talk about that when we meet. We really should meet.'

There was another silence. And then, to Joe Kavanagh's astonishment, five things happened in a row. First, the shocked voice of Kitty Flood came quietly down the line and agreed to meet with him, the following Saturday. Second, it occurred to him that the only reason for this was that there *was* something in Sylvia's story. Third, the phone call ended, and he was back fully in his own home, with a dumpy English woman on the floor in front of him, a broad grin on her face. Fourth, the English woman, Sylvia Porterhouse, turned her Arsenal cap backwards on her head, put her hands on Joe Kavanagh's knees and leaned her lips in towards his.

Fifth. She was a very good kisser.

Kez took his time. He went into town in the afternoon and he got his hair cut at the Dublin Barbershop down on Eden Quay, and he winked at a man he recognised who was waiting after him. He bought new black trousers for fifty quid from one of the

English shops in Jervis Street. He bought the new Populous CD. He ate a cheeseburger and chips in The Ritz on Middle Abbey Street, and felt like a ghost – staring out at the street like he was watching a movie. At home he showered the hairs off him and tried shaving his face. He put on his FOOD IS A DRUG t-shirt and his leather jacket. He stuck a roll of money in his pocket. Just for the feel of it. He watched television until ten o'clock and then he put on the radio and heard the start of the Joe Kavanagh Show.

'Welcome . . . This is Joe Kavanagh . . . On tonight's show we have Peter Sweeney, author of Martyr Music *and* The Liquid Lunch *amongst other things . . . he'll be here for a chat . . . We'll be talking to Alain again about his mother's funeral . . . which should be a laugh . . . We'll be discussing the disturbing phenomenon of child suicide in Japan with an Irish doctor who's based over there . . . I mean they're like seven and eight – it's bizarre . . . And I have two amazing letters from The Joy to read to you . . . That's becoming almost a regular feature . . . We'll have to think of a name for it . . . I don't know . . . Mountjoy Missives? . . . Captive Audience? . . . Joy Division? . . . Requests For Songs With* Free *In The Title? . . . Whatever . . . Suggestions on a postcard . . . in a file . . . inside a cake . . . We might have a special guest later on, I don't know yet, we'll see . . . There's music from Barb Lee, Animate, Danny Miller, Slipper Man . . . The Honeymoon Killers and loads more . . . I'm Joe Kavanagh . . . listen to me now . . . This is Harry Bullfinch . . . '*

His voice sounded cheerful and slightly manic. But the music was slow and quiet and Kez frowned at it.

He took a taxi from his flat down to the river. He liked the night. It was big mooned and it was warm and the air was clean. He walked quickly, his heels clacking, over the bridge to the radio station. In his stomach there was thirst and hunger and the opposite of both of them. It was on the top floor. He went in with his head down and was stopped by a man in a uniform who wanted to know where he was going. To see Barry he said.

'The Joe Kavanagh show?'

'Yeah.'

'And your name is?'

'Danny.'

The man looked down at a clipboard.

'I mean Kevin.'

'Which is it, Kevin or Danny?'

'Kevin.'

The man lifted a phone and hit a button and talked to someone. Kez put his hand over the money in his pocket. He tried to look like he did this all the time. The man put the phone down.

'Right you are. Fourth floor, the lift is there at the back, straight up the top. Good luck now.'

Good luck? Why? Why good luck? In the lift he checked his fly, and fixed his hair in the blurred shine of the door, and he closed his eyes for a moment and thought of his feet in water.

When the doors opened Barry was there waiting for him, which gave him a bit of a fright. For a second Kez didn't know who it was.

'Jesus. Are you not on now?'

'We are yeah. It's in the middle of a triple play though. Sometimes I go off and wander around for half an hour and let it look after itself.'

He smiled, and Kez thought that he probably never did that at all.

'Nice jacket.'

Kez frowned. He stepped forward and looked around him. It was like an office building. Corridors and carpet and pictures on the walls. At a desk in front of them a woman sat, talking on the telephone. The station logo hung huge on the wall behind her.

'What's your name again?' Kez asked.

That was a cruel thing to do. But he was nervous. He saw Barry's face drop, and his smile disappeared, and then reformed slightly.

'Cuthbert' he said.

'Yeah. Right. Sorry.'

'That's ok. Just relax. Don't even think about anything. Come and meet Joe. You'll like him. He's in a very good mood.'

They walked slowly, Barry still limping. He pointed out a picture of Joe. He looked like a twit. Bad hair, bad smile, double chin, stripy shirt.

'It's an old photo, that,' said Barry. 'I should get him to do a new one.'

They came to a door like all the others except it had STUDIO 2 written on it. Kez thought they were going to walk straight on to the radio, but inside there was a small room, all white, with a couple of armchairs, and a sofa, and a water cooler and a coffee machine and a table with some sandwiches and cakes on it. There was a door on the far side, and a big window onto a much bigger room full of machines and tape decks and reels and lights and stuff. In there a woman sat in front of a big desk, with a pair of headphones on. In front of her was another window, and through that he could see the guy from the photograph, Joe, his hair shorter, his face thinner, in a pool of light, in front of a microphone, across the table from a fat man with a bushy beard.

'Ok,' said Barry. 'This guy Joe's talking to is a writer. He's gonna be on for about another ten minutes I think. Then there'll be music up to the news, then the news and the weather and ads and that, and then you, if you want. And if you don't want, that's fine too. When the writer's finished Joe will come out and say hello. Help yourself to anything you want.'

There was another voice in the room, a deep gruff old Dublin accent, north inner city, slightly slurred, and it took a moment for Kez to realise that it was the radio, that it was the writer, talking on the radio.

'It says much, Joe, I think, about modern urban society, that at

night, at night now, a house with all the lights on is much more
likely to be empty than a house in complete darkness – wherein
there are bound to be a clutch of blood relatives surfing the
internet or watching television. And that light has become
therefore, a weapon, a warning, and darkness has become, in
many ways, what we are used to. Now of course lighting as we
understand it today, is a relatively recent invention . . .'

Joe seemed to be looking towards him, towards Kez. He was
smiling. He waved.

'Is he waving at me?'

'Um, probably. I don't think he likes your man very much. He's
probably bored.'

Kez didn't wave back. He half nodded.

'Who's she?'

'Oh yeah. That's Sally, she's on work placement. She asked to
be in here, imagine that. Radio engineer. Trainee radio engineer. She's very nice, but I can get her to leave if you want,
when you go on. If you go on. She's doing my job anyway.'

Kez said nothing.

'Uh, I haven't actually said your name to Joe. I thought you
might want to use a different name, so, uh, do you? Or can I call
you Kevin?'

'No, call me Danny. Or Tommy.'

'Which?'

Kez was trying to think of a name he had never used. He thought
he might have used Danny once before. Maybe it was just that he
had used it downstairs with the security guard. But he wasn't sure.

'Tommy,' he said.

'Ok.'

Barry smiled at him and opened the door and went into the second room. Kez watched them for a while, Barry and the woman,
as they fiddled with things, Barry writing something in a book,

the woman sorting through what looked like video tapes, sliding buttons up and down on the big desk, hitting switches at her side, while in the room in front of them Joe sat with his arms folded, looking really bored now, and kept glancing at Barry and at the clock on the wall. Kez sat down and poured himself a coffee for the sandy feeling in his stomach, but it didn't help, it was lukewarm and just tasted like more sand.

'Read us something then Peter.'

'I'll recite something.'

'Go on.'

'This is from Dublin Is Leaving. It's a song. It's also a kind of vision.'

He cleared his throat.

'Above the sullen river, in the low and listless hills,
The stars appear in honour of the star that night has killed,
And the darkness brings a cover, though beneath it all is chill,
And the silence speaks like drunken men, of love and other ills.

Above the sullen river, where the missing man is king,
A hulking, hollow structure stands, filled with empty things –
Abandoned toys and severed friends and birds with broken wings,
All bundled up like kindling is, and tightly tied with string.

Above the sullen river, in a bonfire of the facts,
The names, the dates, the heights, the weights, the whole
    disgusting tract,
Splintering and spluttering, explodes with mighty cracks,
Which cleave the hills and snap the will and break the city's back.

Above the sullen river, when the first light reappears,
The bloodied ruins of nightime lie where they have lain for years,
And in the scattered rubble that clutters up the ground
Abandoned toys and severed friends and broken birds abound.

Above the sullen river, there stands a battered truth –
Which bloody wars and earthquakes serve, as awful, petty proofs –
That memories, collected griefs, love and loss and yearning,
Cannot be killed or put away by bullet, knife or burning.

Above the sullen river, underneath the failing light,
There is no end to love or lies, there is no end to life,
There is no end to anything that crawls across the night,
For there is no satisfaction here, there is only appetite.'

'Finished?'

'Yes.'

It felt exactly like being at the clinic. He was uncomfortable in his chair. The money felt silly. The look of the wilted sandwiches made him queasy.

'Peter thanks for coming in to talk to us.'

'You're welcome.'

'Best of luck with the beard.'

Joe Kavanagh would probably ask him about his health.

Nothing else was said, music started playing, and Kez could hear doors and voices. He stood up and watched the writer shaking hands with Barry. Joe was still in the studio, but he was standing up, reading something, eating a bar of chocolate. The writer came through the door with Barry behind him.

'Let us know anyway Peter, when it's out, and we'll have you back.'

'Right. Thanks Barry, talk soon, cheerio.'

He took a sandwich from the table, nodded uncertainly at Kez, and left.

Barry stood in the doorway smiling.

'You alright?'

'Yeah.'

'You look well.'

'Thanks.'

'You got your hair cut.'

'Well. Yeah.'

He felt stupid. It was fucking *radio* after all.

'Come and meet Joe.'

Kez hesitated for a second, but Barry motioned towards him, so he went through the door, Barry standing aside, his hand briefly brushing the small of Kez's back, as if guiding.

The woman was concentrating on her controls, and Kez ignored her. Barry stepped in front of him and opened the door to the studio.

'Joe this is Tommy.'

Joe Kavanagh put down what he was reading, swallowed, and came towards Kez, smiling.

'Oh yeah. Great. Hi. Great to meet you. Thanks a lot for coming in.'

He didn't offer his hand. Kez was confused by this, and his arm did an involuntary half jerk at his side. He glanced at Barry and guessed that Joe had been told – *don't shake his hand, he doesn't like that.*

'That's ok. Nice to meet you.'

'Come on through. Come in, come in. I'm not going to talk to you till after the news, but you can sit in. What kind of music do you like?'

Kez found himself in the studio proper, pulling up a chair at the round table, Joe fiddling with a microphone over his head, bringing it down in front of his face. The door had swung shut behind him.

'Anything. I don't mind. Jazz?'

'Really? We can do that. Bit of Coletrane maybe. Barry will have something.'

Kez nodded, felt all kinds of things going on in his stomach. He could feel the money push into his skin.

'I'm nervous.'

'I know. Don't worry about it. Just think of it as you and me chatting. Barry bring the lights down a bit will you, it's too bright in here. It's just you and me having a chat. That's all. Just say what comes naturally. I'll just do a bit of an introduction – nothing specific. I'll just say that my next guest is Tommy and he's, uh, what age are you?'

'Twenty one.'

'Are you?'

'No. But. You know.'

'Ok. My next guest is a young Dubliner called Tommy, and I'll just bullshit a bit, and I won't actually say what it is you do, you know, I won't mention the – actually what do you want me to call it? Do you want me to say that you're a rent boy or a prostitute or what?'

'Rent boy.'

'Ok. First few minutes we'll just chat. You know, just like we met on a bus. I'll ask you what your favourite soap is, like are you watching Coronation Street or Fair City or what, and then we might talk about films or music or something, just chatting. Then at some point I'll just lead into you being a rent boy. It's so that people hear you for a while before they start making assumptions. And it means that we can relax. It'll be fine.'

With the lights dimmed it was better. Through the window Kez could see Barry, but his head was down, looking at the desk. Joe gave him a smile. The money, or his queasy stomach, or something, was giving him a hard on.

'Do you want a cup of coffee?'

'Is there a toilet near?'

He nodded, gave him directions. Kez closed his jacket as he stood to hide his bulges. He went through the door and past Barry without looking at him. He was concentrating on sliders and dials and buttons. Kez could hear the burst of music that came before the news.

As he walked towards the lift he hitched up his jeans and took the money out and put it in his jacket. Downstairs the security guard was on the phone. Kez waited because the door was locked. The security guard looked at him, held the phone to his chest.

'Barry wants to talk to you.'

'Yeah. I have to go.'

'He wants to go,' the guard said into the phone, then nodded. 'Barry says to hang on a minute, he's coming down.'

Kez tried the door. The security guard put the phone down.

'He's on his way.'

'Open the door will ya.'

'He'll be down in a sec.'

'Open the fucking door.'

'Nerves is it?'

'What?'

'A lot of people get nervy. I can understand it. But Joe looks after you. He's alright. Just relax.'

'Will ya open the fucking door for Christ's sake.'

'Ok ok.'

'Jesus.'

Outside, he glanced back and saw Barry come from the lift, and look at him through the glass, and wave at him, smiling like he was embarrassed, and Kez stopped and shook his head. Barry came out, the guard standing in the open door watching.

'What's wrong?'

'I don't want to.'

'Are you alright?'

'Yeah.'

Barry walked towards him. Limped towards him.

'Sure?'

'Yeah. Just changed my mind.'

Kez waited for him to get annoyed, but he didn't.

'Ok. Well. Don't worry about it. Jesus, it's a hard thing to do. I wouldn't do it either.'

'Yeah.'

'I mean.'

'Yeah.'

'Joe comes across as a bit of an asshole sometimes, but he's alright. He didn't say anything stupid did he?'

'No.'

'Ok.'

They looked at each other. Kez could feel the river at his back, as if guiding.

'You still have my number,' he said. 'You could call me. We could, you know, go for another coffee or something.'

Barry smiled.

'Yeah. I'd like that.'

'Yeah. Ok.'

'Ok. I should get back. Thanks. I mean, thanks for coming in anyway.'

Kez nodded. He tried for a smile but couldn't find one. He held out his hand for Barry to shake.

———

Along the river there are walls where you can run your hands over smooth stone, stone that always seems warm like it's alive, curved like something grown not made, as if it has blood flowing through it, as if it might be the spiny back of some creature that

270

lived in the wet ground underneath. Sometimes with your hand on it you might feel a deep tremble, very light, very distant, and you might expect something to rear its head and then you'd realise instead that it was only a train going over the metal bridge, and that the city wasn't a living thing after all – with a spine beneath the river – it was nothing like that, it was brick and muck and glass and stone and water.

Most of it was waiting. Waiting by the river. He daydreamed. He always daydreamed. About monsters under the ground. About a sea captain and a deaf professor. About Singapore and Brasilia. About air travel and endless money. About the path the world took past stars and hot planets. About New York and Rome. In the summer he daydreamed about the cold. In the cold he thought of summer. What was the world after all? It might be nothing but a bubble in a dog's mouth, a light bounced off paint, the paint itself, spilled in a corner of a dead man's room, his clutter room, where all the stars were nothing but the tiny balls of dust that floated close, and then exploded. He thought all history might be over in an instant. He saw men come, many men, many times, weakly and strongly, loudly, quietly, naked, clothed, slowly, quickly, all opposites, every kind, and he thought that the world might be that moment, nothing else, just the muted spasm and the milky way, and he thought that there were probably millions. Millions of men. Millions of women. Millions of worlds, of Dublins, of him.

One night when he had been new to it, he had stood beside a guy who was a bit older than him, who'd been doing it for years, who was a pain in the arse. This guy tried to tell him things, tried to advise him. As if he was wise and Kez was stupid, and needed to be told for example not to get into a van with three guys in the front, which this guy had apparently once done, the fucking eejit, and not to drink from bottles that he hadn't seen opened or that the punter wasn't drinking from as well, which Kez thought was maybe because punters tried to poison this guy quite a lot just to get him to shut the fuck up. Kez stood beside him, facing him, as the guy sat on the wall, and they were away on the other side, opposite the hotel, because the cops had been by, twice, hassling them, and they were doing a walk around, bridge to bridge, and your man had stopped for a burger. And Kez was nodding, and looking behind the guy, over his shoulder, across the river, checking what was happening in the usual place, and the guy was talking, and eating his burger, and sitting on the wall, and Kez was saying nothing, and not listening either, as the guy was telling him particular cars to look out for now, registration numbers even for Christ's sake, and Kez was peering behind him, across the river, and the guy must have noticed that Kez wasn't really listening, and must have wondered what he was looking at, because he turned, swung his shoulders and his head around to look over towards the other side, and whatever way he did it, whatever way he shifted his skinny arse and whatever kind of cheap shiny trousers he was wearing, and whatever way he was holding his burger, leaving no hands to help him, he just slid off the smooth warm stone, just slid off, like a kid going backwards down a slide, and his mouth full of burger, and his eyes turning back suddenly, staring straight at Kez, wide as lights, and his hands going out in front of him, the burger dropped, and his legs straightening, and his upper body bending forward, and his arse sliding out backwards, so that he looked for a second like he was being folded in half, and he just slid off the wall without even shouting, without making a sound, just the face of him staring at Kez like he couldn't believe it, as if to say, *what the fuck is this, I don't believe this,* and then his face disappeared, then his arms and his hands, then his legs, and then his feet, the last thing, his feet, and then he was gone.

Gone.

Kez didn't believe it either for a second. Then there was a splash, and he went to the wall and peered over. He could see nothing. But at least there was water there, because often there wasn't, and the river was sometimes just sludge and supermarket trolleys and bicycle wheels and the smell of dead things. And he might have sliced himself open on that stuff, or hit a rock. At least the river was a river. Kez couldn't see him. He couldn't see anything properly. There was just a swirling in the water where it had been disturbed, and there was the lapping of it against the wall, and there were shadows and shapes and trapped light and flickering dark and he couldn't make out anything really, just maybes and guesses and blurs. He shuffled to his left and stood on the burger.

He thought he saw the guy further down, going towards a ladder, one of those black rusted ladders that hang from the walls like fire escapes. But he wasn't sure. He couldn't see. He thought he heard his curses and his spluttering, but his ears were shocked and he couldn't hear. He looked for something to throw. He couldn't see anything to throw. He knew he should shout and scream and he knew he should get help, but the cops had been by twice already, and he was new to it, Kez was, new to all this, and he thought that if he told anyone anything that he'd have to tell them everything – that is what he thought then. He had not found his voices then. He had not found his names.

He patted the wall and turned, and checked right and left and crossed the road, and he moved slowly to the corner and then he ran. He made his way home with darting eyes.

He didn't see the guy for weeks. All that time he thought he was dead, and he tried to make sense of the lack of news. They hadn't found the body. It had been swept out to sea. It had rotted on the spokes of an old pram. It was lodged there in the slime and would bob up when Kez next passed. Then one night, keeping away from the river, leaning against the hard bars of the Castle gates, touting for 4am business in the pit of Dame Street, he saw the guy get out of a car. Dry as a bone. He scowled at Kez.

'You tell no one right?'

'I told no one.'

'Good. If I ever hear that back I'll fucking know and I'll fucking do ya. Right?'

'Right.'

'Don't know what fucking happened anyway. Loose brick in that wall or a fucking earthquake or something. Jaysus the stink of that water up close. Fuck. It never fucking happened right?'

'Right' said Kez.

He went home straight away and fell asleep, and later woke up laughing.

Delly Roche dozed in the light of the fire and the television, and breathed deep from the cool night which seeped through the open window. It was opened just a crack, just a sliver of the black world, just a bare inch of the planet invading her room. She liked the warmth and the cool hand across it. It was summer. It was not cold. The smell of burning was gone. Seemed gone.

The pain was not bad. It was low and settled, content to raise a simple blade along the inside of her stomach, a little below her chest, like a knife held to the throat of her dozing. But it was easy to ignore. It had not flinched in minutes. Kitty was at work upstairs in the rafters, George was out somewhere, Mrs Cotter was watching television in the kitchen because her husband and the one remaining boy were watching a football match in their house and she wanted to see a documentary about the aggressive tendencies of dolphins. Delly lay with her alarm buttons arrayed on the table beside her, the local one now with a large green tag attached to the string, the more serious one a little further away from her and sporting a red tag. Also there was a remote control for the television, and one for the stereo, and a mobile phone and a bottle of water with glass, and a box of tissues and various drugs.

Drugs were her life, so they would not be her death. On this she was determined. So she had instructed George to keep them to a minimum. Only painkillers, and never enough to dull her senses, despite George's objection that that was what they were meant to do, that it was all they were able to do. But she did not want to be stupid, she wanted to be alert, so in the end she took them only when she wanted to sleep, and for most of the rest of the time, she lived with the pain, and she did not want anything else. He gave her something which performed some tying up function on her insides, some coagulant or calming agent for her bowels, or maybe a lubricant for her clotted heart, she did not know, he had explained it, she had forgotten.

The letter was missing.

Delly had the television on, looking for dolphins, which she could not find, with the volume turned down and the radio at a nice mid ear decibel level at her shoulder. The radio was good, she liked the radio. It was possible to find music which was not terrible, in the sense that it was not too noisy, too insensible, and also, most importantly, music which she had never heard before – so that it did not have any associations, any memories attached. Sometimes she stumbled across a piece – the opening bars, the first swell of a chorus, sometimes just a chord – which entered her head with an odour, a song with shit on its shoe, some terrible decades old waft, and she would hit the remote control, hard, with the heel of her hand until it went away, though leaving behind, often for several minutes, the unpleasant after-smell of that most depressing of things – recall.

She thought that the letter had perhaps been somehow mislaid during the descent. She worried that it had gone into a washing machine, lost in a duvet or a blanket or a pillow case. She would ask around.

She flicked through the channels, each press of a button clicking something very delicate in her forearm, a ticklish, minor pain which she quite enjoyed and which she greeted at each press with a quiet and flat 'ouch'. There was the football match, which she looked at for a while, squinting at the sweaty hair and the spitting and the calf muscles glinting in the floodlights. Then she discovered some pop videos, which she matched with the music on the radio, and found that they fitted, sometimes, quite well. Then there was the news, which she made up, inventing things to match the pictures, such as an earthquake in Cork and the assassination of a cardinal and the sighting of aliens from the deck of a ferry run by discredited politicians evading extradition by staying on the high seas. On the radio she flicked, ouch, ouch, to a station that was newsless and pounding with an endless hammering beat and not much else that she could make out, and she stayed with that for a while, testing to see if she liked it, which she did.

All these things were occupations for her mind. That was all. She was waiting to die, and there was a certain way in which she wanted to do it, and it involved being conscious, that would be best, but free of memory, free of the dregs of her life. She wanted to be empty and washed out and to leave the world as she had entered it, clueless, clean, a glass on the draining board, ready for drying and to go back to the cupboard.

She pressed another button on the stereo remote, forgot to say 'ouch', and found a play, to which she listened for a while, thinking that she heard the suggestion of an affair between two men, and she went again, somewhere else, pressing her finger and going somewhere else, to the sound of The Beatles, whom she had never, ever, ever liked, and then on again, her finger stepping painfully from one island of nonsense to another, each of them simply words and notes and echoes constructed from the static, from the flowing debris of the universe, from the little grey clicking sticks that flowed by the average ear, little islands of rubbish, and it occurred to her, to Delly, her hands slowing down, her eyelids dropping, the television flickering beside the fire, her eyes going crossed, the fire flickering beside the television, it occurred to her, with the radio stations clinging to the wreckage and tumbling in the static, with her eyes gone, it occurred to her, just as she realised that she could no longer tell which was the flicker of the television and which was the flicker of the fire, it occurred to her then, that all entertainment, all the singing and the dancing and the jokes and chatter, all the love and the music and the words, they are all plucked from the static, they stop people from drowning, she thought, she decided, easily, as one would decide what to eat, they stop people drowning in the calamitous, universal fear, terror, fear, terror, fear and terror of death.

She slept.

'We like to think that we are somehow excluded from the horrors, don't we? We like to think we're apart from all that. Neutral. I'd like to welcome Thomas O'Connell to the studio. How are you doing Thomas?'

'Fine thanks Joe.'

Delly noticed first that the window was closed. This she sensed more than saw, for the second thing she noticed was that all the lights were off. And then she noticed that the television was dead and the fire turned down. On the radio there were voices. Kitty had been in then. Kitty with her chewing and her crumbs and her tucking hands. Delly killed the radio sound and listened. She could hear nothing in the house, not a thing. Not step nor door nor breathing. And outside there was nothing. Not the wind nor the trees nor the night nor those parts of the world that were next to her could she hear. Nothing. She raised the radio sound again, and yawned and stretched her painful legs, her needle legs, her pins, stuck into her.

'*The book is called* Hitler In Dublin, *the title alone of which will come as something as a shock to people. Explain please Thomas.*'

'*Adolf Hitler had a half brother. Named Alois. It's quite simple. He married a woman called Brigid Elizabeth Dowling, and for a while they lived in Dublin.*'

'*Wow.*'

She grappled with the other remote and got the television going again.

'*It's truly remarkable how little has been written about this. And I found it very difficult to get anyone to talk about it.*'

She flicked through films and chat shows and found more news, rolling news, which she liked, watching the same stories reappear every fifteen minutes and trying to work out what they were about with the sound turned down.

'*Are you saying there was a reluctance on the part of the authorities?*'

She let one story blur into another, allowed the scenes to become part of the same narrative. So that she watched a mass murderer visit a crèche, a boxer lie down in the road, a small child sign a treaty and go missing then, just a first communion photograph flapping in the breeze, his little death obvious, unstated, linked in some way to the man in the crèche, and his gesturing hands, and his minders. The radio babbled, but she no longer listened. Her thoughts instead tracked the world, which pressed against the glass of the television and oozed past and left a trail, like a snail on the window, while she watched, fascinated, stupefied by the beauty of the natural world, that is, the world that is occurring, our actual place.

A fire in a forest area, people carrying babies to ambulances, some kind of plane crash maybe, into trees, she watched a tearful woman interviewed and construed her as the mother of a lost family. A man talking in a trading room, admitting something, it seemed to Delly, some connection, perhaps, to the downing of the plane, in California, or Ecuador, or wherever it was, and the camera flashing then to a riot, obviously in the man's hometown, obviously, with his house stoned and a boy, who may, despite the skin colour discrepancy, have been a relative, a son or a nephew, almost ripped from the stitching of his young life before the police intervene with bullets.

There was the White House, and she wondered if the President had been shot. Something about space. An asteroid then, or a sun blast of corrective death from the outer reaches.

Why, wondered Delly, did she imagine news that was, inevitably, invariably, worse than the actual news? Why did she fantasise, calculate, both a deeper, more tangled evil and a higher body count, and why did she prefer this, now, this made up bulletin, this fabricated catalogue of gashes in the skin of the world, to the real, turn up the volume, actual, thing. What was it she was hoping for?

'*Do you think*,' the radio man was asking, '*that the Irish are fundamentally fascist?*'

Kitty Flood stared at her telephone. It was a shocking invention. The letter lay before her on her desk. All her screens were dark, switched off. She was not hungry. Her inner panic had staged a coup. It ruled her.

Dearest Delly,

Now comes the time when we are tested. Dan has found us out. Do not panic. Please, love, do not panic. It happened because, firstly, of something I said, something I let slip, and he looked at me, and I knew I'd let something slip, and he looked at me for a moment and then looked away, and said nothing. Later on (this was yesterday), he confronted me about it. You know I cannot lie. I tried to lie. I told him that he was imagining the whole thing, that I would never, that I could not, that it was not possible. But he was angry I suppose and he did not believe me. Somehow then he had found out what calls I have made from my hotel room. There were calls to you of course. Several of them. When he confronted me with his knowledge of these, I could find nothing to say, no excuse to make, and I was silent. So now he knows. He knows about us.

I am not going to try and tell you that this is a good thing. Of course part of me is caught up with the idea that it is. That it is a good thing. That after all these years of silence and of creeping and of lies, that we are out of it, out of that tangle, and we are known about. Does a part of you not feel that? That here comes the truth now, noisy and awkward and embarrassing, but the truth, the truth. Part of me feels that. But I know too that we will face hard times now. There will be a reckoning. Don't think that I don't know. There will be hell to pay. Hell to pay, Delly, hell to pay.

He wants us to return tonight. So we will of course. I will try to call you but I'm not sure that I will be able. And you are most likely out or asleep, the times are all wrong, so that all the time before we travel, while I am alone, I will not be able to reach you, and all the time when we are travelling I will be with him and I won't be able to call you. So that by the time you read this, it will all be out in the open. Much will have been said.

I am in love with you. We may find a way out of it. Never mind. I will find a way out of it. We have shared too much now. Too much to stop.

My love always, Frank

Delly had not wanted Kitty to inherit anything of Daniel Gilmore's because she did not believe she had any right to bequeath it. It was not hers. She had no right to it. She had betrayed her husband. Put him in the air. Crashed him. Killed him. And killed the man she was going to leave him for.

She had about as much right to his money as Siobhan Cullen.

Kitty Flood sat very still.

He wanted to go after him. He stood at the door of the building, with Gerry rattling on in his ear 'you don't usually lose them Barry, still, not to worry, it happens, can't be helped' and watched Kevin head across the bridge, and pause in the middle to look in the river, as if he'd noticed it for the first time, and then go on, as if it wasn't a big deal. He lost him then, in the darkness and the people.

By the time he got back upstairs, a Poofter track they had played earlier was on again, Sally was a terrified shade of white, and Joe was out in the control room trying to pull a cart from the machine with his foot up on the console.

'Three minutes I've been gone. Three fucking minutes.'

Joe burst out laughing.

He was fucked now. Barry was. He was lost and his ankle was broken. The bone had snapped and splintered, and had run in chain reaction up the side of his body like a stroke, powdering his skull, putting shrapnel in his dreams. He could not walk. He could not sit. He could not sleep. He could do nothing but cup his phone in his hand and stare at the stored name of Kevin, and at the numbers that would summon his voice. The push of a button. It felt nuclear.

His ankle was actually much better. His mood had generally lifted, surfaced, and then had dived again, deeper this time, slightly to the left of where he'd been before, into different water, his lungs full of fresh air, his eyes pressed to the aquarium light of his phone's display.

That moment on the surface, in the full light of day, with no one following, with no pain in his body, and no conscience either, had been the handshake. Such a civilised thing. Such a short and partial touch. A fractional embrace. A solid, grown up thing. He pondered the eroticism of handshakes and got nowhere. He wondered why the skin which he had touched – the fleshy palm of Kevin's hand – was not the important skin, the reserved skin, the skin saved for lovers. He imagined some different world, or a parallel one, where the handshake might be the ultimate sensual thing, the consummation, the *act*. But he thought that he would be disappointed in such a world, and gave it up.

It hadn't just been the handshake of course. There had been his face in the light. He had watched Kevin through the thick glass, sitting opposite Joe with his face turned slightly upwards, his eyes nervously seeking the edges to things, and he had seen the shadows fly across his skin as the lights were lowered. He had felt like a complete shit then, Barry had. He had done it before – he had done it quite a lot in fact in the last few weeks – handing over a nervous potential guest to Joe, closing the door and turning a speculative visit to the studio into an on air interview before the junkie or the gambler or bewildered homeless Roscommon man had a chance to flee. But he felt it more with Kevin, because Kevin had seemed to expect it, and because he hadn't been angry. As if it was the usual way of things, not a big deal. Barry was glad that he walked out. At least now that part was over.

And of course, as well as the handshake and the face in the light, there had been that lack of anger. There had been the fact that Kevin had not called him a shit, had not stormed off and refused to talk, had not hit him in the street or flung him in the river. He had nodded and shrugged and shook his hand. All of which made forgiveness, and being forgiven is very seductive.

The light, the handshake. And the week leading up to it. And the shape of his shoulders under his jacket, and his hair cut and the revelation of his neck and the tops of his ears. And his crotch sitting down. And the lift doors opening. And his t-shirt which read 'D IS A D'. And the smell of him, like the smell of warm clothes and wet skin, an after swimming scent, and the cuffs of his trousers meeting his shoes.

Barry was lost to it all, and his bones were breaking, snapping like twigs as lust walked all over him. There were chalky deposits between his fingers. Joe smiled and muttered and smiled again, glancing at Barry, apparently fine tuned just now, to the signals. Was it lust or worse he wondered? He thought it might be worse than lust. He thought it might be that terrible other thing. The start of it anyway. The entry wound. The heart's hard on.

But with all the gulping and the rush of stars, there came a cold breath. The whole thing was hopeless. It was a disaster. It was, at the very least, impossible. He knew that. He could not avoid it. It was not going to happen. Maybe that was part of the attraction?

Of course it was.

If Kevin wasn't a rent boy, six or seven years younger than Barry, then he'd be a different Kevin. Barry wouldn't look at him twice. Wouldn't look at him once.

So of course it was.

If he wasn't a prostitute then he'd never have met him.

So of course it was that. Commerce and the din of the market.

He wondered if he had done anything illegal yet. He felt somehow that he had.

He nearly called him after the show. Two things stopped him. First was the fact that he had nothing to say other than sorry. He needed to work out what happened after that, what could be made of it, what it led to. Second was the realisation that Kevin was probably curved around a gear stick in some bleak suburban car park administering a bleak suburban blow job to a fettered, married, salaried, tethered man in his bleak suburban fifties, who was trying desperately, *desperately*, not to think of his son.

See? It was utterly impossible.

He called him on Friday morning.

Oh his voice was another thing. Dubliners both of them, but there was streets and bus routes and canals between them, and there was years and all, and Barry listened to Kevin the way a banjo must listen to a violin.

He thought he might have woken him. He thought he might be speaking to him in his bed. In his bed. That was all his preparations ruined. The scent in his head changed from swimming to waking, and the skin from wet to dry, and the rustle of sheets filled his ears, though it may have been the line, just the line. He wondered whether he was naked. As if this would make a difference. Which of course it would. He wondered then if he was alone. In all this there was the architect. The architect in all things. He couldn't bear it. So he said,

'Do you really have a boyfriend who's an architect?'

'Studying to be an architect,' Kevin corrected him.

'Do you?'

'No.'

'Do you have a boyfriend then who's not studying to be an architect?'

There was a mighty pause, and the light noise of scratching. What was he scratching? His head maybe, his newly short hair. His cheek, raised up from the pillow. His neck. His chest. His legs. The black hair in his middle. Any part of him. It could be.

'No.'

'Right.'

Well that was the impossibilities diminished.

'Would you like,' Barry started, and his eyes were tightly closed, and he knew what he was doing, 'would you like to have dinner?'

'Huh?'

Oh great. That sound. That sound he could spend hours dissecting. What did that mean? What prompted that? Was it simply that he hadn't heard? Shifting in his bed, sitting up maybe, the covers falling from his torso, the morning light finding him. Or did it mean that he thought the idea was ridiculous, astonishing, mad? Or was it that he was surprised, moved, touched, rendered slightly speechless by the sudden birth of new hope in his street boy heart? Or was it just that, being young, he thought of 'having dinner' as something you did with your parents before you went out and had fun with your mates?

'Would you like to have dinner sometime?'

Another pause. The boy was all gaps.

'Sure.'

The boy was all gaps and single syllables. The horror of it now was a sudden fear on Barry's part that the 'sure' had sounded vaguely sultry, delivered with breath, made hushed and hot, pushed through barely parted lips. Did Kevin think that Barry's invitation was business? Oh Christ. Or had there simply been a little nervousness in his acceptance of the offer – an excited, squeaked out affirmation that *yes, you're on the right track, go on.* Or was he still confused, still unsure what it amounted to?

'I mean, it'd just be a way of me apologising really, for last night, and it'd be nice anyway, and, you know, nothing to do with the show, you know, you don't have to worry about that . . . now I mean . . .'

Ah bollocks he was not doing it right. It sounded like business, or a mugging.

'I'll buy you dinner basically and then we're quits.'

'Ok. You don't owe me though. We'll go halves.'

Aha. Well this was alright. This was him offering Barry a way of making clear that it was not business, that there couldn't be hint of it even. Fair play. The boy was smart.

'Ok. Sounds good. Saturday is best for me, given work and that? I suppose it's bad for you though?'

He had actually thought about this one before hand. What would be the busy nights in male prostitution in Dublin at the beginning of the century, in a time of widespread affluence, during a good summer? Hmmm? It was a hard one to read. The warm weather would mean decent turnover he thought. He wasn't sure though whether good or bad economic conditions would stimulate more demand. If there's money about maybe men can afford to spend endless nights in pubs and clubs and saunas and the poor rent boys have to shiver and wait, wait and shiver. Or maybe the money trickled down to them as well. A man with some extra cash might go to his clubs and his pubs and his saunas and still feel there was enough wad in his wallet to indulge a little trade. Are rich men hornier than poor men? Perhaps in times of recession there was more for your average rent boy to be busy with – his busyness corresponding maybe with that of the St Vincent DePaul Society or The Simon Community or Age Concern. The spirit of the times would come into it too. The nation's sense of its spiritual self, and its place in history. The peace process and the fall of the church. The exposure of Haughey and the retirement of Gay Byrne. Would men panic at the passing of old certainties, and seek solace in a shag from the small ads? A blow job at the side of the road? He thought that there might have been an end of millennium rush, a hedonistic panic, and maybe things were quieter now. Or would that work the other way around? A general purity as the clock turned over, followed by a general lusting after young flesh as the perception grew that we had gotten away with it? He wasn't sure. And in any case, either of these peaks or troughs would surely have levelled out by now, and Kevin looked well fed and well dressed. It wasn't like he couldn't take a night off.

'Uh, no, Saturday is fine. As long as it's not too late.'

'You need your beauty sleep,' said Barry.

'Yeah,' said Kevin, horribly, as if he had tried to laugh but just could not manage it at all.

That was that then.

Except for the endless dithering which Barry went through, loudly, about where they should meet, and where they should eat, Kevin expressing no preferences on either of these matters, laughing at the question of whether or not he might be a vegetarian, leaving Barry to trawl, silently, through the mess of considerations which arranging a dinner date with a rent boy brought to mind. Gay bar or not? Expensive or more expensive? Risk meeting people you know or avoid it at all cost? In the end he compromised on all of them. Not a gay bar, but a bar across the road from a gay bar. Expensive but old fashioned, rather than expensive but bland. And avoiding the definitive haunts of people known to him, but prepared nevertheless to brazen it out, if it came to that. What was he doing after all, other than taking a young man to dinner? They would meet in The Citizen's at seven, for a table in the Bigallo at eight.

Ah it was madness.

They chatted about nothing for thirty seconds, then Kevin said he had to go, and went, and Barry, to his great shame and his great amusement, decided that he had indeed woken Kevin from his sleep, and that Kevin had had to hang up then because he was dying for a piss, which was what he was now doing, while Barry laughed and stood up and limped off to his kitchen for a cup of tea, hobbled slightly by his ankle and greatly by his hard on, and somewhat by his heart.

———

'Do you want to come and meet a great Irish novelist?'

'No I do not.'

They were half way through Friday night's show, and neither

of them could concentrate. Sally kept it together.

'Are you really going to go?'

'Yeah. Sylvia thinks she's uncovered the crime of the century. She thinks she'll win a prize. She thinks we're the new Carl Bernwood and Brian Epstein.'

He glanced at Sally, who was looking down at her desk, then mouthed something to Barry which he could not make out, except that it had *fuck* at the end of it.

'You don't actually believe any of it do you?'

'No. Well. No. But. Why is she meeting us then if there's nothing to it?'

Barry didn't answer. He had been thinking the same about Kevin, in long looping thoughts that had lassoed his day into one endless moment.

The show that night was terrible.

They had woken together for the first time on the Saturday, and he had done the double take on seeing her crushed cheek buried in his pillow. That tiny panic. The initial loss of chronology which made him think for a moment that he was cheating on his wife. Then he had regained the information, and had spent five minutes or so awake in his conscience and his plotting parts, wondering whether this was good or bad.

The first sex had followed the phone call to Kitty Flood. It had been quick but a lot of fun, starting in the living room and ending on the stairs. The second sex had been in her hotel room, and he had exacerbated the injuries to his foot quite considerably, by inadvertently toe poking the headboard with a leg spasm following orgasm. They had both found it hilarious at the time.

She moved in on the Friday. She cooked him something in a wok, which he had not known he owned, and after he did the show they went to a club together, but they had not stayed long, because they were, he soon discovered, a complete disaster on the dance floor (at one point using his walking stick for a bit of limbo, which Sylvia seemed to think was extremely clever), and he was afraid that someone would see him. At home they had fucked in his bed for the first time. The first time since Christine. In their bed. He made a special effort. It was very good.

The next morning she led him from his slumber to his car via breakfast, and caused him to drive south from the river towards the shimmering hills. They shimmered in the morning, which was thinly spread from dawn to mid afternoon, a paler version of the days that had preceded it, suggesting not that the weather was about to break, but that it would eventually break, at some point, sometime, later, in the future.

She was relatively quiet, Sylvia was, reading through notes and newspaper cuttings. She wore a long navy blue skirt and a white blouse, which Joe thought might have been intended to look business like and serious. But her hair was too short, so that she looked like she was faking it. He wondered just how much she was faking. It was too early, in everything, for him to be worried about it, but it crossed his mind. He might have broached the subject right there in the car, as a fun topic, a faux first argument which could be a bit of a laugh – *You don't really like me at all do you? – No not really. – You're just using me aren't you. – Yes I guess. Is that alright? – Yes I quite like it.* Perhaps they could do that. Like a movie couple. As they drove south towards the hills. Follow it with remarkable sex on the hard shoulder. But he was put off by the blouse and the traffic and the skirt, and by her occasional stab at planning.

'We should sit with our backs to a wall.'

'Huh?'

'I want to be able to see the entire venue. All comers.'

Joe had a burning in his crotch, his cock rubbed fairly much raw from all her exertions. His foot was stronger though. It still hurt, but differently. It was fine for walking, sitting down seemed to fill it with blood until he thought it would burst. He had left the stick at home.

The rendezvous was fixed for a remote pub between small towns in the hills on the way to Wicklow. Perhaps in Wicklow, he wasn't sure. Though remote, the place was relatively busy, its vast car park about a third full. As he parked, his foot on fire, Sylvia produced a battered dictaphone from her bag and handed it to him.

'What?'

'Well she won't notice it on you. She'll be talking to me. Put it in your pocket, there.'

She dropped it into the breast pocket of the jacket she had picked out for him. It was the colour of quicksand.

'I don't know how it works,' he mumbled, peering at it.

'Oh for God's sake you work a fucking radio studio five nights a week. Press record.'

She was not fooling around. Sex that morning had been business like and thorough, a kind of pervy workout.

Inside there were a lot of people having soup and reading the newspapers. They were early. They sat with their backs to a corner. They ordered a large bottle of mineral water and three glasses. While they waited they said very little. Sylvia said, 'Just introduce me, then I'll do the talking.' Joe said, 'What if she spikes our drinks?'

Ten minutes late, and with an entrance that caused a brief lull in the hum of conversation, Kitty Flood arrived. She stood in the open doorway, and coughed loudly, and let in no light. She was the shape of the shadow that is cast by the mountains – she was that big. And when eventually she moved forward, into the pub proper, she moved as if gliding, as if on wheels, or little ankle wings, her hugeness oddly gentle, delicate, as if remaking the world as she moved through it, as if she was remaking it all as she went, as if she had a hand in everything, as if she had stayed up late to plan a new shape to the place, a new perspective, from which she was a small and airy creature.

Joe recognised her, but not much. She had grown, she had aged, she had become somehow magnificent, and ruined. Even if he had not recognised her, it would have been hard not to know that this was Kitty Flood. To his surprise, and somewhat to his horror, she walked with a stick – a black cane, the head of it curled slight towards her, unadorned. It looked like an affectation – he wasn't even sure that it was touching the ground, it seemed to dangle. How sad that was – it must have seemed like a good idea at the time, but was gone stupid now.

She was remarkably fat, he thought. Like a marquee. A tent filled with a high gale. She looked blown into, inflated, or holding her breath, as if the stick would puncture her if she fell on it, and she'd whipfartwhizz, balloonish, off out in spirals and whirls and eddies, an isolated current from the river of all her absurdities. Her fatness gone, that would be that. She would look hopeless thin, even thin she would look fat, fatness was in her. Obesely thin she'd be. Hugely thin. Instead she was hugely fat. She was about three times the size of Sylvia. Which seemed to please Sylvia.

'Miss Flood,' she breathed, standing, as if it was some kind of deity which was conveying itself towards their corner table. Joe looked for her feet, but they were lost beneath the hem of some elaborate black gown. He imagined them working like pistons, a dozen tiny steps a second, frantic propellers under her stately bulk.

She came to a halt in front of them. She barely glanced at Joe. Her eyes were fixed, squinting, on Sylvia Porterhouse.

'Who the hell,' she hacked, 'are you?'

From the doorway she might have looked, if you hadn't been expecting her, like she might be trouble. That she might be some raggedy monster with mouths to feed. But she was up close wealthy – bespoke jacket, silk scarf, expensively cut hair. She had that whiff of quality fabrics and platinum plastic, but it was all a little *acquired*, Joe thought, a little put on. He detected an underlying panic. Or unease at least, as if her hidden feet wore holed stockings and flap soled shoes. Her skin looked pampered but seemed to suggest a cover up rather than anything essentially healthy. She had crud on her skirt. On her dress, or gown, or whatever it was. On the skirting of it, on the hem. Mud or dirt or some kind of shit dried in on the hem. Either that or it was part of the design. New Irish, Celtic Wafer. Stepped in it. Rather than steeped.

'Miss Flood, thanks for coming to meet us. This is Sylvia Porterhouse, from London.'

'How do you do Miss Flood?'

Sylvia held out a hand, which Miss Flood ignored.

'Who?'

'I'm a writer, a journalist . . .' said Sylvia, and started to elaborate, but Kitty Flood interrupted.

'Which?'

'Well, both really.'

'Both?'

'Well, yes I suppose so. I'm freelance, and . . .'

'You work for Siobhan Cullen?'

'No. Work for? No no, I . . .'

'What the hell is this about?'

She looked around the bar, as if for assistance. Joe thought that a nod or a glance, or something, passed between her and the barman. She sat down then, a remarkably deft procedure, done without hesitation, of flinging her left hip out sideways, doing something with her invisible legs, feet, and lowering herself, precisely, onto a small stool.

'Well' Sylvia was saying, 'perhaps I should tell you a little about the background to this.'

'To what dear?'

'Well perhaps I should start at the beginning.'

Joe became aware that his foot, which had been filling uncomfortably since they sat down, now seemed to contain all the blood of his body. He looked at it only to find that Sylvia was standing on his toes with a degree of slow ferocity. He coughed, crossed his arms, slid some fingers into his jacket pocket and pressed what he hoped would be the correct button. Record rather than fast forward. The pressure relented, and his foot began to experience a localised version of the bends.

'The beginning of what?' breathed Kitty Flood. She seemed bored now, concentrating on the glass in front of her, and then squinting at the bottle of mineral water.

'I think you know,' said Sylvia calmly.

'Bottled at source.'

'I think you know what this is about.'

'You just get a picture don't you, of little people, little religious people for some reason, people with vocations, running under a waterfall with bottles, and running out again when they're full. All the time with their vespers and their muttering and their sandals slapping on the stones. Don't you?'

Joe liked that. He laughed. Sylvia didn't.

'Miss Flood?'

She looked at Sylvia, rather warmly Joe thought.

'Miss Porterhouse,' she said. 'It was all such a long time ago. I really don't know what Siobhan Cullen thinks she can gain by . . .'

A man appeared at her elbow, the barman, and he placed a tray on the table containing a plate of what looked like tuna sandwiches, a bowl of pale green soup, leek and potato maybe, and a pint glass full of coke.

'Thanks Gary.'

'You're welcome.'

Joe glanced at Sylvia. She seemed a little excited.

'So it's true?' she asked.

Kitty Flood was tucking into her soup. She shrugged as she stirred it with a tuna corner.

'Oh probably. But what's to be gained by going into it now? I mean really? What's the point? Delly is not well, and I'll not have her distressed.'

She could fit one of the sandwiches into her mouth in one go. They were quarter slice things, little triangles, but they were stuffed with tuna, and she followed them, apparently without chewing, with a spoon full of sucked soup. Then there was some movement in the cheeks and the jaw, and then she took a delicate, ladylike sip of her coke. A couple of swallows and she started again.

'Well that's as may be Miss Flood. But I think there are wider implications here than Mrs Gilmore's peace of mind.'

'What wider?'

'Well Jesus Christ, how often was it used?'

Kitty Flood's hand stopped the full soup spoon just in front of her pursed lips.

'Who was it used on? What were the effects?' Sylvia's voice was a little raised. 'Did we all get it? What have we forgotten? What have we missed?'

Kitty Flood's eyes darted quickly to Joe, and then back to Sylvia. She put the soup spoon back in the bowl. She chewed a little. Sylvia started again.

'And I mean, who has it now? Is it still being used? I mean, oh my God, this is a huge thing Miss. Flood. This is just huge.'

Miss Flood took a drink of her coke.

It was at this point that Joe realised they had been talking, completely and utterly, at cross purposes. That Kitty Flood did not have the first idea about a memory loss drug or about Daniel Gilmore's dark experiments or the planetary amnesia which they had induced. She was not reading from the same page. Again her eyes darted to Joe, just for an instant.

'What are you talking about?'

Sylvia snorted.

'The drug.'

'What drug?'

'The memory drug.'

They just looked at each other. There was silence for a minute, and while they stayed the colour they had been before, Joe turned a deep and shameful red. This was not helped by the glances he was still getting from Kitty Flood, as if he had introduced her to a mad woman. He felt Sylvia looking at him too.

'I think maybe we're not . . .'

'Do you know about the memory drug?'

'What drug?'

'I think we're on slightly different . . .'

'Daniel Gilmore's memory drug.'

'His what?'

'I think we're at cross purposes here.'

'We sure are.'

She had another sandwich, leaving the soup. Little cascades of crumbs slid down the silk of her scarf and settled on her breast. She smiled sweetly at Sylvia and shifted slightly on her stool, as if reminding her body that it was still there. Her bulk seemed to slump slightly, relaxing. From somewhere in her jacket she produced a small packet of mints and popped one in her mouth. She didn't carry a handbag.

'Why don't you folks,' she gently croaked, all smiles, 'tell me all about it?'

———

So Sylvia did her thing. Her spiel. And Joe listened to her but watched Kitty Flood, and saw how the giant woman's shoulders sagged, and her shape compressed into something like a laundry pile, and how her eyes seemed to slump as well, and he got the impression that she had her own gravitational system, that she was kept upright only by force of will, and that her will was being severely tested, just now.

But she was perfectly polite, good humoured even, and she fielded all of Sylvia's prompts and queries (as to whether anything rang a bell, or whether Mrs Gilmore might not have mentioned, at some stage, something that might have sounded vaguely like this), with seriousness and solemnity, even though to Joe it now felt that this whole story was crackers, nonsense, barmy, the worst kind of third rate cobbled together conspiracy theory that it was possible to imagine.

She listened and nodded and slumped. When Sylvia got to the bit about Daniel Gilmore possibly having been murdered, she sat up a bit, and her eyes regained their former shape and position on her face. But there was no sign at all that she had heard any of this before. Or that any of it made any sense whatsoever. There was only a mild indication that maybe she found it quite amusing. Diverting. That the novelist in her didn't particularly mind listening to a yarn, over a late morning sandwich in a country pub, just outside the pull of the city. That she was actually a little impressed with it, with the detail and the scope and the sheer ambition of such a convoluted, contradictory tale. Whereas Joe was simply mortified that he had ever even considered believing a word of it. He fiddled with his fingers, monitored his foot, wondered if he should seek out the pause button in his pocket.

When eventually Sylvia reached a kind of conclusion, and brought her hands together on her knees, and peered expectantly across the table, Kitty Flood regarded her for a moment and smiled.

'That's a great story.'

'Is it true?'

'No.'

To Joe's surprise, Sylvia was smiling as well now. The two of them were grinning at each other.

'I'll tell you what though,' said Kitty Flood. 'It might be true. And I might have forgotten about it.'

'Yes I've thought of that. Or it might be true and Mrs Gilmore might not have mentioned it to you.'

Kitty Flood curled a lip.

'No,' she said, sharply.

'Or it might be true and Mrs Gilmore never knew about it herself.'

'Possible. But then why would Siobhan Cullen know anything about it?'

'So what were you talking about?'

'What?'

'Earlier, when you said that it was a long time ago.'

Kitty Flood's smile didn't falter. She just blinked a couple of times and tilted her head.

'Well. Let's just say that I was thinking of something else.'

'Were you now?'

They were, Joe realised, and it renewed his embarrassment full force, causing his face to flush and the throbbing in his foot to ease, they were flirting with each other now. They had skipped forward when he wasn't looking – they were onto something else entirely. He excused himself and went to the bathroom. While there he recorded the sound of himself pissing. He switched off the machine, went to the bar and knocked back a vodka tonic while trying to quantify the extent of the damage to his career if it were to become generally known that this was how he spent his Saturdays. He thought it would not be insignificant. It would be a question of respect, and loss thereof. It would be a question of trust. With the guests, with the audience. The man sleeps with his correspondents. He indulges their fantasies so that they'll indulge his. He doesn't care about the truth. He doesn't care. He's self indulgent. He's self obsessed. He's manipulative and exploitative and crass. He just does what he does so that he can get off on it. There you go. Joe Kavanagh.

The joke wasn't funny anymore.

As he walked back to the table he couldn't actually see Sylvia – she was obscured by the larger woman completely. When she reappeared, emerging from the folds of Kitty Flood's shoulder, she gave him an angry look. He considered for two seconds leaving the pub and letting her find her own way home. But that was his anger shot and spent – just the momentary thought of doing it was enough. Maybe even better. He sat down by her side. They were talking about the bloody internet now.

He thought he would quit his job and go to Eastern Europe, to the Balkans somewhere, and start broadcasting politically subversive stuff so that somebody would shoot him. Or Africa. Some hot place where his shirt would stick to his back and he would be in danger of malaria. He thought he might do that. He sat back and let the idea of it soothe him and renew his self respect.

He could be a good man. He could.

After seeing Kitty Flood off in her huge four wheeled drive tank (rather than looking left and right when leaving the car park she blew the horn and accelerated) they had driven back to town in almost complete silence, with Joe embarrassed and Sylvia scribbling frantically in one of her notebooks. She seemed, Sylvia did, quite content, given the outcome. He tried to ask her what she had made of it all, but she shushed him, holding the dictaphone to her ear like a mobile.

'Did you take this to the bathroom? Aw isn't that cute. I can hear you tinkle .'

She was not embarrassed by anything, Sylvia Porterhouse, or so it seemed to Joe. He tried to think of things which might shock her. Nothing sexual anyway. She had pretty much got through his entire repertoire in about an hour. Even things he hadn't done since before his marriage. Then she had done things which he had never done. Then she did things which he hadn't even imagined. Well, just one of those, which had kind of freaked him out. Because he had imagined, in the course of his imaginings, many things. But this thing she had done, on the stairs as it happened, was a thing he had never thought of. As something that a woman might do to a man. As something that a woman might do to him. When he thought of it, which was about every ten minutes since she had actually done it, he felt a kind of exquisite embarrassment, and a belief that it was probably the best thing that any other human being had ever done to him. As if the death of his father and the loss of his wife had not been in vain. But when she had started doing it he had been momentarily disorientated and had even protested, with an 'Oi!' or something, but she had simply slapped his arse, hard, and continued.

'Were you not supposed to see uh, what's her, um, I can't remember her name, sorry, were you not meant to see your daughter today?'

'No. It's every second weekend. Nicola.'

'Every second weekend?'

'Yeah.'

She drummed her biro on the dashboard. He drove beneath the arch of Christchurch.

'You're not a very good father are you Joe?'

'No.'

She wrote in her book. He blinked at the river.

'I like that in a man,' she said.

That night they stayed in. She cooked and he drank. She made a few calls. He watched television. It was all deeply boring, a little embarrassing, hollow, as if they weren't sure what to do with each other. There was no sex. It was inevitable. That the physical side of things would diminish. They were not, after all, kids.

The Citizen's was packed. The doors were open and Barry could taste the heat. The noise too. The music was loud and the crowd shouted and the traffic roared through the open door and Barry made it to the bar and decided that he'd better buy two drinks because it would be hopeless if Kevin had to go off up to the bar himself when he arrived – he could be gone for ages. So Barry had to decide what to buy him. He settled on a bottle of lager and got one for himself as well. Then he made his slow way back towards the door and found a space where he could stand without touching anybody else unless they wanted to get past him, which they did, about every ten seconds.

Kevin showed up fifteen minutes late. Which was just long enough for Barry to have begun to worry that he wasn't going to turn up at all, but not so long that he was pissed off. He was wearing a tight off white shirt under his leather jacket, and a pair of belted black jeans, the buckle flat against him like a magnet, stuck not tied. He looked very young. For the first time Barry thought of the possibility that he might be turned away at the door of some places. Not here evidently. He smiled broadly, and thanked Barry for the beer and sipped it. They gawked at each other. Then for a while they shouted out the names of pubs they liked, and Kevin seemed to like pubs slightly out from the centre which Barry had never heard of, places on Thomas Street or Clanbrassil Street or The South Circular Road with unlikely names such as 'The Florida Inn' or 'McFannigans'. Maybe it was the noise. Kevin scanned the crowd a number of times, running his eyes over the faces, and Barry wondered whether he would be able to ask him, at any point in the course of the evening, about that thing that he did. For a living.

They stayed for two drinks, Kevin insisting on buying the second and proving quite good at getting to and from the bar quickly, as if he understood the dynamics of crowds, as if he could slide in and out of people without their noticing.

On the walk over to the Bigallo, in the calm of the streets, he seemed quite chatty, telling Barry that his mother was the kind of woman who couldn't stand any noise at all, who couldn't bear to be in the city centre unless it was first thing in the morning, who couldn't bear crowds or crushes of any sort, who had once burst into tears in the middle of Dunnes Stores one Saturday before Christmas. He told Barry that he lived in Dolphin's Barn. He seemed happy. He smiled. Then at the door of the restaurant he went silent, and he refused to hand over his jacket, and when they sat down he looked around himself as if he expected some kind of trouble.

Barry saw his discomfort and his own was therefore doubled. Because this was the wrong place. This was entirely the wrong place.

What the hell had he been thinking?

The last time he had been in the Bigallo, he realised, had been with his father. Sitting hardly talking, with his father. His father having decided, apparently, that they could have a man to man conversation out of the way of the women, in a city centre restaurant, beneath old photographs of Cyril Cusack, David Kelly, Maureen Potter, Noel Purcell. His father had been wrong. What the hell was he up to now, following his father?

He thought, as they each studied the menu, that he had somehow got it into his hidden head, his underside, his occluded brain, that the best way to behave towards Kevin was in a fatherly manner. Indeed. Was it indeed? Somehow in his mediocre mind he had made that assumption. He knew what it was based on, but it surprised him nonetheless. It was based on the knowledge that he could not, under any circumstance, under any circumstance at all, have sex with Kevin. He could not. He could not because that was what Kevin did. He could not because it would not be new. It would not be novel. It would not be fun. It would certainly not be special. He would be used to that kind of carry on. He would know all about it. He would know a damn sight more than Barry did, or ever would, and there was nothing, Barry felt, that he could do with Kevin that Kevin had not had done with him before, a million times, a thousand times, a hundred times, a dozen times. He could not impress. He could only reveal to Kevin that he was no better in the end than a punter. That all he wanted really was a fuck. That it was the same old thing. Except he didn't want to pay. There was no way around it. Sex was the business, not the leisure, of Kevin's life. The only thing Barry could do with Kevin which might make an impression, which might connect them, which might bring them close, was to not want to have sex with him. That might interest him.

It was solid logic, he knew it was. He had been aware of it.

What he had not been aware of, and which now made itself painfully clear to him, was that his idiotic subconscious, trained as it was by pop culture psychology, and fed by the Freud in our communal food, had decided to go *in loco parentis* to the object of his desire. It was an arse ways Oedipus, horrid to behold. What did it involve? The restaurant, his father's booth, beneath Rosaleen Linehan and Ronnie Drew, listening and nodding, offering advice – *here let me choose the wine; you wouldn't like the monkfish; would you not think of buying, renting is such a waste; are you not worried about disease; must your jeans be so tight; I could lend you some money to get you on your feet.*

Kevin shifted on his seat, as if sitting on stones. He looked over each of Barry's shoulders. He looked over his own. He considered the ancient waiter for a moment. He looked at the ceiling. He looked at the wall. Something on the floor won a glance from him. He didn't like it one bit. Not one bit.

'Can we swap seats?' he said.

'What?'

'Sides I mean. Can we swap sides? Can I sit where you're sitting?'

'Oh. Yeah. If you like. Sure.'

So they swapped each other over, Kevin's hand touching his arm as they were gliding around the table, his ducked head and his three eight's smile and his jacket in his hand, and they reformed themselves then, in reverse, in to the booth they'd been given. From this side Barry could see signed colour glossies of Tony Kenny and Red Hurley and Mister Pussy. And over Kevin's shoulder he could see a clutch of other diners, all variously progressed through their meals, peering this way and that, in and out of conversation, glancing.

'Who was it?'

Kevin's head was back in his menu. Or Barry's menu. They had not swapped menus. Or rather, they had. They had not taken their menus with them.

'What?'

'Someone you know?'

'Oh. Yeah. Sort of.'

So, Barry thought. So. He went through the faces. Saturday night suits. A couple of mixed tables – husbands and wives; three elderly ruins; old chorus boys; a priest and a little old lady. It struck Barry that they were the youngest people there by about thirty years.

'Which one?'

'It doesn't matter.'

'No, tell me. Which one?'

'Uh, the really good looking one.'

There was none such. Kevin's smile had diminished somewhat, and his face had coloured. Barry thought he should leave off. The odd inflated features of Danny La Rue looked sideways at him. The waiter hovered. One of the elderly men was staring at their table, or, more accurately, at the back of Kevin's head. He wore a high collared jumper beneath a tweed jacket. He looked like a poet or civil servant. He was the one. His eyes were watery steady, and they had in them the right mix, it seemed to Barry, of sadness and lust and malice. Dirty old queen.

'Very nice to see you again Sir how are you?'

This was the waiter now, and just as Barry was levelling his surprised eyes at him, he heard Kevin say,

'Very well thanks. How are you?'

And he heard the waiter say,

'Hale and hearty thank God. It's a great summer and it does me wonders. Will you have it still or sparkling?'

Kevin asked for sparkling, and the waiter went off, and Kevin barely glanced at Barry and went back to considering the menu.

Bloody hell.

'You're a regular then?'

'No not really. I've been here about three times. But the last time was only last week.'

Barry glanced at the old guy. He was now staring directly back at him.

'On, uh, on business?'

Kevin flashed him a quick look that was not exactly full of love. 'Yeah,' he said, quietly.

'That's ok. I mean, sorry, I'm being nosy. I didn't mean to ask really. Sorry.'

His father came to him then, in the blotched and combined visage of Twink and Jimmy O'Dea and the ancient waiter, who served them sparkling water and Kevin's choice of Chardonnay and a basket of oily bread. His father stood, with his autograph sticking out of his shoulder and into the air, with a sparkle in his eyes and the reflection of the footlights in the gleam of his smile, and considered him a moment and roared at him then, *YOU'RE IN THE FUCKING BIGALLO! WITH A BOY WHORE! AND YOU'RE AS VISIBLE AS LIBERTY FUCKING HALL! AND BAD AS IT IS, IT LOOKS TEN TIMES FUCKING WORSE! YA GOB-SHITE! HAVE YA NEITHER SHAME NOR SENSE?*

No, answered Barry. I have neither of those.

'Sorry,' he said again.

Kevin looked up. He was open faced. In the way of honest horses and new-borns. His eyes were deep, and the brown in them was the brown of winter forests and the walk home. His mouth was generously smiling.

'That's ok,' he said, and nodded once. 'I don't mind.'

From then on it was marvellous. Barry decided that that's what it was. Marvellous. He paid no further attention to his companion's paying partners, nor to the ghosts on the wall or in his head, nor to his upbringing or his caution or his fear. He let himself go altogether. He found that he could be entertaining. He found himself adopting slightly the persona of Joe Kavanagh, and reined it in after a couple of stories about the girls who drove the jeeps, and was quieter then, more honest, and allowed himself to wander into a potted history of himself, in the hope of some return.

He didn't get that.

But he got the easy laugh and the relaxed manner, and Kevin told him little things. He told him about his mother. About his brother. His brother's wife, or perhaps partner, Barry wasn't sure. About their child. He told Barry about his flat. He told him about the clothes he had his eye on, and about places which he wanted to visit. He wanted, he said, to travel a lot. He asked him things as well. About how he had got his job. About the qualifications he had needed and the courses he had had to do. About the pay and the hours and the kind of people he had to work with. He did not ask about Joe.

He was perfectly pleasant company. Never once did he mention what it was he did for a living. His only allusions to it were the broad and passing references he made to having once been told something 'by some guy', or of having heard of some foreign place from 'some guy' he had met. That was all. For an eavesdropper there would have been no clue. The conversation was therefore stilted and unreal, but that didn't matter. Because he knew, Barry did, that there would be something after. And as their second bottle of wine was opened for them, he started to wonder whether he would invite Kevin back to his place, or suggest first that they go for a drink, or a dance. And in this wondering, it has to be said that there was really, honestly, no thought in Barry's mind, about breaking his own rule so early – of having sex with Kevin. Or not much thought anyway. Instead he thought that they would talk, and talk more, and more and more. And that eventually they would get to the point of it. And he was, as he listened to Kevin's odd account of some minor earthquake in his youth, composing in his mind, a little speech, which might, when the time came, be good to have to hand. Along the lines – *You have autonomy over your own body and I make no claim on it, but I like you, and I like being with you, and I would be interested, pursuant to our earlier conversations, in embarking upon some kind of relationship with you, which I am entirely relaxed about, and from which I expect nothing other than the opportunity to be a friend to you* – etc etc.

Barry was a little drunk. Before the first course arrived he was a little drunk. By the time they were starting on the second, he had forgotten all but two words of his speech – *your body* – and was trying to start a half hearted argument over the fact that Kevin was eating veal. What he objected to chiefly was the irony of it, which he was sure existed, and he did not like irony, he preferred poignancy, and would have preferred therefore that the old tweedy queen across the room was the one eating veal, while Kevin worked his youthful way through a plate of honest pasta. But Kevin loved his veal.

'It's from *calves* you know,' Barry whined.

'I know.'

'They're not allowed to *move*.'

'Yeah.'

'They're in *crates*.'

'Uh huh.'

'They're *babies*. In *pain*. Tortured. They're *tortured babies*.'

'Yeah they're lovely.'

And if in his head Barry was comparing Kevin to a tortured baby, was Kevin in his own head accepting the comparison and licking his lips and claiming to like it? Was this their conversation? And if it was, did that mean that it was ok for Barry to think about getting in on the torturing at some point? Was that why Kevin had ordered veal? To indicate to Barry that he'd like to have sex with him?

Shouldn't he just ask?

'Kevin . . .'

'Barry . . .'

They stopped eating and looked at each other, Kevin with a face which suggested that it would be ok now to ask whatever Barry wanted to ask, to suggest whatever it was that he wanted to suggest; that now would be a good time, for example, to declare an interest, emotional, erotic, whatever, and to lay down some cards and clear up any misapprehensions, and to be generally open and honest and straightforward. All of this, Kevin's face suggested.

It was also possible that it suggested a level of horror at what might be said next. That Barry's exhalation of his name had caused Kevin some alarm, and that the face which he presented was intended to convey a warning – don't ruin a perfectly nice evening with some hopeless declaration. Leave it.

'We should,' said Barry, 'have more wine.'

He watched for the reaction, and missed it really, or couldn't quite catch it, or couldn't quite read it. A slight drooping of the muscles? A kind of disappointment in the tendons of his cheeks and his mouth and his eyes? Or was there a hint of darkening, a pigment alteration, an alarm being sounded or silenced? Barry couldn't tell. He nearly asked.

So it went on, and became a kind of fractional conversation. A handshake conversation. It was not what Barry wanted. He knew this. But it was marvellous all the same, for it contained all the possibles. The impossibles as well, admittedly, but the wine was going to his head, and he was optimistic, and looked favourably upon the unknown. And he enjoyed himself, and he felt that Kevin enjoyed himself as well. That they got on well together. They laughed at each other's jokes, they carried the short silences easily, without any flapping. They found a store of things to tell each other and exchanged them with ease.

So it was with some pain and not a little surprise that Barry heard Kevin say, as he knocked back his coffee and looked at his watch,

'I have to go.'

'Where?'

Kevin frowned, and seemed to hunt around for an answer.

'Oh,' said Barry, 'I mean, really? So early? That's a pity?'

'Well I did warn you.'

'Yeah I know you did.'

Did he? Had he? Somehow Barry had translated that into a get out clause, only to be invoked in the event of Kevin becoming bored. Had this happened? Or had it been genuine? And if it was then was it work related? Well what else would it be?

He found it suddenly appalling.

'Do you have to?' he asked.

'Go? Yeah, sorry.'

No, he tried to say, I mean do you have to fuck for money? But he nodded and stuck his finger in the dregs of his espresso.

In the first uneasy silence of the evening, he realised that he had all the power here. He realised that it would take some perseverance to manage any kind of relationship with Kevin. It would take a surplus of attraction, a long term lust, an utter absence of jealousy, a deep emotion, to stay close to him. Love, he thought that amounted to. Love. That thing. Hard to come by. And he thought that it was maybe Kevin's only chance of a non-paying shag. Ever.

———

Imagine that.
  Either love or money.
  Imagine that.

––––––––––

He looked at him and wondered how aware he was of the problem. His face was small and expectant and poised, as if he was waiting to be hit or hugged. Barry was drunk. He was prone to sentiment when drunk. But he thought that Kevin's was the most beautiful face he had ever imagined, never mind seen.

He had the power, but that only meant that he had the trouble. The responsibility. He scanned the walls and thought about his father, who wouldn't get involved. He saw the smilers and the actors and the make up and the lights. Showtime.

Back at Kevin's face there was still the expectancy, and maybe the reason that Barry could not read him was because there were always two things there at once – hope and its opposite. He swirled his mind and could not decide. Kevin spoke.

  'Can I call you tomorrow?'

Barry nodded before he thought. You can call me anytime. Any time. Don't not call me. Don't ever not call me. Not yet anyway. Don't decide for me. Don't rule it out. It might happen. Don't think it won't. Don't torture me. Baby.

Kez loved it. The doorways and the black sky. The smell of drink in the stones. He loved it. He loved the air in the streets, the cars in the road, the feet on the pavements. He loved the wine in his body, charging around him like traffic. Here he was, Kez in the city, on the corners, waiting for the man and his money. It was his place, stand up homeless, trader.

They had gone speechless from the restaurant, and wandered speechless up the street, towards the Green, past groups of drinkers and eaters who travelled from pub to pub, propelled by voices. Barry was very quiet. Almost sulking, thought Kez. He couldn't decide if that was cute or annoying. He wondered whether he would change his plans if Barry asked. He wondered if he would give up the easiest money of his week if Barry said, you know Kez, I mean Kevin, I'd really like you to come home with me. He wondered. But Barry never asked, so he didn't have to pin himself down on it. He might have though. He might have.

The guy was one of Vincent's. He paid a hundred quid to watch Kez have a wank in the passenger seat of his posh car. One hundred. He didn't even seem to enjoy it much.

Barry was polite. He was polite like a much older man might be polite, as if there was nothing that he deserved, or as if he deserved everything but wasn't going to be vulgar by asking for it. He wanted things offered. Which was polite, in a way. And in another way was just really annoying.

Kez liked him though. He was funny. He had a nice smile. That kind of thing.

On his mobile there were two messages from regulars, one of them cancelling the following day, the other one confirming a date for Monday. There was one message from an out of towner who sounded English and had wanted a call back earlier on. There was a text message from Vincent reminding him that it was Kathy's birthday on Wednesday, to send her a card.

He looked at his watch. He was a little late. He was outside the 747 travel agents on the corner of George's Street. He wondered whether Barry had really gone home. It was early still. And he had been disappointed. Hopeful then disappointed. He might have gone up to The Pod instead, or double backed towards The George or something. These gayboys had their places. Kez beeped through his address book and found Barry's name. Just as he pressed the call button the car appeared at the lights across the street and he had to cancel it. He switched the phone off and put it in his jacket, hitched up his trousers, blanked his features, then smiled, waited. He couldn't see the guy's face, but he knew it was him. When the lights turned green the car eased its way over to him, and he lent forward and opened the door and got in.

He liked this guy. So easy. So moneyed. And it was good, after the experience of Chester Haft, when he thought he'd never speak to one again, never mind get into a car with one, to be doing business once more, with an American. A skinny American in a BMW.

Easy.

Death

Cars, houses, streets. The wind whip, the slap, the hunkered down temper of the traffic. Growling under the negative lights, the darkroom lights, at the corners and the intersections, the blood red lights. By the glow holed dwellings, the rows of windows – lined up, occupied or empty, who knows? They go up and they go across. Grid work. The clattering concrete and the stained pavements, collecting footfalls and litter, vomit and phlegm, money, dogs, children, shoe parts, animal shit, debris, bad air, car smoke, scrapings, minor infestations, little wispy nothings that we drop and don't miss. The huddles, the doorways, the single palm, the invocation. The blanket and the chewing gum box. The sleeping bag and plastic cup. You know them. The mild roar of the weekend drinkers. The clump of hormones at the corner – all crotches and dribble, all gagging for it. The confused, the queues, waiting for the bouncer to give them the once over – no work clothes, no sports gear – mixed nerves and bravado, all smelling the same – cheap, hopeful, scared. Shirts, skirts, jeans, seams, skin, hair, scents, mouths, slap, tickle, snatch, tackle, come on, c'mon, you on for it, you up for it, you out for it, you in on it? That's the crunch, the hope of violence. That's what they're all after, a fight or a fuck, something howled out, vicious, bitten. It's the weekend. It's Dublin. It's showtime.

––––––––

Dr Addison-Blake, clever him, had filled a poppers bottle with chloroform. Spillage was a danger, as was over sniff. So he had diluted significantly with lemon, vanilla and an ester of benzocaine and nitric acid. It smelled about right, though perhaps a little sweaty, like incense. In tests it had rendered Dr Addison-Blake unconscious within about 10 seconds and had kept him out for nearly an hour. It had left his head nicely spinning, with sound, so that he felt he was a finger being slowly drawn around the rim of a wineglass. A little longer and he'd sever and bleed. That lasted a couple of hours – he took nothing for it.

The city doesn't care. The city doesn't even notice. It's a heavy rumble by the side of the sea and the heave of the hills. It takes years to form a thought. Its blinks are generational. It takes the long view, hypermetropic, not bothered with the details, with the single dramas or the brief scenes, not bothered with the clutter of iteration. *Accumulate,* it says. *Accumulate.* Lay down your life. Add what you have. Then piss off. It's history that the city's after, not the clicks and squeals – not you, not you and your notions. Not you and your aspirations. Your grime. Locked in petty murder and the day to day. Piss off with your memoirs and your plans. Aspire elsewhere.

We are the city. We are the city, like we are the church. Like we are the neighbourhood and the street and the houses and the spirit. We name these things and live in them. Owner occupiers we are, upkeep and admittance, rules and humours. Without us there's bricks and silence and all the names are ended. We are the city. And the city doesn't care. It just squats and deep breathes. It lets people move through it. It doesn't care what you do. Do it.

Do you think that the names will survive us? Do you? Do you think that the rats and the roaches will call this place Dublin? Or that the machines will? You think the dust and the cold light will whistle out the street names and the songs? That we are making something permanent here? Well we're not. We're building a midden. And nothing much will trouble it after we're ruined. Unless a spaceship comes a digging.

Or do you think that we will always be here? In some form, recognisably ourselves, with our rancour and our porn and our opposable thumbs? In new clothes, one colour, peaceful, sorted? You think so?

No neither do I.

———

Dr Addison-Blake drove the boy through the streets.

They headed for the park, the Phoenix Park, which was where they had gone the time before, even though Kez had told him there were better places – he seemed to like the trees and the darkness, that's what he said, or seemed to say, and just as they got towards the park, instead of going into it, up the hill and into it, he drove instead down the side of it, towards the side gate, even though Kez told him that the side gate would be closed by then.

––––––––

Letters, phone calls. It's time people talked to each other. In all the corners of the world. E-mails, text messages, answering machines, voicemail. Conversations and asides. Small words. Big talk. It doesn't matter.

Why can't we all just get on?

Why the violence?

Why so much violence?

––––––––

Earlier.

Barry's phone rang once as he turned the corner off the Green, doubling back on himself. By the time he got it out of his pocket it had stopped. *One missed call* it said. *Kevin.* He called him back, but it went straight to his answering machine, as if he'd turned it off. He didn't leave a message. What was that about? What did that mean? Was that some kind of signal? Barry decided that it was some kind of signal – some good kind of signal – and he felt good about it and nearly went home, but didn't.

––––––––

Later.

Dr Addison-Blake stopped the car. Not in the park you under-stand, not there. It was too dark there, there were too many trees. He stopped instead in the large forecourt of a furniture ware-house. These things ringed the city like forts. He told the boy to put his seat back.

'What?'

'Put it down, so that you're lying down.'

He took off his seat belt and was fiddling around at the side there, trying to find the lever, the lever that lowered the seat.

'It should be there.'

'I can't find the . . .'

'Like a small lever.'

'Yeah . . . I can't . . .'

'It's just like a lever, you know, just pull it up.'

'Ok. Hang on.'

'Got it?'

'No, it's . . . I can't see . . .'

311

Oh for fuck's sake. I mean for fuck's sake. You know?

He half caught him with a backwards swipe, left hand, knuckles into the cheek bone, just a flail, a slap, nothing. He tried to wind him bringing his right hand around fast but the punch seemed to land on a hip. The kid was being smart, he was scrambling for the door handle, not even wasting time being surprised or trying to defend himself or hit back at all. Door was locked though. Door wouldn't open.

———

He'd been stupid, Dr Addison-Blake, just impatient and rushed. He had to learn calm, had to learn manners with the method. It was all about timing and determination. Like comedy or surgery or cooking. Why lash out at the kid because he couldn't find the seat back lever when he could simply have waited a couple of minutes until his pants were around his knees, handed him the poppers bottle and had him out cold in about twenty seconds.

———

Earlier.

Barry was busy typing out a text message to Kevin, having trouble remembering the abbreviations for certain words – was Thanks for example txs or tnks or just ta? Ta? Tnks 4 this evng. Was that right? Tlk 2moro? xxx? cu? What was the text version of 'I'm not jealous I'm just taking my time with it.' What was the three letter equivalent of 'every penny you make breaks my heart but it's your body and I won't tell you to stop even though I'd like you to stop and then be my boyfriend even though realistically you're far too young and I'm far too naïve.' Was there an emoticon representing 'Are we at cross purposes, or is this a possibility?'

Message sent.

———

Joe Kavanagh and Sylvia Porterhouse were taking a bath together, sitting in the steam with their legs entwined and a glass of wine each and Joe with the tap between his shoulder blades, feeling like a bit of a fool. She had lit candles. She had put a CD of *Aida* on the stereo in the bedroom. It was all too beautiful.

———

Delly slept. She did not dream. But in her fingers little ghosts played hopscotch.

———

Earlier.

Kitty Flood celebrated. Oh with what relief! She danced in the cleared spaces of her mind. She let the air move through her. She tittered and smirked. She drove in circles, she drove at speed, she drove her horrid failings over a horrid cliff, and wheeled her heavy, graceful car through the capillary lanes of the Dublin suburbs.

No one knew. No one.

On her mobile, one handed, her eye up ahead, she booked a table for herself in her favourite restaurant. Then she remembered her second favourite restaurant and booked it as well, as a back up, as a fail safe, as a maybe. And she thought of a third, which had been recommended, to which she had never been, and she booked that as well, as a why not, as a possible, contingent on parking, on the parking situation, and she called her love, her Delly, and she told her that she would be late in, not to worry, everything was fine, utterly fine, completely fine, and that she was eating out, and that Mrs Cotter would take care of her, would look after her, and she was not to worry about a thing, that there was nothing, utterly nothing, about which she should worry.

She had spent the time since the phone call, since the smooth voiced man had interrupted her, in a permanent tremor. She had driven to the meeting feeling that she was on her way to identify a body. That it all presaged loss. That Siobhan Cullen was after a recompense, a reckoning, justice. That she wished vengeance on the woman who had taken her husband from her. That it would mean ruin. The end of the house. The last of the money.

She felt foolish now, and shook her head and smiled, and took the turn for the city, tired finally, of running through the carefree minor roads. In the same way that she was tired of her own pettiness, her resentments, her selfishness. She had realised, through this scare, that she was a fortunate woman. One who should be grateful for her place. One who should return the letter to her companion's side and say no more about it. One who should enjoy what she was given, and have no care for what was given to others. Dr George was not her enemy. He was an orphan and he was young and he had given up his time to come and care for Delly. She should not resent his reward.

She had liked the English woman. The journalist. She had been

313

wonderfully confused. Hopeful. She had chased after the ridiculous and had not been embarrassed. Such people are worth knowing.

Kitty Flood drove in magnanimity towards the little city. She considered her dinner reservations. There might be time, she thought, looking at the sun folding down on her left, to honour all of them.

———

Later.

In the car, as Kez was driven toward the hills and began to realise that this was serious, this was not a joke, this was not a misunderstanding, he managed to get his hand into his pocket, his left hand, into his right jacket pocket, inside pocket, while he held his bleeding right hand between his thighs, squeezing it there, though it seemed now that it wasn't as badly cut as he'd thought, that it wasn't his wrist, it was in the palm, and though it stung like crazy he didn't think he was loosing a huge amount of blood out of it, and the stinging of it was eclipsed anyway, now, by the state of his cheek, his right cheek, which was swollen enough for him to be able to see it, invading his vision like a space vehicle creeping onto a TV screen.

The American, this guy, this nice simple straightforward, money-eyed guy, was quiet now, listening to the news on the radio. He'd stopped the muttering, the low American mutter, he'd stopped all that. He had seemed to take no pleasure from it. Which was freaking Kez out. Because that meant the pleasure came later. That this wasn't over. Not at all. His hand closed around his phone. He tried to moan at the same time as the start up beep, and seemed to succeed, because the American didn't even look over at him. He thought about trying 999, but he couldn't reach down far enough into his pocket to get a finger on the nine. He hit the redial. He couldn't hear ringing, or anything, so he didn't know when to start talking. He tried to be smart.

'Where are you taking me?'

'Shut up.'

His smartness stopped there.

'I'm being murdered.'

'Naw you're not.'

'I don't know where I am. Car. Country. BMW.'

314

The guy looked at him, saw him twisted in his seat, talking into his chest.

'Fucker. Fuck's sake.'

His hand came flying off the steering wheel and smacked right into the phone in Kez's pocket, and Kez heard a crack, and felt like he'd been shot, and the guy braked, and at the same time his hand was tearing through the jacket, tearing it off him, getting to the phone, and by the time he'd brought the car to a stop, with the sound of horns passing them at speed, he had the phone in his hand and he was banging it off the dashboard, bits of plastic flying everywhere, the light staying on until it gave a final beep, like the beep it gave when a text message came in, and it died, broken, crushed, and fell at his feet.

After that there was silence for a moment, just the two of them breathing. Then the American turned to face him, and he had a little bottle in his hand.

———

'I'm being murdered.'
'Naw you're not.'
'I don't know where I am. Car. Country. BMW.'
'Fucker. Fuck's sake.'

———

Phone
goes
dead.

The thing was simply this. Barry missed the phone call because his phone was switched off because when he went to Incognito for a shag after leaving Kez at the corner, and after sending him a text message which stated, simply,

Tnks 4 2nite. Tlk soon. xxx B

he switched off his phone and put it in the locker with all of his clothes. So at the time Kez called him he was actually phoneless, sitting in the steam room wrapped in a towel, wondering whether he was there too early or too late or whether he was just too ugly by now – ignored as he was by the cute, vaguely north African guy who was getting up to leave, and pawed at by the scrawny old bloke who smelled almost overwhelmingly of cigarettes and beer, like the aftermath of a gas explosion.

When, three rotten hours later, he left for home with nothing much to show for his efforts but a flustered ten minutes with some overly decent country boy from Leitrim or Letterkenny or Laois, he didn't even think to switch his phone back on. Why should he, at that hour, with the streets starting to collapse, the sirens splashing in the shallows of the sludge, with the clattering feet and the sliding traffic? So he didn't hear the message. He slept well. He slept soundly. The house was quiet. He dreamed of no bad thing.

Even in the morning it took some time to get to it. There were things to do. Sleeping. Then dozing. Then getting up, listening to the radio, making coffee, eating, turning on the TV. He showered. He got dressed. As he went out to get the papers, he thought of his phone, and it even occurred to him that he should turn it on, because Kevin might call, but he was half way out the door and he was only going to the shops, and by the time he came back he had forgotten about it. He was distracted by the silence in the house. There wasn't a sound. And there were no smells either. Just the still air and the vague sense that he had missed something. That the building was to be demolished and everyone had been evacuated and they'd forgotten about him. Or they'd assumed that he was gone already, because nobody could be in bed that late. Or that war had broken out. He scanned the papers but they contained no news whatsoever.

It was only as he considered going out, going into town maybe, to have a drink, and thought about who he might call to go with him, that he finally, close to three o'clock in the afternoon, turned on his phone. And even then, he just switched it on, and was fiddling with his toaster, thinking that he should clean it, that it was probably about to bring an extended family of mice into his life, that the thing made that elongated beep to indicate that someone had left him a message. So he turned his toaster upside down and made a small mountain of crumbs and crusts and the burned black lumps of melted bread molecules which his mother had always told him were carcinogenic, and he spent a few minutes messing with that, knocking about a third of it onto the floor, clogging up the sink with the rest of it, getting a brush out, putting the toaster back where it had been, wishing he'd left it alone, picking bread dust out his shirt sleeves, and it was only then, with his mind involved in all this utter unimportance, with food debris, with the fear of small animals, that he called his voicemail and listened, with his hands paused over his cuffs, with the phone clenched between his shoulder and the side of his head, just at that point where ancient executioners must have aimed their axe.

'You have one new message. Message sent today at twelve forty nine am.'

'M been murdered.'

'Naw yaw naw.'

'Dunno air yam. Car Cunt EBM woo.'

'Ucker. Uck's sake.'

'Press two to play the message again. Press seven to . . . '

He played it again.

'I'm being murdered.'

'Naw you not.'

'Dunno where I am. Car Cunty BM woo.'

'Fucker. Fuck's sake.'

Barry stared at his phone.

'Press two to play the message again. Press seven to save it. Press nine to delete it.'

He pressed two. Then again. Then once more. Then he pressed seven.

'Your message will be saved for three days.'

Three days. Three days. Then what? What happened then?

————

He found himself, later, going through all the hours and all the minutes from 12.49 that morning as if they were years and he was old and he was dying and he'd never done anything except clean toasters and doze and use the bathroom and wander round saunas staring at shoulder blades and nipples and cocks. He was ashamed at the waste. He went through the minutes and the hours in his head and imagined, while trying not to, all the ways that pain might be inflicted over that length of time. Because what he felt, and this made total sense, was that because he hadn't heard the message until nearly fourteen hours later, that it had *continued to be true for all of that time*. That Kevin had been murdered. And because Barry had been chasing ass and sleeping and fiddling with his fucking toaster, the murder had taken fourteen hours, give or take, from start to finish. That, Barry felt, was a lot of pain.

But this came to him later. The first thing that came to him was adrenaline, a peculiar thing in the circumstances, redundant and brazen, charging in with all kinds of nonsensical notions, a piece of human software hopelessly out of sync with the notion of recorded telephone messages. It wanted him to run. It wanted him to pick up a weapon. Run or pick up a weapon. Instead he uttered a noise of some sort, almost certainly primal, and flapped his hands about and felt sick to his stomach. He beeped through his address book and called Kevin back.

No ringing. Then,

'Hi. Thanks for calling. I'm busy at the moment, so please leave a name and a number and I'll call you back as soon as I can. Bye.'

The voice. The voice was Kevin's. It made Barry gag slightly.

'Uh, Kevin, hi, this is Barry. I just got your message just this minute. It's, uh, it's like three o'clock on Sunday, and I'm, I, I just hope you're ok. Will you call me please? Call me as soon as you can. I'm worried. Please call me.'

He hung up.

Run, or pick up a weapon.

Oh the deep love of women. The bed like loving of women. The enveloping love of deep folded women. The arsenal of caresses and stroking and touches in substantial women. Their love lore. Their ways and means.

Joe Kavanagh lay half on the bed and half off it, the edge of the mattress engraving a beaded stripe between his shoulder blades, one foot pointed at the carpet, ready to intervene, the other entangled in Sylvia's lower calf muscles, caught somewhere there in the heat. He wondered how he managed to stay on at all. He thought it may have been because his heart and his genitals were all slightly to the left – were all inclined towards the snoring woman who lay spread-eagled on her stomach, on his bed, filling the void which had lately appeared in place of his wife.

He hadn't realised the void had been so big, bigger by far than his wife had ever been. But maybe there was something in abrupt departures which left an exaggerated space behind them. Some law of physics.

$$\text{Absence} = (\text{Former Presence} \times \text{Level of Panic} \times \text{Level of Guilt} \times \text{Degree of Anger}) / \text{Sense of Relief}$$

Or,

$$A = (Fp \times P \times G \times A)/R$$

He had not been good at the science subjects. Nor very good at the non science ones either. His father had greeted the arrival of each school report with a deep sigh of 'Oh Christ', uttered prayer like before opening the envelope.

Sylvia's snoring was sonorous and scary, and made it impossible for him to sleep. But he liked it. It was regular, rhythmic, warm, alive. It was a comfort to know that she was completely involved in sleeping, that she wasn't lying there plotting or debating or listening to him. That she didn't, largely speaking, care.

He moved slightly, trying to gain a little more purchase on the cover – a single summer sheet – and considering how much louder Sylvia might be if she was lying on her back. His head was in her armpit. That was ok, but it meant that he couldn't really turn and face her. He tried turning the other way, but there was an alarming loss of balance involved, and his arse seemed about to topple him off the edge as soon as his tried to twist his hips. The only real way that he could see of becoming comfortable was to get out of the bed and then get back in. Or to shift her. Prod her or pinch her or poke her in the ribs.

He didn't want to disturb her though. It was too early. She would sit up and start talking. She would want more sex. She would want more food. She would want the newspapers and the radio on. Breakfast and information. So he stayed where he was. Balanced on the edge of his bed, clinging contentedly to her noises.

He hadn't slept very well.

He tried to describe her to the audience in his head. But he couldn't really manage it. She's here, he said. She's here, just now, she's here. In my bed. In its centre. Resting. At rest in its centre. It was the best he could manage.

Another reason that he didn't mind his relative discomfort was the fact that she was going to leave. She was bound to. She was going to pack her things and go. It was inevitable. Wasn't it? After the mess they had made of their meeting with Kitty Flood. After that elongated farce in the foothills. Sylvia had no more use for him now, not after that. It had been embarrassing – excruciatingly so – but only, apparently, for him. Because the two women, one large, the other even larger, had seemed to understand each other, despite the misunderstanding. As if he had been the cause of that.

He didn't want to think about it though. It made him feel peculiar.

The foothills. He had made it to the foothills of Sylvia Porterhouse. It was time to be turned back by inclement weather and difficult terrain. And even if the weather stayed good and the terrain got no worse than it had previously been, he thought he'd turn back anyway. It had been a good hike. It had cleared his head. A little. Time to come down.

He thought on balance that he'd be glad to see the back of her.

Of Sylvia Porterhouse. He'd be glad to return to his study of the television, to his foodless kitchen, to his renewed experiments with masturbation – a teenage hobby which he had sadly neglected, but which had begun again to be a source of great, if melancholic, diversion. She had been in his house for three days now, and that was enough. He was keen to get back to his keening.

He wondered what time it was. There was a full light, but there was silence also, so it was early. As he listened for traffic or church bells or some Sunday noises, the telephone rang, making him jump. Sylvia stirred. Joe slid. He landed in a kind of kneeling position at the side of the bed, his hands dragging Sylvia's pillow from under her cheek. She opened an eye and regarded him.

'Get that will you doll?'

He picked it up on the third ring, still kneeling by his bed.

'Hello?'

'Mr Kavanagh?'

'Yes?'

'It's Kitty Flood. We met yesterday.'

Oh Christ.

'Good morning,' he managed. He could see Sylvia's wristwatch on the bedside table. It was exactly eight am.

'May I speak to Miss Porterhouse? To Sylvia?'

'Um, yeah, yeah, hang on.'

He pressed the receiver into his chest.

'It's Flood. It's Katherine, Kitty Flood.'

She didn't seem surprised. She smiled. She sat up, brushed her hands down over her breasts, coughed to clear her throat and slapped both hands to her cheeks. Twice. She took the receiver without looking at him again.

'Hello Kitty,' she chirped. 'How are you?'

Joe stood and left the room, limping naked across his landing as the voice of Sylvia Porterhouse followed him cheerfully.

'I'd be delighted to,' it was saying. 'I'll get Joe to drive me. No no. Drive.'

And there was laughter then, English and measured.

———

He dozed while she dressed. She opened the curtains and switched on the radio and moved back and forth from bathroom to bedroom, talking, half to him, half to herself. She made no attempt to conceal her excitement at the prospect of meeting Kitty Flood again. She cooed and whimpered and fussed over outfits. Joe farted under the duvet and wished he was brave. He thought about having a beer, but couldn't bring himself to actually want one. Eventually she was ready. She told him so.

'I'm ready.'

'Ok.'

There was silence. She was standing by the bed.

'Are you?'

'What?'

'Are you ready? I can't be late.'

He didn't answer for a moment while he considered what he was going to do about this. He was basically, he knew by now, a coward. If he drove her to her rendezvous, at least that would be it. He could forget about it for a few hours. Maybe sort out his house. Move all her crap into a corner. Book her into a hotel while she was out. Pack for her. Then tell her politely, calmly, after she returned, that it was best, he thought, if she left, that he had of course greatly enjoyed the last few days, and that he looked forward to resuming their professional relationship once she had returned to London. But for now, he thought it best if she stayed somewhere else.

Whereas, if he refused to drive her anywhere, he'd have to say all that right now, with none of the sweeteners like packed bags or booked hotels, or flowers for example. He could pick up some flowers later. Do it all with a bit of class. A little bit of style.

'Ok,' he said. 'Just let me get dressed. Then I'll drop you.'

———

By the time he'd returned home he was weary entirely of his life and his progress through the world and of all that ailed him. What was he playing at? Where was it he lived? In the wreck of his home or the virtual bubble of his radio studio or the dark damp depths of his dreams? Or did he live, and this seemed most likely now, in his car? Caught in constant traffic, between places, always travelling and returning, always checking the mirror, surprised that he was not being tailed.

She had left little things all over the place. Little items. There were pencils and notebooks and hats and shoes. There were jars and bottles in the bathroom which suggested the presence of a fugitive, disguising herself, rather than a woman and her make up. His kitchen radio had been re-tuned to RTE. His milk was all gone, and there was a carton of pineapple juice in his fridge. The washing up had been left in the sink. The dishwasher was empty.

He was sitting on his toilet thinking to himself that she had sat there too, when the telephone rang, and at that point he began to actually hate her. Which was, he knew, not right. Not classy. Not stylish. Things were beyond his control, which was not good. He was drifting somewhere far from the place he'd been before Sylvia's arrival, and he was miles distant now, whole mind-frames and patterns of thought and sets of emotion away from his intended place. Which was, he reminded himself, a place where his dull ache would be sharpened to a point, with which he could pierce through the cotton wool which had surrounded him since he was about fifteen, slash his way out of his nest, burst his bubble, and carve out a new path through the jungle, becoming a better man, a better presenter, alert, smart, active, doing things, moving forward, slash, cut, rip, prick. He had been distracted. By his lower urges. It happened. These things happened. It had just been a couple of days. She'd be gone soon. He could get back to The Plan. He could concentrate.

He let the phone ring. It rang out and then started again.

Whole sequences of thinking he'd have to go through now, to get back the urgency. Including Sylvia. He'd have to account for her. Learn from her even. Because she was, he had to admit it, forward moving. That had probably been the attraction. There was, he thought, a certain lack of precision to her methods though. They were decisive, that was true, and they were determined, so that she could move things on before you noticed that things were even moving at all. But there was also a kind of scatter gun feel to it. She didn't know what the outcome would be. She didn't know where it was she wanted to get to. But she went on her way all the same, full throttle.

The phone stopped. Then he heard the horrid trill of his mobile, somewhere downstairs.

He was second stream now, he was sub plot, plan B, extraneous, an add-on. He'd been useful for approximately three days. But she'd left all her stuff in his house. He admired that. It was all forward momentum, all progress, jerky and haphazard, but progress, active. Movement. Whereas he was a wait and see man. If unsure just sit it out. He was static.

The mobile phone stopped. The static one resumed. Jesus Christ. She could get a fucking taxi. He'd had it with her.

'Yeah hello?'

'Don't say anything okay, just listen to me.'

It was Barry. On the telephone. Not Sylvia at all. Barry. Which was a good thing. It was a good thing simply that it wasn't Sylvia. That in itself was an excellent thing. But it was good too because Barry knew about the plan. Barry could remind him. He started to talk but Joe didn't really understand what he was on about. And he was thinking too, while Barry was rattling on, that his relationship with women might be described by some people – like Barry for instance, in one of his regular *insightful* moods – to be homosexual repressed kind of behaviour. Which it wasn't. But he might appear to be, ultimately, not interested. In women.

They made him static. He drew too much comfort from them. They *unmanned* him.

'Joe?'

'Yeah. Well. I mean. I'm not. Are you sure. That. I mean.'

'I'm really fucking worried.'

'Yeah. Well. Call the police I guess.'

There was silence.

'Or go around to his house, you know. Where does he live?'

'I don't know. Dolphin's Barn somewhere.'

'Well there then. Go, you know, around there or something. I don't know.'

'Joe wake the fuck up will you I'm asking you for the first ever fucking time, seriously now, will you please think about this properly – I seriously think he's in big trouble or was, and I don't know what to do. Joe, please . . .'

Barry sounded like he was going to sob.

'Well what do you want me to do Barry? I don't know anything about him.'

'Yeah, I . . .'

'I have no idea what you should do. I don't think there's anything that you can do actually.'

'I keep on calling his mobile, but it's turned off. I left another message, and I don't know what the fuck else to do.'

He sobbed.

'Barry Barry, take it easy man. He's bound to be okay. He was probably fooling around. He'll call you. He's bound to call you. Take it easy. Just stay where you are. He'll call you. There's nothing you can do. Just wait.'

They didn't talk much more. Barry apologised. Joe accepted his apology. Said he'd see him the next day, not to worry. He went back to the bathroom. He took a shower and thought about static. Static was the worst thing that could happen to a radio show. It made everything seem delicate, prone to failure. If you heard static you anticipated loss. Static led to loss.

He stood beneath the water and he thought about electricity and interference. He thought about sparks and spikes and white noise. Thought about the fuzz of standing still. He thought about the useless, noisy blur of standing still, and of the ringing clarity of movement. He washed himself clean.

Then he got dressed and got into the car and drove towards Barry's place.

Dr George had disappeared. The house was in turmoil. Kitty was late.

No one had seen him since the previous day. Though Delly, with her talk of screaming and her generally wide eyed, blanket gripping demeanour, may well have seen him and not noticed. His car was there, parked where it usually was, and locked. But his bedroom door was also locked, which he tended to do only, Kitty had observed, when he was out, and there was no answer to her knocking in any case. He was not in the music room, he was not in Daniel Gilmore's old offices on the ground floor, he was not answering his mobile, he was nowhere to be found.

Delly meanwhile, was behaving like she needed a doctor. She was pale and shivering, her skin was cold and she could not remember whether she had taken her morning pills. Kitty managed to get her to sip some weak black tea, but she would eat nothing.

'I've had enough Delly. Really. I really have. Tomorrow I'm

325

organising a 24 hour nursing staff for this house. Because I have no idea what's wrong with you, what I should do with you, George is nowhere to be found, you're not eating, you're cold, and it's just not fair to expect me to know what to do.'

There was no protest. She gripped her blankets and squinted into corners.

'It was bloodcurdling,' she muttered.

'It was a dream.'

'I wasn't asleep.'

'I heard nothing.'

'How would you hear anything up there in the attic?'

Kitty had slept well, relieved, contrite, resolved, full. She was going to start to take this seriously now, this looking after Delly. It was her responsibility. She had cried for a while before sleeping, as if she had come close to something horrible, and had made it by. As if she had been in a car crash or a plane crash or had swum from a sinking ship. She was going to look after Delly, write her book, and stop worrying constantly about the bloody money.

'I don't even know how to take your blood pressure. You look like a woman who has no blood pressure. I should probably be ringing the alarm. But I haven't a clue.'

She scanned the table by Delly's bed, and picked up some tissues and an empty glass. She would look after Delly, write her book, and get out more. Less time spent on those bloody computers. Less time spent channelling her creative energies into chat room characters who wandered aimlessly and unheard, like lost saints, out in the desert, on stony ground. In the morning she scolded herself for her sentiment and her religious imagery, but the strength of her conversion remained.

'Maybe I should call Dr Mullen.'

'There's nothing wrong with me.'

'You haven't eaten in days.'

She had a date with the English woman, the journalist. Why had she done that? She had been interesting. Funny. She had been friendly, plump. She had worn nervous clothing, she had been respectful but cheeky too. She had presented a preposterous story but had not been embarrassed. She had, as her theory fell, not fallen with it. She had stayed there standing, smiling, asking cute little questions about life in the big house. Kitty liked all that. She liked the English woman asking the Irish woman about life in the big house. And her eyes had been a sparkling blue.

Though Mrs Cotter, strictly speaking, took Sunday afternoons off, Kitty was fairly sure that she wouldn't mind coming up to the house to keep an eye on Delly until either Dr George or Kitty herself returned home. It was not, she knew, the perfect start to her new regimen of care and creativity – to be going out for Sunday brunch with a journalist – but still, it was social. It was active. It was, she supposed, exercise.

'When was the last time you saw Dr George?'

'I don't know.'

'Yes. Well.' She didn't want to criticise him. It wasn't part of her new approach. But what else could she do? In the circumstances. He had left no message. 'It's not good enough really is it? It's a dereliction of duty.'

'Ssssh!' Delly hissed.

'What?'

'Shush!'

They were silent for a moment. Kitty could hear nothing but the slight breeze rummaging in the gardens. The windows were open. A dog barked in the distance, and Kitty peered out through the gap in the hedges and the garden walls and out over the fields towards the country that Delly didn't own in the distance and the far sea beyond it. The sun glinted there, the miles shimmered with the early heat. There was not a movement.

'It's just the guard dog.'

'Not that. There was . . . Did you not hear something else?'

'No.'

'You're deaf.'

'You're daft.'

They left it at that. Kitty went to kitchen and called down to the Cotters' house and told Mrs Cotter of the situation. She didn't seem surprised.

'When was the last time you saw Dr George?'

'Yesterday afternoon Miss Flood. He was in the swimming pool.'

'What do you mean, he was in the swimming pool?'

'He was down in the bottom of the pool Miss, having a look at it.'

'I thought the pool was covered.'

'Well it was but Dr George asked Mr Cotter to take the cover off. So he could have a look at it. Mr Cotter thinks he wants to fill it again.'

He had not mentioned it to Kitty. Just as well. She would not have agreed to it, not before her conversion anyway. She hated the near naked etiquette of places by water. She hated the meritocracy of skin. She hated the smells and the damp warmth and the furtive glances. She hated the splash she made when she jumped in. She hated the waves that rolled away from her moving body like mountain ranges, slapping against the pool-sides with great seismic cracks. The last time she had swum in a pool had been in France, about three years before, with only Delly and Jean Paul and Thomas in attendance. Conversation, which had been loudly good humoured before she jumped in, seemed to have died by the time she resurfaced. Thomas had excused himself and fled into the house. Jean Paul and Delly had turned onto their stomachs. When she emerged she had noticed that Delly had had to move her book from under her chair to avoid the overspill. The water did not settle for a good ten minutes – it sloshed and bucked and splashed. She had not been in a swimming costume since.

Now though, she considered Mrs Cotter's news and thought that maybe it wasn't a bad idea. Delly had been a great swimmer. It might persuade her out of the house. She had loved to sit by water.

'Well. If Dr George comes back you call me.'

'Yes Miss Flood.'

She thought that if he re-appeared she might take Miss Porterhouse for a drink or a drive or for an early tea or something. If he didn't then she'd come straight back.

'Otherwise I should be back by about four.'

She might take her to the German cemetery or to Powerscourt or something. Where they could walk and get to know each other. She wondered whether she should tell Delly where she was going to. She didn't usually. But this time she wondered whether it should not be part of her conversion – to keep Delly up to date on her movements.

Tomorrow she'd start that. Tomorrow would be fine.

Barry kept going on abrupt and horrible little raids into the creepiest corners of his imagination. The things he found there shocked him. He couldn't understand how he'd constructed them, or where their parts had come from. He saw, particularly, lateral and deep cuts in Kevin's throat and stomach. Ragged, bleeding. He saw internal items. He saw emergent bone, blood on his teeth. He saw three quarter severed limbs. He saw sexual damage, precise, surgical, a kind of slasher calligraphy – part Hollywood, part holiday thrillers, part his own intuitive savagery. He saw tears on the face and the eyelids pinned back. He saw, most of all, abject terror. And he felt sick in his stomach. And he entered a double state, a dialogue, a useless little conversation, between his hope and his fear. *You're being ridiculous.* I AM FUCKING NOT. *It was a joke.* THAT SOUND LIKE A JOKE TO YOU? *He's fast asleep, the little prick.* HE'S FUCKING DEAD.

He plugged his mobile into the charger. He turned the ring volume right up. He stared at it. On the landline, which he hadn't used in months, he called first his sister, who had been, the last time he'd talked to her, dating a policeman, but she wasn't in; then Joe; then the radio station, on the fractional chance that Kevin might have called there, or turned up at the door, battered and confused. No. No messages. No one there to see him. Then he called a friend of his whose brother worked in the ambulance service, or at least so Barry had thought, but it turned out that he actually worked for the fire brigade and was in any case on holiday in Florida, at Disney, with his kids, two girls and a boy, for two weeks. Then the mobile rang. Which made his heart stop until he answered it and it was his friend Will, asking him did he want to go out for a drink, but Barry just frantically told him to shut up, gave him his land line number and told him not to ring the fucking mobile, don't ring the fucking mobile, and he cut him off and checked for messages and there were no messages. Will didn't call back.

He turned on the television and checked the teletext, but there was nothing. He didn't know what it would look like if there was something. 'Body found, police investigate.' 'Grisly discovery in

Dublin'. But that would be wrong. The country, he'd said. 'Grisly discovery in the country.' Where in the country? Where for God's sake? He turned on the radio news. They didn't mention anything that sounded even vaguely like a murdered rent boy. There was a fisherman missing off the Donegal coast. There was an argument with Europe. There were worries about coin security. A man had crashed his car in the centre of Limerick, knocking down a statue. In Peru an earthquake. That was the list. That was the state of the nation. Maybe there'd be more later.

Then the door buzzer sounded, and he thought he'd ignore it, but then he thought Christ, it might be Kevin, even though Kevin didn't know where he lived, and he grabbed his mobile in case it wasn't Kevin, and he galloped down the stairs, ignoring the pain in his ankle, in case it was.

It was Joe.

They stared at each other.

'Any word?'

'No. Nothing. Why are you here?'

'Well. I'm not doing anything. You know. Might as well. Is it ok?'

He had some expensive looking sunglasses sitting on his forehead. Barry could see his car parked in front of the house. He had only been there once before, dropping Barry back after work one night, a little after Christine had left him.

'Sure.'

He nodded, stepped in to the hallway.

'You've ditched the stick then?' Barry asked him.

'I've what?'

'Ditched the stick.'

'Oh, yeah. Jesus I thought you said something else.'

'How's your foot?'

'Healed. I think.'

He looked down at it, wiggled it about.

'How's yours?'

'It's, uh, it's a bit better I think.'

He led his boss up the stairs.

'I should have brought it over for you. The stick.'

'Like I'd use it.'

'It's very good – excellent physiotherapeutical properties.'

'It made you look like a gobshite.'

330

'Oh well. Mock the afflicted. Taste of your own, you know, medicine. Jesus this place is a mess.'

It was not a mess. It was, in comparison to Joe's house, neurotically tidy. Neat. But Barry understood Joe to mean something more than that. The place was a hole was what he had wanted to say, and probably would have, had it not been for the circumstances. The circumstances.

He was quite good, Joe was, at being sensible and calm. He poured himself a glass of water and sat down on the sofa and asked a series of questions, making Barry retell what he had already told him, but slower this time, in sequence, without any sobbing at all. He pursed his lips. He nodded. He rubbed his eye. He sipped. He asked to hear the message, so Barry called his voicemail and handed the phone to Joe. Even when the phone was stuck to someone else's ear he could still make out Kevin's voice. Muffled now and distant, it sounded worse, as if he was trapped, unchanging, in a looped moment, reduced to a pulse on a circuit board, bouncing around, pinball, endless.

'Yeah,' breathed Joe, handing back the phone. 'That's not really funny is it?'

Barry shook his head.

'You don't recognise that voice in the background?'

'No. But I mean how would I? It's got to be a customer, client, whatever.'

'He never said anything about who he was meeting or where?'

'No.'

'Where did you leave him? I mean, where did you, you know, go your way . . .'

'That street. Parallel to Grafton Street. Up there.'

'Dawson Street?'

'No, the other side, where Break for The Border is.'

'Oh yeah. And he went?'

'Left. Right I mean. Towards George's Street.'

'What time?'

'No idea.'

'Half eleven? Midnight?'

'Closer to midnight I think.'

'He called you at ten to one. So that's fifty minutes for him to get basically anywhere.'

331

'Yeah.'

'Shit.'

Barry regretted that he had not been more drunk or more besotted, or both. Maybe then he would not have let him go. Maybe then he would have followed him.

'You turned your phone off when you got home?'

He thought about telling him the truth but didn't see that there was any point. It would just distract him.

'Yeah.'

'Thing is though Barry even if you hadn't, you'd still be none the wiser you know? He wouldn't have been able to say any more, tell you anything. He just said what he could before he was, uh, cut off. You answering it wouldn't have made it any easier.'

'It would have . . . At least I would have known.'

'So you could do what?'

'And at least he would have known that I knew.'

'But still.'

Joe was right of course, and Barry was not unaware of how horrible it would have been to have taken the call, at 12:49am, and not known what to do. Not knowing what to do in the middle of the day is less scary than not knowing what to do in the middle of the night. So there was a terrible thought trapped by the weight of his panic, like a spider under an upturned glass. Relief. That what was done was done by now. That there was less urgency now. That if he was being murdered then, he was dead by now. There was nothing to do. Not now.

Joe asked him what static was.

'What?'

'What does static mean?'

'It's uh, electricity, not flowing. Not in a current. Just, you know, around. It builds up in . . . . Why?'

'Can people be static? I mean, can you say a person is static, you know, not moving.'

'Yeah.'

'Right. I thought I had the wrong word. You know when that happens? You're using a word, quite happily, thinking it's the right word, and then suddenly for no reason you don't know why, but you think it might not be the right word at all. That it might not mean what you think it means at all.'

'Right.'

'So static can be a person? Or, I mean, a person can be static?'

'Yes.'

'Which means not moving. Stationary.'

'Yes.'

'Right. Good. I know there's a reason, but, um, to clarify, why are we not talking about the police here?'

'Because we have nothing to tell them. I don't even know his name. You know, just Kevin. Mightn't even be his name. Because it might, ultimately be nothing, or not nothing, but nothing that is any longer, you know, a problem. It just might have been a moment. Maybe he's home in bed.'

Joe nodded.

'I wouldn't know what to tell the police,' said Barry.

'Would they not be able to do something with your phone? Trace the call or whatever. No?'

Barry shrugged uselessly.

'Well we have to do something,' Joe sighed.

'What though?'

'What do you know about him?'

Barry shook his head. Nothing. Not much anyway.

'He has a mother who lives, um, I don't know where she lives. Northside somewhere I think. She doesn't like crowds. He lives in Dolphin's Barn. He drinks in pubs I've never heard of.'

'What pubs?'

'I can't remember. I'd never heard of them. Not in the centre. South Circular Road, places like that. I don't know.'

'What else?'

'He has a brother. Half brother. Older. Who has a girlfriend and a child. He wants to travel. Wants to buy a suit. That's it. He likes veal. He likes to eat veal.'

Joe frowned at him and shook his head.

'Right. Ok.' He sat forward in his chair. 'We have to find out more about him. We have to find out where he lives. To do that we need to find someone who knows him. So. Therefore. I think we should go down to where you found him, you know, originally, on the quays there, or wherever, and we should ask around.'

He shrugged.

'Ask other rent boys I mean. They'll know about him. More than we do.'

It was a good idea. It was way too early, they'd have to wait until close to midnight probably, maybe a little earlier given it was a Sunday. But it was a good idea.

'Do you not need to be, um, elsewhere?'

'No.'

'Sylvia isn't . . .'

'No.'

'Ok.'

'Can we eat first? I'm starving.'

'Yeah. We can't do it till late anyway. There'll be no one there. Why are you doing this?'

'I don't want to be static.'

'Static?'

'Yeah, don't worry about it, you'll understand when you're older and you have kids of your own, oops, maybe not, forget about it, what food have you got? I've had no breakfast you know. There's no food in my house, just fruit and yoghurts and something called skimmed milk. Do you have sausages?'

Barry thought that maybe he had caught Joe on a good day, or a bad day, depending on how you looked at it. A different day. He seemed a little cowed. Less like himself, more like himself. Something along those lines. He thought about it for a moment and was then distracted, backwards, reminded, as if he had forgotten, about Kevin and the missed call, murdered Kevin and the voice in the car.

'No' he said. 'I'm sorry. Really sorry. I don't.'

Delly cowered. She thought now that she could be seen by malignant air things. Air creatures. Birds. She thought that they could see her on her pyre like food and they'd sweep in low and get her. She feared mostly for her eyes, useless as they were – she had a fear for the safety of her eyes.

The scream had been a single moment that seemed now to have carried on somewhere and she thought what it was was that she was remembering it and it sounded like it was happening again, when it wasn't, it was just that she was remembering the sound and her mind replayed it and she thought she was hearing a new one, not the same one, repeated. It was short, the scream. It was not like in the movies. It was not harsh and pin shaped. It was low like a cleaver. It was a short broad blade, awful really. Terrible. It reminded her of something and for a long while, worried by birds, she didn't know what it was that it reminded her of. And then she remembered. Damn it.

She pressed the alarm. The house alarm. It wasn't an alarm. It was a bell. A buzzer. A summoning thing. She pressed it, expecting Kitty to arrive, but it was Mrs Cotter who came through, in her dusting pinafore, not smiling so much as not frowning, as she appeared at the door, then disappeared across the room, coming closer to Delly like a mist.

'What day is it?' she asked.

'Sunday Miss Roche.'

'What's happened?'

'Nothing Miss Roche. Dr George and Miss Flood are both out this afternoon, so Miss Flood asked whether I might come up to the house.'

'Where are they?'

'I don't know Miss Roche. Miss Flood left only recently. We don't really know where Dr George is.'

'What do you mean we don't know where he is?'

'He's not answering his phone Miss Roche.'

Kitty was right. She should get a nurse. It was not fair. She shuddered.

'Can you close the curtains?'

'Alright. Will I leave the window open?'

Good God. She hadn't realised it was open.

'Yes. Christ. I mean no – close it is what I mean. God.'

'It's a lovely day though Miss.'

'It's always a lovely bloody day,' said Delly quietly.

Mrs Cotter clarified herself and closed the door behind her. That was all. In the gloom Delly rested her eyes, stood them down, tried to get them to relax, unwind, blur. Danger past. No birds now, shattering the glass, finding the gap, clawing at her breast. She heard the scream replayed, a machete blow of a scream, a broad blade in the arm, a male scream, abrupt and fore-shortened, clipped, cut off.

That night, as the thing came down, the whirligig thing, the fly-ing thing, the bird. No. The helicopter. As the helicopter came down she heard a scream. No she didn't. Did she? No. Did she? She wasn't even out of the house by then. She was on her way. She couldn't have heard anything like it. But that's what she remembered now. She squeezed her wrist and tried to think about the curtains and Mrs Cotter, and Kitty gone off like that. But she could hear the old scream, replayed and replayed. As if it was a thing she remembered.

Maybe there had been a moment, as the engine cut out – did the engine cut out? – while the storm drew its breath, a moment of near silence, of a hesitating world, three quarter turned, paus-ing, Delly at the windows, heading for the terrace and the steps down, going towards the garden and the concrete circle with its yellow H, maybe there had been a tiny silence then, in which she had heard this scream. This scream. That one. Low and knowing. Here we go. Into death.

That's what it reminded her of. That's what she remembered.

It was curious to her now, that here she was, lying in the gloom, remembering that night, and the pain in her no greater than when she remembered nothing. Curious, that was.

🍴

Kitty Flood gave her full attention to her driving, trying not to kill anybody. At traffic lights she took sips from her can of Fanta. At roundabouts she whimpered and the tyres squealed. The radio was on and off, off and on, depending on what she needed to know. She turned it down to hear if she was in the right gear for example, or whether there were problems in the suspension or the axle or the pistons or the valves. Those were the words she knew. She also knew how to drive assertively, how to be confi-dent in the race, how to be safe towards children and cyclists and elderly drivers. But she did not know how to park. She was not good at corners, particularly. She disliked the semiotic clutter of road signs. It confused her. She was in fine form all the same, and sang when the road was clear. She had a lovely singing voice.

As before, Sylvia Porterhouse was waiting for her, alone this time, in black trousers and a green top, looking fresher and younger than she had before. Oh yes? Hmmm. Her shoes looked cheap against the chrome and the steel blue carpet. The setting was better though, far removed from pub sandwiches and lager pooled tables and low stools. It was air conditioned, waiter service, a view of the sea, the low sound of strings, the high scent of money – all of that. Paul Rafferty on the terrace with a government minister. That film director fellow eating scrambled eggs alone in a booth. Red leatherette. String quartet. Some other of the bloody brackets were filled with anonymous wealthies, and varied names, some of which Kitty could remember. A table near the window stopped their chat and stared at her. She had no clue who they were.

Sylvia was at the bar, sipping a Bloody Mary and pushing a single olive around an oily bowl.

They greeted each other with a handshake, though the English woman leaned forward as if for a kiss, and Kitty pretended not to notice, and smiled and averted her gaze, as if taking in the room for the first time, remarking that it was a while since she'd last been there and they had changed the layout of the place and she was not sure that she liked it. This was an untruth. The bar was unaltered, she had been there the previous Tuesday for a pasta lunch on the terrace, alone.

They found themselves a booth, the next along from the scrambled egg director, Kitty unwilling to risk the climb onto the bar stool or the possibility of sweating in the sun.

'Do you smoke a pipe?' she asked Miss Porterhouse.

'Do I . . . ?'

'Smoke a pipe.'

'Is this some euphemism?'

Oh dear.

'No, not at all. I just wondered whether perhaps you smoked a pipe. I believe it has become fashionable. For women. Again. Or is this a new thing? In London. Magazines. Tell me this.'

She smiled too widely and laughed too lightly and her hair shook brightly, against the red leatherette.

'No I don't smoke a pipe.'

'Alright.'

They ordered, Kitty ordered, some orange juice, a pot of coffee, a ham and cheese omelette, some sautéed potatoes, toast and butter. Sylvia ordered some orange juice, a pot of tea, two Spanish sausages and some granary bread. Together they ordered a bottle of sparkling mineral water and a bowl of pistachio nuts.

They talked about :

- Traffic.
- The location of the house. Kitty was a little vague on this, determined to be suspicious of all questions which could possibly relate to Delly. She was protecting Delly now. She was in a new place.
- Property prices.
- London.
- New York.
- Spanish sausages. What makes a good omelette.
- Neapolitan coffee.
- The Amalfi coast.
- Skin cancer.
- Delly. Cancer of the colon. Caught late. Careful. Kitty cut it short with an oblique reference to her general good humoured perseverance and the quality of her care.
- Love.
- –
- The Celtic Tiger.
- Europe.
- Currencies and monetary policy and the European Central Bank and sterling.
- Taxis, the lack of them and their cost and their difficult and unpredictable shape, size and quality.

Suddenly,

'Where are you staying?' asked Kitty.

'I'm, um, in a hotel in Temple Bar, Dean's or something. Some literary illusion.'

There was a little silence. Kitty simply regarded her, prised apart a nut, popped it in her mouth, held steady, said nothing, regarded.

'Allusion I mean – don't I?'

Kitty chewed and slowly nodded and raised an eyebrow.

'Last night,' said the English woman, her accent blowing stronger in the sigh, 'I stayed with Joe.'

'Last night?'

She frowned.

'And the night before.'

'Is that a sexual relationship?'

It seemed to Kitty that she spent half a second considering whether to tell her to feck off with her cheek; and another half second, the first question having been answered negatively, whether to tell her a lie; and another half second then, in light of this double negative, considering whether the truth would be to her advantage; and another half second, in the light of this affirmative, considering what formulation to employ to provide the fullest possible answer to the question asked as well as to at least three others not asked but certainly, definitely (and Kitty arranged her face to confirm it) implied.

'Oh for him it very much is yes, though for me it is more a question of free phone calls and keep fit.'

Kitty allowed herself to giggle and blush and make a charmed face. Her weekend had altered significantly.

'So do you have a, partner then? In London? Hmmm?'

'No I don't. Not currently. Not at the moment.'

'As does, and does your preference . . . do your preferences tend towards, uh, men or women?'

Sylvia blushed now. Was she doing this right? Kitty? Was she? She had never done it before. Not really. She had read about it and written about it and she had brought herself to the point of doing it, to the brink, but she had never, actually, as such, done it.

'Or children?' she added, as a joke.

'I'm, uh, ha ha, I'm, I suppose, if I had to name it, a bisexual. Officially.'

Kitty nodded, threw a pistachio in her mouth without de-shelling. Realised immediately. Didn't want to take it out or spit, due to the intensity of the gaze, the importance of the moment. She rattled it around a bit. Big damn thing.

'And you?'

'Mwe?'

Sylvia gave a lovely buttery smile. Her cheeks were cherry red, English rose, leatherette.

'I'm muffly a momam . . .'

The nut propelled itself from the back of her tongue in a kind of skimming stone way, ricocheted off the underside of her front teeth, shot straight through the conditioned air and splashed, *plop*, into the natural fizz of her mineral water. Bottled at source.

'Oh dear,' she breathed.

Sylvia laughed, but in a nice way, in a funny way, in a way which forgave her her spittle and her fat mouth and her indelicate manner. In a way which suggested that puking a pistachio nut into her water was not the end of the matter. No it wasn't. Not by a long way. There was more to be discovered here. Amongst these women.

There had been a time, shortly after they had come together, Delly and herself, while they were still astonished by their situation, while they were still utterly convinced, when a man had come from somewhere in the mid west or the north or the Canadian Rockies and had courted Kitty Flood, in the belief that she was about to become very famous indeed, like an Irish Martha Pullman or a woman Tom Porter or a white Aysha DeLoite. He had been misinformed. His misinformation was considerable. She was not about to become any of those people. Those things. But he courted her assiduously. He was after fame. That was all he wanted. He was thirty, thin, earnest, black haired, handsome, and had no sense of humour. He wanted the fame of being her lover. The lover of the woman who had written some masterpiece – which existed entirely in his head. She was not about to do any such thing. But he persisted, courting her all the time, every day, with flowers and phone calls and sudden lovelorn appearances outside shops and cabs and theatre doorways. Flowers and chocolates and phone calls and a puppy. Which she had refused, damn animals, she'd never liked them, not even as a girl – horses and dogs and rabbits and boys. Delly had quite taken to him, strangely enough. Not the puppy, the man. Jaunty, she called him. Jaunty. Though he was in fact called John T. Falkirk, out of Wisconsin or somewhere, north country, after fame and nothing else, courting her assiduously, charmlessly, as if romance was an argument. He wrote her long letters which spoke clumsily, endlessly, about her use of language and

340

her understanding of the human condition and her place in history. She told him that he was barking up the wrong tree, he had the wrong end of the stick, she was playing for the other side, he was not her cup of tea, and yet he continued to insist that she had a marvellous way with words. Eventually Delly took matters in hand and for the first and only time in their relationship they slept with a man. Together. In the same bed at the same time, they had a man together. It was not a success. No. He was confused, Jaunty was. There was too much of them. There was too little of him. He tried to involve himself, he tried to partake, and they tried to encourage him, they tried to involve him, they tried to be generous and patient and kind. But he was hopeless and they knew what they were doing and he seemed overwhelmed by the options and they were laughing too much, and they were talking too much, and they had a shorthand by then, a physical gift, an understanding, which he lacked, and all he could think of to do was to stick himself into whatever gap opened up, so to speak, even though the girls (a long time ago, this) were much more interested, what with all the new-fangled equipment they had in their possession at this time, in turning the tables and seeing how he liked accommodating rather than being accommodated, at which he loudly (too loudly) protested, and was pretty much, in that case, no fun whatsoever, so that Delly, eventually, even though it had been her idea, in the first place, and even though she had taken it upon herself to convince first Kitty, and then Jaunty, that it might be a laugh, even though she was, without a doubt, the main instigator of the whole mid Saturday afternoon Park Avenue seventh floor guest bedroom experiment, she put a stop to it, Delly did, by telling him finally, and with some determination, to piss off back to Duluth, or wherever it was he was from, and not to be bothering them again with his supplications, seeing as how he couldn't hack it in the real world, repressed North American milk drinker that he was, out of his depth with the European women. They felt bad afterwards. They felt bad and they worried that he would kill himself. He did nothing of the sort. He tried instead to sell his story to the New York Post, who decided not to run with it after Delly made a call. Jaunty disappeared then. They never saw him no more. That had been Kitty's last experience with a man. Delly's too, as far she was aware, though they had, out of curiosity, watched Thomas fuck Jean Paul on the balcony one evening in France, thinking they were invisible, only to have Thomas cry out, as he came in a terrifying arc which vaulted the entire length of Jean Paul's body, landing like bird shit on his hair, 'See what you're missing, bitches.' It had become such a familiar phrase that Jean Paul had it embroidered into the backs of a set of dressing gowns which he gave them the following Christmas.

That was all they knew, together, of men. Delly knew more of course, from before, on her own. But before was before. It was not since.

———

'I'm sorry, that's very embarrassing.'

Sylvia laughed and flapped her hands.

'Oh don't be silly. Not half as embarrassing as it going the other way and you choking. Embarrassing would be me trying to do the Heimlich manoeuvre on you. In this place. You turning purple doll. Imagine.'

She was really quite sweet. Kitty found herself drawn mostly to the sound of her voice. London, definitely, but variable. It sounded easy. Human.

'So?' she asked.

'Women,' said Kitty, and Sylvia nodded slowly and her gentle smile remained. 'All women, since years and years.'

She had used the plural, but there had just been Delly. Why had she used the plural? There was some compulsion to accumulate. She didn't correct herself.

A telephone rang. They both rummaged in their bags as if in a race, but it was Kitty's. The display read 'Home'.

'Yes?'

'Miss Flood it's Mrs Cotter.'

'Hi.'

'Dr George has turned up. He said he was asleep – that he slept late. Well, anyway, he's here now and says he'll be here all day. So I'm going to head off back home if that's ok?'

'Yeah that's fine. Thanks. I'll be back later on. Is Delly alright?'

'Yes Miss Flood, she's been dozing, and she even ate some fruit.'

'Really?'

'Yes. She said she was hungry and asked for a banana.'

'Great. That's great. Ok. I'll see you tomorrow. Thank you Mrs Cotter.'

She smiled broadly. Things were looking up. A banana.

'Things are alright?'

'Oh yes. Absolutely.'

'It must be a strain, with Delly so ill.'

'It can be, but, oh well, we're a good little team. Mrs Cotter and myself. And the doctor, um, he's um, Delly's adopted . . .'

'Oh yeah. What's his name?'

'George. Addison-Blake. Doctor.'

'Yes. What's he like?'

'Between you and me dear? I don't like him. He gives me the creeps. Skinny. But Delly is so hopeless – she refuses to have a full time nursing staff or to see any of her regular doctors. As soon as she got out of hospital, after all she'd been through I suppose it was understandable, she just wanted to lie in her bed and fade away. She was terribly depressed, silent. It was horrible. She didn't want to live. Then Dr George arrived, almost unannounced, and just started treating her, without even waiting to be asked. Took one look at her and immediately had her on drips and drugs and potions and powders and God knows, and gave Mrs Cotter instructions on her food, had the bathroom converted, bought a wheelchair, so, to be honest dear it was a huge relief. She improved for a while, became more chatty, more positive, but slipped back into her depression then. Physically she's better though, than she had been.'

She paused. Considered. Said it:

'If he hadn't come over I really think she'd be dead by now.'

There. She thought it was true. She sipped her water. She wanted more nuts but was afraid of them now.

'It's been a battle. She was due to return to hospital for various tests, and to have her colostomy situation sorted out, but she's refused all that. Just point blank refuses. So he's had to look after all that as best he can. Which I think he's done. He's not hugely optimistic though. He thinks maybe a year. That was about a month ago. I haven't really discussed it with him lately.'

'When is he going back to New York?'

'Oh God knows. That depends on Delly really. On how she is. She stopped eating a couple of days ago. Got it into her head to

343

stop eating. I think she'd seen a documentary on the H-Blocks. Anyway. She's just this minute had a banana. Isn't that the business?'

'Great. What about his hearing?'

'Funny you should ask. She's started hearing screams. Probably nightmares. Or daydreams I suppose. Perhaps vivid dreams are a side effect of something. One of the drugs. There seems to be several.'

'No, sorry, I mean, Dr Addison-Blake's hearing?'

'His hearing? It's fine as far as I know. Though he may be somewhat tone deaf. He plays the piano very badly, on the floor below me, when I'm, uh, trying to work. Of course he can't hear his phone when it doesn't suit him either.'

'No,' she said, pinching one eye shut and pursing her lips, trying to hide laughter Kitty thought. 'I mean his hearing in New York? His, you know, disci . . .'

'In New York?' What the hell was she talking about? 'I can't imagine his hearing being any better or worse in New York. Hmmm? Is there something I'm missing here?'

'Yes.'

She laughed, Sylvia Porterhouse did. Not attractively. It brought blood to the bags beneath her eyes.

'What?'

'His, um, what is it called? It is called a hearing isn't it? Like a court hearing? You know?'

'What hearing?'

'He's facing suspension isn't he? Or his licence is, oh what is it? Did you not know this? Disciplinary proceedings. Hang on.'

She was rummaging now in her large bag.

'I think I have it here.'

Kitty felt a chill, a predictable, ugly sliver of unease, enter her from the fingers and crawl rapidly, like a multi-legged thing, towards her heart.

'Here we are.'

She pulled out a large file, a cardboard document folder, and leafed through its many pages.

'What the hell is that?'

'Oh I just put together all I could find about . . . where is it? . . . about Gilmore . . . here we are.'

She handed Kitty a photocopy of a newspaper cutting. Handwritten in the margin was 'New York Times, Metro Section, Page 12, February 14th.'

Drugs Giant's Son Suspended

Dr George Addison-Blake has been suspended by the State Health Department, pending investigation of his handling of three admissions to the emergency room of St Agnes & Angels Hospital in NYC, where he was attending in emergency medicine. His licence suspension continues until such a time as a hearing can be arranged before the disciplinary board of the State Health Department. The board has so far been unable to arrange a date for a hearing. It is believed that Dr Addison-Blake, the adopted son of the late Daniel Gilmore, is out of the country. Daniel Gilmore established Gilmore Pharmaceuticals in the late 1950s, and was chief executive of the company until his death in a helicopter crash in 1979.

The company remains one of the top five drugs giants in the world, and was recently the subject of speculation concerning a merger with Italian rival Ridolfi. An unnamed source within the company has said that Dr Addison-Blake has no association with Gilmore Pharmaceuticals whatsoever. It is believed that the doctor may be in Ireland, where Mr Gilmore's widow, Fidelma, is believed to be seriously ill.

'Jesus Christ' said Kitty Flood.
'You didn't know?'
'Jesus Christ.'
'You didn't know. God.'
'I mean Jesus Christ.'
'You had no idea.'
'Jesus Christ though.'
'Sorry.'

'Where did you . . .? Why did you . . .?'

'I was just chasing up all references I could find to Gilmore Pharmaceuticals. This one didn't really stick in my mind, because it's you know, not directly related. Sorry.'

Kitty read the clipping again. How had this happened? How had she not known about it? They had friends in New York. They had a bloody lawyer in New York. How could they not have been alerted to this? How had he kept it from them? She read it a third time. Three admissions. Three. The guy was a damn danger. They had an incompetent in charge. A deceiver. A fraud.

'Jesus God,' she said.

She tried to work out dates. The date of his arrival, the newspaper date. It didn't say how long. How long since. She tried to work out the chronology, the sequence, the plot. He had left after being suspended? Yes? She didn't know. Had he known? Was he suspended after he left? No. Why would he leave otherwise? They had not summoned him. Kitty had not called him to her. He had come unbidden. Out of the blue west. Skinny like a needle. Weirdo was on the run. He was a fraud. He was deceiving them. He was discredited. Undeserving.

Her mind galloped homewards.

Undeserving.

Chased by money.

'I have to go.'

'Oh.'

She gathered her things. Threw the clipping in her bag.

'Give me that,' she said, pointing at the file.

'I can't give you that.'

'Why not?'

'It's mine.'

Kitty sucked a lip.

'Is there more?'

'More what?'

'Things I should know for example. The gardener is a rapist? The security men are wanted for robbery? That the Cotters make their own . . .'

She was going to say 'porn movies' but she stopped herself. There were weird associations forming in her head. It was money. Everything was money.

346

'Give me it.'

'No.'

She made a lunge across the table for the folder, knocking water and nuts all over. Sylvia Porterhouse gave a little shriek, and half rose, her grip on the cardboard firmer than Kitty's, and they tugged at it a couple of times.

'There's nothing in there. Nothing like that.'

'Then give me it.'

'I'll make copies. I'm not going to just hand it over. I'll make copies. Jesus.'

Kitty hesitated. She sensed a general lull. A communal gaze directed at their table. She thought she probably had resources sufficient to this.

'Ok,' she said, and let go. 'Make copies. When you have a full set of copies call me on my mobile. I'll have them picked up.'

'My trousers are soaked.'

Kitty pulled her purse from her bag. She threw two fifty pound notes on the table.

'My resources are sufficient,' she said. 'Don't call the house.'

She prised herself from the red leatherette and proceeded, stately as she could, but swiftly, towards the exit.

Joe asked him about the mechanics of being a rent boy. As he understood it.

They sat in the warm room, fending off the sunlight with half-hourly curtain adjustments, listening to a quiet Hark Angels CD and their various dumb phones – useless silences, cups of tea.

Barry felt defensive on Kevin's behalf, ready to insist that it was no less dignified than being, for example, a radio presenter, an on-air chatter, a *DJ*. It was no more exposing than that. He was not called upon to actually say it, but felt that he would have, if pushed. But he did feel somewhat under the glare of Joe's heterosexual family man perspective. Maybe he was being paranoid. But he thought that Joe thought (though would probably never say, not unless stupefied by drink or dope or boredom), that really this kind of kidnap/murder scenario was an occupational hazard, something to be expected really, when you spent your time offering up your ass to total strangers, and which couldn't be all that remarkable, and should not be taken too seriously and that sitting around worrying about it was something of an over-reaction.

'I mean, you just hang around in particular places and guys come along?'

'Yeah. I suppose.'

'What happens then?'

'I don't know. Sex of some description.'

'In the car?'

'I suppose.'

'Yuck.'

'You've never had sex in a car?'

Joe thought for a moment.

'No, as it happens. I don't believe I have.'

He had gone out for something to eat and had returned with a sweating bag of Thai food and a six pack of beers. He was on his third. He poked around in the remains of his Pad Thai and scooped up some bean curd. His phone had rung twice. Both times he had stared at the display for a moment and not taken the call. Now he'd turned it off.

'But how,' he said, 'how do you have sex in a car? I mean man man sex. You know. How do you do that?'

'How do you mean?'

'I mean it just seems to be difficult, angle wise, in terms of, you know. Unless you have a big car.'

'Same as for man woman sex I imagine.'

'Well that's going to be a lot easier isn't it. Cars are designed for that. Lower the passenger seat, there you are. But bum sex is different isn't it? You need, like, more space, really, like one of those big family things. Cruisers.'

He laughed at himself.

'Cruisers,' he said again.

'Christ Joe. Bum sex?'

'Whatever.'

'You can do other stuff as well.'

'Not me. I can't do any of it. I can barely be in the same room as you.'

He seemed about to continue, but his smile faded and he stared into his beer bottle.

'Does he advertise?'

'What?'

'Do they place ads in magazines and stuff?'

'Who?'

'Rent boys.'

'Yeah. I hadn't thought of that.'

'No you hadn't. Ok. Write me a list of male whore mags and I'll go mortify myself down at the newsagents.'

Barry sent him into town so that he could pick up some gay free sheets as well from a bookshop. He went off with his list, looking like a man going off to war. Barry was terribly tempted to give him a peck on the cheek at the door of the flat, but he was afraid that he wouldn't come back.

———

Male escorts advertised in the pages of various Dublin listings and event guides, as well as gay and straight, mainstream and marginal publications, and one 'Adult Contact' magazine (duplications excluded):

- Jason, 19, swimmer's body. Friendly, unhurried service, out calls only, 087 ——
- Brendan, 24, guaranteed satisfaction, in/out, WE, massage, call : 086 ——
- Paul & Sean, 25 & 26, visit our dungeon, for full S&M service, CP, CBT, TT, etc, no red. Please call if interested, references available. 087 ——
- Grant, 18, smooth body, nine stone, 5'10", brown hair, blue eyes, WE, versatile, out calls only. 087 ——
- Muscular Mike, 28, body builder, toned, XWE, broad minded (bondage etc), in/out 24hrs, 086 ——
- Visit HE-MALE, for a refreshing massage. Dean, 22, or Henry, 27, will provide you with the best service in town. Relaxed, friendly, no rush. Out call also by arrangement. Call us now! 087 ——
- Luke, 28 – for the time of your life! Sensual massage, indulge your fantasy! Call 086 ——
- Fintan – 25, smooth, very handsome, luxurious city centre

location, full service, in or out calls. Call the expert, on
087 ——-
- Lee – Asian guy, 23, out calls only : 087 ——
- Edward, 19, will visit you at your home or hotel, for sensual,
  un-hurried massage. Great body, WE. 087 ——
- Steve, 18, good looking guy, versatile service, central
  Dublin. 087 ——
- Boss Boy – 20, versatile, 7″, slim, smooth, most scenes,
  bondage, role playing etc. Call 086 —— – ask for Matt.
- John – 27, hairy chested, man's man, in/out, 9″, top, go on,
  spoil yourself. 087 ——
- Pete – 18, btm, good looking Dublin guy, 7″, bubble butt,
  satisfaction guaranteed.
- Gene – Black guy, 25, massage expert, top, exotic, out calls
  only. 086 ——

'You can call them.'
'We'll take it in turns.'
'We fucking won't. You're the homosexual.'
'So?'
'So I wouldn't know what to say.'
'Joe I've never done this before.'
'Yeah but there'll be, you know, terminology, with which I am,
unfamiliar.'
'You're unbelievable. What happened to your great quest?'
'My what?'
'You were seeking out the underbelly of Dublin last I heard. Is
that on hold?'
'I'm the one who went out and bought them. That Adult
Contacts thing cost a tenner. A tenner for Christ's sake. And the
look I got from the guy at the check out in Spar. Jesus Christ.
There's terrible homophobia about. What does WE mean?'
'Well endowed?'
'See? See? I wouldn't have known that.'
Barry dialled the first one. There was no answer.
'Look at these ones, Jesus, in this thing. What is CBT?'
'You don't want to know. It rang out.'
'No, tell me.'
'Hang on.'

'Hello?'

'Yeah hi is that Brendan?'

'Yes, hi.'

'Um, I saw your ad in, um, in something or other, I was wondering if you could help me.'

Joe was giggling.

'Sure. I'm 24, twelve stone, smooth body, six and half inches cut. I can be active or . . .'

'No, uh, I was . . .'

' . . . passive. I'm available tonight up to midnight.'

'No, I was just wondering whether you could help me with, uh, something else. I'm trying to get in touch with someone called Kevin.'

'What?'

'Well I know this guy called Kevin who is a rent boy and I'm trying . . .'

The line went dead.

'Seriously, what is CBT?'

'You really don't want to know. What am I supposed to ask? They're all going to tell me to fuck off.'

'You can only try. None of them says GSOH. I think that's a failing. If I was trying to find a male prostitute I think I'd need to find one with a really really really GSOH.'

'Paul and Sean.'

He got an answering machine.

'Is there any point in leaving a message?'

'Only if you're happy for The Dungeon to have you in their little black book.'

He hung up.

'CP is corporal punishment right? Spanking and that? So what's CBT? And TT? What's TT, Barry? Is that, like, Isle of Man stuff? Motor racing leathers? Oh I get it. I Love Man. Like the ads they used to have. Is that it?'

'Joe shut up.'

He dialled the number for Grant, 18, smooth body, nine stone. He was greeted by the recorded voice of Kevin.

'Hi. Thanks for calling. I'm busy at the moment, so please leave a name and a number and I'll call you back as soon as I can. Bye.'

'Shit. Hi Kevin, it's Barry again. Um, I'm really worried about you? So if you get any of these messages call me on my mobile ok?'

Joe was looking at him.

'What?'

'Grant is Kevin.'

'Wow. Really? Is it the same number?'

Barry looked at it. Checked the number stored in his phone. They were the same.

'So now I have to ask these guys if they know someone called Kevin or Grant.'

'Or God knows.'

'Shit.'

'Do you have a photo of him?'

'Joe. Christ's sake. No I don't.'

He proceeded. It went like this:

- Muscular Mike – told Barry to fuck off and hung up.
- HE-MALE – answering machine.
- Luke – answered, listened and politely told Barry that he really didn't know what he was talking about.
- Fintan - answered, listened, claimed to know someone called Grant, but that he wasn't on the game, didn't know anyone called Kevin, offered Barry a Sunday night discount.
- Lee – no answer.
- Edward – no answer.
- Steve – answering machine interrupted by Steve, listened, said he knew Grant, gave a description which sounded plausible, said he didn't know his second name or where he lived or anything else about him, promised to tell him that Barry was looking for him if he saw him.
- Boss Boy – Barry recognised the number as he dialled it. Kevin. Same number, same message. On the notepad in front him Barry now had Kevin/Grant/Matt.
- John – answered, listened, hung up.
- Pete – answered, listened, claimed he knew Matt well, that they often 'doubled up', said he hadn't seen him in about a week, but then gave a description which was clearly not of the same person.
- Gene – no answer.

Barry accepted a glass of white wine and wished Joe would produce a joint.

'You think you should call back that one who said he knew him, who gave the right description?'

'I don't know if it was the *right* description. It just sounded, you know, like it wasn't a completely different person. I'm confused about age though now. He said his guy, Grant, was about 22. The ad for Grant says 18 but the ad for Matt says 20. And I thought Kevin was maybe 19 or twenty.'

'Jesus, well, it's all the same kind of area. Jesus.'

They did nothing else for a while.

During the course of the afternoon and evening, his sister called him back, Will called him back, and two other friends called him on his mobile. His sister had dumped the policeman over a disagreement regarding drugs. She liked her dope and he felt compromised, insisting that he might have to arrest her. This was played out to its full sexual fantasy potential and had then become tiresome apparently. So that was that. She offered to get a number for him but Barry declined, thinking that it would be the same as just formally calling the police, given that he'd only met the guy once and had been rude to him, and that he and Joe were in any case already doing what the police would probably do, eventually, after they did nothing for a long time.

Will was looking for a drinking buddy, his girlfriend having decamped to Rome on business. Barry declined, apologised for earlier, semi-explained the situation, leaving out any detail which might have made him sound sensible, and hung up. With the two friends on the mobile, he just shouted the land line number at them, in a way that Joe seemed to find hilarious, and though they both called back, they seemed slightly put off by Barry telling them that he was looking for a rent boy and asking whether they knew any. He tried to explain. They didn't seem to get it. Neil hummed and hawed and confessed to having once visited a male brothel in Amsterdam. Terry declared that he would never pay for sex, not on his salary, and offered to sleep with Barry for drugs. Barry explained again. They were silent, pensive, they didn't like to hear of it. They were no help.

Joe watched television, flicking between stations, yawning.

'What time do you want to go down there?'

'About eleven I suppose.'

Joe checked his watch.

'You don't have to wait around,' Barry told him.

'No it's ok.'

'I can go down there myself.'

'No I want to. You'll need the car as well. We might have to hang around for a while. I want to.'

He settled on a documentary then, about the loss of a ship, about the sinking by storm of a passenger ship, about the sudden flood and the list, and the flowing dark and the horror of creaking things. Barry sat still and watchful, his mobile cupped in his hand, its green light winking at him like a rescue beacon, bobbing on a high swell.

Joe had switched his phone off when he'd gone into Barry's flat. She hadn't called before then. When he left to get the food he'd switched it on again. She'd left two messages.

'Joe hi doll. Weird world isn't it? She's walked out on me, don't ask, I was the bearer of bad news. Listen, I'm gonna get a cab back to your place, save you hassle, so I hope you're there and just not answering. If not, call me will ya? I don't have a key doll. Later.'

And:

'Joe where the fuck are you? I'm standing outside your house. Call me will ya?'

That had been twenty minutes earlier.

So he'd called her, and she was, at this stage, in the local pub, an indescribably dodgy place two streets away from his house where he had once been asked whether he was the guy looking for 'a piece'.

'Jesus be careful in there.'

'Yeah. It's tame doll. Should see my local. Where are you?'

'Something's come up? Bit of an emergency situation with Barry. I'm with Barry basically. It's an emergency.'

'Jesus, what's happened?'

He really didn't want to tell her. He didn't think it would stand up.

354

'His brother's been killed.'

'*Oh Jesus.*'

'Yeah. So I'm with Barry, you know? I have to be with him. What I'll do is I'll drop over there now, let you in, you can pick up your stuff, we'll get you back into your hotel. Ok? I'm on my way.'

There was a big silence.

'Sylvia?'

'*What happened to his brother?*'

'Oh, car crash. Early hours. Head injuries. You know.'

Another big silence.

'*And why am I moving back into a hotel?*'

'Well. I have to be with Barry. You know. I won't be . . .'

'*Is he not with his family?*'

Jesus.

'No. They're all . . . They rejected him. They threw him out when he came out. When he informed them I mean, that he was gay. Is gay. Hello?'

'*Yeah. Are you bullshitting me?*'

'No.'

'*You are aren't you?*'

'No.'

'*I'll give him a call. Offer my sympathies.*'

Jesus.

'Ok look. Shit. Ok. His brother isn't dead. I can't tell you the nature of the emer . . .'

'*Fuck's sake Joe.*'

'Look it's an emergency.'

'*Yeah right. That's so fucking lame Joe it really is you know? Using Barry to get me off your back. You wanted me out of your house all you had to do was fucking ask. We're adults Joe. At least we're meant to be. Jesus Christ. It's not like I'm ooh, Joe's so sweet, I'm just falling head over heels, ooh. I wasn't moving in Joe. Fuck's sake. It's not like you're much fucking good at the fucking, you know?*'

He could see her in the pub. The guys twisted round in their bar stools to look at her. The pool game paused, her raised voice the only sound now. Oh they'd love this.

'Sylvia for Christ's sake. I'm not making it up. Barry has a real genuine fucking emergency in full fucking swing. Unlike your

355

bad episode of The fucking Avengers which has had me traipsing around the entire country the last couple of days having – no, not having, taping – taping bizarre conversations with enormous women.'

There was a gap. Horrible quietude.

'You're jealous!'

'Oh right. I'm jealous. Of a vast lesbian.'

She started to laugh.

'Oh Joe you're so pathetic. Really. It's beyond pathetic. You're like a ten year old. You're world's so small. You're terrified. You just want to be left alone don't you? With your toys and the odd wank and no nasty girls to come and frighten you.'

There was a horrible sneer in her voice. It transfixed him. He felt ten years old and terrified.

'Oh fuck off,' he managed, in a voice like his daughter's.

'Yeah right. I will.'

She hung up. He could picture it. The entire pub, bastards all, breaking into sustained and whooping applause.

🍴

She drove too fast for the first five miles, then slowed as things grew colder. Don't go charging in.

She stopped in a woodland lay-by and rummaged in her bag and found a number for Dr Mullen. He was not answering. Sunday. She left a message to the effect that she wished to talk to him as soon as possible about Delly's care, about nursing staff, about palliative facilities, about arranging, with alacrity, a home visit. She rummaged some more and called their New York lawyer, Elliman. He wasn't there either. Time zones, Sabbaths, all were against her. She left a message which, she thought, communicated sufficient dissatisfaction and alarm without actually, directly, going in to detail. Call me, she told everyone. Call me on my mobile. Anytime.

She sat and did nothing for a while. She determined, eventually, and with some regret, not to say anything to him. Not yet. She thought she would talk to Mullen first. And Elliman. Get the facts. Legal, medical. Get the chronology. Get it right. And then tell Delly, and then, when there were men around, tell the weirdo to piss off. Back to New York.

Because, frankly, he gave her the creeps.

Delly had eaten food. She had taken it upon herself to eat. This had not been forced.

She understood that something was different. That she was perhaps, finally, with a little hunger and a lull in the senses, getting ready to die. Her mind was preparing her body. Her body was bracing itself. Something like that. She tried to think of nothing, to open up a clear space where death could put its foot, but there was a clutter of old words and dead faces and other days. A swirl of things.

She chewed her apricot slices. This was practically a second meal. She peeked into the garden. It looked nice.

George had come and had changed the bag and had asked her how she was and had rushed off again without giving her any of her tablets. So she had to ring the bell to get him back. Then he took her temperature and listened to her chest and took her pulse and asked her whether she had any pain.

Any pain.

'Not much,' she said. 'Not so much today.'

'And your head,' he wanted to know, 'is that clearer?'

'It is,' she said, and this was true. Her head was clearer.

So he told her then that he was taking her off a couple of things, just to see how it went, a couple of the stronger things, just to see how she fared, and she could go back on them anytime she wanted. Just let him know.

So she didn't get any pills at all. Not a one.

It meant he was giving up on her. That there was no longer any point. She was on her way. She would soon be leaving. The alternative – that she was getting better, a little better, and he was testing that to see exactly how much better – was simply not possible. Though she found, irritatingly, that there was a part of her that wondered, or held out hope, or clung to that sliver of life, or did some other bravely noble horrid useless thing. Death, she declared to her rebellious parts. It's death come to get you. Ready or not. Shut up and listen.

But she could not make herself interested. Not fully. She day-dreamed and drifted off. She yawned and stretched her legs. She played with the television. She felt okay. She felt clearer than she had. The pain was vague and hard to place. It seemed to lie doz-ing on the left side of her body, making small and gentle move-ments sometimes to the right. There was nothing alarming. Maybe pain had given up as well. Life was leaving, and maybe this was how it happened. She sat there, propped up in her bed and peeked out at the garden and the lowering sun. She remem-bered riding horses with her husband. She remembered Frank in the stables. She remembered the pool. The memories caused no pain. A comfort closed around her.

Death was very gentle. Relaxed. A little boring, if the truth were told.

Kitty calmed down. She drove out to the sea and looked at it for a while from the sand. It pawed at her and she took off her shoes and went and put her feet in it and stared out towards Britain and conjured up an English village and a bicycling vicar and wished to be there. Or elsewhere. The house in France would be gor-geous now. All that blue water. Their friends coming down from Nice. Their old friends. She hadn't heard from Jean Paul in more than a year. She would call him. Maybe invite him over. He would like that. Fussing about Delly. He would be the expert now on death as well as everything else, his accent sliding over English like the sand slid over her feet. Thomas was dead three years.

They had lived long lives, she thought. All these people she had found. They had lived long, unlucky lives.

In the water she saw the flick of some living thing, a crab or a fish, and she backed away to the frothy shallows where the tiny ripple waves broke, one after the other, endlessly. There had been a lot of distant deaths. Lizzie Gibbs had fallen under a cab on 7th Avenue. Karl had died of cancer at the age of 62. Paul Walker had shot himself in the mouth two days after retiring. Thomas's heart had failed him in his sleep – a stupid death for such a man. All this during Delly's illness. All this on-going. Kitty had travelled to the funerals alone, black dressed, awkward. It had come to that now. Airports were bad news. Their travel agent had learned to adopt a solemn tone whenever she called. What was it this time? A car crash in Nevada. A heart attack in Monaco. Liver failure in Rome. Little ripple waves, one after another, on-going.

Now this.

She wanted to throw him out. She felt no motherly feelings. She never had. She felt no gratitude. Deeply and instinctively she wanted to eject him. With curses and injunctions and threats of some vague and sinister kind. She wanted this to happen in full view of Delly, with her imprimatur and her encouragement. She wanted her voice to be both their voices. She had this thing turned round. He was the fake now. She had to rethink her notions of provenance. Didn't she? Damn right. He did not deserve Delly. He did not deserve to be in their lives. He did not deserve (she stepped on a stone and it hurt) the money.

The problem though. With this. The problem was Delly's guilt. Delly's stupid deathbed sleight of hand. Her righting of wrongs. Her handing it over. She would need convincing of his unworthiness. Next to her own. It was what it was all about. Kitty wondered how it balanced. Would Delly's old affair, its discovery, the death of her heartbroken and despairingly reckless husband, be outweighed by his adopted son's disguised incompetence and his flight from responsibility? Which one of them deserved the old man's money less? Or more?

She could not say how it would go.

She let her feet dry by standing still and watching a container ship glide southwards on the very line of the horizon, as if doing a trick on a wire for her benefit.

———

Her telephone rang as she cornered doing sixty through a housing estate somewhere west of Bray. She was lost. Everything looked the same. The streets, the houses, the people, the dogs. One road after another like a terrible suburb of hell. She pulled into a driveway where a child pedalled a kind of plastic tractor on an A4 lawn.

359

'What?'

'Miss Flood, Kieran Mullen here, I got your message.'

'Ah God, yes. Dr Mullen. How are you? Thanks for getting back to me.'

'No problem. This is surprising news I have to say, that you want to discuss a nursing staff, it really is. Has her condition worsened?'

'No. It's improved a bit I think. Dr Addison-Blake has taken her off some of whatever it was she was on,' (she thought she heard, as she said this, a kind of muffled '*harrumph*', which she interpreted as Dr Mullen indulging in a mildly disguised expression of contempt for George) 'and she seems a lot brighter. Not exactly what you'd call cheerful, but certainly more, um, bright.'

'Well that's good news. Very good news. Is she experiencing any pain?'

'She complains about it but she doesn't seem particularly uncomfortable. She was off her food for a couple of days but she's eating again now apparently.'

He made a humming noise.

'Yes. I'll have to discuss the situation with Dr Addison-Blake at some point of course. I'll need to know about her drug regimen and her recent treatment. He told me that he had her on amitri-optyline for example, which I would certainly be concerned about in conjunction with various palliative, um, with pain management care.'

'I don't know anything about any of that.'

'Ok. Can I talk to him?'

'No, well, I'm in the car. Actually.'

The child on the tractor was sitting on the driveway in front of her now, staring through the windscreen while picking his nose.

'Dr Addison-Blake doesn't know about this at the moment. He's been unavailable.'

He said nothing.

'It's really just been a matter of . . . ', what could she say,' . . . a lessening of Delly's resistance to the idea of nursing care, and my own initiative.'

'Oh yes?'

Lessening. Perhaps. She had stayed silent that morning. Maybe she hadn't heard.

'And other factors. Which we can discuss. Can you come?'

The kid was blowing saliva bubbles and rocking back and forth, the little black tractor wheels sawing at the ground.

'Of course. Yes. I'll come. I have to say that there is nothing more unedifying than two doctors at odds over patient care Miss Flood. I'm sure it won't arise, but I'd prefer if at all possible that Dr Addison-Blake is told that I'll be examining Mrs Gilmore, and that it's her wish that I do so.'

She briefly considered asking him what he knew about licence suspensions in the state of New York. About whether that was a serious kind of trouble to be in. But she wanted to retain control. She would wait until she had talked to Elliman at least. And besides, and bizarrely, his tone annoyed her. She thought he might crow.

'Yeah I'll look after all that. The important thing is just to get the arrangements in place.'

'Of course. Believe me Mrs Gilmore will feel the benefit of a professional and full time nursing presence. Which is not to suggest for a moment that you have been anything other than marvellously dedicated . . .'

'No I know.'

The kid's nose was runny. He wore navy shorts and a red t-shirt. He was freckle faced and nasty.

'It's just that she needs the expertise . . .'

'I know. She's been against it.'

'Would Tuesday suit?'

'Perfect.'

'About 11am? I may have to call for directions.'

'That's fine. Thanks. I'll see you then.'

The kid had lost interest in her. He was dragging his tractor back towards the front door between his legs, looking horribly like an insect with a catch bigger than itself. Kitty thought it incredible that he would be allowed to play unsupervised in front of the house on a Sunday afternoon, at the mercy of any passing weirdo or stray dog, and in danger of being confused with the other wet faced children who wandered the estate like evening slugs, and lost forever in an unidentifiable confusion of snot and saliva and tears.

She felt a great and shameful urge to run him over in her great

361

off-roader. But she backed away instead, and sought a way out of the maze by turning right at every corner, until she ended up, she did not know how, on a main road running west.

———————

Delly thought she was dying again. She insisted that she would not last the night. But for all that she was looking better than she had in weeks. Her eyes were bright. She was alert and upright. She argued with the television.

She reported that Dr George had looked in on her twice since his early afternoon visit, and had brought her some fruit and then tea. She said she felt little pain. She said she knew it was the end approaching.

'I don't need you with me. I'll be fine.'

'Do you not want me to wave you off or anything?'

'You think you're funny.'

'Should I not be here to wail? You'll need keening and the ringing of bells . . .'

'A kind of blasphemy . . .'

'To alert the villagers . . .'

'In the face of death.'

'And the network news.'

She put on a new bag. She brushed her hair. She told her about the traffic, even on a Sunday. She kissed her forehead and told her to cheer up. Not to be too disappointed if they met again in the morning, if there was more to come between them.

———————

He was sitting in the big office with the Sunday papers folded out on the table, a pot of coffee by his side. He smiled at her. Thinly.

'I'm so sorry Kitty I believe you were looking for me.'

'Yes well . . .'

'I was sleeping. Slept right through until one o'clock or later. It's not like me really. And my phone needed recharging and . . .'

'I knocked at your door.'

'I was out cold.'

'Well it was Mrs Cotter who ended up having to . . .'

'Yes I've apologised to her. Won't happen again.'

He smiled still. She looked at his pointy knees. He was challenging her to say something further. To be unreasonable. She had a terrible fear that he would not be bothered that she knew of

362

his American difficulties. That he would shrug it off. Explain it away. That he would win Delly over with the way he spun it.

She would say nothing. She would let him be until she had everything in place. She would talk to Elliman. Find things out. Do some digging. Already she was winning. She knew that.

Upstairs, while she searched the internet for information, and talked twice to Elliman's wife, and waited for him to call her back, she ate a bowl of cold cocktail sausages and a small sliced pan and drank a pot of tea and a Lucozade. She had missed dinner. In her fridge there was a Bewleys chocolate fudge cake. The kettle was on. She was in control now. She was active and involved. She was taking back her life. She checked only her own e-mail. She made notes about George. She made notes about nurses. She worked out a wheelchair route from the long room to the pool.

She thought briefly and regretfully of Sylvia Porterhouse. She thought now that it would not have amounted to much. Kitty had too many responsibilities. Towards Delly. Towards the properties. Towards Daniel Gilmore's money. Towards the future.

When Elliman rang at nearly midnight and admitted that he had known of George's suspension but had not passed on the news because he assumed they knew all about it, she called him a fuckwit, insulted his wife and told him he was the worst lawyer in New York and that all of the city would know of it by dawn.

Control.

It would take up his time. If he was going to do it properly, which he might as well. The thing was, he wasn't a bad chemist at all. Couldn't have got that from his father unless his father was Daniel Gilmore. It gave him a headache. The whole thing gave him a headache.

The kid had been heavy. You think a kid like that is going to weigh practically nothing, a skinny kid like that. But he was heavy. He was slumped and heavy. He'd hauled him out of the front seat to put him in the boot but he was too heavy. So he'd got him in the back seat instead and covered him with a rug. Guys on the gate didn't even look. Assholes. Then at the house he'd just left him there and gone scouting around for the women. The Roche was sleeping, her hands on her blanket like flat fish on a deck. Fat Flood's snores could be heard from half way up the stairs. He'd gone to the basement then and checked the two bedrooms there, where sometimes Mrs Cotter overnighted, thinking she'd be needed. She wasn't there. He called the guys on the gate and told them he'd seen a light near the west wall, like a flashlight, and they were all to go over there and check it out. Assholes. Then he'd hauled the kid through the front door of the old offices, and dragged him to the passage, and more or less thrown him down the stairs. Kid was out cold. Completely. He'd pissed himself too. He stripped him and hosed him down. He cuffed him to the bench. Took a couple of pictures with his new digital camera. Made sure nothing was broken. Made up something to keep him wiped out for the night. Good looking kid. With a big black eye coming up.

He slept in the little office next door. Woke at eight, eight thirty. Spent the morning waiting for the kid to wake up. Nothing would do it. Couldn't make too much noise. He hadn't tested the sound proofing. Wasn't sure that he'd put it on the right way around. Fucking kid just wouldn't wake up. He'd given him too much. It'd take a while to get used to him. To the kid. Doses and times and that. The Roche was more or less useless now. There was no point. She was permanently wiped out, and he couldn't tell any more if that was because of him or just because she really was dying, or whatever. He'd leave her off everything maybe, for a while, see how she did. Like a control. A what? A placebo. No. A control.

He slapped the kid around on his narrow cot. He hosed down the area. The drains seemed to work. The kid just lay there, wheezy breathing, sometimes a low moan, all baby white and pink, like bone and split tissue. He didn't know what was wrong with him. Damn kid.

He was a good enough chemist, but he was a lousy fucking doctor.

They left at a little after ten thirty, with the mobile fully charged, the land line number stored into Joe's, so that they could check for messages, and some paper and a pen, in case someone gave them an address or something. Barry felt that they should have rope, torches, waterproofs, guns. He sat and watched Joe's driving like it was the most delicate of skills, where the tiniest of misjudgements might kill them. They drove in silence, not even the radio, and he stared out at the streets and saw dead cars and stumbling people and fast dogs and spills of rubbish and the curves and hills of their road like the aftermath of great heat, of melting, and he saw the moon and the yellow lights and the swill of neon and he felt a bit sick, like a child on a difficult journey. Towards a new school. A dying grandparent. To spend a weekend at a cousin's. That kind of self centred dread.

'Where? Here?'

'Go straight.'

They crossed the river in the centre of town, and went along its northern bank for a while and turned and crossed it again, and went along its southern bank, westward, Barry with his eyes out for boys and parking spaces, and discovering neither. They went around again.

'There's no one there.'

'It's early. We'll wait.'

They crossed the river twelve times all told. Past the shops and the Custom House and the union building and across one bridge and another, O'Connell and Talbot, Talbot and O'Connell, past the hoardings and the train station and the pubs and the theatre and the travel agents and the superloos and the monument and the corners and the doorways and the altering light and diminishing crowds. It took that long, moving slowly, low on the road, past the reeling groups of people, the solid single people, the people; past the parked cars and the crawling cars and the hurtling cars, and the screamed at taxis and the hissing buses and the lurching trucks. Northside southside northside south. Then a space opened up in front of them, suspiciously convenient, per-

fectly placed. Joe dived into it before Barry could warn him of
traps and hides and the possibility of ambush. As the engine died
Barry discovered that he was breathing hard, loud, like that had
been a bad landing.

'Are you alright?'

'Yeah.'

'Don't worry. We're here. Stop fretting. You'd swear we were a
fucking SWAT team.'

It had occurred to him.

Beside him was the road. Across the road were buses. Beside
Joe was the footpath and the wall. Over the wall was the river.
Barry looked at his phone. It blinked at him.

'They're not going to approach two guys in a car.'

'Well presumably we'll be approaching them.'

'They won't like that.'

'What?'

'Two guys just, you know, get out of a car, approach, like that.'

'Well how do you want to do it then?'

'You stay in the car. I'll get out and . . .'

'Approach.'

'Yeah.'

They watched two girls and a boy walk across the road
towards them, arms folded, dodging the traffic, beeped at, and
continue past them, on the road, beside the parked cars, laughing.
One of them was saying, the boy was saying, *Yez are fucking mad,
I never fucking said it, me bollix I fucking said that*', the girls were
shrieking, *Ya did! Ya did!*'

Ahead of them, a woman climbed into a jeep.

'Can we . . .' said Joe. 'Can we . . . can we be, you know, get in
trouble for this. Be arrested?'

'For sitting in a car?'

'For approaching. Kerb crawling isn't it?'

'In the circumstances.'

'Yeah.'

'I don't think so, in the circumstances.'

'Yeah. Ok.'

A bus revved its engine. A police car passed them. In the side
mirror Barry could see a guy pissing in a doorway.

'It's all a bit weird,' said Joe.

'What is?'

'This. Who could tell that this was going on, right here, just here, right in the middle of town.'

'There's nothing going on at the moment.'

'But it's weird. It's like one city inside another. Parallel cities.'

Barry spotted an anoraked boy slouching down the footpath on the other side of the road, looking around, hands in pockets, on his own, sober, slow moving.

'It's like an episode of Star Trek.'

'I must have missed that one.'

'It's *like* I said.'

'Here we are.'

'What?'

'That guy, I think.'

'What guy?'

'That guy. Kagool.'

'Ok. Really? Ok. Are you sure?'

'No.'

'He's pretty ugly.'

He hesitated at the corner of the street that opened up to their left, across the road there, by the monument. He looked around a bit. All the buses were still waiting. The parked cars were lined up, dead. He turned and went away from them.

'No,' said Barry.

'No.'

Nothing happened. He couldn't see anything. Then nothing happened. Then he couldn't see anything. Then he heard something below him, but he didn't know whether it was below him or above him or to his side, and he couldn't work out if it was loud or not, or whether it was human or animal or machine. He had just heard something. Nothing happened. He could see something. It was like a tiny speck of light, but it wasn't light at all, it was just less dark. Less serious dark. As if the dark had been painted on and they had missed a bit, a tiny bit, maybe just on the second coat. That was all. It wasn't anything with a shape. It was just a speck of less dark. He tested to see whether it was something on his eye, some kind of speck on the ball of his eye, which would mean that it would move with him as he looked around, but it didn't, it stayed where it was when he had first seen it. It wasn't his eye. It was a blemish in the paint work of the dark. Then nothing happened. The speck of light was either above him or below him, he couldn't tell. He couldn't tell if it was to his side or over his head. He didn't know where it was other than that it was at eye level.

Everything was at eye level.

> After a while Joe took his phone out, and turned it on.
> 'That was off?' Barry asked him.
> 'Yeah.'
> 'All day?'
> 'Yeah.'
> He looked at the display and dialled his voicemail and listened. Barry could hear beeps and voices. Female voices. Then Joe spent a couple of minutes sending a text message.
> 'Everything all right?'
> 'Oh yeah.'
>
> ———
>
> After about twenty minutes Joe's phone rang. He looked at the display and didn't answer it.
> 'Who was that?'
> 'No one.'
> It rang again. Joe sighed and opened his door and got out of the car. Barry could hear his voice as he leant over the river wall, but not quite what he was saying. He talked for about five minutes. Quietly. Then he got back in the car.
> 'Ok?'
> 'Yeah yeah. The river smells like, you know, tomato soup. Anything?'
> 'No.'

All the pain in his body had left him. Except for one small dull ache in one of his elbows, he couldn't tell which one. The rest of his body was lovely. Soft and warm and comfortable. He didn't move. He didn't move at all while all around him nothing moved and he didn't make a sound while all around him there was silence and he didn't open his eyes while all around him there was nothing to see except the blemish in the paint work of the dark, which he tried, softly, gently, to put out of his mind, because it was the only wrong thing. It was the only thing that happened.

Another ten minutes. A boy appeared on the footpath by the river wall. He walked past them slowly, smoking, peering in at them.

'Right,' said Barry, as he went behind the car. 'I'll go have a word.'

'Are you sure he's one?'

'Can you see him in the mirror?'

'Yeah. He's standing by the wall.'

'Ok. I'll go see.'

'Ok. I'll cover you. One false move and he's a dead man. May God go with you.'

'Shut up.'

The outside of the car was warmer than the inside. It was noisier too. Then a breeze came and cooled him, and the traffic hesitated, and he could hear voices and footsteps and the lack of sound that towered over the river. He walked around the back of the car onto the footpath.

The guy was nursing his cigarette, leaning his arse against the wall, his arms half folded, his legs crossed at the ankles. His head was very active, this way and that, up and down, watching the street. He watched Barry approach him and at the same time he watched everything else as well. He stood opposite an empty space. He was slight, dark haired, young looking. Barry was thinking he'd just nod and walk past him, just to be sure that he wasn't just lingering by the river for a smoke on his way home, all innocent and pure, but just as he entered nodding range the guy spoke first.

'Lookin' for business?'

Immediately Barry thought that he'd need money. That you'd have to pay these guys for information, that's how it worked on the telly, he should have got some money from Joe. He thought he had about a tenner on him.

'Do you know someone called Kevin?'

'Wha?'

He was looking at Barry with huge sneery puzzlement. The jerkiness of his head seemed to move itself down to his shoulders.

'Kevin. Or Grant. Or Matt.'

'No,' he said, and turned to look off down the river towards a train going over the railway bridge. He drummed his hands off the wall. In a rhythm that his hips followed.

'About 19 or twenty, looks younger sometimes, brown hair. Slim. Not skinny.'

The guy looked at him.

'Brown eyes,' Barry added.

'You police?'

'No.'

'You lookin' for business?'

'No.'

'Whaddaya lookin' for?'

He was still doing his dance routine, though his hands now were stuffed in his pockets like it was cold, and his torso was swaying.

'A guy called Kevin, or maybe Grant, or maybe Matt.'

'Are they rent?'

'He. There's only one. It's one guy. I'm just not sure what his name is. He uses Grant and Matt but I think his real name is Kevin.'

'Yeah?'

'Don't know that he hangs out here much. He has ads as well.'

'You meet him here before?'

'Yeah.'

'Why are ya lookin' for him now then?'

Barry hesitated. Scratched his neck.

'I'm worried about him.'

'Ah he'll be alright.'

'Do you know him?'

'Dunno. What's he look like?'

'About my height? Brown hair. He got it cut, but it was quite curly, you know? He's, um, you know, he's a good looking guy.'

'Ok.'

'You know him?'

'Dunno.'

Was he meant to offer money here?

'Why d'ya wanna find him?'

He had no money. The guy was jerking his head again, leaning against the wall now, looking at Barry like he was simple, with a half smile. On the road the traffic passed and paused and passed, the buses lingered, footsteps came and went, voices bounced, reflected, so that they seemed to come from the river sometimes.

'Uh, it's, uh, ok. Forget it. Thanks.'

The whole thing was stupid. His mouth moved as he walked back to Joe's car. *Fucking stupid, fucking stupid*. There was a silence for a moment, a dearth of traffic, an absence of movement, no people near. He expected then that the boy would call him back and tell him something. But nothing happened. He opened the car door and climbed inside.

'Yeah well' Joe was saying. 'I can't.'

He glanced at Barry. Barry shook his head. Opened the glove compartment in the hope of mints or sweets or something, but there were tapes and an empty bottle of water and a driver's manual and a four inch teddy bear wearing a bow tie.

'Yeah well. You'll have to wait I'm afraid. No. Sorry. No. No. Ok, bye.'

'What's up?'

'Nothing?'

'Are you needed somewhere?'

'No.'

'This is stupid anyway. Go if you want to. We're not going to find out anything here.'

He told Joe some of what had been exchanged between the boy and himself. He found himself imitating the boy's voice. Making him sound stupid, sticking his tongue into his lower lip. *Mwaw mwaw mwaw*. Why did he do that?

His phone rang.

He banged his hand off the side of the door, off the handle for the window, trying to get the thing out of his pocket. It came up green, noisy, lit up, vibrating, in his suddenly sweaty fingers, like it was something that had jumped from the river. The display said *Unknown Caller*.

'Hello?'

'Hello is that Barry?'

'Sylvia?'

Beside him Joe muttered something.

'Yeah hi. Look sorry to disturb you.'

371

'Sylvia, I can't stay on this line. Can you call me back on Joe's ok? Bye.'

He hung up. He didn't know why he still bothered doing that. But he thought now that he would probably do it forever. That he'd never talk to anyone on his mobile ever again unless it was Kevin.

'Fuck's sake. Tell her, will you, that I'm helping you out and that it's none of her fucking business what we're doing and that she'll just have to fucking wait.'

'What?'

'Just tell her to fuck off basically. She's gone all weird . . .'

His phone rang. He handed it to Barry.

'Just don't be nice to her.'

'Hello?'

'Barry?'

'Yeah.'

'So he is with you. Sorry about this. I thought he was bullshitting me.'

'We're, um, Joe's kind of helping me out with something. Is there a problem?'

'Well just that I can't get into his house all day long to get my stuff you know? I'm in a hotel now but I have a flight booked for the morning and all my stuff is in his place. You know, like clothes and notebooks too and that kind of thing. He's being a real pain in the ass about it.'

Barry was looking at Joe, who was shaking his head and making wanking motions with his hand.

'Um, well, I, you know, don't know anything about that.'

Thumbs up from Joe.

'Yeah I know doll. I'm not getting at you at all. I just actually didn't believe him when he said he was with you, you know?'

'Ok. Well he is.'

'Yeah. Fine. Well you just might remind him to give me a call when he's finished so I can get my stuff.'

'Ok.'

'Thanks doll. And good luck with your emergency situation, whatever.'

'Ok.'

In his dreams the American man came and fiddled with him. With his straps and his clothing. He didn't say very much. Some instructions and curses and things Kez couldn't understand. He thought he spoke German. German or something from a film. Sometimes he injected something into Kez, or made him drink something. Kez never saw him because the dark was ruined when the American came in. It was ripped apart. And it was loud and noisy and it hurt and he hated it. So he kept his eyes closed.

When he woke up there was nothing.

He handed the phone back to Joe.

'What have you done?'

'Absolutely nothing. I've been a gentleman.'

'That'd be a first.'

'Cheers. Is that by any chance one of your urchins?'

Across the road, back against a wall, can of something in his hand, was a tall thin guy in tight white jeans and a tight black top. He was staring at passing cars.

'Looks likely doesn't it?'

'Want to give it a try?'

'Fuck it. I don't know what I'm doing. I'm probably just wasting everyone's time. I tell you, if we're sitting here and Kevin walks around the corner I'm gonna kick his fucking head in. I'm gonna throw him in the river.'

Joe smiled at him.

'Go on,' he said. 'Or else I have to go face Saliva.'

'You need to sort that out.'

'Go.'

'Seriously though Joe. Why don't you just go over there now? I'll wait here.'

'Oh yeah. Make a little pocket money while you're at it.'

'She has to get her stuff.'

'It's just stuff. This is more important. Go.'

He went. He skipped across between buses. He glanced behind him to see that the jerky headed guy had moved further down along the wall. There were fewer parked cars. Everything was a little quieter. He was a little more depressed. The new guy's jeans were remarkably tight. They just looked like a plaster cast of everything underneath, from his clothes hanger hips to the skewers of his ankles. Barry couldn't help wondering how he got them off and on again several times an evening. Was there flesh beneath or bare bone? He thought he'd try talking first.

'Hi I'm not a cop and I'm not a punter . . .'

'What?'

He'd started too early. The guy just hadn't heard him.

'I'm saying I'm not a punter or a cop or anything, I'm just looking for a guy who's a friend of mine he's called either Kevin or Grant or Matt he's about my height curly hair, not very curly but not straight you know, and he's had it cut, last week. Brown eyes, good looking about nineteen or twenty. Does most of his work through the ads I think. But he does come down here the odd time.'

The guy had backed away slightly, startled at first. But he'd stopped then and had seemed to listen. He looked him up and down, and checked over his shoulder as well, before he answered.

'Why are you looking for him?'

His voice was surprisingly calm.

'I'm worried about him.'

He smiled, astonished, and then made a face that was a perfect caricature of sympathy.

'Aw. Have you brought him a vest?'

Hard as nails thought Barry. Nail thin, nail sharp, nail hard.

'I think he might be in trouble.'

'Why?'

'Do you know him?'

'I don't know.'

He half yawned, looked over Barry's shoulder.

'Is this him?'

Barry swung on his heel. The first guy was crossing the road towards them, hands in pockets, moving sideways through a bit of traffic like he was on his way up to the bar. Barry glanced towards Joe, and could see him peering through the passenger window. He didn't want to be mugged. He didn't particularly want to be standing on a corner in the middle of town with two rent boys either. Something told him he should be making decisions, but he couldn't work out what they were, how to frame them.

'No. I talked to this guy earlier.'

The jerky boy dodged a car that turned into the side-street and crawled past them all, and he bent down slightly to catch the driver's eye while he walked along the kerb unsteadily, his hands still hidden. He greeted tight jeans by throwing back his head sharply, once, and tight jeans said something that might have been a *'Hiya'* or an *'Alright?'*, and they stood turned half away from Barry, looking down towards the railway bridge and the approaching traffic. They ignored him. They started a quiet, muffled conversation, of which Barry could catch nothing apart from *'fucking weirdos'*, which he thought he was probably supposed to catch, and the words *'ciggies'*, *'blow'* and *'money'*.

He stood there for a while, but felt like a fool, and was conscious that there were definitely a couple of cars now, prowling, coming around more than once, with their drivers staring, their anxious eyes very wide, and that one of them had given Barry a good going over.

'Look,' he announced, and he knew he sounded rich and comfortable and ignorant and completely fucking stupid. 'If either of you thinks you might know who I'm talking about, I'm in that car over there. Just opposite. I'm not a weirdo, I'm not making it up, I'm not trying anything on, ok? I just think this guy might be in trouble. I mean he might have been picked up by someone who's not letting him go, or might, I don't know, who wants to hurt him.'

He heard a fault in his voice, like it was going to crack. He stopped talking for a moment. Swallowed. Tight jeans was looking at him over his shoulder. Jerky head was looking everywhere else.

'I'm over there. I just need to find out another way of getting in touch with him. 'Cos he's not answering his mobile. Which he should be. Right?'

They said nothing.

'Fuck it. I'm over there.'

And he walked back to Joe, pissed off suddenly, and unfairly, that of all the people in his world, of all of his wide circle, the only one he had to rely on in his crisis, in his disoriented state, in his floundering and his thrashing about, was Joe Kavanagh. It was a joke.

Once when he had been very little and he had wanted to cough he hadn't coughed because he was in a car being driven somewhere by some adult, being driven to swimming or to the cinema or back from somewhere, from the school or the hospital or the shops or something, by someone else, with other kids in the car, not his mother, a man, someone's father, and he had wanted really badly to cough. Just to have a big cough, because his throat tickled him and he needed to cough, but he didn't, he stopped himself, he just held it in, and he was gasping a bit, and probably turning red, but he wouldn't cough, and the man driving turned to him and told him, nicely, you know, kindly, Kevin, cough if you want to. So he coughed. A lot. He coughed all the way home.

He didn't know why he hadn't wanted to cough. Maybe he had thought it was rude or something. As if he'd confused it with farting. Or as if he'd just been to the cinema and the man driving the car had complained about someone in the cinema coughing. Or maybe he hadn't wanted to cough because the man wasn't coughing. Maybe he thought coughing was a kid's thing. That men didn't cough.

Barry had a bit of a limp. Joe could see it as he watched him come across the road, looking like he'd just asked someone to dance and was now, you know, not dancing. He thought that Barry was thoroughly miserable, with all the bad things come at once. Fear. Uselessness. Incompetence. His limp was worse the faster he moved – getting out of the way of a taxi for example. Self disgust. Paranoia. Suspicious of his own motives. He couldn't even open the door properly. It slipped and caught, so he grabbed it again, and there was yanking and muttering and collapsing in and slamming.

'Fucking stupid fucking stupid.'

'They don't know him?'

'They don't know whether they know him and they've decided that I'm some sort of weirdo. Fuck's sake.'

This was the problem. This was the kind of thing you had to

expect, to make allowances for, when you embarked on the course of action that Barry had now embarked on. In the same way that Joe would have to endure a whole series of indignities and sly looks, and at best pity, at worst scorn, if he went looking for any of the people missing from his life. His daughter for example. His wife.

His father come to think of it. Especially his father.

Imagine the raised eyebrows at that.

'It's just not done,' he said.

'What?'

'It's a step too far. It breaks one of the rules of social intercourse, forgive me, between these guys and us guys. The system does not allow for it. For you turning up and being concerned for the health and safety of one of their number. They are rattled. They are regrouping. They don't know what to make of it.'

'Right.'

In the same way that he, Joe, would be breaking various rules, guidelines, procedural etiquette, if he were to demand for example, or ask even, to see a little bit more of his daughter, to try and mend things, to try and make some kind of connection between the two them that would ford the gaps, that would last the years, that would mean something – something of what it was supposed to mean – in the end. Or if he tried to change the mind of his wife, who, after all, he had loved, to see if it was not possible that he might still love her, after all. Or to seek the forgiving spirit of his father. However that was done. A loss too far perhaps – that. But nevertheless, this was his desire, wasn't it? To redress the balance in these things.

Barry was looking at his phone, as if missing people called you up.

He thought, Joe did, that he was perhaps the worst possible person in the world. Because he knew what was wrong with him. He knew why he was bad. And he liked it there. When all was said and done he liked it there. In the hollow place. Single. Disconnected. He didn't love his wife. If he ever had, he didn't now. She was selfish, self satisfied, cold, humourless. All those things which had probably brought them together. He liked his daughter. He loved his daughter. But he was no good with her. Sylvia was right. When had been the last time he had called her?

377

He hadn't. He hadn't called her since they'd been together the weekend before. It was not that he had forgotten. It just hadn't occurred to him. Instead he had done his show, healed his foot, in fits and starts, taken up sexually with an English woman, helped her interrogate a fat writer about a covert chemical weapon and a cover up, had locked the same English woman out of his house, and was now cruising rent boys with his producer in an attempt to solve the possible murder of one of them, known by several different names, with whom his producer was besotted.

He was bad at the good things. Good at the bad.

There was a whistle, a movement. Barry looked. There were three of them now – tight jeans, jerky head, and a new one – blond, dark jacket, pale blue trousers, smiling. He had whistled. Big grin on him. He was looking over at the car, waving at Barry. Gesturing him over. *Come here. Come here.*

'Looks like you're wanted,' said Joe. 'Will I come with you?'

'No. It's alright. Just keep an eye out. Actually maybe just get out of the car when I'm nearly there. Just sort of be seen. Lean against the bonnet or something.'

'Very Starsky And Hutch.'

'But don't come over unless I'm being,' where had he heard this before? 'murdered.'

He took his wallet from his pocket and put it in the glove compartment. It was all he could think of. Not his phone. He wouldn't leave it and he wouldn't let them take it. He thought he'd die first. He thought he'd be dead before he'd relinquish his phone.

The traffic was thin now. It came in shallow waves from the lights down by the train station. There was none due for a moment. So he could stroll across, and see the way of things. The buses were gone as well. The parked cars few now. There was someone in one of them, looking at him. You can't afford me, he thought, to cheer himself.

Blondie regarded him, smiling still. Tight jeans slouched by a wall. Jerk head sat on the kerb, doing something with a shoe.

'Who are you looking for?' asked blondie, friendly enough.

Barry told him, as he had told the others, and the others seemed to cock an ear and listen better than they had before. Blondie said nothing. Tight jeans lit a cigarette. A car crawled by them and jerk head stood and his hands framed his crotch for the duration, but the driver didn't stop.

'Lads use all kinds of names,' said blondie. 'I don't know anyone called Kevin or Grant or Matt. But that doesn't mean I don't know your guy. Did ya rent him?'

Barry took his phone from his pocket.

'I work for a radio station right? And a couple of weeks ago I came down here looking for one of you guys to come on and talk on the radio about what being a rent boy was like. And I met this guy who told me his name was Kevin, and I gave him my number, and a couple of days later he called me and we met and had a chat and then he agreed he'd come onto the radio show, or, at least, well, he came down to the studio, but that's not important. What is important is that I met him a couple of times and we got to be quite friendly I think and then last night, we went out for a drink and whatever, and after I went home he left a message on my voicemail. He left this message on my voicemail.'

He held his own phone up to blondie's ear. Up to the ear of a stranger. Blondie made no attempt to hold it himself. He just turned his head and put his ear to it. As if to a door. He squinted.

'Fuck,' he said. 'Can you play it again?'

He was naked. He had no clothes on but it was okay. He could feel the shape of the air around him, could feel where it had to bend and curve to cover him, to touch him all over. It had to follow his skin. He knew that if the air wasn't touching him he would die. He knew that he'd die if the air fell asleep and didn't follow him when he moved, or if the air moved away, or forgot about him or made a mistake. So whenever he moved he had to do it slowly, carefully, so that the air would notice what it was he was doing, which part of him was moving, where it was going, and it could follow him there and keep him covered so that he wouldn't die. If even a small part of him, like his foot, were to move suddenly, sharply, from where it had been to some new place, without warning, it might create a gap in the air, because the air might not move so fast and even if it were only for a second, even if the air realised what had happened and rushed after the foot and covered it again, even so, the skin would blacken and wither and die. The skin that had been without air. It would rot. So he had to be careful. He had to be so careful.

Barry played it again. This time blondie closed his eyes. His lips seemed to move. Tight jeans came over. He stood craning his neck towards Barry's outstretched hand.

'That sounds like Gerry.'

'Let's hear it,' said tight jeans. Barry replayed it. They listened to it together, their heads touching, one of them wearing a cheap aftershave that smelled like burning plastic.

'That's Gerry,' said blondie, and tight jeans said 'Ya sure?' and jerky head came over and said 'Who is it?' and blondie produced a phone of his own and pressed a few buttons and looked at it and asked Barry what number he had for him, for this guy, for his Kevin. Barry recited it.

'That's him,' said blondie. 'That's Gerry.'

There was a change then, and Barry could not help but be impressed by it. He was no longer a punter or a problem or a creep. He was interesting now. They gathered around him, they looked at his phone, they looked at him – with something in their faces approaching respect, or at least the absence of contempt. They asked his name. They asked about times, days, dates, chronologies. Blondie seemed the smartest. Tight jeans seemed the most appalled. Jerk head was, Barry now decided, definitely on something.

He gave blondie his phone. He handed it over. The guy had one of his own, much flashier looking than Barry's, so where was the danger? He listened to Kevin's message a couple more times. He handed the phone back. He called Kevin on his own phone. He shrugged.

'Gerry. Gis a call will ya? Pronto. Ray.'

They stood there then, the three of them. For a moment. Said nothing. Barry was relieved. Ray was evidently not. Tight jeans was pale. Jerk head ceased his jerking for a moment. He was the only one to continue to monitor the passing traffic. Then tight jeans began a low muttering of *fuckfuckfuckfuckfuck*.

'Barry?'

'Yeah?'

'Who's that over there?'

'That's a friend of mine. Gave me a lift. He's alright.'

'He know the story?'

'Yeah.'

'Ok. Let's go.'

He started walking towards Joe. Barry hesitated.

'I know where he lives,' Ray called back. 'Paulie you call me if Gerry shows up here or if anyone shows up who's seen him. Or anything. Right?'

'Yeah.'

Barry followed his new pal. Who was, he thought, in his early twenties, and who seemed to possess a confidence lacking in the others. This guy knew what he was doing. Ahead of them Joe was losing his nonchalant air. Barry trotted a little to get to him first.

'This is Ray, he knows where Kevin, or Gerry apparently, lives.'

They regarded each other briefly and Ray went to the back door and tried the handle.

'It's locked. Hello? Are we going then or what?'

Joe peered at Barry, a slight question on his face. He shrugged.

'Right,' he said, and climbed into the car. Barry did the same, sticking his hand in first to pull up the lock on the back door and admit the second rent boy of his acquaintance, who, Barry thought, was very trusting. They could after all, Joe and himself, be the abductors, getting together a collection – the killers, on a spree. But if he had thought it he had obviously dismissed it immediately, as improbable, or even ridiculous. Barry wasn't sure whether to be pleased or embarrassed that he could not be mistaken for a maniac, a stalker, a danger in the world. He would possibly have liked, given the situation, to have a more intimidating air at his disposal.

They drove off along the river, the three of them. Up river. Towards the source. But they turned too early, to Dolphin's Barn and the empty flat, with the neat wardrobe and the hidden cash, and the getaway bag beneath the bed.

He heard a baby crying.

A light came on and shone in his eyes when he thought his eyes were closed. He tried to open his eyes to get away from the light but that just made it worse and then he did not know whether his eyes were open or closed so he didn't know what to tell them to do, and his eyelids buckled and strained and he could feel them bruising.

Then the light went out and there was water on his chest and his stomach and his eyes were no longer working.

He was thirsty. But nothing happened.

The dark is fuller than the light. There's more in it. It's thick and dense and etched with detail – carved, curling, complicated, endless. It is a thing by itself.

Light is nothing in itself. It just shows you where the shadows are.

'He has a brother.'

'Yeah. Do you know where he lives?'

'Nah. But I know where he drinks.'

They stood on the street, the three of them, having rang the bell marked JD, and then all the others for good measure. It was a three story semi detached house. Five bells. Junk mail spilled over the porch like sick in a doorway. Barry had it in his mind that Kevin might have had a fall. Like an old person. And be incapable by the side of the bath. Joe thought this unlikely. So did Ray, but nevertheless it was he who did all the talking when a sleepy looking man eventually came to the door. Yes he knew who they were talking about, no he hadn't seen him all weekend, and yes they could come in and try the door if they wanted, he didn't care. He stood on the stairs with his dressing gowned girlfriend behind him as they knocked and called and peered through the keyhole. Nothing. To Barry it seemed all askew, and he felt foolish. He was calling out *Kevin*, and Ray was calling out *Gerry*, and Joe was looking sceptical and alarmed. The place was bland. Barry couldn't see Kevin there, at that door, coming and going. He'd wanted to kick it down, not so much now because he believed that he might be in there, but because he wanted some proof that this was actually the place where he lived, and that he and Ray were definitely thinking about the same guy. But Ray was against it. As were the couple on the stairs, who began to talk about calling the police. They left the building.

'Will it be open?'

'Don't know.'

They piled back into the car. Joe was being silent now, had glanced at his watch a couple of times. Barry knew he was liking this a lot less than when it had been just the two of them. He was shy now, and nervous, and he wasn't the boss anymore.

'Can't remember the brother's name. He's a serious sort of bloke ya know? He's into some strong stuff. Trying to remember his fucking name. Danny or Anthony or something. Turn left here. Get whatever ya want. Hangs out with certain people. I've been on a couple of gigs he's set up. Straight ahead. He's alright but you wouldn't want to be on the wrong fucking side of him. He's got some serious fucking friends. Right at the lights.'

Barry was wondering what a gig was. Joe was driving so slowly that there was angry revving coming from behind, a roar, *get on with it*.

Eventually, Ray directing them, leading them, they arrived at a blank wall in a side street off the Coombe, with two high small curtained windows and a single caged lamp. It looked to Barry like something in Belfast, on the news, scene of a sectarian gun attack. There was a battered plastic sign, the back light off, which read 'Pony Bar'. The door was like a house door, complete with stained glass panels, behind which there was an orange glow, twelfth of July, gunflash. A metal shutter box gripped the wall above it. Ray told them to stay where they were. They watched him try the door and then knock. It opened a crack and then it opened fully and he was admitted into the dim light and disappeared.

'You sure you've got the same guy then?'

Barry was no longer sure of what exactly was going on. He felt creepingly suspicious that he and Joe were being taken for an elaborate ride. That this was some convoluted conspiracy, some con, and they were the dupes, the fall guys, the patsies. It was all very American, Chicago, convoluted, mob related, drug related, possibly fatal, like the movies. The fact that they had nothing worth stealing made him think it likely that they would end up dead.

'Oh yeah.'

'You know this place?'

'Christ no.'

'It's a gay bar?'

'I doubt it. Certain lack of, um, frills.'

'Could be, you know, hardcore.'

'Hardcore what?'

'I don't fucking know. Hardcore rent boy drug den bondage leather thing.'

Barry stared at the door. He couldn't hear anything.

'Hardcore,' said Joe. 'CDT.'

'CBT.'

'CBT. What does it mean?'

'You don't want to know.'

'I fucking do.'

'T,' said Barry, 'is for Torture.'

They said nothing then. That was enough.

The Pony Bar

In February 1996, Michael Guiney, 38, known as Midge, and 'well known to the gardaí', was shot three times in the back as he entered The Pony Bar in south central Dublin. He fell to his knees with his face against the glass, and his body blocked both the attempted entrance of the gunmen and the attempted flight of several of the customers. No one saw a thing. Three days later Paul Kilbride and David Masters were arrested and held for 18 hours in connection with the murder before being released without charge. David Masters was shot dead two months later in a pub car park in Tallaght. Paul Kilbride was imprisoned for twelve years in 1997 for drugs related offences. No one was ever charged with Michael Guiney's murder.

POLITICIAN'S NECK

In a fight in The Pony Bar in 1982, the local Fianna Fáil TD, Neil Keegan, suffered a broken collar bone and a neck wound which required surgery. Although newspapers reported that Mr Keegan had been close to death, that his throat had been cut and that his life had been saved only by the prompt actions of a barman, no one was ever arrested in connection with the incident, which Mr Keegan himself later described as an accident. Mr Keegan briefly became a junior minister in 1987 but resigned his job due to ill health. He left the Dáil at the next election and now lives in Leitrim with his wife.

MONEY TO BURN

The butcher's shop next to The Pony Bar was burned down in 1979. Arson was suspected and the insurance company refused to settle a claim made by the owners, who were also, at that time, the owners of The Pony Bar. In the subsequent legal wrangling, the owners of The Pony Bar were revealed to also be the owners of three retail outlets around the city which had all burned down within the previous eighteen months. They lost their action against the insurers. The Pony Bar was sold to Maurice Hanlon some months later for what was reported to be a bargain sum. Mr Hanlon, the owner of several city centre pubs, set about refurbishing what is one of the oldest bars in the city, and had the original late 18th century frontage removed and the 1840s oak bar ripped out and replaced with modern, fire resistant furnishings. The work led to protests, and indirectly to the formation of The Dublin Pub Heritage Group, which picketed the re-opened Pony Bar throughout 1980. Maurice Hanlon closed the pub in November 1980 and sold it in March 1981 to the Tiernan brothers, Arthur and Patrick, trading as APT Ltd.

EATING CHILDREN IS ILLEGAL

Three men were arrested on Thomas Street in July 1997 and charged with a breach of the peace, after leaflets were distributed at the fringes of a Pro Life demonstration, purporting to show 'semi eaten foetuses' and 'partly digested child remains'. Complaints were made about the nature of the leaflets to the attending police officers, who arrested the three men immediately. They were taken to the Bridewell Garda station and questioned for several hours before being charged. In court the next day the men stated that the pictures in the leaflets had been faked by them, but that their purpose was to point out the need for a constitutional ban on the eating of human babies. The judge fined the men £20 each and bound them over to hold the peace for six months and to refrain from what he described as 'an unfunny and quite obscene practical joke, whose intent was to mock and belittle those genuine and sincere protesters who were concerned with the problem of abortion'. The men were named as Arthur Tiernan, 43, Patrick Tiernan, 40, and Raymond Gannon, 19.

A second city centre entertainment venue has been acquired by APT Ltd, the company which bought out the troubled *Sputnik* club when its English owners ran into difficulty last year. The new acquisition is the *Digital* night-club and performance space on Crowe Street in the Temple Bar area. *Digital* was opened only six months ago by Phelim Doyle, son of the former Foreign Affairs Minister Lawrence Doyle, and has been one of the more successful of the recent spate of club openings in the city, attracting a mix of fashion conscious young Dubliners and artists, as well as establishing a reputation as a place to spot both home grown and international celebrities. APT are believed to have paid over £5 million for the club, which some sources were yesterday saying was some way below market value given the club's size, location and its already solid and lucrative market position. Other sources however pointed out the fickle nature of the entertainment venue business, which is largely at the mercy of rapidly changing and unpredictable fashions, and insisted that the investment was a considerable risk for APT Ltd, who also own two Dublin pubs. Indeed the *Sputnik* chain is a case in point. From small beginnings in London the business expanded rapidly, opening several clubs in the UK as well as outposts in New York, Prague and Dublin. *Sputnik* in Dublin was plagued with problems from the start, from staff disputes to drug arrests and a death on the premises, and a fire which closed the club for nearly two months. The failure of the Dublin venue marked the beginning of the end for the chain, which is now in receivership. APT have however made a success of the Dublin club (renamed *Twenty Three*), largely by booking bands and DJs from around Europe and the United States at just the right moment, after they have won the attention and respect of the critics but before they achieve large scale success and graduate to playing larger venues and commanding larger fees. *Twenty Three* has hosted the European debut of New York band *Character Map* and the first gig outside Germany by the now hugely successful *DJ KMark*. APT Ltd has announced that there will be no change to the running of *Digital* and that Phelim Doyle, who will have profited considerably from the sale, will be staying on to manage the venue for the immediate future.

'Give me your phone.'

It was Ray, at the window, his hand on the bonnet of the car, crouching.

'What?'

'Give me your phone.'

'Why?'

'He wants to hear it. Hear the message.'

'Who does?'

'Jesus. Vincent. Gerry's brother. Vincent. He wants to hear the message.'

'No.'

'What?'

'I'm not giving you my phone.'

'He's a bit pissed. He doesn't really know what I'm talking about. I need to play him the message.'

'Tell him to come out and hear it.'

'Fuck's sake. Just let me have it for two minutes. Here . . .'

He rummaged in his pocket and produced his own phone and held it out to Barry.

'You hold on to mine then. You can keep it if I don't come back.'

'No that's not it.'

What was it then? It was the voice. He didn't want to give away the voice. Three days he'd have it for. Three days only. The first one of them was nearly gone. He didn't want to lose the voice. He couldn't say it.

'Fuck's sake.'

Ray put his phone away. He slapped the car lightly. He sighed. Shook his head. Walked back to The Pony Bar, kicking at the road.

It was utter dark where he found himself.

He thought he was dead. Which brought a whole parade of emotions, one after the other, slowly: fear, stock still fear; then calm, relaxing into it, thinking that maybe it was ok; then relief that it was over, it was all fucking over; then sadness that it was over, and that he wouldn't see certain people again – Vincent for example, his mother, Radio Boy; then resignation – what the hell; then boredom, and the thought that maybe he wasn't dead at all.

389

Not dead. Not yet.

He thought that he might be in the boot of a car. That was his thought. That it had happened. That the bad thing, the final thing, had happened. That thing that always happened to his type on the telly. Some half good actor on the way up as the doomed rent boy – pale and sick and sucking off-screen cock and fucked up and druggie and pretty quickly dead, stabbed usually, sometimes shot, sometimes strangled. Though it was mostly the rent girls that got strangled for some reason, maybe to do with heterosexuality, he didn't know. Some rare times he was horribly pulled apart by razors and throttles and cleavers and knives. Usually right at the beginning, because he'd seen something he shouldn't have seen. Kez tried to work out what it was he'd seen.

So he thought he was in the back of some gangster's smooth saloon, on his way to the city dump or the reservoir, having being knocked over the head with a length of drain pipe or a cudgel or a heavy crystal ashtray. It took him a long time to work out that the nausea he felt, and the sense of motion, came not from car fumes and the turns of the road, but from the same source as his needle point headache. They were symptoms of the damage already done to him. They were aftershocks, and they were on-going.

This was not a car.

Those rent boys on the telly were always too old looking, always, sometimes by years, sometimes by just that sad six months. They were always supporting a habit. They were never *really* gay. They did stupid senseless things like trying to rob the gangster (there were always gangsters) or getting into vans or starting up a bit of blackmail.

He was not in a car. He was in a dark room. Pitch dark.

They were always blond these guys. Dirty blond. Fair.

He tried moving his hands. These seemed to work. He sniffed at the same time, not meaning to, and thought that his nose was bleeding or possibly just very runny, and he lifted his hand towards his face but it stopped just above his waist, paralysed, like it was in a bag. His hands were tied.

He couldn't work out what way they were tied. They didn't seem to be tied to each other. He could move them apart and up and down a bit, from his mid thigh to his mid stomach, and he could lift them up away from him by about six inches maybe, but he couldn't put them together. They must have been tied to whatever he was lying on. He tried to feel for his belt but it was gone. He was naked. Which came as a surprise, because he was so warm, comfortable.

They were always ugly. Shivering. Best got rid of, quickly. Best remembered.

He tried to get past the headache and the sick feeling and the spinning and swaying to discover what else was wrong with him. There were aches all over his face. And his chest hurt. He remembered the parts of dreams. Or he just remembered. He had been there a while. He had had such weird dreams. He tried to lift his head. There was nothing to see and his neck ached. More things ached the more he moved. He tried to lie still. He wanted to piss. He was thirsty.

He went through the contents of his getaway bag. In his mind he sorted through it, checking that everything was there – counting the money, counting the underwear, the pairs of socks. Looking at the unopened shirts, nervously, thinking that maybe some of those would be a bit out of fashion by now. He checked the maps and the addresses and his passport and his birth certificate.

Everything there. Ready.

He didn't know how far he was by now, from his getaway bag. But it calmed him to think of it. To list the things he had collected. To list the cities he could go to.

He remembered the American man. That's where he was. For a moment he thought that he might be in America, and he was somewhere in his mind excited, that he was in America. But then he knew he wasn't. He couldn't be.

391

The American guy in the BMW. He'd hit him. Knocked him out. Taken him somewhere. Tied him up.

Ok.

He'd always just assumed that when the moment came he'd be able to get back to his getaway bag. He didn't know why now. Why he'd assumed that. He just had. He thought it was stupid. He'd been stupid. He should have taken it with him, everywhere. Like Chester Haft. So that he wouldn't have to go back to get it. He should have had it with him. He should have made it smaller, made it a shoulder bag, taken it everywhere.

He could see nothing whatsoever.

He thought then that he was blind. That he had been blinded. That the American man had thumbed out his eyes, or had skewered them with his car keys, bursting them like balloons. Or had sucked them out, swallowed them, whole, not daring to bite down on them for fear that they held everything that Kez had ever seen, and his mouth would be broken then and his stomach burst, from the multitude of things and people sudden there, the whole world instant in the gut. Plosive.

This was not fucking funny.

In the thick dark Kez screamed.

It had not occurred to Barry that Kevin's brother might look like Kevin. He had not considered it, as if he had thought that there could be only one, as if the very notion was absurd. But here he was, older, heavier, taller, different. But nevertheless, *like*. It was in the face, of course. The body did not compare at all – it was bigger, wider, probably a lot stronger, worked on. And in the face it was mostly in the eyes. The mouth was different, thinner lips. The skin was not as good. The nose was broken. The hair was shorn. The eyes, and a little in the overall shape and colouring. Similar. Recognisable. Proof.

Barry thought first simply that Kevin had been the lucky one, that he'd got the looks. Then he thought that maybe this was Kevin in a few years. Filled out, battered. Which gave him pause. He didn't know. He put it aside.

The brother walked steadily enough, peering at Joe as he crossed the road. Then he followed Ray around to the passenger side, and he stared at them both through the windscreen as he went, looking a little annoyed but also a little nervous, as his brother had, about these guys behind the glass and what they intended.

There were no introductions. He just started talking.

'You know my brother?'

'Yes.'

'What's his name?'

Straight into it. Like that. He needed proof of his own. Guys like this, they always did. They were always aware of the legal situation, of alibis and aliases and burdens of proof. Of evidence and accusations and reasonable doubt. An entire life spent checking your own story, testing it, touching it up, would inevitably lead to a reluctance to believe anything anyone else ever said to you. Barry was on the spot. He'd know now, where he stood. He wondered whether they had worked it out specifically – whether Kevin had told his brother his name was the key to trusting strangers who spoke of him. Or whether it was a simple awareness on the brother's part that punters never got the real name. That punters and other rent boys and inconsequential passers by never got the real name. And maybe there was a hierarchy of names. Maybe he would know Barry precisely by his answer. Gerry. Matt. Grant. Each of them signifying something. Indicating the level reached.

'Kevin.'

He didn't react. Not a flicker. Barry pushed the buttons on his phone and held it out. Vincent glanced briefly at Ray and took it, held it to his ear. He looked at the ground. There was a flicker of his eyes, then a single exaggerated blink, and his head ducked and rose and he stared at Barry.

'How do I . . .?' he started, looking at the phone now, bewildered.

'Press 2.'

He listened to it again. Then again. He turned his back on them all, stuck a finger in his other ear. He listened again. He crouched on the ground. He muttered something. He listened again. He stood. Put the phone on the bonnet. Barry got out of

393

the car. Vincent produced a phone of his own, pressed a quick dial.

'Kevin. Call me. Now.'

Then he stared again at Barry. There was something stricken there. His eyes were widening, blinking. He hand wiped his mouth.

'Fuck,' he said. 'Fucking American fucking cunt. Oh Jesus Christ. Oh Jesus.'

He kicked Joe's car, hard. A wail started low in his throat and came at them like an animal noise, trapped in a corner, desperate, wild.

Barry split evenly. This was serious now. This guy looked like he might not be scared by much. But he was scared by this. And if he was scared, Barry was terrified. But he had been given the name. He had been given the right name. Kevin. In all of this, if nothing else, there was that.

'I know that guy,' said Vincent, the heel of his hand pressed to his temple. 'Fuck it.'

'Gerry?' said Ray.

'His name isn't fucking Gerry it's Kevin.'

Ray seemed to Barry to be experiencing a sideshow disappointment equivalent to his own sideshow joy. Kevin was someone people liked to feel they knew.

'I mean I know the fucking American guy.'

Joe was out of the car now. All four of them stood on the footpath as if there had been an accident. Barry got back to the point. This was serious.

'Who is he?'

Vincent was about to answer but shook his head. He stood still for a moment then, concentrating.

'Right,' he said. 'I have to get hold of Deano. What time is it? Shit. Ok. Ray, you stay with me right, I need you to drive my motor.'

He turned to Barry.

'Listen. I'm taking your phone right? I'll get it back to you. I need to have that message. Don't do anything ok? You did the right thing finding me. I'll sort it ok? I mean it. I know who this guy is. I just need to get in touch with someone to find out where he is. Then I'll sort it. Thanks for coming to me. I'll let you know what happens and I'll return your phone.'

394

He had already taken it from the car bonnet and put it in his pocket.

'I'll come with you,' Barry heard himself say.

'No you won't son.'

Son. They were about the same age.

'I appreciate it but this isn't your business right?'

'He called me.'

'Yeah well. He'd want me to look after this, not you ok? Go home. Your home number in here is it? I'll call you. Promise.'

He walked away from them, back towards the pub. Ray followed. Barry hesitated. He'd met Kevin three times. Four times. He didn't know anything about him except his name.

'Let me know.'

'I will.'

'Please.'

They ducked through the pub door and the street went quiet.

———

Joe drove him home. They barely spoke.

'Look I better go and sort out the Sylvia thing ok?'

'Yeah.'

'Do you want me to come back after?'

'For what?'

'I don't know. To wait.'

'No. I can do that on my own.'

'You sure?'

'Yes.'

He forgot to thank him. He remembered as the car sped off, and almost shouted it, but didn't. He went into the ragged building and climbed to his home, fragile and empty, suspended above the street like a nest over a rising river. He examined his door out of habit. He sniffed the air. He could hear nothing but a low television somewhere below him. He checked his phone for messages. There were none.

———

He tried not to sleep but failed. He woke in the small hours to a knock on his door. His dreams had been such that he was not startled. It seemed entirely reasonable. It was solid. Persistent. It was not imagined. Barry pulled on a pair of jeans, and felt somehow that this was the end of it, one way or the other. He hoped that it would be Kevin. That the end of it would be Kevin.

It was Annie's husband.

He was pale, and his hair was wet, and his eyes were a dogfight red. He swung a fist at Barry, but waywardly, and his shoulders rocked, and his fist hit the door. Barry hadn't avoided it. The man had missed.

'She's gone . . .' he said.

'Dead?'

He looked at Barry with a twisted confusion, as if he thought Barry was trying to trump him.

'No. Fuck it. She's gone. Back in. Fuck's sake.'

And he sobbed fully, and stood there not moving, and Barry looked at him. Crying. He was a chubby man, his skin was bad, his eyes were ringed and his hair was lank. He wore a grey sweatshirt and blue trousers and old brown shoes. At once, Barry understood that this man had followed him, had knocked at his door, had called his name in the street. He had tried to haunt him. He worried suddenly that this would be his future.

'Do you want,' he said, 'a cup of tea?'

And he took him in.

Sylvia glared at him. Stamped through his house and took her things. It was a minor re-run of his wife's departure, and he was glad of it, given that he had slept through the real thing.

Joe let her go. He said nothing. He accepted all the things she called him. She was right. It was true. He owed her an apology, an explanation. But she was way down his list and he said nothing. She shouted all the way to her hotel. She slammed the car door. She was gone.

He drove home and told himself that he knew what he had to do, but that he had to start close to home. At home. He had to sort out the domestic arrangements before he could have a look at the world. The world after all, was a scary place. It was not family. There were people out there. In trouble. Lots of them. In lots of kinds of trouble.

Not all trouble, Joe decided, is the same.

He tried to think of Jesus. Of things that would help him. He tried to think of things that would help him. In the darkness and the quiet, with nothing but his own body, which was nothing, with nothing but his own body to see or smell or hear or touch, he tried to remember. Words. Stories. Songs. Things which would help him. He tried to imagine strength. He tried to imagine love. Being loved. He tried to remember that. Or imagine it. He tried to think of Jesus in a warm bright place, on a hillside in the sun, surrounded. He tried to remember what was said. Then. What were the words?

He had tried to escape. Jesus had. He had tried to run away. When he found out. When he was a kid. He found out who his father was, and he saw what was ahead of him, and he saw the messiness and the nails and he was frightened, because it was frightening, and he had tried to run away from it. He had run to the house of his friend, Ben, and he had hidden in the grain cellar, grain room, with the cool air and a rat that had worked its way through one of the walls and was too fat now to leave by the way he'd come. Jesus crouched there in the dark and he smelled the grain and he heard the rat and he waited for the world to forget about him and he refused to believe that it had anything to do with him, and he waited and waited and tried to be quiet, but the rat annoyed him and eventually Ben came in, looking for him, knowing he would be there, because they had hidden there together before, when Ben's father was angry, when Ben's mother was drunk, when they had wanted, the two of them, a little peace and quiet for God's sake. And Ben crouched beside him in the dark and asked him what the matter was, and Jesus told him that there was a rat in the grain room that couldn't get out, and Ben listened, and heard the rat, and with his practised eye, which was used to the dark (because, and Jesus was not sure how he knew this, but he did, because Ben knew the grain room very well indeed – he had spent many hours there, hiding and not hiding, mostly alone, listening, waiting, thinking about the light, thinking about his life and his future, worrying about his mother, afraid of his father, feeling great nostalgia for his friends, Jesus included, whom he could sometimes hear outside the wall, on the other side, playing in the sunshine or the early dark), with his clever eye and his quick hand, he killed the rat with a single throw of a small rock. The rat did not even yelp. He simply ceased his chomping. And Ben asked Jesus again, what the matter was. But Jesus could not burden his friend. It was not in his nature. So he berated him instead. He gave out to him for killing the rat. And in this way he settled into the idea of being God's representative on earth, through the deployment of deception and sentiment.

Kez thought that he was perhaps not on the right track. That he was badly facing. That he was not tolerant or just. He could not remember. He could not remember the reasoning, the formula, the rigid way, the tunnel out of himself which he had found as a child, between two eternal sheets, as if he were there on an endless plain, bordered above and below by smooth hard surfaces, like dark glass, like dark marble, impenetrable, but somehow not threatening, as if he was small enough not to feel crushed, buried, but he could not honestly say what size he was, big enough, small enough. He could not say how he moved. He was not his body – there was nothing to feel uncomfortable with, nothing to be squeezed, restrained, limited, crushed. So, comfortable then, unnaturally so, strangely so, but a strangeness which is not unsettling, not dangerous, not sharp. He was able to see a great distance. For the horizon was vast and endless. He didn't mean his bed. He meant his wall. He was in the wall. He was in that place. Endless place. Wonderful. There. That place. Travel. Travel was a place. There was a place which was also travel. This travel. This place.

You could be dead soon.

You could be dead soon.

A matter of hours. A matter of minutes.

Who's to know?

Would he remember the moment of dying? From where would he remember it? From where would he remember the parts of his life? From where forget? As if all was random. That couldn't be it. That it was all just a throw upon. A mistake. A burden. A wholesome weight. To be thrown off. He would be content to remain. For a moment longer. Just for that.

———

He tried to feel the fear Jesus felt, but he could not gain the comfort. He was left almost idle on the edges, lost in the darkness, a weight on his chest, a noise in his mind. His awful idle ruminations. He could not get the comfort of knowing anything. There was nothing he fully knew. Nothing he fully understood. There was nothing he fully.

———

Sound was missing. So he heard strange sounds. He heard his mother chop potatoes. He heard his brother singing. He heard a punter slap his arse. He heard the doors of the pro-Cathedral. He heard the Markievicz baths and his feet in the verruca pool, splashing. He heard the wind around the Custom House. He heard his running feet and his breath in the air. He heard the whistling of the national anthem, repeated and repeated, and kisses and farts and the bell of a bus. He heard the Angelus and the six o'clock news. He heard a baby crying. He heard the rattle of a chain and a knock at the door.

No one.

Sight was missing. So he saw strange things. He saw the body of a boy. Skinny in the corner, turned to the wall. That was not what he wanted. He saw his cock bigger than the rest of his body, like a missile that had been fired into his middle, pinning him to a table, killing him. He saw three trees in a gale, blowing one way then another. He saw rain. He saw a bird on a roof. He saw the body of a boy.

A voice came out of America. Out of the dark hollow air. Out of nowhere. Kez shifted on his shoulder blades, his head rolling round to look at that part of the dark. There was nothing there. There was something there.

At first there were just words. Just words coming across the room, thrown, handfuls of bright debris, things he should duck from, dodge. He thought they would hurt him, if they hit. He tried to sit up. A weight held his head down. He thought of yoghurt. He thought of a black bag full of rubbish. He thought of rubbish, rotten food and sweaty plastic. The bad breath tang of a split sack of rubbish. It held his head down and he could not rise, he could not duck. American words.

. . . sleep . . . rake . . . use . . .

Something like that. Small, fist sized words. Small fists. Boy fists. He thought then that he was a rat in the dark, too fat to get out now, and that this was a friend of Jesus, with an American voice, throwing bright yellow, red, blue words at him, hitting his face with them. Children's bricks.

ford . . . howl . . . pit . . .

Something like that. He thought he saw a face above his own. Or below. Or beside. Depending on how he was facing. A face next to his own.

yell . . . up . . . fuck . . .

He was lifted, he thought. Something raised him up. Mostly he was afraid of the drop back down – of being let go. He thought that his neck would surely snap and his head come off. His head would roll in the corner. Dark thought. He breathed and wondered had he been doing that all the time or had he just remembered?

'Well?'

A man was supporting his shoulders, propping him up. There was light. All the dark had whimpered off. That had been the sound he'd heard. Maybe. He wanted to be sick.

'Aw snap out of it will ya.'

The voice. That voice. It was wet and it smelled bad. Something was pressed against his lips. Okay. He knew how to do this. Suck cock. It was one of his skills. It was an easy thing to do. He should save his fight for the hard things. That was a joke. He opened his lips but he opened them the wrong way for the rim of a mug and the cold fresh water that followed. He spilled it down his chest.

'Aw Jesus Christ. Drink it fuck's sake.'

But that was okay. That was fine. It hit his skin and snapped. Bit him. Baby teeth. Cold. Very cold. It must, he thought, be warm, where he was. His eyes picked out a doorway, open just a crack. He adjusted his notion of upright – a little more slanted to the left than he'd thought. The hand that held the mug was thin but strong. He had perfect nails this guy. Americans are like that – perfect nails, perfect teeth. All the rest of them rotting.

'Go on.'

He took a sip, then another. The mug was blue or green, wide rimmed, cold in itself. And the water was superb – obviously some kind of special water available only to rich Americans, because he'd never tasted the like of it before, not ever.

'You done?'

He was almost gentle, the fucker.

Kez decided to say something. This was a very sudden decision. He felt that it would be right that he said something. That if he remained silent he would regret it later. That it was appropriate for him to speak. What to say though was the problem. He wanted to say something about his brother. But he couldn't work out what that was. He swallowed and opened his mouth again and tried to push out words. *My* and *brother* were his starters. They were the first ones. He'd see how he got on with those. They were bright blue, rectangular, their corners caught in the soft part of his mouth as they climbed from his throat. They hurt. They made him cough and gag. He couldn't spit them.

'Yeah yeah.'

His shoulders, or his forearm, or whatever part of himself it was that supported Kez, began to withdraw. Kez went down. The dark lapped at his eyes, but it did not cover them. There was still a chaos of colour. He saw a face above his own. It was triangular and banana yellow, first one way up then the other. It had eyes and a mouth but no nose that he could see. It smelled of land fill. It was too close. He thought it might be paper and he wanted to rip it up, but it spoke to him, in a television

accent, all corners and edges and sharp straight lines that connected with his face like bridges, and the words ran over, an
army of them, swords and spears all flailing.

'You'll feel better in a while I guess. Don't make any fucking
noise though. Okay? I'm not going to hurt you either. This is not
about that. I'm washing your clothes and you can have them
back. You're completely safe here. Okay? Couldn't be safer. So
sleep. Asshole.'

It withered then, the yellow mouth. Receded leaving vapours.
Kez wished to exhale but could only hold to what he had and
wait, hoping half that he would not die, and half that he would
– just so this American would be in the maximum kind of trouble, in this world and the next, for all eternity, without Jesus.

What new trick was this? This spectacle. This Catherine Wheel
and lantern light. It was an attack, a riot, an assault on her senses.
It was intricately strange.

Delly Roche had woken to an odd and clarifying thought – that
she was not dying. She suspected this had come to her in some
dream, the details of which fell flailing from her grasp as she
emerged from it, leaving her with nothing more than a terrible
lucidity and a loud insistence that she was not dying. *You are not
dying.*

Her hands felt different. Cool and untroubled. She found herself looking at them, examining the multitude of tiny scratches on
her fingers and palms, all of them hard and healing. They surprised her. She had not noticed them before. It was then that she
realised why she had not noticed them before. She had not been
able to see them before.

Her eyes. There was something right with her eyes.

She closed them immediately, and yelped, and retreated
beneath her blanket and twisted and turned. What the hell was
this? She ran her hands over the parts of her body that she could
reach, feeling for leaks or lumps or other signs of trouble. There
was nothing but the clammy bag at her side and a cold stomach.

She was hungry. Hungry and alert and not dying.

This was a lifted siege, and she felt an awful fear.

She peeked at her table. She could clearly see a radio, an empty glass, a box of tissues with one protruding from the slot as if escaping, a remote control device, the alarm button, a clock. All these things were simple. She looked again at her hands. They were old, spotty, scratched. Her veins looked fragile, tired, only half full. The bedspread was blue, dark blue, with a pattern of chequered squares at the corners. Her night gown was cream and silken, with red and gold needlework flowers around the wrists and the neck. To her other side the curtains were plain and heavy, the colour of honey with the first sun behind them. She looked at all of it and then looked again. Her mind was calm and clear, like a fresh day. She thought, for the first time in months, of the sea. And then all sorts of other thoughts appeared to leap at her, wanting her attention. Old things. Names. Faces. All the lists of living. They formed a jostling queue.

This was not dying.

The kid was alright. He'd been worried, a bit, that he was actually going to croak. That he'd screwed up some dosages, or had hit him too hard, or some combination. But he was alright because he was angry as hell. Which George had to admit, was funny.

'Get me the fuck off this fucking table.'

'Shut up.'

'You're a fucking maniac.'

'I washed your clothes. You want your clothes? Fag? Huh?'

'Just let me go. Please.'

'Cocksucker.'

'Jesus Christ.'

The kid wouldn't swallow his morning mix.

'Look kid. This will be a hell of a lot easier if you just stop acting the asshole. I am not going to hurt you. I do not have any interest in hurting you. I am not going to rape you. I am not a fag. You're naked cos you messed your pants. And I cleaned them. See?'

He opened the door but the kid couldn't see a thing.

'You take this calmer downer and I'll give you your clothes, let you get dressed.'

'What do you want me for?'

'Research.'

Eventually he had to smack him a couple of times and hold his nose and force it. He hoped he hadn't put too much diazepam in there, but he wanted him pretty much out of it for the first few days. After that, when the main thing kicked in fully, it'd be easier.

'Ok. What's your name?'

'Matt.'

'Matt what?'

'Matt Molloy.'

'You're making that up. What's your name really? Really really?'

'Kevin.'

'Ok. Good. What's the worst thing that ever happened to you?'

'This.'

'Before this.'

'The earthquake.'

'You were in an earthquake?'

'No.'

He was drifting off. Shit.

'Here. Sit up. Shit.'

He unlocked the wrist shackles and tried to prop him up, but he kept on slumping. He undid the ankles as well.

'Here kid. Stand up. Stand up. That's it. Walk a bit.'

He shuffled pathetically towards the wall.

'What was the earthquake?'

'A guy.'

'What guy?'

'Chester.'

'Chester? Chester is a guy? Chester who?'

He reached the wall and put his head against it and didn't move.

'Oh fuck's sake you're out of it already aren't you?'

He got him back to the cot. He left him unshackled. There was nothing in the room anyway, and he didn't want him shitting himself. He left a pot in the corner.

He had to be smarter. There was only so much of the stuff left.

Kitty set her alarm for seven. She was downstairs by half past. In time to see, from the cool hollow chamber of the hall, Dr George's car turn a crunchy circle in the gravel and head off somewhere. He seemed always to be ahead of her somehow.

She looked in on Delly and found her sniffing suspiciously at a de-crusted piece of home made brown bread. On her tray was a pot of tea and the remains of an apple.

'How are you?'

'Do that again.'

'Do what again?'

'Go back over there and walk towards me again.'

'Why?'

'Go on.'

She turned around and headed back towards the door.

'From there. Come from there.'

She did so, and saw on Delly's face a puzzlement and a deep concentration.

'That's baffling.'

'What is?'

'My eyes are much better. They're nearly working. I can see you almost. I can make out your features Kitty, where the things are on your face. And you standing right beside me. It's nearly normal.'

She was frowning. Her voice tripped over itself slightly. Her eyes flashed.

'Really?'

'Do it again.'

'Oh stop it.'

'It's strange to have you walk towards me and not disappear.'

Her colour was better. She bit into the bread. Chewing seemed an effort.

'I've been neglecting you Delly.'

She looked surprised at that.

'No I have. I've been neglecting you, neglecting my work, I don't know what I've been like at all. But I'm going to do better from now on. Really I am.'

Delly swallowed. She seemed to be staring at Kitty's mouth. She addressed herself there.

'You've been very good to me Kitty Flood. Don't make me say any more.'

'I have not.'

'Oh Jesus Christ you have so and you know it. Yourself and George. You have kept me . . .'

She trailed off, put down the bread, looked elsewhere – towards the floor. Kitty knew that she resented the care, the minimal care, the keeping of her. At least sometimes. And that at the same time she was grateful for it, afraid of herself and her wishes. Kitty had not liked being roped in with Dr George though. She'd have to wean her off that. Slowly.

'This bread is awful.'

'Do you not want anything on it?'

'Are there things? Go on then. I don't mind. I suppose I have to eat. I have to do these things don't I? Or else you and George are wasting your time. Today I can see. There's good news for you. The eyes are not themselves completely. But I can use them. There is less fog. My mind is clearer. Which I can only accept. I can only accept it. What else can I do? It'll all shut down in the end. Do you remember . . .?'

She stopped, looked horrified.

'Do I remember what?'

'Nothing. But. Do you remember the sea? Of course you do. But that bit of it, in France.'

'Of course I do.'

'That bit of it though. That square of it.'

'What square of it?'

'Nothing. Never mind. This bread is awful.'

Kitty buttered her a slice then, and one for herself, and they sat in the bright morning with the southerly world laid out before them, and they battled through some reluctance on Delly's part, to talk first about France and Jean Paul and Thomas, whom they had not talked of in what seemed to Kitty like months, and then about the pool and the possibility of Delly going out there, in time of course, the practical nature of this part of the conversation seeming to ease Delly a little, encouraging Kitty to raise once more the subject of nurses and doctors, about which Delly seemed, if not

406

entirely keen, then at least relaxed about discussing.

'Dr Mullen is coming tomorrow.'

'Oh?'

'Is that okay?'

She shrugged. Hummed.

'I'll be dead by tomorrow.'

'Well he can pay his respects then.'

She nodded, her eyes squinting out at the greenery.

'I haven't told Dr George yet. So don't mention it.'

Delly glanced at her.

'Why?'

'Oh just because. He'll be offended. I'll tell him later. But it's what you want isn't it?'

'I don't know.'

'You know you do. You've changed your mind. I know you. You want to be more comfortable . . .'

'I hate nurses.'

'You'll have approval. You can interview them.'

'I don't want to interview bloody nurses.'

'Well I'll interview them. No battleaxes. No funny voices. Only pretty young things. Sultry. I'll try and get ones who have some experience of erotic dancing.'

'You want me dead.'

'Bed baths will be a lot more fun than they are with me.'

She nodded and did not sulk. She stared out the window. She seemed fascinated by the view. She muttered that there was always a chance of a decent accident outdoors. A nurse might tip her in the deep end and the wheelchair might sink her. Though she worried that the bag would make her float. When Kitty laughed at her she did not frown, she smiled. Then hid it with a piece of bread and an exclamation that she could see as far as the gardens, and a bit of the field beyond, where trees were dotted along the sloping grass towards the stables in the distance.

Kitty was surprised at the small, bright change in the woman she loved, and at the gentle reminder that she loved her still.

But it was not yet 9am.

––––––––––

Mrs Cotter fed her poached eggs and toasted cheese and a pot of coffee and a Danish pastry in the kitchen while they listened to the radio and argued about economic indicators and the astonishing weather. Mrs Cotter seemed pessimistic about the future of all things. Kitty let her in on the news of the nurses, and she was plainly delighted. But Kitty warned against saying anything to Dr George and she nodded solemnly and seemed to understand something, though Kitty was unsure whether they understood the same things exactly. She did not know, as it happened, where Dr George had gone that morning, only that he had said he would be away until lunchtime.

Kitty took the last of the coffee out into the gardens and wandered amongst the flower beds and the weathered steps. In the distance she could see either Mr Cotter or his son fussing about a tree. The day was heating up. She turned and looked at the back of the house – at the stone and glass and the width of it. The width of it and the height of it. It looked sleepy. Benign for the moment. Like a monster in the morning, dozing still, waking, about to stretch and raise itself and shake its great domed head and give a lazy roar. A thing like that would terrify.

On the way back through the kitchen she told Mrs Cotter to go home. To take the morning off in recompense for the day before. She seemed delighted. Kitty smiled and watched her go, brisk and business like down the path that led towards the old tennis courts and the Cotters' house far beyond.

———

She went to the music room first. Something about the idea of sneaking into his bedroom made her slightly queasy. She hoped she wouldn't have to. Dr George had been using the music room as a kind of personal office and it was full of his things – some books, a lot of newspapers and magazines, and various folders and files. A bureau she did not recall having seen before sat against a wall. She frowned at the keyholes in its drawers. The piano stood in the centre of the room, and she noticed that there were two small speakers lying flat on its closed lid. She ran her eye over the pile of papers that sat between them. There were bills from his New York apartment. There was a letter from an Irish bank about a replacement credit card. Something that looked like a receipt for work on the car. Travel brochures for the far east and South America. A clothes catalogue. On a half empty bookcase by the window she saw various medical texts and pharmaceutical guides. Travel books. A couple of thrillers. A telephone directory for Manhattan and another for Queens. A mobile phone instruction book. A Let's Go guide to Ireland. Three spiral bound notebooks, all empty.

From this side of the room she saw that there was a miniature stereo system on a table right beside the piano. It seemed oddly placed, at a difficult height. Why wasn't it on one of the empty shelves around the walls? There was a cassette tape in the deck with *G.A.B.* scrawled on the label. Kitty turned the volume down considerably and pressed play. It was piano music. Stuttering. Unaccomplished. Repetitive. It was immediately familiar. It was the music that constantly bothered her as she sat in her office up above. It was Dr George, on tape.

She switched it off and turned the volume back up to where it had been, which, she immediately realised, would be loud enough to give the impression to anyone outside the room that George was within, playing the damn piano. This also explained the positioning of the speakers.

She tried the bureau drawers. They were all locked. On top were a couple of what looked like old files from the downstairs offices, but nothing which looked like Dr George's own. Nothing about disciplinary hearings or suspensions or St Agnes and Angels Hospital. Nothing. She tried all the drawers again. She rummaged for a key on the tops of things, finding only dust and dead spiders. She circled the room seeking hiding places or cubby holes. Nothing. Back at the bureau she had a look at what it was he had relocated from downstairs.

There was a folder with a faded, handwritten *Adoption Documentation* on the cover. Inside was a collection of letters from the State Adoption Board of Alabama and lawyers in New York and Montgomery and Daniel Gilmore's old Dublin solicitor. Another, much thicker folder was labelled simply *House*. It contained plans and drawings, and correspondence from contractors and the architect's office. There were black and white photographs of the foundations, with Daniel and Delly standing in what looked like the start of the dining room, and more photos of the house in various stages of its construction. There was also a large white envelope with *Mäckler Letters!* written on it, in what looked again like Daniel Gilmore's hand. Inside were three sheets, typed.

Dear Mr Gilmore,
I see of course the necessity of an independent access door to the suite of office. I do not argue this point whatsoever. My objection is to the idea that a front door requires a 'hall'. It does not. The idea of an area of reception is directly in opposition to the philosophy which I explained to you of integrated desire. This absence of demarcation operates to your satisfaction in the traditionally female areas of the residence (the sitting room, the dining room, the bedrooms) but meets your resistance in your own domain which you seek to control such as a rabbit or a rat controls the underground. You already, to my pain, have your hole in which you may bury yourself. This is enough. My designs for the office space are no longer amenable to adaptation to your patriarchal anachronisms. I do not have a secondary position, this my word is final.
Yours,
M. Mäckler

Dear Mr Gilmore,
The entrance to your lair must be as it is as
it is not part of the house which I have
designed and am building — am spending so
much of my life building. It is awkward
because it is not integral. It is a <u>hideous
appendage</u> which has no place in a home
intended for human beings. If you fall on the
steps you will be falling on your own swords.
Yours,
M. Mäckler

Dear Mr Gilmore,
I do not wish to amend invoices or invoicing
structures to incorporate the dishonest basement. I do not wish to be associated in any
way with this cancerous growth beneath my
design. The men who have constructed it are
not, believe me, interested or impressed by
your Medici delusions. Your concerns in that
regard are nothing more than a display of
megalomania. I do not wish to enter into any
further correspondence on this matter and I
consider it closed. I do not intend to charge
you for this monstrosity, in much the same
way as one does not charge the dog in whose
turd one steps.
Yours,
M. Mäckler

Kitty read them three times. She read them three times and then stared for a while at the stereo system beside the piano. Deception and history, she thought, and the secrets of men. Bad music, all of them.

Delly was pacing her room. In her mind she described it thus. *Look at me, pacing, damn it to hell, stamping up and down like a girl.* She was trying to go too fast, attempting dizziness, half hoping for a fall. In truth she was more shuffling than pacing. Her movements were slow, and despite her half hopes, they were well planned, considered, mapped out in advance, with all kinds of possibilities taken into consideration. *If I fall to the left I may bang my head on that table. Which would certainly hurt. But not as much as falling to the right and being impaled on the bare breasted bronze goddess with her cherubs and her empty plate.* She was dimly aware, but did not mind, that this debate was ridiculous, and that rather than walking herself into unconsciousness she was probably getting some decent exercise, which would be good for her. She did not mind because the whole rigmarole, her quickened breath, the heat in her joints, her darting eyes, distracted her somewhat from the terrible thoughts which gathered, legion, around her, like wild animals around a campfire, like lions around meat. A new siege.

She was under attack. Memory stalked her. Her past was present.

She did not concentrate on it. She sought refuge in movement and the corners of the room. She was like a woman in flight from a dream.

She used what she could as support. An armchair. A low table. A sideboard. So that when Kitty came in in a clattering rush, Delly was way off to her left rather than anywhere near, never mind in, the bed, which was slightly to Kitty's right. She was clinging, Delly was, to a lamp stand near a bookcase which she had not previously noticed, and was losing herself, as best she could, in her somewhat alarming ability to read the spines. She had not known that they had a full set of O'Casey. Fancy that.

413

And look! Three histories of the Easter Rising! The collected poems of Peter Sweeney! Two novels by Serageldin! Yeats in a leather bound volume!

'Jesus Christ,' breathed Kitty. 'Now what?'

'I'm over here dear.'

Kitty swung, or rotated swiftly perhaps, and stared at her.

'My God. How did you do that?'

'I can walk you know.'

'Yes but you're miles away.'

'I know. It's mostly balance I think. The pains are all smaller when I move. Useless little things. What's wrong with you? You look rattled.'

She had started towards her, but her large frame could not find a way between the heavy coffee table and the winged armchair.

'Nothing's wrong with me. I should get you my stick. Why didn't you ring if you wanted to go wandering around the place? What if you'd fallen?'

'I have it with me – look.'

She held up the button which hung around her neck. She was sure it was the full scale disaster button rather than the cup of tea request button because she could see now, with her miraculous eyes, that it was red, and hung on red string, and had **PANIC** written beneath it in big black letters, while the other one, which was on a much shorter, blue string, was green, and had *Attention* written underneath it in fake handwriting like, she thought, a name plate outside a small Parisian hotel. Any one of several where she had briefly lain with Frank Cullen.

Oh Jesus Christ. Stop it. Leave me alone.

'But Delly, still, God.'

'I thought you'd be pleased.'

'I am, I am. I'm surprised.'

She had thought better of her route and had come around the long way, and stood now beside Delly who was aware, for the first time in quite a while, of just how fat she was.

'I'll sit down I think.'

'Ok, here, no there, ok, there you go.'

Her hands were gentle. She sat opposite.

'It's tiring. Being up. And about.'

'Are you ok?'

414

'Yes I am. More's the pity.'

'Ok.'

They looked at each other. Before she knew where she was Delly found herself remembering, Jesus, remembering a random New York day, a Battery Park walk, fireworks, something about the statue. Reagan in town, watching fireworks, night time. A Wall Street roof top. She chased it away, damn thing, before she had it clearly. She pinched the skin on the back of her hand. Hard.

'Delly, is there a basement in this house?'

Was this a trick question, she wondered? To check on the state of her mind?

'Yes dear. Kitchen, store rooms, two bathrooms and a bedroom. And a laundry room.'

'No I don't mean that. I mean another basement. A hidden one.'

There had been terrible tantrums from the architect. Mäckler. Daniel had found it all very funny.

'The hidden basement. Daniel's den. It's under here I think. Underneath us.'

'You're joking.'

'No. He insisted on it.'

Delly pinched harder, but details came none the less. They presented themselves. Kitty looked terribly surprised.

'You never mentioned it.'

'Well. You never asked. I forgot about it. I don't think I was ever down there. I can't remember. I don't want to remember.'

'What was it for?'

'Oh men. You know. I think he had a little lab down there. I don't know. Leave me alone. Why do you want to drag me over this old nonsense?'

'I found some letters. Never mind. How do you get into it?'

'From his office. His private office. The inner one. There's a secret door. He loved all that. Mäckler didn't. Mäckler was a very strange man. I think he became a priest. Oh stop. Daniel claimed he was a genius. I think he did some work in the UK after here. Then he did a seminary in Wales. My God. This stuff. And became a priest. Or was that someone else? Leave me alone. Where are you going?'

'To have a look. Are you alright there? Do you want to get back to bed?'

'Stay. Talk to me. We have to work things out. Ramps. We'll need ramps. Where will the nurses sleep? Will they stay over? Should we interview them? Kitty? We have to talk about the future. Kitty!'

'I'll be back in a minute. Promise.'

And she kept her promise too, dashing back almost immediately with her walking stick, retrieved from somewhere in the hall, which she presented breathlessly to Delly with some mumbled instruction not to trip on it.

She practically ran from the room, huffing and puffing and flushed. Refilling the pool. Nurses. Doctors. Exercise. Kitty needed to lose weight. Delly tried that. Tried to think about that. She'd get her to walk everyday. Around the estate. Get her to swim. Swimming was good. Very good exercise.

It was no use.

Daniel hadn't liked to swim so much. Or he didn't like the pool. The sea was fine, but the pool, he said, was full of chemicals. He understood it too well. It spoiled it.

There.

He preferred to whack tennis balls at her, or cling to a galloping horse. She had been good at tennis, but she'd never been able to take it seriously. She was reduced to giggles by his serious, grunting serve. She annoyed him by not arguing over points, by forgetting the score.

What was the point?

The horses scared her, which meant that she kept her mouth shut and concentrated, while Daniel careered around her, telling her fragments he remembered from his boyhood adventure stories. Cowboys and Indians. Lost explorers. Armies on the march.

Daniel.

Daniel Gilmore.

There had been snow for a while. Every year, a deep layer of it would fall, to rouse them from their January or February depression, and Daniel would have the horses brought up to the house and he would take her, walking pace, through the white glare to the walls, or to stand in clouds of horses' breath beneath the great oak in the west field. He loved to go slowly on a horse through the snow. He loved the silence and the blank country and the far distant curls of chimney smoke. He would say quiet things to her then. Quiet and solemn things – based on joy. Based on joy and a house to go home to.

Lucky years, those.

Her hand was pinched raw. But there was no point.

She rose with difficulty, the problem being concentrated mostly in her knees, which were sore and noisy. She thought that she might not have made it at all without Kitty's stick. She shuffled back towards the bed, taking her time, stopping along the way to have a look at pieces of furniture or knick-knacks or pictures, seeing if she couldn't remember where they had come from.

She could. Of course she could.

There was a jewellery box which she knew contained a turning ballerina, pirouetting to the wind-up chimes. She wondered whether there was any jewellery. She didn't want to bend and check. There was danger in her joints. There was a tiny piece of beige card in a plain silver frame. On the card, under a roughly sketched lopsided face, was Salvador Dali's autograph. Apparently. Daniel had come back from Spain with it, and with an elaborate and improbable story about a bizarre hotel in Madrid and an actress whose name she could not recall, and the mad artist on a balcony, throwing crusts of bread to the trams.

Why did she forget the details? The actress's name. And remember the useless things. That he had sent flowers every day of his absence.

There was a porcelain statuette of a dancer in a green gown, and a matching one in red. They inclined towards each other, two slim women, their faces averted. Germany, she thought. He'd brought back a ridiculous clock as well. She couldn't remember where that was. He had always brought back something. For her. They were her things, he'd said. *Everything is yours, and these things are extra. Because I love you. Because there is no end to it. No end to it. Never.* He had gone away and come back. He had taken her riding in the snow. He had written her letters while she was sleeping. He had built her a house to live in. He had filled his head with her. He had not stopped. Ever.

'Delly!'

Jesus God what?

It was Kitty, filling the doorway.

417

'Don't do that Kitty, you gave me a heart attack.'

'Sorry. Are you okay? I found . . . do you want me to help you?'

She came and assisted with Delly's climb back into bed. It was a hurtful procedure, and gave some relief. Parts of her body seemed to balance very shakily on others, like spinning plates. They got it done, with some grunting, Delly at one point, she thought, gaining a foothold in Kitty's stomach, which was of great assistance. She lay panting on her podium.

'I found it.'

Delly merely looked at her.

'I think I found it. There's a safe dial. Behind a light switch. In the small office. It must be it. I can't see the door but it must be it. Right?'

Delly took a moment to remember what it was she was talking about. Her confusion was remarkably brief.

'It must be I suppose.'

'Do you know the code?'

'No idea.'

Kitty sighed disappointedly and sat down. Delly was breathless still, but it was slowing – she could feel her innards calming, calming down. And all the muck was flooding back. That she had been, for example, she knew, so lucky. To move from one love to another. To have been found like that. Twice. Three times. She should not complain. Yes she should. She should not push it away from her. Yes she should. Her heart resumed its rhythm.

'It'll be something memorable,' said Kitty. 'Or some chemical thing. Or something.'

'Are there trams,' asked Delly, 'in Madrid?'

'What?'

'Trams. Or just buses and trains?'

'You know I really don't remember. Why dear?'

'Nothing.'

He had been, Daniel, like a force of nature. He had blasted through the world. He had taken her with him. He had made her feel lazy but had never once asked of her any single thing other than she stay with him, be with him, that she remain. Frank Cullen had been a kinder, slower man. He had not been so determined. So driven. He would have settled for a quiet life. In a small house. Somewhere sunny. With Delly.

Oh not Frank. Don't start on about Frank. Please. Leave it.

The telephone rang. Kitty answered.

'Yes? No he's out. Who are they? Well I don't know where he is. Was he expecting them? Well go and ask them.'

She looked at Delly, dropped the mouthpiece slightly.

'There's people at the gate for Dr George.' She stared into space. 'Just numbers,' she muttered. 'Maybe a telephone number or a date.'

Delly watched her thinking. Her forehead pulsed and her eyes narrowed and twitched. She had had the quiet life. The sunshine. She had seemed content with it. Had not perhaps written as she should have, but that was her concern. She had never asked for anything other than to stay. To be with Delly. To remain. She had passed, Delly had, from passion to love to comfort. Was that it? Like a single relationship, but with three different people? Was that it?

'What? No well tell them they'll have to come back. He's not here. No. No they cannot. Never heard of him. He'll have to go and come back. We know nothing about it. Right. Bye.'

Daniel had loved her. He had scratched her name in church stone. He had sent her daily postcards from the world.

'It'll be my birthday,' she said.

'What?'

'If it's a date it'll be my birthday.'

Kitty sat forward.

'Are you sure?'

'If it's a date. Yes. Of course. My birthday. It would have to be my birthday. What else would it be?'

He had built everything for her.

Kitty rushed back to Daniel Gilmore's old office. It sat at the front of the house. Its window gave a good view of the drive. There was no sign of him. Dr George. She went to the dial hidden in its little recess in the wall. She had found it by banging. A single slap had released it.

She tried firstly the month, the day and the two digit year.

Nothing. She tried the month, the day, and the four digit year. Nothing. She realised she had it backwards, American. She tried the day and the month, and before she could try the year something shifted with a thud beside her. She jumped. She thought she'd been discovered. But it wasn't that. She had got it. The wall to her right had come an inch or two closer, or part of it had. A central section protruded, emerging from the panelled wood lower half and the cream upper. Plasterboard. She touched it and found that it slid easily and quietly and smoothly to the right, revealing a wide doorway into a black space. Hinges hung from the wall on the left, and a doorframe was clearly visible. A second door had obviously been removed.

Perhaps he had not been able to get in. He would not have known to try Delly's birthday. Or maybe it was obvious. Maybe it was the kind of thing that would appear on any list of possible code numbers, given a little bit of intelligent thought.

She stuck her head in and sniffed. There was a musty kind of odour. There was silence. There was no light. She ran a hand over the walls on either side looking for a switch. She could not find one, but in her moving about something brushed her face. She shrieked and went backwards, and stumbled, catching herself on the wall, realising as she did so that what had brushed her face was a pull cord for a light.

She regained her feet. She moved back to the edge of the darkness. She pulled the cord. She was surprised that it worked, but with her surprise came the almost certain knowledge that Dr George had been there before her. He had changed the light bulb. He must have. Either that or it had stayed in working order, and the electricity had stayed connected, since 1979. In front of her were steps that twisted downwards and towards the left, taking a strange misshapen route. It was all bare concrete, rough edges, cold walls. Nothing was painted. Nothing was finished. None of it seemed at all related to the house. The smell was bad. The silence was sweaty.

She went down a couple of steps. The naked bulb cast a glare and she wanted to see past it. The steps were uneven. Her hand caught on the walls and came away dusty. Her feet crunched a little. The steps seemed to go left and then right, and then left again, for no apparent reason. They went quite deep. She stood and stared towards the bottom. She could see only a concrete floor, in darkness, but with another pull cord just at the edges of the shadow. She climbed back upstairs.

It had been constructed in a sulk – she could see that clearly. Mäckler had decided to build it as he believed it to have been conceived – as a dirty little secret. A bunker. She wondered suddenly whether Daniel Gilmore had been worried about war. Whether he had imagined Delly and himself escaping the fallout in their concrete cave – living on tinned food and bottled water. Mäckler hadn't mentioned it. But it had been the era after all.

She called the front gate. If there were people looking for him he might be back soon.

'I want you to call me on my mobile when Dr Addison-Blake arrives. Ok? As soon as you see him. Ok? As soon as you see his car on the road.'

She checked that her mobile was turned on, and went back to the stairs.

She thought of whistling to herself. Of humming. She thought of talking aloud. Of cracking jokes. She expected to find, at most, at worst, a kind of den. Maybe a television and some porn movies. Funny stuff like that. Maybe some details of the trouble in New York. Some evidence. But in the back of her mind, working away in a corner, raking and mowing, hammering and heavy lifting, was the Cotter boy. His disappearance. That.

She pulled the cord on the light at the bottom of the steps. There was a corridor. She saw three doors to her right. She saw a washing line slung the length of the passage with a pair of jeans, a shirt, a pair of underpants, two socks hanging from it. On a table at the end there seemed to be a jacket thrown. On the floor beneath it a pair of shoes. Young man clothing, all of it. Her mind emptied suddenly of all expectations. She was here now.

The first room was a bathroom. It stank. The sink was stained brown. A huddle of dead spiders occupied each corner. There was a brand new bottle of mouthwash and two rolls of toilet paper. There was a towel taken from upstairs. It looked horribly significant, like a marker left for her. You're getting warmer.

The second room was a lab or office of some sort. There were work benches. Papers. More sinks. Glass jars. Bottles. Trays. Racks of test tubes. A fridge. Canisters. Charts. She saw scattered pills and a tub of white powder. She saw little tiny envelopes opened and empty. She saw syringes in a bin, and more in sterile packets in a steel tray. There was a stethoscope. There were books, opened at pictures of muscle groups, diagrams of internal systems, cross sections. She wanted to look through some of the papers. But there was a third door. She checked her phone. There was no signal.

Kitty Flood cursed and turned, and came out in to the dim corridor and looked towards the steps. There was nothing. She could hear nothing. She hesitated for a second and went to the third door. What could he do if he caught her? Fume and sulk. Be embarrassed. But she was not in the wrong.

The door was locked, but the key was there and she turned it and tried again. The room was dark. She reached for a cord but could find none. There was no noise. She felt for a light switch. It was to her left. She flicked it.

He was naked and his skin was blue and grey and he was as still and precise as a photograph. His head was turned away from her, fallen to face the wall. His hair was matted, his feet dirty, his chest a blooded purple. There was blood like rust on his stomach and his thighs. His fists seemed clenched. Nothing in him moved.

Kitty thought she might faint. Her elbow hit the doorframe. She was moving backwards. His feet were dirty. She was moving backwards. She had never seen a dead body before. His mother was over in her cottage. Washing windows. Preparing lunch. Telling Mr Cotter the gossip. Thinking of him. Jesus Christ. Kitty Flood backed into his jeans that hung from the line in the passageway, and she became entangled briefly, and she screamed, and cut it short, realising where she was, backed into a corner, in trouble now, entangled now, the things he could do to her now, and she turned towards the steps that led upwards, and she fled.

Dr George Addison-Blake drove along the nondescript lane which led past his adoptive mother's estate. He drove slowly, taking a look at the wall, checking for breaches and damage which the security assholes would invariably miss. He was worried about access. Getting in and getting out. He thought, not for the first time, that he should get rid of the current security firm and organise it himself. He knew people now. Who could do that kind of thing. As he turned in to the gate one of the assholes was in the box hut on the phone. Another one, unusually, stood in the wide entrance.

'Dr Addison-Blake. Those gentlemen there have been asking to see you. They've waited a couple of hours.'

He ducked and looked out through the passenger window. He gaped. Something in his lower insides went a sudden cold. Walking towards him from a parked Mercedes was David Martin. David 'Deano' Martin. Who he had never seen outside of the city. Who had never even telephoned him in person. Deano Martin summoned – he did not visit. With him was a younger guy who looked a little familiar. There was no way in hell, in any conceivable circumstance, in which this could possibly be, at all, good news.

'Go away,' he said.

'Pardon sir?'

'I'll deal with it. Go away. Open the gate.'

He shuffled off towards the box hut and the gate in front of George swung slowly open. As it did so the younger guy broke into a swift jog and made it to the passenger side before the car could go anywhere. He rapped on the window.

'Hold the fuck on.'

George held up a assuaging hand, tried a smile.

'Yeah, yeah. No problem. You wanna take your car in? We can go up to the . . .'

'Open this door.'

He opened the passenger door. The guy got in.

'Right asshole. You are so fucking dead. I swear to God.'

And he hit George, hard, on the side of the head, with a tight fist, once and then twice, the second blow sending his head cracking into the window.

'Jesus Christ what the fuck are you doing?'

He had his hands up but they were just defence. He wasn't going to mess with this guy. Deano's guy.

The back passenger door opened and Deano climbed in.

'Ok Vince that's enough. Drive us up to the house George there's a good lad.'

He started the engine. He tried to work out what he'd done. It couldn't be drugs. They gave him what he wanted. It couldn't be the guys he'd fixed up for them. He'd done a good fucking job. He'd made sure of that. The porn? They didn't care about the porn. Deano had thought the whole porn thing was hilarious.

'You've got my brother.'

'What?'

'You've got my fucking brother.'

In the rear-view George could see the Mercedes following. He looked at the guy in his passenger seat.

'What are you talking about?'

He got punched a third time. This one caught him full on the nose. He lost control of the car – it started off somewhere to the left. He braked but was conscious that they were on the grass. He thought his nose might be broken.

The young guy grabbed George, by his shirt collar. He pulled him over the gear stick.

'If you've hurt a fucking hair on his head I swear to God I'll fucking kill you.'

'Will you wait Vince for Christ's sake.'

George was looking at Vince. He looked familiar. But he couldn't place it.

'Let him go Vince. We'll do it proper.'

Vince pushed him away. George looked at Deano.

'On please George, there's a good lad.'

'What the fuck is this about?'

'Just drive.'

As he drove, the Mercedes following, through the clumps of trees, past the pathways and the rolling grass, towards the low solid bulk of the house in the distance, George Addison-Blake, breathing blood, tried to work out exactly what it was that he had managed to get so completely wrong.

🍴

Kitty slipped on the stairs. Twice. She bruised a shin on the steel. She was breathless, so much so that she could not think. She had dashed through the office, into the hall, sliding on the marble floor, to the main stairs, moving faster than she'd moved in years.

Her brain was struggling in deep water. She reeled. On the first landing she started to cry. But it took even more oxygen from her system, so that something in her chest burst into flames, so she stopped crying, lest it kill her.

She must call the police. The police. There was a murdered boy in the basement. She must take Mrs Cotter to her home. She must comfort her and keep her husband from thoughts of revenge. She must get protection for Delly. She must call the gates and tell them not to, not to, under any circumstances whatsoever, not to admit Dr Addison-Blake to the house. Security alert. Panic button. Bells. Ring the bells. She hit the second flight of stairs with force, as if trying to stamp it level, and felt for certain, something go in her hip. She reached for her phone and could not find it. She had clutched it in the basement. Perhaps she had dropped it there? She searched in the folds of her clothes and the holding places of her body but there was no phone. She stood over three steps. Looking up towards the second floor. His room was there. He might have returned. Her phone, after all, was elsewhere. How would she know? She looked down at the first floor. The music room. He might be there.

In her head a ghost arose. She saw herself murdered in the dusty dark. She saw her head caved in. She saw blood caked on her skin like a mask. She saw herself naked and dead in the concrete. Buried alive.

She tried to go both up and down, her indecision vast and endless. Her long suffering feet could not please her. They tangled and tied and tripped her. She fell headlong, hip wide, face first, onto Mäckler's concept staircase, rendered in steel, inspired by early 1920s Soviet cinema, in a way that only he had understood, and she came to rest, Kitty Flood, upside down, still, in semi-realised fulfilment of her vision, without dignity, useless, in a trickle of her own tired blood.

'You don't remember me do you?'

'No I . . .'

'Fuck's sake.'

'I don't remember you. I don't know who you are or what the hell is going on and I think my nose is broken.'

'Georgie, Georgie. Calm down. Vincent here is a pal of mine. He's a good lad. You'll have met him a couple of times, but I'm sure you've met a lot of people haven't you? And you can't be expected to remember them all.'

'I met you at Deano's. Twice. Second time you asked me whether I could fix you up with a boy. Remember?'

'A boy? What are you talking about?'

'Don't fucking play with me.'

'I don't like . . . I'm not a fag.'

'I couldn't give a shit what you are. You asked for a boy. And I gave you a number. You remember now?'

'No.'

'You fucking do.'

'Deano, what the hell is this?'

'Just listen Georgie.'

'I gave you a number. My brother's number. And I know you called that number because I asked him. And he said you did. Shut up. You called it. He's my fucking brother. And this is you . . .'

George thought he was being punched again. But it was not a fist, it was a mobile phone, held up to his ear. It hissed at him.

'I'm being murdered.'

'Naw you not.'

'Dunno where I am. Car Cunty BM woo.'

'Fucker. Fuck's sake.'

He made his face go blank. But maybe it was blank already. He should have let the little fucker go, as soon as he'd seen the phone. Brothers. Jesus Christ. The city was so fucking small it was like being at a private party. Look at this guy. Pimping for his own brother. That was some special kind of sick.

'I'm being murdered.'

'Naw you not.'

'Dunno where I am. Car Cunty BM woo.'

'Fucker. Fuck's sake.'

'You need to hear it again?'

'That could be anyone.'

This time it was maybe two punches, one quickly after the other, he wasn't sure. He thought he blacked out for a second.

When he was next aware, his eye, his left eye was closing. He thought back to having the kid in the passenger seat where his brother sat now. He thought it was clumsy, stupid symmetry. He thought that they'd probably kill him.

'Get out of the car.'

He fumbled for the handle. He couldn't find it. Then Deano opened the door from the outside. George half fell. Vince came and dragged him onto the gravel, where he slumped, got to his knees, had trouble standing. Vince hauled him up. They were talking to each other. Deano and Vince. George couldn't hear them.

'Who's in George? George? Listen to me. George. Who's in the house?'

His mouth hurt. He thought he wouldn't be able to speak, but he could.

'Flood, maybe. Delly. Cotter woman. I don't know.'

'Are there security guards in the house?'

'No.'

'Are you sure?'

'Yes.'

'Right. Where is he George? Hmm? Where's the boy?'

'Inside.'

He heard Vincent moan, a terrible, long sound.

'Where inside Georgie?'

'Downstairs. In a basement.'

He thought he heard sobbing. He didn't know if it was him or the kid's brother. He thought it might have been both of them.

'What have you done Georgie?' Deano asked him, and his voice was all there was. 'What stupid fucking thing have you done?'

They thought he'd killed him. They thought he'd killed the kid. It wasn't until he was able to look at Vince, able to focus on his face, and he saw the horrified eyes, and the grief, and the small flash of hatred that he was trying to cling to, that he realised. *They think I've fucking killed him.*

Which meant of course, that things were not as bad as they had seemed. Not by a long way. Because if he had actually killed the kid. If he had actually been some kind of sick fag serial killer, he was sure that Deano and Vince would kill him. Not here. They'd take him somewhere else. Somewhere remote. And Deano would hand Vince a gun or a knife or a hammer and Vince would kill him, probably as slowly as he could. And they'd bury his body where it wouldn't be found. Easy.

But he hadn't killed the kid. Sure he'd, he supposed, kidnapped him. Tied him up. Slapped him around a bit. And true, the kid, now that he thought of it, was still naked (unless he'd actually thrown his clothes into the room and the kid had been together enough to put them on, but he couldn't remember whether he had or not), and was going to look pretty bruised and be pretty much out of it, but there was no real harm done. He hadn't broken anything. He hadn't *done* anything to him. A couple of cups of coffee and a hot bath and the kid would be right as rain.

He tried to tell them.

'He's fine you know, he's fine. I just needed, you know, someone healthy, fit, you know, he said he'd be willing, I'm paying him good money, it's research, you know, it's important.'

He took them across the gravel. As he fumbled with his keys he saw drops of blood on the small stones. His blood. Deano was looking around, looking up at the house, his hands in his pockets, like he'd come for a viewing. Vince was at George's shoulder. He was shaking his head, wiping his eyes.

'Shut up.'

'It's my father's, you know, work. His work. It's his work. I'm just carrying on. Continuing. With it. The kid was willing to help. The phone call. He was. You know, just a little apprehensive.'

'Shut the fuck up.'

He got the office door open. Two locks. Both open. He pushed at it and left a red smear on the wooden frame.

'But he's fine. I mean him no harm. No harm. Just a couple of weeks. Ten days. Just a week maybe, probably less than a week. Just taking the tablets. Just one a day. Just to see. Because with my mother.'

They stepped in. His nose seemed to be melting down his shirt front like a dinner candle.

'I mean with Delly. She's not my mother. With Delly I just can't tell. Can't figure out if it's the tablets or whether she's just fading anyway. Losing it anyway. The kid is great. Is a great help.'

428

A mobile phone lay on the floor. George picked it up. Put it on a desk.

'It's important work. Could be very important. My father you see. He had this idea. He was a great man. So your brother is playing an important . . .'

'Just shut the fuck up.'

'It's research.'

He stopped in the inner office and stared at the hole in the wall. It was open. The door was open. The panel had been slid away. To the side. George moved slowly. He said nothing. The lights were on. All the way down the lights were on. He went down. Vince followed him. Closely. Deano came behind. George trotted down the last of the steps. He went for the last door. It was open. It was open and the key swung in the lock. Inside the cot lay empty. There was no one there. He was gone. He swung around and pushed past Vince and looked in the lab. Nothing. Then the bathroom. The fucker was gone.

'Well?'

'I don't understand.'

'Where the fuck is he?'

On the line behind Vince's head there hung two socks, like little black question marks on the pale grey walls.

He dreamt that he was cold. He dreamt that he was cold and he was sitting on a pier and the waves were breaking below his feet as he swung his legs over the edge and stared out to sea. He dreamt that ships passed by in the distance, and that when they saw him they blew their whistles and sounded their horns and the passengers stood on the decks and waved at him and cheered. But he was cold. He was cold and miserable. He dreamt that all the boats came towards the pier and they hung out flags and they turned in foaming circles underneath him and the crowds waved and cheered and bands struck up and orchestras played but still he was cold. All the harbour and all the bay and all the sea as far as the horizon tried to warm him. Fish jumped. Yachts set sail. Ocean liners nudged each other. Trawlers filled their nets. Whales and dolphins sang and danced. Captain Bird's Eye winked at him. And still he was cold. Closest to him of all was a girl on a wooden raft. A raft of sticks and branches, tied together with vines. She smiled at him. She touched his feet. She reached up and touched his feet. She stretched herself to full height, held his feet and roared his name.

He woke. Startled. The light was on. He was freezing. There was noise. Some noise. Or there had been some noise. He sat up. He was able to sit up. He was not tied. His wrists and his ankles were free. The light was on. The door was open. Someone had been there.

He stood up and fell down. He banged his arse on the side of the bed and it hurt. There were no bedclothes. The whole room was just a concrete shell, like a room on a building site. He stood up again, holding on to the bed again. Which was not a proper bed. The noise had been like shouting and running. He held the bed and stared at the door. There was nothing in his head but thinking. He was hungry. Thirsty. He couldn't tell which was which.

The key was in the lock on the outside. He could see the same concrete out there. He could see a floor and a wall. And he could see his jeans, hanging upside down from a clothes line, swaying back and forth, moving like they were being touched by a breeze.

He tried to make a run for the door, afraid that if there was wind then the thing might slam on him. But his legs were fucked, and they buckled and he only stopped himself falling by doing a kind of splits and by leaning a hand on the edge of the open door, aware that if he fell a certain way he could well end up slamming it shut himself. Everything hurt. But mostly now his throat hurt. His mouth was dry and his throat ached and he wanted a drink of water more than anything else in the world. He climbed upright. He moved slowly and went through the door. His head swam. But he could make out his clothes floating in front of him, a corridor to his left, steps at the end of it. A couple more doors. Concrete. Bare. No one.

He grabbed his pants. Getting into them was an ordeal. He realised half way through that he shouldn't have bothered. He should have gone straight for the jeans. But he got them on. His shirt too, though he couldn't button it. He put on his jacket, then tried the jeans. Eventually he lay down and squirmed into them. His shoes as well. Then he just rested, exhausted, lying on the floor staring at the ceiling, thinking that it looked like a cloudy day, that it looked like rain, and that that would be good – rain would be good. He was afraid that at any moment the American would reappear, but he was too tired to move.

He knew he was in a basement. That was all. He tried to think of strategies but his mind was hopeless. It held nothing but steam and hunger and thirst. He knew that he needed to get out. That was all. He may have dozed off, because suddenly his heart leapt, as if he had woken again, and he was terrified, and he climbed to his numb feet and stumbled down the corridor. The middle door was closed. He avoided it. He moved by on the opposite side. He listened for sounds. There was nothing. The last door on the left was ajar. It was a bathroom. He could see a sink. He spent a long time listening. His head bowed, his eye on the gap. Then he shouldered the door. It was empty. He ran the taps but there was no water. His throat clawed at him and he wanted to cry out.

The steps took forever. He kept misjudging their height. He took them like an old man, having to put both feet on each one, clinging to the wall, sometimes just leaning against it, getting concrete dust all over his jacket, scraping the leather. There were twists. He banged his head. Eventually he reached the top. He seemed to be in an office. There was a carpet. It was warm. There were wood panels and bookcases and a desk. He stumbled to the window. He saw grass. Flower beds. Trees in the distance. Lots of empty grass. There were birds in the blue sky, or black dots in his eyes – he did not know which. There was a gravel driveway. There was a big Land Rover. There was no BMW. He didn't recognise anything. He turned and went through another door, and into a bigger office. More desks. More bookcases. There was no sound. There was a door leading to the outside. He tried it, but it was locked. Double locked. He turned and walked, bumping into things, towards the big doors opposite. He was afraid now that they would be locked as well. But they opened onto a hallway. There was no sound. The floor was tiled. Big checkerboard black and white tiles. To his left there was a closed door. Ahead of him was a closed door. Slightly to his right was a staircase. Up and down. Further to the right was a gloomy wide passage way which seemed to lead to a bright area, a hall.

He stood and listened. There was something. A low constant noise, a murmur. A television. He was sure it was a television. It seemed to come from in front of him. He moved towards his right. Away from it. Then he heard, clearly, unexpected, a woman's voice raised above the tinny canned applause – *Oh for God's sake leave me alone can't you* – and he halted, and waited, and turned.

He thought about knocking. But he didn't see that there was a point. He opened the door a little and peered in. He could see a long room stretching off into the distance. Furniture and pictures and views of a green world. Beneath one of many windows there was a bed. Beside it a table where some bottled water stood. Water. He moved forward slightly and heard a gasp to his right.

An elderly, thin woman, his height, with long grey hair, stood startled in front of a large television. She wore a dressing gown. She was pale but her eyes were deep and dark. In her skinny, scratched hands she held a remote control and a walking stick.

'Who the hell are you?'

'Please help me.'

She reached for her necklace, but her hands were full.

'Are you a Cotter? You're not are you? Who are you? What's happened?'

'I was taken. I'm . . . I was down in the . . . I was in the basement. The American man. I'm thirsty. Please can I have some water. My name is Kevin. Except . . . That's my name. Except . . . I have another name, but I can't remember it.'

He was tired. He had been a long time scared. He was so tired. He didn't mean to or want to, but it was high time he did. He began to cry.

The boy stood on her carpet and he wept. His shirt was open. He wrapped his arms around himself. He was black eyed and bruised. He trembled. He was utterly lost.

Delly's hands hung in mid air, her stick half raised, the remote control pointed upwards. She knew she should drop the remote and keep the stick as a weapon. Then she should use her free hand to press the button that hung from her neck. But she was prevented from doing this by his choice of words. *Basement. American man.* These were ominous. And the ragged state of him. As if he had travelled a great distance to bring her bad news. Perhaps he had come from the terrible television. From the wounded family on the day time talk show. Perhaps her invocations had been heard and he was the angel of death. A battered angel, caught in a storm on the way down, here to take her skyward. His hands twitched. Perhaps she was supposed to take one of them – to grasp his shaking hand. Perhaps she should ask him.

'Are you?'

'Can I have some water?'

He walked towards the bed. He shuffled. His legs seemed triple jointed but useless, and his face was pained. He wept still and his nose ran and he sniffed. She set off after him.

'Yes,' she said.

She found that her greater knowledge of the furniture allowed her to catch up, even though she paused to switch off the television and throw the remote control on a chair. She was horrified then to discover that her shuffle was faster than his. Passing him made her dizzy. While he continued his terrible advance she poured him a glass of water. He came to her side and stood panting and drank, spilling some. She could see dried blood on his chest, glowing at her through his open jacket and his shirt.

'Thanks,' he breathed.

Her fingers fiddled with the string around her neck. Perhaps she was dead now. Perhaps death was a boy. A hurt boy. Perhaps death was a hurt boy who you had to look after.

'Sit down. Sit down on the bed. Have a tissue. Are you alright?'

'Yeah, thanks.'

He clearly wasn't. He wiped his nose.

'Are you,' she asked, and found her finger pointing at her neck, 'going to kill me?'

He looked astonished.

'No. No. God.'

'Who are you then?'

He sniffed. Looked to his left. His voice was quiet and frightened and came broken and uneven, in a rush at first, then faltering. He gulped great sobs which made her want to help him. But his words were shocking strange. He looked often towards the door. His trembling eased, but did not stop. He bit his lip. He told her that his name was Kevin, though he seemed dissatisfied with this, and that he was some kind of prostitute, though she thought perhaps that she'd misunderstood that bit, or misheard it, or somehow got it garbled.

She listened to his story. She listened, and after a while she sat beside him on the bed, and as the tale was told she joined him, distractedly at first, but with increasing bafflement and horror, in glancing at the door.

'Be smart now Georgie. This is a bad kind of situation to be in.'

Deano stood in front of him, his hands in his pockets, his face creased blackly, criss-crossed with anger and loathing and distrust. He was powerful and still. Nothing in him moved.

Vince was standing sobbing by the open door. In his hand he loosely held a gun. Small calibre, snub nosed and ugly. George thought that it might have a home made silencer attached. He thought that Vince's mind was probably elsewhere. That he was thinking his own thoughts. That he might just shoot anyway, anytime, just out of blind white repulsion.

'Where is he Georgie?'

'I don't know.'

Vince raised the gun. Spluttered something. Lowered it again. Raised it. Lowered it. Took a step forward.

George was tethered to the cot, sitting, but hunched over, his feet on the floor, his torso twisted sideways, his head down, his wrists held by the ankle ties which he had used on the boy.

Which he had used on the boys.

Vince moved again. George felt the gun on his head. On the top of his head. On the crown.

He was going to die now.

'Where the fuck is he?'

It was still Deano talking. But his voice seemed attached to the gun. The whole thing felt like a drill.

'Where the fuck is he?'

The gun disappeared for a second. The drill disappeared. Then there was a hot bright explosion that lit up the side of George's head, and he felt everything there go numb. Vince had hit him with it. His ear bled. From the inside. He couldn't hear anything. He couldn't hear Deano's voice. He looked up and saw his lips move.

'Where the fuck is he?'

He had done terrible things in his life. George Addison-Blake. From the start. He had not intended these things. But he had done them. He saw them lined up behind him like road signs. Like markers. Milestones. They lined the road behind him, going back into the distance, over the horizon where he could not remember being, back to the start, of which he had no knowledge, of which there was nothing but a blank space. An erased name. Something forgotten. He tried to tell them.

'My father,' he said, and a red bubble formed on his mouth. 'My father,' he said again, and it burst, and he shivered, a sudden cold approaching. 'He made a drug. It makes forgetting. You can forget. So that people can forget. Where they come from. Where they are.'

He was hit again. He didn't know why. He was telling them.

'It's fucking true. Imagine it. This drug. In Northern Ireland. In Palestine. Balkans. This drug. This forgetting. Imagine it. Imagine it.'

They were going to kill him. He could see them talk to each other. He could see Vince looking at the gun. They didn't get it. No one would get it. It didn't work. It couldn't work. And when all that he had done was discovered, and a light was shone upon it, and it was lined up and shown to the world, he would not be able for it. There would be no escape. No way of not being himself. He would have to give the whole world his father's drug,

435

and hope the world forgot him. He didn't think it could be done.

It was alright. It was okay. He deserved it.

'He's in the wall,' he said.

His hearing was gone. He couldn't hear them. Vince held him up, almost gently, and stared in his face. He was like his brother. In the eyes. George pointed. With his bloody head.

'Out there,' he said. 'At the end.'

They were gone some time. He breathed. He heard his broken lips whistle in his head. His heart sounded like a train pulling in to a station. He was something arriving. It was only fair. He watched the small drops of blood fall on the floor. He shouldn't have done it. It had been stupid. There had been no need. The Cotter boy. His name had been Michael. He had come sniffing and poking and accusing, with his crowbar and his grievances. Shouting and pushing and threatening things. Stupid angry kid, losing his dirty little sideline to a yank. He should have dropped it. He just should have dropped it. He'd broken into the tennis hut. George had led him back to the house. They'd fought in the main office. George had knocked him out. He'd impressed himself with that. Then he'd given him a massive shot of morphine and watched him sweat and go cold. He should have kept him. But he only thought of it afterwards, as the firemen stamped through the ashes looking for bones. It would have saved all this mess.

Peace. His father's work. His blood turned black on the floor. Peace through forgetting. His father's work. That was all. He was leaking blood now, but his hope had been peace. In his heart. Somewhere deep. Peace and the road home.

Michael Cotter was curled up behind a plasterboard partition at the end of the corridor. That's where they'd find him. And any dead boy by this stage would look like any other.

When they came back in the room he raised his head to see whether it would be straight to the gun or whether he'd be punished first.

It was straight to the gun.

Kitty's head lay in blood on the fifth step up from the first floor landing, and her body occupied the four steps above that. There was silence where she was. There between floors, high over the heads of others. Her blood dropped through the perforated steel and fell to the steps on the flight below. When a small pool had gathered there it dropped again and landed on the marble of the main hall, the drops splashing, sending tiny specks of blood in wide circles.

One shoe remained on a foot – the left. The other had come to rest by her head, and was peculiarly upright, as if she had stepped out of it for a rest. Her skirt was bunched up around her thighs. Her tights were ruined. Her blouse was ripped a little where a button had caught in one of the holes in one of the steps which she had slid over before coming to a halt.

She was dead.

She was not dead.

She couldn't decide.

She thought that the absence of all pain, other than that of the axe lodged in her skull, was a sure sign of death. But the taste of blood and the sight of her shoe, and her damp and stinging crotch, seemed to indicate that she was still in the world. Of the world. This world. The blood and piss world.

She could not raise herself. Not that she tried. She was convinced, utterly, of the impossibility of movement. Even the opening of her eyes had been a terrible, troublesome thing that had taken days. Why had no one found her in so long? It might have been weeks. Perhaps she was dead. Perhaps this was death. To become part of the place where you fell. So in a garden you became the soil. In a forest you became the mulch. In the sea the water. On the stairs the stairs. On the steel the steel. She had been reborn as a girder.

It was her own damn fault. Running. At her age. With her weight. What had it been this time? Was she late for something? Hungry? She was always hungry. Sprinting down to one of Mrs Cotter's breakfasts. She thought that she should be nice to Mrs Cotter today but she could not think why. Perhaps because she would feel guilty for having caused this carnage. She would feel bad about the blood. Something about the blood. She should be nice to Mrs Cotter and she must be good to Delly always – that should be her first priority in all things. And there was something else. But she couldn't make it out.

She moved a knee and her whole bulk slid a little. A step. Downwards. Her cheek slapped against the edge of something. It hurt. She tried to use her hands to stop herself, but they seemed not to be working. Lifting them in fact made her slide again. Her head was in an uproar. Stop this now. But she slid faster. There were one, two, three more slaps to her cheek and then a horrible thud, and the hollow cavity of her skull came to rest on the first floor landing. She fell into a sudden sleep.

Her unconscious body settled itself on the level by use of gravity and a single roll. She lost the one remaining shoe. The chief gash in her head was now facing upwards, and the bleeding lessened somewhat. Her breathing, though strained, was not impeded. She was out for about a minute.

When she came to she was convinced that it was the next day. The evidence was the increased light and the fact that she was feeling a little better, as she would after a good night's sleep. She had to use her hands to check that her body was still attached to her head, as her head was really the only thing that she could feel. She wished it were otherwise. Her chief confusion, rising above all the others (her father's first name, the colour of Delly's hair, their telephone number in New York, the location of her shoes) was that no one had come to help her. How could no one have used the stairs in so long? And all that noise she had made the day before, when falling, and then again. It had been like a train derailment. It should have brought them running. But there was a deep and edgeless silence. Nothing came to her at all.

She tried raising a hand. It seemed to work. She had a sensation of lifting something impossibly heavy, and her blurry eyes caught a movement in roughly the right kind of place. She tried the other. A sudden piercing pain shot through her, reminding her brain that it had an arm and a hand and fingers out there, exposed, prone to damage. She whimpered, and unconsciousness made a rush at her which she dodged at the last second. Something was certainly snapped.

438

It took about four weeks in pain time. First to roll over. Then to haul herself on to all fours. Then up to her knees. Raising her head was simply horrendous. She expected it to burst. Her vision was altered, but she found that if she wiped the blood out of her eyes and then half closed them, it was sufficient. One arm was broken. She thought up near the shoulder somewhere. There was swelling over her eye. She was afraid to prod her head too much, but knew that the chief problem was at the front, on the left side, just above her hairline.

On her knees she proceeded across the landing in the direction of her bedroom, thinking of nothing much more than getting to her bed. Her progress was terribly slow. The pale green carpet over which she travelled revealed itself to be a vast and complicated land, filled with warring peoples and isolated tribes and unlikely wildlife. Several civilisations rose and fell in the course of her painful advance. Knee forward, ball of hand forward, clawed fingers, forward, forward, sliding more than lifting, causing with her frictional tights and her fleshy hands, firestorms to be raised on the plains, wiping out whole villages, settlements, cities. Bored, troubled, hurting, she imagined these people on the pale green swathes below her. She invented names and languages and architecture and culture and songs. Some tribes recited, others sang. Others danced in strange formations, senseless on the ground, revealed from her awesome height as complicated, dizzying patterns, designed to catch her eye, beseeching her, praising her, declaring obeisance and loyalty and fealty towards her, pleading with her, begging. The great crawling God of the carpet. She did not quite know what they wanted. She advanced so slowly that a carpet lifetime was passed without her seeming to move at all. But in that lifetime a vast lake of blood might drop out of the sky to prove that she was indeed all powerful and terrible, and over a generation a fire might rage and the villages disappear from the path of her divine knees, her miraculous hands, the trailing revelation of her bare feet.

She thought she would sing to help her on her way. She would sing to her people. It would be, perhaps, what they were waiting for. A sign from above. She had not sung in so long – she didn't know why. She considered. Something cheerful, rousing, fun. To make them dance. She liked when they danced in their huge circles. She liked the patterns that they made of spirals and corkscrews and wheels within wheels. She started quietly and found it eased the pain in her head. So she became louder and drew strength from the beautiful sounds she could make, as she trailed her blood across the carpet world, and her people danced for her, in rings and stars and conga lines of millions, and she saw what she had made, and she saw that it was good.

'Truly Scrumptious
You're truly truly scrumptious
Scrumptious as a cherry peach parfait.
When I'm with you – it's so delicious.
Honest, Truly, you're the answer to my wishes.'

She thought he looked a bit like Frank Cullen. He was far too young of course. But it was there. Or maybe it was in the voice, or the body language. Or maybe it was the way he kept looking at the door, terrified. Or maybe it was something in the way she found herself reassuring him.

'He's out. He's still out. I would have heard the front door. It's okay. It's alright. He's not here.'

His hair came down from his head and stopped on his neck and his skin re-emerged. She could see the start of his collar bone. She could see his chest. He was very handsome. Frank had been more handsome than Daniel. She thought. Though he was younger. Five years younger.

'I'll lock the door.' She thought she remembered saying that to Frank. I'll lock the door if that makes you happy.

She shuffled off.

'Where are you going?'

'To lock the door I said.'

'Can I use your telephone?'

'Yes of course.'

Something in her had turned to liquid. To water. Some part of her, inside. She could feel it as she walked. As she shuffled. It moved in her like a sea. Or a lake, probably. More like a lake. It had edges. But the edges, where it stopped, was where she stopped as well. She couldn't work it out.

Nothing hurt.

It happened in Rome. It had been a stupid thing. A stupid idea. That she could go with Daniel where he went and not be bored. That she could follow him and listen and feel involved. She had gone with him to London a few times. In Paris she had felt stupid. She went to Rome. Thinking that she could look around while he had his meetings. And Frank had been there and they had met many times of course, before that, and he had stayed in the house, with Siobhan, a few times, and she had liked them but had thought them a little dull, polite, respectful. Siobhan was not in Rome. And when Daniel went to see the chemists and the pharmacists and the researchers to have his technical talks, his drug discussions, his 'brainstorming' he called it, Frank had taken her out – because he was the accountant and he didn't need to know any of that stuff, or he didn't understand it – she wasn't sure.

They went to the Vatican and they laughed. They stood in the Sistine Chapel and they giggled. Laughter. It was always laughter that got her in trouble.

She locked the door.

'Now press it.'

He pressed the minor alarm. He held the telephone in one hand. He pressed the alarm with the other. She could hear a distant buzzer. She hadn't heard that before. So that was how it worked.

'Now you see. If it's him he won't get in. But Mrs Cotter and Kitty, they will. Have you been to Rome?'

'Have I what?'

'Been to Rome?'

'No.'

He was sitting on the edge of her bed. This strange boy. He was just sitting there now looking at the telephone receiver lying in his hands. He had told her terrible things. She knew she had to think about them. She had to decide whether she believed him or not. She had to decide what was the truth.

'Why are you not . . .'

She gestured, as she shuffled, at the phone.

'I can't remember any numbers.'

'But you're young.'

He looked at her. He seemed to find her fascinating. He looked at her the way birds looked at her. The way birds in their trees and God on his ceiling looked at her.

'I use a mobile. I don't know any numbers. Just the names. I have them stored. It's broken. It's gone.'

He started to weep once more. She had to deal with this now. She had to focus on it and work it out. He replaced the receiver and scratched his hands. She had to concentrate.

'I have,' he sniffed 'a getaway bag. I need to go home for it. Then I can leave.'

'What's a getaway bag?'

'In case of trouble. It has everything I need in it. To leave.'

He was a little confused, she thought, as was she.

'Where will you go?'

'I don't know.'

She handed him a tissue. She had limited resources. Mineral water. Some moisturiser, aspirin, a view.

'Are you sure you didn't see Kitty?'

He shook his head.

'She went down there. She let you out.'

'I didn't see anyone.'

Delly stared through the window at the noon day world. Looking at the boy was distracting her. She recalled her husband as a young man. His body. His body in the sun by the sea. In the far distance she thought she could make out the water, but it was only a fault in the sky. When Frank had first kissed her they had stopped laughing. When they first made love they had cried. In a Dublin hotel room in the middle of winter, with the rain hammering, with the rain pounding on the walls. They lay there and they cried.

The boy clutched his chest. He was not well. Terrible things, he had told her. About her putative son; her tentative life. He was a ghost. A spirit. He was come from the walls. A snotty nosed boy with a black eye and blood on his chest, in damp clothes with news from below, and her life was altered and amended and would need to be rethought. Just like that. A burst of words, sitting on her bed. There. A few short minutes.

And on top of everything else.

Frank and Daniel and everything else.

Where the hell was Kitty?

She was in a world of her own.

When she had sung for some time she felt better. It was during the third verse of *Luck Be a Lady Tonight* that she realised she had passed her room and was beside the secondary staircase, the conventional stairs, which led down and up, and having named 'down' to herself she remembered something odd involving Dr George, a moving wall, someone else's blood.

She needed, she thought, to perform some kind of task. Some essential service. There were deeds required of her. She studied the carpet. What deeds? There was no one down there. Just a blank and barren vast expanse. Her people had abandoned her. They doubted her existence. She was cast out. Her head hurt. She wanted to sleep. Now that her singing was stopped, she wanted to sleep. But there was something she was supposed to do. She looked at the start of the stairs. The top. It looked difficult. She had a go at it forwards, and changed her mind, feeling there was an incorrect distribution of weight – that her bulk was behind her, pushing her, pushing. She came back and turned around. All of it taking hours, a re-alignment of planets, a shift in the shape of the heavenly body. Great was her torment, and her knees were raw.

She recalled a naked man. She confused this a while for her own history. So that down several backward, nervous steps she forgot that the interest she had in the bare flesh of men was negligible, academic, reserved for the great gay artists and their notions of beauty. She thought she was a woman in love with a man, and this man was somehow tethered, naked, to a high platform, in an empty field, by a rushing river, and it was her task to rescue him, clothe him, heal him. Why then was she descending, arse first, down some kind of stairwell? She paused, heard her breath, felt the pain in her head.

Delly.

443

Delly Roche.

Why did she want to die so badly? Had life with Kitty been so hard?

She'd have to ask her. She'd have to ask Delly that. Sit her down and ask her. Ask her out straight. About whether Kitty should take it personally that she was keen to be gone. Maybe it was because Kitty was fat. Because she was certainly fat. There was no doubting it. Not at all. She was definitely fat.

She set off again, not able to see very much – even when she ducked her head and tried to peer upside down underneath her body, through her legs, towards the next step, and the one after – so that when she reached the little half landing, where the stairs doubled back on itself, the next flight going from south down to north, her lack of downward potential shocked her a little, and a great gob of blood fell from her head, onto her hand, and she stared at it, silent, without a thought, before remembering (and it came with a sound, a whoosh, which brought bells and klaxons and chaos dragging after) that she had seen the dead body of the Cotter boy and that George was a killer and Delly was in danger and that the whole sudden world was gone horrid, violent, weird.

She rushed then. As much as a fat woman, concussed, on all fours, backwards, with impossible news, could be said to rush. She used the banisters in the later stages. She paused when she thought she heard a crack, as if one of her knees had finally snapped, but the pain remained constant, and she soon got going again. She had to rest on the half landing between the first floor and the ground, simply out of desperation, out of sheer exhaustion, out of the knowledge that her heart was loose and had fallen, and was pressed against her rib cage like a boxer on the ropes. She tried calling out, but nothing came of it that she could tell, and it hurt her head too badly.

Eventually she reached the ground floor. A phone. Delly. These things. The door to the long room was in front of her. She tried to stand. Using the banister. She made it, but her head was a remarkable, extravagant agony. She inched forward, put a bloody hand on the wall, breathed as if she had been underwater, not upstairs, and gripped the handle.

She was obviously too weak to open the damn thing.

Either that or it was locked.

She rattled it. It did not give. Her breathing just got quicker. It was as if the air was thinner down here. As if it was running out. A phone. She needed a phone.

She turned and stumbled to the offices. She shouldered the open door and it swung and banged the wall. In front of her, through the glass, she could see figures in a car, in a Mercedes car, two at least, maybe three, as the car turned in an arc on the gravel drive and headed off towards the gates. George's car was there too. Parked. Empty. Just sitting there looking at her.

She headed towards the phone, but through the open door to the inner office, Daniel Gilmore's private office, she caught a glimpse of her own mobile, sitting on the desk. She headed that way. She'd be able to call the house phone, reach Delly through the locked door. Her lumbering body bumped into everything. Her breathing didn't seem to work. It frightened her, the noise of it in her head. She felt dizzy, sick. Her vision was frayed at the edges like old cloth. It was only when she was in Daniel Gilmore's office that she remembered his hidden basement. The sliding wall. The cold concrete. The dead boy. It did something to her heart.

She looked that way. There was nothing. There was no door there. Just a wood panelled wall. A light switch. That was all. She held her phone. She didn't know, she wasn't sure. She swung her head to clear it, and to check the other corner. There was nothing. It was all gone. All gone. Finished. She couldn't work it out. Where was she? This big house. This sunshine. These things were not real. They were not hers. She was blood and fat and she reeled, dizzy, and sought her own name in the list she had invented. She needed her own name. What had she made up? What was her story?

As she fell she tried to grab the door, but managed only to slam it shut. Her head caught the solid mahogany arm of a chair which stood against the wall. Her collar bone cracked on the parquet flooring. Her bare feet caught in the delicate legs of a nest of small tables, causing ligaments to tear. None of this mattered.

If her head had not killed her, her heart would have.

They clung to each other and stared at the knocking door. It was Daniel, she thought, and snapped a correction at herself – don't be bloody stupid he's dead more than twenty years, it's his son, his mad son, his adopted son. *His*, she noticed. *His* son.

'Who is it?' she called out. There was no answer. She could feel the boy tremble.

'It's him.'

He made no move. They listened. There was no more knocking. Silence came back.

'That's him. I know it is.'

There had been just the one time, in just over three years, when they had come close to being caught. It had been in this very house. Frank had been down for a meeting, and had stayed, and that night, while Daniel slept, they had met each other in the smallest bedroom on the top floor, and had lain there for an hour, in silence, awake, until they heard Daniel's voice somewhere below, calling Delly's name frantically. She had sprinted to him. He sat up in their bed with a look of terror on his face. She told him she had been to the bathroom. He told her he had had a nightmare in which he'd been lost, on a ship, and could not find her. He thought that she had fallen overboard.

When she told Frank the next day he had been suspicious that Daniel knew what was going on. That he was teasing them. That he was playing with them. But Daniel could not have behaved like that. He was not so deliberate, so careful as them.

'What happens when you press the panic button?' asked the boy.

'I don't really know. Doctors come. I think. An ambulance. Should I press it?'

'Yes.'

They regarded each other.

'I'm very sorry,' she said.

'It's not your fault.'

'Maybe it is.'

She pressed her panic button. Bells rang. Through the house, and beyond, bells rang out, loudly.

'Wow,' said the boy.

'I'm very rich,' said Delly.

He was cold. He was cold and scared but he thought now he would probably be alright. It hurt him to remember things. He wanted to forget them. He wanted to forget the basement and the dark. He wanted to forget his brother and the American man. He wanted to forget what he did for a living. He wanted to get to his flat, get his getaway bag, and get away. The plan had always been Dun Laoghaire, and a ferry. That would do. He couldn't remember how much cash he had. If he had enough he might go to the airport. He needed to rest. He needed to eat. He needed to get away.

The bells rang in the house. The woman was talking now about her husband and horses, and she was trying to apologise to him but she was going about it the long way, by explaining her whole life to him, and he wasn't really listening. He needed to get away.

He wondered what the bells did. He thought that police would come, and that he'd be asked endless questions, and that there would be trouble.

His body hurt him.

'George wasn't mine. He isn't mine. I never wanted him. That's not my fault. Maybe Daniel suspected. Or maybe he knew. No. He didn't. I am you see. I would have. Given everything. Everything. Nothing matters. None of it. I would have given it all up. In a moment. Frank Cullen. He had such a laugh. I don't know why. Don't ask me why. How can I know? But he found out. And he killed them both. Or the storm. How do I know? In front of me. As if on purpose. Both of them. Dead. On my nightie. Blood. Over there. Over your shoulder. Yes I know. Horrible. Horrible. And look at me now. Still here. Still in my nightie. Still with blood. Your blood now. No that's alright. I'll write you a cheque. Where is it? My eyes are almost perfect. I don't know why. If they had managed, in that storm, if they had managed to land, to get that stupid thing down, onto the ground, in all that noise. If they had done that. And come to me across the grass. Across the gardens and the grass. If they had come to me and offered me a choice I would have chosen him. Here it is. I would have. If it had been up to me. It

447

would have been my choice. I would have given all of it. All of it. But they died. Over your shoulder. Horribly. I could almost laugh. And ever since. Ever since. I've had George to remind me. Of what I was about. Of what I was up to. Of the choice I would have made. And ever since. Ever since. I've had Kitty to distract me. From what I was. From all of this. But it's over now. I'm back. I'm back in my nightie. And I'm waiting. Just waiting. With the blood. Let me tell you. Let me tell you this. You have to regard your life, you have to mind it, you have to use it up. Because one of these days you'll wake up and realise that you're fifty.'

She paused. There was more silence. Deeper silence. Always noise then quiet, quiet then noise. It was a damn parade of stupidities.

'What is your name?'

'Kevin.'

'Kevin what?'

He told her. It was a nice name. She wrote it down. A good Dublin name.

'You'll wake up and realise that you're fifty. And you'll think to yourself – Jesus Christ almighty is it not over yet? Is there more of this to come? How much more of this? How much more? You might only be half way through it. Imagine that. Imagine that. Half way. And don't believe what they say. It does not fly. It crawls. Once past twenty five it crawls. It cannot run any more. After thirty it can't even walk any more. It crawls on its stumps and it bleeds and it leaks and it hurts and it smells. So regard what you put in the path. There will be no way around it. Here.'

She held it out to him. He took it.

He thought he could hear voices in the house. Voices and footsteps. The bells stopped ringing. She was standing at a desk with a cheque book and a pen. He was confused. He had another name. He was sure of it. It spun in his head, moving so fast that he could not catch it or see what it was. It made him dizzy.

He didn't want to do this anymore. This job. He couldn't keep track of all the names.

'They're coming,' he said.

'What?'

She listened. There were noises outside. Then a knock at the door.

'Jesus,' said the boy.

'It's alright. It'll be Kitty.'

'No. This. The cheque. Is this for real? You have to be joking.'

'Oh take it. It's nothing. For what you've. For what happened. It's nothing. Really. I'm very rich. And I've nothing left to do. With it. And Kitty has all she wants. Apparently. And George can forget it. Really. It won't bounce. There'll be questions of course. But I'll look after all that. Don't you worry. You look awful. You look like death.'

There was a shout.

'Miss Gilmore! Are you alright?'

'I'm fine,' she called out, sure for once that her voice would carry. 'The door is locked. Hold on a minute.'

The boy was looking at her like she was mad.

'That's Mrs Cotter. It's only money. It doesn't do any good. But it might help. With your getaway bag. My God, my strength is awful.'

She began her shuffle to the door. It resembled a walk. The boy coughed. He wasn't interested in her story. She was barely interested herself. But it's all you have to offer when the time comes. It's politeness to tell what ails you, when the time comes. At the door there was a babble. Maybe Mr Cotter, or his son, or some of the security men. The bells, she assumed, would call them over. They would have a procedure. She could hear neither George nor Kitty. She could hear, she thought, the sound of a helicopter. Like drumming fingers on the sky. Memory playing tricks on her. She had asked death into her house so often. She had thrown open the doors and the windows. She had repeated the invitation so many times that it was practically the only thought left to her. Death. Come in. She had prayed for it. She had willed it and wanted it and it had stood its ground. She had summoned it in. But it had not entered. It was stubborn and proud and it let her be. She was stronger than a boy. She was fully alive. Death had somehow missed her.

She turned the key in the lock and opened the door to the long room and looked out at the little crowd. She sought out certain faces. But they weren't there.

Lastly

They take him as instructed. They lead him, his weak frame, from the long room, and as he passes, Delly touches his head, his hair, as if in blessing, and she leans forward, to whisper something in his ear perhaps, but stops herself, as if she has remembered something, as if something that was clouded is now clear. She shoos them away, tells them to take him, to lead him, to help him. Mr Cotter and his son, Paul, Paul Cotter, assist him gently, puzzled, and direct him, and when he stumbles in the main hall, Mr Cotter holds him up, while Paul goes and gets a chair from beside the wall, near the bottom of the stairs, where he notices drops of blood on the marble, and a pale shallow pool, and thinks to himself that that's odd – perhaps the boy has come this way – that he'll have to investigate that. They wait there, father and son, silently, in attendance on the feeble youth with the blood on his chest, while the two security men go to fetch the paramedics. This is like a dream.

Mrs Cotter fusses and flaps at Delly Roche, who demands, as soon as she realises what's happening, that the curtains be closed, that the horror of the helicopter be shut off from view. She slumps then in an armchair and bids Mrs Cotter be gone. To go and find out where Kitty is, and where George is too, and to bring them to her. She has words for both.

They lie him on his back. The damaged boy with the black eye. They give him a once over and some oxygen. They talk to him, they use his name. They are gentle and polite and they secure him to a stretcher and he lets them. They wheel him from the main hall down the corridor to the elevator at the far end, where they take him down, and all the time he tries to figure out what it is that has happened to him, and whether it's real, and if it's real, just how real is it, and whether it's bad or good and whether he should be sad or happy. How much is ended?

They take him out into the blue world. His eyes hurt, but he makes himself look at the sky, he makes himself sure. He sees the house, the size of it. He sees the gardens. He sees the empty cube of a swimming pool. He sees the blades. For a moment he does not understand. He thinks that there is some mistake, that he is still in danger. But a man holds his shoulder and explains. This is for you. We're taking care of you. Everything is going to be okay.

Mr Cotter follows. He watches the casualty being loaded into the great hollow bell of the helicopter. He hasn't seen one this close up in over twenty years. The memories are not welcome. He shudders and his confusion sticks in his throat. His son Paul goes back to follow that trail of blood from the hall.

Mrs Cotter is following the same trail, but from a different place. A bloody handprint on the long room door. A speckled progress towards the offices. In the outer room there is a heavy silence, broken by the noise of the helicopter's engines starting up. The blood goes left, unsteadily. She tries to open the door to Daniel Gilmore's office. It seems to be jammed.

And meanwhile, miles away, Barry's heart can bear it no longer, and it instructs his head to remember his mobile number, and instructs his hands to dial it, and he listens to the ringing tone and he does not breathe. He is alone again in the growing discomfort of his home. Annie's husband stayed much of the night, telling his story, telling hers. It took hours.

This is a new world.

And in another part of all this, Joe Kavanagh lies on his back on the grass of his garden, and he stares at the sky and he thinks of his daughter, and he sees a high plane and wonders whether Sylvia is on it, but decides probably not, that the ends of things are never that clean, never that pretty.

Delly closes her ears to the drumming fingers, the rotary blades, the reminders. She will have none of it. She will not let it in.

Too late.

She hears, at the same time, the rising howl of the memory engine, and Mrs Cotter's scream.

454

Kevin tries, with his eyes closed, to remember all his names. Nothing comes to him. He has never flown before.

The machine rises up. It lifts. On the ground below, a metre or so east of the restored tarmac pad, with its yellow H, hidden beneath the short sun burned grass, there lies a shard of fibre glass, twenty two years old. And a little to its left, an inch or so beneath the hard soil, is one of Daniel Gilmore's teeth. And beside it, as if approaching, is a button from Frank Cullen's jacket, and further to the left, as if escaping, is a cuff link which he received, as a gift, from Delly Gilmore, née Roche, on the first anniversary of the start of their affair.

The machine hangs, nose bowed to these relics, and turns a semi circle to the north, and moves as if searching, towards the air over the house. Kevin lies on his back, but he can turn his head, and does so now, forgetting for a moment all the things he has forgotten, and he sees the high chimneys which rise from the long room where Delly sits, her face awash with frightened tears, suspecting now, at last, too late, that her longings have been clumsy, ill directed. Underneath her feet, in the dishonest basement demanded by her husband, their adopted son lies dead and undiscovered. Near him is the decomposing body of Michael Cotter, waiting quietly for his brother. And his brother isn't far. He stands beside their mother, his shoulder at the office door, shifting the dead weight of Kitty Flood, hoping uselessly that there might be life within. Kevin moves above him, gathering speed. Security guards run backwards and forwards, their dogs barking at the sky, their walkie-talkies useless.

They go on. They continue. Kevin, on his back. To the city. They pass over the Mercedes in which David 'Deano' Martin and Kevin's half brother Vincent consider the possibility of getting away with murder, and think it unlikely. For their attempts at deception have been rushed. Untying Dr Addison-Blake. Putting the gun in his hand. Sliding shut the wall. Wiping off fingerprints. And their departure, half calm, deliberate, witnessed by the two men on the gate, had the look of a completed con, and the feel of a funeral procession. Though Deano's chief worry, just now, is that Vincent's guilt at having left the body of his brother where they found it will cause him to blurt or blab or otherwise reveal, at the wrong time, to the wrong people, what it is he has done. For he is sobbing now, making a mess in the back seat, muttering, '*Kez, Kez, Kez*', like it is a prayer. Deano knows silence is their only hope. This is not silence. He will have to have a think about this.

Kevin flies over them, and for a second he remembers something about his name, but he loses it then, it's gone, as blurred and as strange as the ground below him.

On he goes. Over the dual carriage ways and the green fields and the edge of the island. On towards the start of the city. With his pocket full of money and his body full of chemicals and his heart emptied out by living. He stares at the passing air. He twists to see the ground. It hurts but he does it.

In the city there are people living. There is Barry, about to hang up, but hearing at last the strangled voice of Vincent, repeating again and again a single syllable that makes no sense, and crying loudly when Barry asks what's happened. Crying out some wordless news that Barry cannot fathom. What is this place? Back down the road, Vincent has rolled down the window and has thrown the phone away. It cracks on the roadside and its pieces scatter on the grass and all the voices in it cease.

Joe Kavanagh stands in his garden and tries to chat with Albert's wife over the wall. He wants her to like him. It's so simple that it makes a stuttering sob rise in his throat which he has to swallow back. He asks about her children, and she asks about his.

Kevin is in the air. All of him. And the number in his pocket is more than he can count to in a life as short as his. It will be paid. And he will get away. They'll patch him up, they'll fix him. He'll go and get his bag and he'll head for the airport and he'll leave. Because he's had enough of this.

Annie's husband is called James. Barry goes down to the basement and he knocks on his door. He needs to tell someone what he's lost.

Kevin looks down on the city and he tries to see it clearly, all of it, expecting that the height will tell him something he doesn't know. That from up here it'll be different. He recognises roads and streets. He can make out buildings and houses where he has been, where he has passed by. He knows the open spaces and the parks. He knows the walls and the corners. He knows the doorways and the lights, knows what's hidden there, and what isn't. He knows it all. The river comes down out of the hills where he's been. He can see it pick its way through the clutter. He can see where it's going. He can see that it's always going there.

He lies back, rests his head, checks the sky. He wonders what the city sees, when it looks up, when it looks at him. Always these machines overhead, always, going somewhere else. Always there, going somewhere else. He smiles. Kevin smiles and looks for someone to say it to. The man at his shoulder leans forward, nods, turns his ear to Kevin's mouth. It's a good thing to say.

'Here we are.'